ILLICIT LEARNING CURVES

Keith Warren

Published 2010 by arima publishing

www.arimapublishing.com

ISBN 978 1 84549 421 6

© Keith Warren 2010

Printed and bound in the United Kingdom

Typeset in Garamond 11/14

In this work of fiction, the characters, places and events are either the product of the author's imagination or they are used entirely fictitiously. The moral rights of the author have been asserted. Any resemblance to actual persons, living or dead, is purely coincidental.

Swirl is an imprint of arima publishing.

arima publishing

ASK House, Northgate Avenue

Bury St Edmunds, Suffolk IP32 6BB

t: (+44) 01284 700321

www.arimapublishing.com

PROLOGUE
February 1994

As I begin this, I hardly know how to make myself write your name. Deep in velvet nights and across the pastures of the day, I have whispered and called it so often that to shape it now, here, is somehow to measure the impossibility of the distance. I am not ready for that yet. If I form the letters that are you, I shall have to stop again to weep. Forgive me then if I just begin to write. You know this is for you. It could not be for anyone else. There is no one else. There can never be anyone else.

For an eternity of time, it seems, I have waited for your letter. It is more than a year. It is eighteen months since I saw you last, tearful at that window. And so now, the heavy steps of the postman; the knocking at the door one always dreads. Remember that terror? I did not want to touch the cold, white envelope. I put it, unopened, on the table in the window, the one with the view of the river you said you liked on the one sad occasion you visited. Then I brought it here, to our place on the stony beach in Devon. I will not write that name either. But you remember? Of course you do. You will not forget.

Perhaps names are not so important now. We were in this place and we were one, you and me. It happened; it mattered. It cannot be erased. It lives on.

I could not read the letter at home. I thought that to bring it here would somehow close the circle. It seemed to take me all day to drive here, the envelope waiting, silently beside me on the passenger seat. A final, futile but romantic act. Or just sad?

It is cold. No one comes here in February unless they are seriously deranged. The chalets are empty so I took one for a week. The same one. 'Seagull'. On the West Beach under the cliff. Just like before.

Of course, your letter made me cry. How else? I read it sitting on the pebbles, just where we sat on that beautiful sunny morning. Oh, so long ago; and yet...the same place. Leaning against that rock with the funny white cap. You said it was fossilised snow; remember? Maybe today it is just that: it is so, so cold down here and the sea is gun-metal grey. Perhaps it was a mistake to come here. Maybe I torture myself.

I sit in the same place now, this morning, writing this. You are close to me here. I can see you over there, throwing stones into the sea. Watching the seals in the swell. Your laughter comes to me with the clean salt spray on the wind. You turn and wave to me, beckoning. I see your smile. I go to you. You hold me close and put your lips to mine. This is all I am - is you.

At night you are beside me, as then. I reach out and touch the dark tresses of your hair while you sleep. I lie awake, listening to the softness of your breathing. I watch the stars shift across the window while I wait for you to wake up too. Your dawn is my beginning. I don't want to miss a single second of your day. What you are – is me.

What else am I to do? On this beach, I know where I can find you when I need you in the lonely hours. There are many lonely hours and there will be more. You will know them too. The darkest hour is just before dawn, remember?

Of course, I shall return to my home. What will you do with your life, I wonder? You know I still do not fully understand what has happened to us. You have consigned me to darkness. If I caused you pain or if ever I hurt you, I am sorry. I did not ever mean to hurt you; it was my own terror that you felt as I stared into the abyss. You do not deserve to hurt. There is no blame.

I will not try again to make you change your mind. I have to try to understand that it's too late, isn't it? Perhaps you are to suffer in this more than me, for you have to bear your own pain as well as mine.

Thank you for the love you brought me. It was a precious garment to wear. I have it still, here beside me on the hard rocks. I love you now as before. Yes; don't be surprised. I will not stop loving you even if I never see you again.

I must bid you farewell, then? But...you are still here! Nothing on this beach has changed and yet I know that all the grains of sand have re-arranged themselves, just as you said they must.

And so, now, I have come to that deep, dark place. Turn, turn, turn. There is a beginning and there is an end in all things. Because you wish it to be so, this is the end. So be it.

Mike

I BEASTS

THE MONKEY HOUSE
October 1990

With heavy heart and heavier briefcase (for it contains thirty books and thirty blotched and dog-eared essays) Michael Chadwick, PhD., early middle-aged English teacher with a mortgage, a pudding of a wife, itching hell-fire in his loins and another twenty years to do before he gets his pension, threads his way through the clatter of corridors to C Block.

The noise reverberates and hammers the skull. A thousand adolescent voices raised in screeching inter-lesson communion push the decibels beyond levels considered acceptable by the Health and Safety Executive when it visits the nearby paper mill.

Michael pauses at the top of a staircase and glowers around him at the lava flow of children, seething, steaming, bubbling and squabbling their way to lesson six.

" 'Lo, Doctor Chadwick! Orlright, Sir?"

"Yes, Gavin, I'm fine, thank you so much for your concern. And tuck your shirt in, lad!"

Room 28 is at the end of a peeling corridor, its plaster gouged, sculpted and defaced by generations of disconsolate children. The featureless, colourless room is a mess of strewn paper, pen tops and mud brought in on countless feet. The desks are askew; the blackboard is not wiped clean. It smells like a monkey house. Michael winces.

"Blimey, Sir, what a stench! First years, I expect."

"No doubt, Gary. Baked beans for lunch, was it? Open a couple of windows, will you? Or we'll never make it home for tea. What are we all waiting for? Come in and sit down; just don't breathe for a while. Half an hour should do it; less for the asthmatics among you. Mark! Spit the gum in the bin. Louise? Sit at the front, please and do your blouse up properly, there's a good girl."

Despite his despairing, glum mood, Michael's humour is there. It is instinctive; part of his style. It is a teaching tool; he carries it with him like a stick of chalk. The class responds as he knows they will, by chuckling with him against the now departed, offensively flatulent enemy. They acknowledge admiringly his blunt reference to that which most teachers would pretend to ignore. Immediately, he has them on his side. But he knows he has to keep them there. One little victory is never enough.

As he empties his briefcase and distributes books, he gives Louise a look to ensure she complies with his instruction. He'd like to write on her end of year report, "Louise's future does not lie between her ears", but he doubts he'd get away with it.

As the class settle, he prepares himself mentally for the struggle ahead. He doesn't need to review his material; he knows his subject. Like an actor who knows his lines, he must psyche himself up for the performance. For modern teaching is a kind of performance and it can be exhausting, especially if the audience has been forced to buy tickets.

They watch him for ten minutes. They are not being disruptive or even silently obstructive. They smile in the right places, but they are reluctant to be engaged in any kind of dialogue.

Sensing that he's not getting through, he wonders briefly whether he's losing his touch and whether they can tell he's on auto-pilot. He tries a different approach, forces some more energy into his tone. Even clowns around a little for effect.

They continue to exist in front of him, without opinion, mute, lumpen behind their desks, faces expressionless, eyes glassed with indifference. He sighs with the recognition that today it's not going to happen.

One or two of the shrewder girls at the front watch him carefully, noting, assessing his mood, calculating and speculating over the reasons for his evident unease. When he is busy at the back of the class, one whispers to her friend.

" 'Ere, I reckon there's another woman!"

After all, they watch the soaps and read the magazines. They know about these things.

They sit at the front because they like Dr. Chadwick. They have a crush on him. He is clear and authoritative. There's no messing with Doctor Mike. They are drawn to his assured, masculine power. They warm to his inclusive style; they enjoy being teased by him. He makes them laugh, he is kind and understanding. He is in good physical shape and he is handsome in other ways which they cannot quite define. They pretend to swoon behind his back at the smell of his aftershave, just like they do in the adverts and they know about them too.

Most of all, they are subconsciously aware that he is a sensitive man. He has a strong female side to his personality. They might not be able to articulate it or even understand the concept but they are female and so, somehow, they divine it.

8

He has an aura about him which makes some of the girls shiver. They draw comparisons between what they sense as his calm, considerate, mature sexual allure and what they know as their boyfriends' insistent coaxings, manipulations, lies, threats and pressures; their inexpert and selfish fumblings and probings. They want to believe it does not have to be like that. Yes, they know about these things and they believe Dr. Chadwick knows too. His wife is a lucky woman, they think.

The more experienced and bolder among them wonder aloud between themselves how he might be in bed. Their parents, as well as being horrified by the speculation itself, might be even more alarmed by the detail and varied experiences that their daughters are able to bring to such a discussion. Their mothers would have had crushes in their day too and might even have wondered, as their daughters now openly assess and dissect, but only a very few of them would have had the experience to take them beyond fantasy.

These young girls' conversations are graphic, intense, and physical. They are alive with brutal, anatomical slang; the arithmetic of sizes and frequencies; replays of frantic, thrusting, back-seat couplings; the odours and fluids of adolescent sex. They have done all these things. Perhaps they have done more than Michael himself. They know, with the wisdom of age.

Michael has learnt, like all teachers of older children, that the schoolgirl crush is part of the undercurrent in all secondary schools. In a sense, it is unremarkable. Not an issue. As a raw, young teacher he was alarmed and even frightened by it. A tall, dark, handsome young graduate, he was the pin-up of many an adoring pupil, some of whom would try to corner him at the school disco or in the shadowy places behind the scenery when he was stage-managing the play.

But he soon learned, as most do, how to put it in its place and not allow it to run out of control. He is used to these things. He can handle it. He always has.

Ellen Fortune has a crush on Michael and has had since she was fourteen. No one knows that this is so except her good friend Tracey. For almost a year, Ellen keeps a little notebook of thoughts about her English teacher, romantic and often racy stories and cartoon drawings in which they are the main characters. Towards the end of the book, there are some stories where she and her teacher go to bed together. Just a fantasy. She writes in her notebook nearly every day. One day she shows Tracey. It is their secret. She knows she has a crush. It's just a teenage thing. No big deal. Passing; transient. She can definitely handle it. It's a bit of a laugh. No problem.

He has set the class some pointless writing task to occupy the last twenty minutes of the lesson. He knows that and so do they. It falls clearly within the accepted rituals of the system. Now he has time for his own thoughts. They are many and varied: tomorrow's timetable alterations; get the car serviced; the twins' birthday next week - discuss with Barbara. Phone Mum.

And Ellie Fortune who has asked to see him after school. He is surprised to find that the thought keeps bobbing up in his mind like a cork in water; it should not be a significant event but it seems that it is.

Never mind; he can handle it. He always has.

THE OWL
October 1990

Out of his study window, Michael sees a grey sky with a bruised underbelly that threatens rain.

Bob Menzies has a third year class on the far field. They are pinball size figures; a shoal of boys pulled by the ebb and flow of the game; garishly striped kit, an incongruous contrast with the dun of the hedge and brown, churned filth of the field. Some, mud-daubed, harry one another for the ball. Others shirk on the touch-line, welcoming the shrouding fog sidling furtively into the valley. An obese boy scrapes clods of sticky earth off his boots, hoping for an early end to his suffering.

Bob is shouting something angrily at him and he lumbers reluctantly back into the edges of the swim. From this distance, Bob's voice is a series of yelps and indistinguishable bellows. The sounds are muddied by the afternoon mist.

Michael turns his attention back to the papers on his desk: timetables; scribbled notes; memos; sixth form essays handed in for marking weeks ago.

*

How he hates bloody autumn afternoons! The season of piss-wet mists and mellow, mouldering fruitfulness. The calendar's penumbral zone with its long shadows, clammy fogs and vague outlines. This morning he could smell it in the air: the murky dawn. He had allowed himself a childish fantasy: had some mischievous joker draped grey muslin around the bedroom during the night? Ridiculous of course; there was no one else there, except Barbara and she was snoring like a hog as usual. Ah, but during the night? The sandman cometh! Good for the sandman; Michael reflects that it's a long time since he cameth during the night.

He is in the late summer of his life, or so the twins tell him, the cheeky buggers.

"I am only forty-four," he says.

As far as they are concerned, that is old because they are eleven. Since he is their father, it follows that he must be old, regardless of the arithmetic.

"Anyway," chuckles Hannah, "look at your hair! You're old, Dad! Period."

"I am thinning on top, but only a bit," he retorts, running a hand over his head.

"A euphemism, Mike," offers Barbara. "You're going bald."

Lucy, with one of those little phrases that she delights in creating and then singing out loud, says that once long ago, he was barrel-chested but now he is thermal-vested.

" You fall asleep in the armchair on Sunday afternoons, just like Grandad used to do. I rest my case," Lucy says with a dismissive flounce.

*

Grimly, sighing reluctantly, he once more endeavours to focus on the papers on his desk. He has his study door open, although he would rather it was shut. Some of the younger teachers have complained vociferously that neither he nor the Head, John Sutcliffe, are sufficiently accessible. Their doors are shut so that they cannot see what is going on in the classrooms and corridors. They have deliberately divorced themselves from the real business of teaching, walked away from the chalk dust to an upholstered swivel chair. Ergo, they are not real teachers. They are interlopers, renegades, over-paid administrators who are not doing a proper job. They have forgotten how to teach.

Michael is irritated by this. His record as a teacher in three previous schools is impeccable and impressive. He is a born teacher, a gifted communicator. His results with examination classes have been enviable and his pupils have always regarded him highly, the older ones invariably referring to him affectionately as, "Doctor Mike".

In his previous school, where he was Head of Department, he was regarded as especially academic and scholarly. That, coupled with the fact that he favours horn-rimmed spectacles of a rather old-fashioned kind, earned him the soubriquet, "The Owl". He didn't mind that, but prefers "Doctor Mike", especially when he considers some of the savage, crude or offensive nicknames bestowed by children on many colleagues. He once taught with an old historian universally referred to by generations of boys as, "The Tosser".

Promotion to a Deputy Headship has divorced him from the classroom for half the week, so perhaps the staffroom critics are right. He is not sure about this. He is not sure about many things these days.

In any event, the levellers of the staffroom have won the most recent round. Whilst he has been on compassionate leave, John Sutcliffe has agreed (unwisely and weakly, in Michael's view) that their office doors will be open whenever possible so that both of them are visible and accessible.

"Available and accountable," Sutcliffe had intoned. "Those are today's watchwords. The mantra of modern schools."

"Watchwords? Mantra? You mean the bollocks-speak of management courses," Michael had replied.

So far as he is concerned, the result is that he cannot order his day, especially not now, with his emotions in a spin. This is annoying, for he has a tidy mind. He is constantly being interrupted with "urgent" matters. Everything is urgent now. The new bloody mantra.

*

He throws his pen onto his desk, kicks a filing cabinet drawer shut with a vicious slam and stands up to watch Menzies' group clumping back from the far field in the soupy dusk.

He is unnerved by the shortening days: the beginning of the end of light. The fear is a primeval thing, like hurrying home when it begins to get dark or cleaving to the fire on a gloomy afternoon.

And only five weeks ago he was basking in the warmth of the Provencal sun. The summer holiday – a holiday almost long enough to forget that you are a bloody teacher! Almost; because at the back of the mind is forever the rough beast slouching towards Bethlehem to be born – the inevitable return to the classroom: a terrible, black, sinking feeling in the pit of the stomach. And something else too: nameless; the anti-Christ! The same sense of foreboding that Marlow had chugging up the Congo into the veritable heart of darkness looking for Kurtz.

He mutters to himself wryly, "The horror! The horror!"

And now he has exchanged the smell of wild thyme on a scrubby Provencal hillside for the rotten whiff of unlocked classrooms! Michael allows himself a wry smile as his mind develops the theme. The odour of foetid spaces shut up for six weeks. The bottled stench of adolescents! Indescribable! No brand of disinfectant or cleaning fluid known to man or caretaker can forever banish that unwashed, damp blazer, cabbage-fart, dried semen, soiled underwear, virgin juice odour.

"You can call it mellow fruitfulness if you want, Keats my boy; leave me out of it. Virgin juice? Where's that thought come from? Good Lord; talking to myself again; cracking up, Chadwick!"

WHERE IS THY STING?
6th September 1990

After a fitful sleep that night, I awoke suddenly, a leaden feeling in my stomach. Rain was lashing against the window panes; there was a clammy, musty feel to the air in the cottage. The stones, dried in August's heat, were sucking up moisture from the sodden earth. Cows down by the river were lowing mournfully.

The first day of term! I lay still for a moment, collecting and ordering my thoughts, bracing myself for the onslaught: the noise, the administrative demands, the relentless requests and expectations from pupils and junior staff alike. I knew it wouldn't be long before someone phoned in sick, requiring timetable amendments under pressure. Bastards!

I shifted uneasily and warily, anxious not to waken Barbara who was snuffling and muttering beside me. I didn't want another "serious discussion" about our marriage.

I didn't want to talk about it all, and certainly not early on the first day of term. I didn't want to talk about anything to anyone, let alone Barbara.

On cue, the phone began to shrill. I jumped out of bed and stumbled onto the landing. I glanced at my watch and saw it was only six. For fuck's sake! I didn't want Barbara woken up and I was also annoyed to think that some feeble sod was phoning in sick at six on the first day of the year.

It was Mum, telling me that Dad had been admitted to hospital after a fall.

"A fall? How do you mean, exactly?"

"I don't know, exactly, dear. He'd gone to the bathroom and then there was a bang and I heard him calling. Fortunately he hadn't locked the door. He said he felt dizzy and thought he'd sit down and then he found he was on the floor wedged between the bath and the toilet. Banged his head, I think. That's where I found him. He couldn't get up, dear. I had a hell of a job to get him into the bedroom."

"Christ. Why didn't you call me last night?"

"I didn't want to worry you, Michael. Anyway, I was at the hospital until two this morning and I didn't think you'd want me to call then."

I suppressed my irritation.

"OK, OK. Look, does Dr. Mortlock think it's, well, you know, serious? What about the hospital? What did they say? If it's bad, of course, I'll come up."

After making a few further reassuring noises, I replaced the receiver and went to wake the sleeping Leviathan. I explained briefly to the twins that Grandma needed my help because Grandad was not too special, phoned Sutcliffe, threw some clothes in a bag and set off up the M4. During the two hundred mile journey, I wondered, rather guiltily, whether I was grateful to Dad for postponing my return to school. Not that a late start to the new school year was ever going to be fun. Twice as difficult, in fact.

I arrived mid afternoon. A grey drizzle was sliding in from the Estuary and the gulls were shuffling disconsolately on the rooftops. I noticed, as I pulled into the drive, that the horse chestnut was already shedding its leaves. As I got out of the car, a wet leaf blew against my neck, its decaying dampness causing me to shiver involuntarily.

Dad was sitting on a metal commode in the bedroom. He looked up as I entered the room, although I noticed that he seemed to be struggling to lift his head. His neck seemed thin and stringy, like a turtle's; his head ungainly and too large for his body. His voice was clear, but strangely tight and reedy.

"Hello, Mike. There was no need. I'm alright. Your mother makes a fuss, you know."

"Don't be daft, Dad. You don't look too chipper to me. She was right to call. Andy's on his way, too."

"Is he?"

Dad was silent for a moment, his watery eyes tracing the edges of the room before coming to rest on my face.

"I see. I thought as much. I've deteriorated quite a bit since you saw me in June, haven't I? I'm on the way out, aren't I?"

It's not really a question, I thought, it's a statement. How to respond? We were not a family that minced words or told lies to one another. Yet I just couldn't say, "That's right, Dad, according to old Mortlock, you're dying. Your kidneys are shot. Ten days at the most, he reckons."

So, I remained silent and tried to smile.

"It's alright, Mike, you don't have to say anything. I know. They say you know when it's your time. I always thought that was crap! But they're right. It's my time, all right. I can sense it. The Grim Reaper is just parking his car; he'll be here in a bit."

For a moment, our eyes met. I could see resignation in his gaze and anger too. Raging against the dying of the light. I looked down as tears came unbidden. I saw that Dad's hands were shaking; his skin was slack and yellow. There was an odd, sour smell in the room.

*

As Dr. Mortlock predicted, it took Dad two weeks to die and he fought it every inch of the way. He refused medication, he drank and ate but little, he tried to pull out the catheter, he struggled to get out of bed when he shouldn't. The home-help nurses were afraid he'd fall again and break bones. He had no balance. Andy and I sometimes took it in turns in the early days forcibly to hold him down whilst he cussed and abused us. He kept us awake at night, yelling that he wanted the toilet, oblivious, apparently, to the fact that his bladder was being drained continuously.

Immediately after the first dose of the morphine that Mortlock prescribed, Dad was on a high, and insisted that the three of us sat on the bed around him. He was calm and coherent for the first time in several days.

"I suppose you think I'm on my bloody death bed? I'm not. I'm not going yet."

He paused and smiled. It was his little joke. He was going and he knew it but it felt good to stick two fingers up at the Grim Reaper who was already waiting on the landing, polishing his blade.

"Piss off! And mind that bloody scythe on the wood panelling, otherwise there'll be fucking great gouge marks!"

Mum dabbed at her eyes.

"I'm sorry I'm dying. In fact, I'm more than pissed off about it, but there it is. Look after your mother, boys. Oh, and keep that stinking bloody cat off the chairs, will you?"

He said no more, closed his eyes and died later that day.

I returned to school nearly three weeks after the beginning of the term. Things had already fallen into their new pattern but I couldn't adjust. It felt like a three-dimensional maze; as if I'd never been there before.

Of course, it wasn't just Dad's death which threw me. It was also those last few days in Provence.

CAT'S EYES

"Sir? Doctor Chadwick, could I see you for a few minutes, please?"

He turns. There is a sixth form girl standing in the doorway. He recognizes her from his 'A' Level group but he cannot recall her name. He noticed her long, curly, brown hair yesterday and the extraordinary green eyes. His late start to the term and his troubled state of mind have interfered with his customary ability to remember names after one hearing. But he remembers the waterfall of hair because he was vaguely disturbed by it.

"Well, I only have a few minutes, er? I'm teaching at half past."

He looks at the wall clock.

"Well, OK, come on in and sit down."

"Thank you, Sir. I'm really sorry to bother you. I can see you're busy."

He is surprised by the demure apology which is better than that which many of the staff might muster. Instinctively, Michael is aware that the girl in front of him is concerned about something serious. He knows the signs. She is pulling at her fingers, worrying at her bag strap, adjusting that luxuriant hair nervously. This is not just a query about the essay he has set the group, although he expects that this is how she will begin.

"That's alright. I'm sorry too, because although I know I should know your name, I'm afraid I have forgotten it."

He opens his hands, palms up, in a joking gesture of hopelessness.

"Ellen Fortune. Ellie."

She smiles and looks him straight in the eye, her pupils dilating in translucent green pools.

"Ah! Er, right. Ellie Fortune? Are you? Didn't I teach you in the third year? Or was that your sister? Or am I suffering the early stages of senile dementia, Ellie?"

The girl laughs.

"Yes, that's right. I mean, you did teach me in the third year. Mr. Rutherford taught my sister, Sir. It was me."

He is surprised because the Ellie Fortune he remembers was a stunted, mousey little thing with rather lank hair, braces on her teeth and not much self-confidence. He could hardly get a word out of her all year. He remembers an aggressive, religious zealot of a mother who gave him a hard time about the third year reading list at the parents' evening.

"And I don't think you're senile, Sir. Nothing like it."

"I'll ignore the flirtatious comment. Probably," he smiles. "Well, Ellie, I would never have guessed. You've changed considerably since then. Of course, your third year was a long time ago."

"Everybody seems surprised by me these days, Sir. I'm getting used to it."

He glances at her, silently acknowledging her beauty.

"Yes, it's coming back to me now; I remember that I had a fairly vigorous discussion with your mother about the literary virtues or otherwise of, 'Of Mice and Men'."

"I know, Sir. I remember. So embarrassing. She's like that. I don't think she was able to see any virtues in that particular novel. With it being, well, like a bit explicit, Sir."

Michael registers the confident, articulate answer.

"Anyway, Ellie, what is it you want? I have to get myself organised for the fourth year mobsters in a minute."

"Well, it's that sort of stuff that I've come to see you about, Sir."

"What?"

"My mother and what we're reading, Sir. She doesn't approve of 'Tess'. She told me to tell you she'll be making an appointment to come and see you."

"Are you sure that's what this is about? Your mother doesn't approve of Thomas Hardy's 'Tess of the D'Urbervilles'? Why? On second thoughts, never mind, Ellie. I'm sure she'll tell me. But I will say, and you can tell your mother this, I don't intend to justify every book on the Exam Board's set list for the next two years. If she's going to get excited about Thomas Hardy, God help us when we reach Philip Larkin!"

"I'm really sorry, Sir. I'm very, well, you know, angry about it. She's always interfering. We had a big row about it last night, Sir. But I thought I ought to warn you."

"So I can prepare my case? Thank you! Incidentally, there's no need to keep calling me 'Sir' every three minutes now you're in the sixth form, Ellie. Just once every half hour will do, in case you forget who's in charge."

"Alright, Sir."

They both laugh at the inevitability and absurdity of the reply. He waits. The girl makes no move to go. Michael looks at her and raises an eyebrow.

"Ellie, would you like to tell me what you really came to see me about?"

"Well, er, it's a bit difficult, Sir. Sorry, Sir, I didn't mean to say, 'Sir'. Oh!"

She laughs a deep, gurgling laugh and puts a hand to her mouth in embarrassment. She hesitates and seems about to reveal the true reason for her visit, but then changes her mind. She looks at her watch.

"There is something, Dr. Chadwick, but if you don't mind perhaps I could come back later?"

"OK. Might be better, since I have to go and cast pearls before swine shortly. Four o'clock suit you?"

"Yes, thank you. I'll see you later then. Sir."

She grins and gathers her things to go.

As she stands briefly in the doorway, her form is silhouetted in profile by the last of the afternoon light coming from a corridor window. She smiles and lifts a hand to push her hair off her face, the action pulling her blouse taught across her bust.

Michael swallows hard and wonders whether the movement is unconscious or deliberate. She is wearing a reflective metal clip to hold back a fringe. It catches some light, transmutes it into flickering diamonds and spills them through her fingers into the room.

Michael blinks. Shifts in time and place. He squints against the light, trying to focus, trying to get his bearings, to regain equilibrium, some sense of now.

Now he has it: Provence! And emerging from the sea is the girl with droplets cascading from her brown hair; the girl at Gassin.

MEDITERRANEAN CICADA
August 1990

Barbara loathes Provence and is always saying she would like to try somewhere cooler like the Norwegian fjords. But the girls and I like the sun and the beaches. The warmth.

"You're suggesting freezing my codpiece in the land of the midnight sun?"

"For an educated man, you sometimes show a remarkable ignorance and prejudice, not to mention vulgarity, Michael."

Educated and vulgar: that's about right. So far, I have resisted successfully a visit to the fjucking fjords.

Going down through France is always tiring but exhilarating, nevertheless. L'Autoroute du Soleil! We sing all the songs we can think of with the word 'sun' in them. Well, the kids and I do. Barbara just sits there and then once we are south of Lyons, she starts grumbling about the heat.

"The sun has got his hat on, hip, hip hoo-effing-ray, the sun has got his firkin' hat on and he's coming out to-pigging-day!"

"Mike, must you? I really don't want the girls running up and down the beach singing that, thank you very much."

"Alright, alright. The French won't understand it anyway. You know what they're like; they don't do English."

"Not all of us appreciate your perverse and warped, so-called sense of humour."

"We think Daddy's funny, Mummy."

"Be quiet, Lucy."

We usually only take two weeks holiday away but this year, we took four. Last school year was especially turbulent. A bastard, in more prosaic language.

During the first week of July, I checked my bank balance and found with surprise that there was a little more cash in the current account than I had thought. That decided it. I booked a villa for a whole month.

"Oh, we're going to Cap Camarat?" said Barbara with typical sarcasm. "What a nice surprise, Michael. That will make a pleasant change."

"You'll be fine when you get there."

The villa was last-minute expensive, booked through a holiday company, sight-unseen. It was a splendid stone construction, probably originally a grape store or some such, in the Var hills, above St. Tropez , with a panoramic view of the bay. It was simple but comfortable and clean.

To start with, things were fine. Or as fine as one could expect them to be. In the evenings we sat on the stone terrace, sipping the local, rather rough, red plonk and gazing at the boats and jet-skis far below us in the bay. The rattling fusillades of cicadas in the olive trees, the smell of the vines, the perfume of the dry thyme, the setting sun rimming the sea orange and gold and, of course, the mellowing effects of the wine all conspired to bathe the year's wounds. I suppose those were the best times, massaging the senses and, at the beginning of the month anyway, doing something to ease my exhaustion and quell my emotional turmoil and dissatisfactions.

During the day, we ambled aimlessly through the markets, buying bags of olives, ice creams or souvenirs made from cork, entirely as the whim took us. We'd have a disgracefully expensive coffee in the square in St Tropez and then, because it's Lucy's favourite thing, we'd go and have a look at the street artists by the harbour. She's happy to stand and watch them for hours. We'd leave her there and go along the harbour, gawping at the ostentatious craft moored and watch the jet-set big-dealing it on the deck.

Well, I did. Fat, old, manicured guys, oozing money and fondling young, long-limbed girls with huge breasts, tiny waists and pert backsides! Envy, I suppose, at what money can buy! If we could drag Lucy away, we'd think about lunch at Gassin or Ramatuelle or, if Hannah got her way, at Port Grimaud.

If the idea of traipsing was too much and we were bored with the pool, we'd throw towels into the car and head for the beach at Pampelonne. The girls would swim, sunbathe, run up and down the water's edge or disappear on a pedalo. They're at that delightful, innocent stage and not really of an age where self-consciousness or the need to preen will inhibit their fun.

I know Barbara finds the Mediterranean heat and sun less tolerable as each year goes by and I suppose that doesn't help. She says she is afraid to indulge in anything too active in case it dislodges a vertebra again. Repeatedly, I suggested that joining us at the water's edge or catching a beach ball occasionally are not generally life-threatening activities. It is not a remark that she took to especially kindly.

The situation made me feel guilty, I suppose. I knew I was probably being selfish but then I'd look up and she'd be lying lumpenly under the umbrella, covering her ballooning form with towels or t-shirts, griping and whining incessantly about the heat, reminding us of her Norwegian preferences. My anger and impatience would come storming back.

In our college days, she was a slim, pretty, vivacious young woman. But after a few years of marriage, I started looking at and lusting after other women. That's all it was to start with. Like most men, probably. After we'd been married for five years, I had a brief affair with a school colleague; a much younger woman who was a probationer in the Geography Department. I can't blame her. I made all the running.

The affair was brief - she got bored and moved on - but while it lasted it was intensely physical and quite disturbing in drawing a stark contrast with what was happening in my marriage bed. Not a great deal. Sex is rather perfunctory and our half-hearted efforts mean that the delirium, the resonances of youth have gone. By contrast, Ann was uninhibited, energetic and enthusiastic.

I think there is some weakness or immaturity in me that precludes me from adapting to the calmer middle years of marriage. My sexual template, as they say, is set somewhere in my late teens or early twenties, unable to progress. I look at younger women and constantly recall the intense pleasures of youth. Society views men like me as dysfunctional. Aberrant. Shameful. We are 'dirty' old men. But I don't think I'm any of those things. I just happen to prefer younger women. I am aroused by teenage girls; not when I'm wearing my professional hat; that's different. Usually. I mean those knowing teenage girls you see out of school. And I don't mean little girls either, let's be clear.

I can't help it. It's not something I set out to do bloody-mindedly in defiance of society's expectations, like, I don't know, wearing pyjamas in the street or deliberately farting like a klaxon during a wedding ceremony. No, it's how I was made.

Barbara must have put on a stone in weight in the last few months and somehow I hadn't noticed until we were in France; because she was wearing fewer clothes in the heat, I suppose. Her once trim waist has been swallowed whole by rolls of quivering blubber. Repulsive. The brutal truth has to be admitted. It isn't that things have gone a bit stale. It's much worse than that. I no longer find Barbara in the slightest bit attractive.

So, I spent a good deal of my time watching the French teenage girls on the Pampelonne Beach. Most other middle-aged men were doing precisely the same thing. I'd pretend to be reading but from behind the book and the sunglasses, I was watching the girls, driven half insane with desire for their topless, ripe and rounded perfection. Jesus! French girls on a beach!

"Bon jour, monsieur! Mon Dieu! Vous avez le boner formidable!"

"D'accord, mademoiselle. Aimes-toi le lollipop?"

I looked at them furtively, naturally. Glancing sideways; pretending to take a break from my book; that sort of thing. Let's face it, you don't want young girls taking you for a pervert. Their fathers get protective when they're not too busy lusting after other men's daughters themselves. French men seem to have fewer qualms, so why did I worry?

Cue Barbara.

"Because you are a married man of forty four and you are a teacher. It is not seemly. Not acceptable or appropriate in a man your age, that's why. I mean, for Christ's sake! They could be your pupils!"

"Yes, dear. As always, you are quite correct."

When you're young yourself, it's alright to lust after teenage girls; then after a while it isn't. Bloody unreasonable shift in perspective, I think. When you're a young man, people call it "getting interested in girls" and chuckle indulgently or breathe a sigh of relief that you're not a closet shirt-lifter. But when you're middle aged they call it "leering" or being a "sexual predator".

I noticed one particular girl. To my great surprise, it seemed she had noticed me. She and her family sat in the same place each day and I caught her glancing in my direction more than once during our last week there. Or I thought she was. Sometimes I was sure of it and other times I thought maybe she was looking further up the beach to where the bronzed young bucks were hiring out jet-skis. More than likely, I thought; I should stop kidding myself.

Her eyes were an extraordinary dark brown, almost black in the light bouncing off the sea. Her features were delicate, clean and precise, the teeth almost too good to be true. She was tall, slender and had lustrous, dark hair which tumbled and rippled down almost as far as her tiny waist. She usually wore a bikini top, for the sun was particularly fierce, but one morning she did not. I could feel myself swallowing time and again. She was perfectly proportioned and needed no bikini for support. She seemed aware of my admiring glances but she made no effort to conceal herself.

She was a few days shy of nineteen and her name was Simone. That much I deduced, for her family called to her up and down the beach in that raucous and insistent way of the French. My knowledge of the language is sufficiently good to understand their conversation about her forthcoming birthday party in Paris.

After a while, I decided that I was imagining things. Perhaps it was the effects of the heat? A beautiful young French girl was hardly likely to be interested in me, a pale-skinned Englishman in his forties who was beginning to thin on top and thicken in the middle?

"I must be going down with bloody sun-stroke."

"Pardon? What did you say?"

"Nothing, dear. Talking to myself."

"I think you're dribbling as well, Michael."

Someone like that gorgeous young woman could have taken her pick from the thousands of men on the beach. Old or young. No doubt. I tried to take my eyes away from her and concentrate on the book but I couldn't. David Lodge is good, but not that bloody good. Choose: his undoubtedly superior narrative - or a half-naked teenage girl with long legs and perfect breasts? No contest, David, sorry. So, my gaze returned time and time again as she ran in and out of the water with her sisters, rolling in the surf and sluicing wet sand from her loins. Loins! That's the word. "Legs" does not get anywhere near it.

She returned from the water's edge. She smiled and pushed the wet hair out of her eyes. She stood in profile with the sun behind her. The light caught the water droplets as they arced in a cascade of diamonds from her hands. I was mesmerised. Any healthy man with blood in his veins would have been. I was meant to be.

She gently lowered herself onto her stomach. She glanced at me. Not by accident. She looked my way deliberately; I wasn't quite sure what to do and so, being British, I self-consciously and quickly averted my gaze. But didn't I detect an ironic smile on her lips? I would probably have done well to have gone for a cold shower.

She dozed for a while and the sun quickly dried her back. She said something to her little sister who reached for a sun lotion bottle and began to smooth oil into her shoulders. She turned her head and looked at me looking at her. She knew what I was thinking, absolutely no bloody doubt whatsoever. She raised one quizzical eyebrow. Oil me, baby.

"It's the heat bouncing off this beach. I'm hallucinating now."

"What? I think you should think about drinking less, you know. And you're still dribbling."

"Yes, dear."

Simone levered herself onto one elbow, reached into a bag and produced a large peach. She turned the fruit around in her hand, looked at the erect little stalk and deftly flicked it off with her thumb. She looked at me again, put her mouth to the globe and sank her teeth slowly into the fruit. Juice ran over her lips and began to trickle down her fingers.

I almost laughed out loud at this barely disguised suggestiveness. Oh, come on! A bit of a cliché, ma petite belle, isn't it? Yes, I get the message. We're all trained in Hollywood symbolism now! Next, cut to a shot of an express train thundering into a tight, dark tunnel.

I couldn't watch any more. I rolled to one side, hoping that I wouldn't embarrass myself by outgrowing my trunks. I shook myself like someone waking from a compelling dream and ran down the beach into the sea.

"Michael?" called Barbara, no doubt surprised by my sudden grunts and violent movements. "What the hell is the matter with you today? As if I didn't know! The heat bouncing off the bloody beach, is it?"

I swam furiously out into deeper water, dipping my head time and time again into the cooler patches beneath the surface, willing the dramatic change in temperature to subdue me before I was carted away by the gendarmes for questioning.

I dived down to the bottom and plunged my fingers into gritty sand, letting the grains wash out of my clenched fists as I rose slowly to the surface again. I looked back to the shore. Simone was lying on her back, propped on her elbows, her knees up and, provocatively, slightly apart. She was watching, waiting for me to surface, I swear it. She let her head fall back a little and, although I could not be sure through the water in my myopic eyes and the reflected light on the sea, it seemed to me she was laughing.

Later that same afternoon, she hired a jet-ski and with great skill and aplomb, pushed the thing to its whining limits across the waves a few hundred yards off shore. She eventually brought the craft slowly in shore, gently beaching it on the sand in front of where we were sitting.

There was a pause. She was looking in my direction, waiting until she was certain that she had my attention. She didn't need to wait for more than a nano-second; just as long as it took me to check my elastic waistband for signs of escape. Then she dismounted, holding one leg in the air just a little longer than was necessary. Water riveted down the inside of her smooth thighs. She smiled coyly, well aware of exactly where my gaze was resting.

I looked her straight in the eye and grinned. There could be no mistaking that. If nothing else, she needed to know that I knew what she was doing. And that given half of half a chance, I was ready if she was. She smiled back and raised the eyebrow again. And then she re-mounted the jet-ski and set off once more towards the hire jetty, turning to wave as she went. I lifted my arm to wave back.

Suddenly remembering myself, I looked across at Barbara. The transgression had not been logged. She had fallen asleep, her mouth open. Her arms rested heavily across her middle and a lobster-coloured calf poked out from under a towel.

"Beauty and the Beast," I said quietly to myself and then felt ashamed at my cruel disloyalty.

Barbara wanted to make love that night. It was the inflaming effects of the wine. I was surprised she was even interested, so she caught me off-guard. But I couldn't do it. No matter how hard I tried to go through the motions, I just could not make it happen. It was quite humiliating.

She had drunk far too much and began to behave in what she thought was a seductive manner. She found a tape of old hits and quite deliberately selected, 'Witch Queen of New Orleans'.

The tune is significant. A rutting call. Years ago, I was Social Secretary at college and charged with the responsibility of organising the annual Students' Revue. Andrea was in her first term and offered to do a dance to that song. Eye-watering. She had a delectable, feline body and was years ahead of her time in what she was prepared and able to do on stage to music. Sexual magnetism - and I was the iron filings.

After the finale on the first night, when everyone else had sloped off to the student bar, I dashed into the gym, which the girls had used as a green room, to turn off the lights. Quite innocent; I didn't realise she was still in there; but she was, in just in her bra and pants, taking off her stage make-up. The skimpy underwear didn't stay on long. There followed ten minutes of frantic, pumping, hollering sex on one of those sweaty gym mats. Let it not be said that courtship and romance are dead.

Barbara never knew for sure what happened on that occasion (and several others) but she suspected and so 'Witch Queen' in her mind had a special quality: the song that would, apparently, automatically release animal lusts in me.

"It was the body, not the song, dummy!"

Anyway, she began to wriggle and writhe in front of me in what she no doubt thought was an alluring display. Gradually she disrobed and revealed herself for my delectation. What could I say?

"No, that's alright, dear, no need to trouble yourself; it's very kind, but actually I had a hand-shandy earlier; what about some Horlicks before we retire?

Don't turn the lights out, Mother, wait 'til he gets in bed and grabs his…Horlicks is very good for you!"

No chance. She was keen. "On one," as the twins would say. As the parody of a stripper's routine progressed, pudgy shoulders give way to collapsed breasts, somehow calling to mind two piles of grey dough, part-kneaded by a thick-fingered baker. Tyres of flesh around her middle fell from under her blouse like the deceased contents of a snake charmer's bag, sans charm and then, the piece de resistance: a mottled backside quite frightening in its elephantine proportions. A living lardy cake. Each buttock seemed to have an identity and life of its own; each had declared unilateral independence from the mother state.

I became increasingly distressed and uncomfortable. Well, who wouldn't? When she was gruesomely stark naked, she leant forward and sidled her fingers playfully into the top of my beach shorts.

"I'm really sorry, it must be the wine, I don't think I can," I muttered.

This was not the approving assessment of her dance routine that she expected. She was very insistent and tried to arouse me by groping clumsily at my groin. There are times when having one's groin groped clumsily can be the apogee of a day's silent lechery but it depends, in my estimation, on who is doing the groping. When it was clear she would not succeed, that the scud was in the silo for the night, she turned on me savagely, accusing me of infidelity of thought, even if not of deed. Naturally, I was cut to the quick by this stain on my character.

"You can read my mind as well as everything else?" I retorted irritably.

"You spent all day leering at those teenage girls. There's no point denying it, Mike. I was watching you. You think I don't notice? Your tongue was practically on the sand. You had a great lump of lead pipe in your trunks most of the afternoon! What that French family must have thought I dread to think. Do you do the same at school, for God's sake? Eh? With your pupils?"

She began to cry, but it wasn't caused just by an excess of vin rouge. In between sobs and harangues, she began to gather up her discarded clothing.

"Look, most men on the beach watch the girls, Barbara. It's what they're there for. I am not "leering". It's perfectly normal. It's biology in fact. We are mature males of the species. Our genes must survive. They are ripe young females in the first flush of sexual maturity and their pheromones are calling for a mate. We are still in good shape, so, we watch. Look at the pride of lions. Same principle: the strongest, biggest old lion has his pick of the young females until he's too bloody knackered to get it up. Then the next strongest takes over and so on. Yes?"

I paused for a bit and felt a grin forming on my mouth.

"Well, OK, maybe we lust a bit. So what? It doesn't mean that we're going to do anything about it or, indeed, that we're interfering with ourselves under the Hawaiian-design beach linen."

I thought my riposte quite witty and hoped it would deflect her anger. Of course, it didn't. She wasn't in the mood for humour. From her point of view it wasn't funny anyway. It was probably just cruel and thoughtless. I had mis-judged the moment, like so often before. We men always do, I'm told, because we are thoughtless, feckless bastards.

"There's no need to be crude all the time. And who are these "we"? I'm talking about you, you shit, not bloody lions. I know you're in good shape. You've still got the shape you had twenty years ago; well, more or less and they know it too, the little tarts. But I'm not in good shape, am I?" she wailed. "I'm fat and forty and you're not attracted to me any more, are you?"

I could not answer, or at least, I could frame no answer that would have satisfied. It was the same as the, "Which shoes do you prefer?" conversation when you're going out for the evening. "Look, I don't fucking care, just make a decision and let's go!" is never the required answer but it is the only one I seem to be able to muster in the circumstances.

Barbara sniffed but said nothing more for some time. I hoped that the moment had passed but I was wrong. Again.

"You shouldn't be interested in ripe young females in the first flush of, whatever you said. It's disgusting. You shouldn't have those urges at forty four!"

"I'm sorry. You are, as ever, quite correct. I know. But it seems I do have those urges. Like lots of other men of forty four."

"Make love to me then. If you have urges."

"I'm sorry. I can't. Look, you're missing the salient point here. I need...Anyway, as I say, I'm not the only one. Half the middle-aged men on the beach are watching Simone." It was out of my mouth before I realised the stupidity of the remark.

"Simone? Simone? Who the bloody hell is Simone?"

"No one, I mean, she's that girl who sits with her family near us...that's her name. I've heard them call her that. You're getting hysterical unnecessarily."

"So it's not just ripe young females in general, but one particular ripe young female, is it? That's why you had a pistol in your pocket? You sneaky, lecherous bastard!"

With that, she slammed out of the villa and sat sobbing on the terrace. I should have gone out there to her and apologised but I couldn't. I was being entirely unreasonable, I know. I think the frustration I felt about Simone's unattainability was somehow Barbara's fault. I wanted rampant, climactic sex with Simone but the person offering coitus was a rolling sixteen shadows of her former self.

I stayed inside; I couldn't bear the accusations and the tearful pleading for reassurances which I knew I couldn't give, even insincerely, at that time. I stomped off to bed and left her to get on with it. Later, I woke up with a dry mouth and an insistent bladder. Starlight filtered through the bedroom window and slowly, my head thumping, I made my way into the lounge. Barbara had fallen asleep on the rickety sofa. I suppose she was hoping to make her point about rejection by suffering there rather than returning to the bedroom. She snuffled and whimpered to herself in the half light.

I went back to bed and in the early hours, I dreamt that I was riding Simone's jet ski with her. I straddled the pounding machine, Simone's trim waist between my hands as she forced the craft ever faster across the tops of the waves, smacking and chopping the water, spume engulfing us in a tunnel of silver mist. My thumbs could feel the sublime tautness of her spine. My fingers caressed the rise of her rump. My thighs could sense hers on the seat ahead of me, her flexing buttocks repeatedly pressing into my groin as the craft pumped and pounded its way out into the far reaches of the bay.

When I woke up, I could taste salt in my mouth.

THE VIPER AND THE MOUSE
Gassin, 31st August 1990

On our last night, we went to our favourite restaurant on the terrace at Gassin. We sat under a vast white parasol and ate a sumptuous meal by candlelight. If I hadn't been feeling so utterly pissed off, it would have been a delight. Romantic even. I certainly would have liked for it to feel that way.

The twins were decked out in their best white tops and pedal-pushers, saved for this special occasion. They giggled, make rude remarks about the effeminate waiters and counted the little lizards which scuttled along the walls. I suppose that by silent mutual agreement, Barbara and I took our cue from the girls' enjoyment and tried to join in with their chatter. Just for a few hours we attempted to push into the background our own sadness. We were not entirely successful.

The argument on the night of the drunken strip-tease had left a gaping wound. I confess that I made little effort to try to heal it and Barbara kept it open with periodic bouts of crying and reproachfulness. She insisted that when we went to the beach, it was to an altogether different part so that we were nowhere near Simone. That made me bloody angry, but what choice did I have? Even though I pointed out frequently that I had not even spoken to the girl, she was not negotiable on the issue.

"I know what you're like, Mike. You can fuck a girl just by looking at her. Words don't seem necessary in your case."

"Well, thank you, my sweet, for those few kind remarks, although I don't believe that the technique to which you allude has any basis in anthropological studies."

I was surprised to find that I was more disturbed by this enforced separation than I would have imagined. We sat a good quarter of a mile further down the beach, so, of course, I was constantly looking up and down the shoreline, hoping that I might see her or even that she might stroll along the sand, curious to see where I had got to.

"Michael? Are you listening? Hannah is asking you what you liked best about the holiday?"

Barbara's voice had a pointed edge. I realised that for some several minutes I had again been in a lustful reverie, completely oblivious to what Barbara and the girls were talking about.

31

"As if we didn't know," she added in a venomous hiss whilst the girls were giggling between themselves.

"Sorry, Hannah, I was miles away!"

It wasn't the girls' fault that their father was fighting middle-age lust and yearning for the impossible. Or what seemed like the impossible that evening.

"Oooh, well, let me think," I said with forced cheerfulness. "I think snorkelling round the rocks. Oh, and maybe the ice creams at Port Grimaud!"

The girls laughed and put forward their own favourite things. They agreed about the ice cream. There was a dispute about the relative merits of swimming in the sea or the pool. Lucy, always a surprise, did not nominate the artists at St Tropez as expected.

"I like the one with blond hair who's in charge of the jet-skis," she said after a while, a little embarrassed.

I was both amused and slightly horrified by the remark. I think that men rarely concede that their daughters will one day forsake them for another man. In fact, I wonder whether Lucy was correctly alluding to her own probable future with a series of blond, muscular, surfer types. Every one of them a consummate arsehole, no doubt.

"Yuk! He's so gross!" Hannah squealed.

Barbara looked censorious.

"Lucy! You're only eleven! He must be nineteen or twenty; a grown man!"

Lucy shrugged her shoulders.

"He winked at me," she said softly.

"Just admiring him from a distance, eh? Checking the merchandise? No harm in that is there? Anyway, nineteen's only a kid, isn't it, dear? I thought that's what you said the other day?"

I couldn't resist ramming that one down her throat.

Barbara scowled at me.

"You know, Mike, sometimes you're too bloody clever for your own good."

We all ate far too much. I leaned back in my chair and patted my swollen stomach.

"Phew!"

"Yuk, Dad! Gross!" Hannah affected nauseous revulsion, pretending to put her fingers into the back of her throat.

"Hannah! Don't you dare do that again!"

"Sorry, Mummy."

"And your conversational skills seem a little restricted this evening, Hannah," Barbara snapped peevishly.

"Don't worry, the belly's not permanent, I hope," I said. "Now, I think I shall have to risk the French facility before we drive back to the villa, even if it is the customary overflowing, rank, cockroach-infested croucher in total darkness. I'm busting!"

The girls giggled again and Barbara sighed at the lavatory humour. A mincing waiter directed me around the end of the building at the far end of the terrace. As is the way of things in France, the path was not well lit or obvious. A track looped down between a cluster of olive trees. I could see the roof of a smaller building through the branches and a glimmering light mobbed by moths and mosquitoes. I decided that must be it. Fortunately, there was a full moon, otherwise I'd have needed a torch.

As I was gingerly making my way through the trees, heading for the light, my bladder enlarging by the second, I was aware that someone was coming the opposite way on what I took to be the path. I was reassured that I was not mistaken in my direction. We met head-on at the narrowest point of the track in a pool of moonlight.

It was Simone.

"Bon soir, Monsieur!"

I was momentarily struck dumb. Although I'd hardly stopped thinking about her for days, at that particular moment I was concentrating hard on finding the toilet and she was out of my mind completely. My mouth opened and closed. My tongue seemed paralysed. If she looked attractive on the beach, she looked even more stunning in evening wear. Eventually, I managed to splutter something in my feeble, schoolboy French.

"Ah, bon soir, Mademoiselle, um, Simone? Alors, je crois que…merde! I thought you had gone back to Paris?" I said, smiling and hoping her English was better than my French.

"Tomorrow. I too zought you had gone. I look for you; we miss you on…ah…le plage?"

"Well, we…it's just that…ma femme…"

I gave up the explanation. I couldn't say that, well, my wife thinks I'm a pervert and, apparently, I've been fucking you vigorously with my eyes, so she's put me in detention at the further end of the beach.

Simone grinned. She knew what I meant.

"Ah, oui, la femme!"

"You look very beautiful," I said. Suddenly the pressure in my bladder seemed to have disappeared only to be replaced by a different, more pleasurable pressure in an approximately similar location.

She chuckled but said nothing. She just looked into my face and raised that eyebrow again, just as she had on the afternoon of the jet-ski. She held my gaze for some time. I felt like a mouse mesmerised by the eye of the snake.

Then she began to move rapidly, just like that snake and something happened which at the time seemed hardly possible and seems no more credible now.

She glanced up the path behind me and looked quickly over her own shoulder. She grabbed my hand and pulled me off the track and into the smudgy darkness under the olive trees. I was shaking; said not a word, did not resist. What for? What was there to resist? She leant with her back against a trunk and pulled me towards her, putting her arms around my neck as she did so.

Naturally, my hands come to rest around her waist. Superb. Divine. Perfect. Sublime. Not a centimetre of surplus flesh but at the same time, not like embracing a sack of sticks. I felt a shudder run from my throat to my crutch. She hesitated for a second; not out of doubt, I don't think but, it seemed to me, simply to savour the moment.

Vive la France! Vive la bagatelle!

My head was swimming with the sense of her pulsing vitality under my hands, the fragrance of her perfume and her hair, and the intoxicating, nocturnal sounds and smells of Provence. There seemed to be a sound of waterfalls in my head. She brushed her mouth against mine and I heard myself whisper her name.

We kissed. Of course, it was a French kiss; how else? It was a long kiss, the kind that makes a grown man dizzy with desire. And dizzy does not really begin to describe the sensations taking hold of me. I ran my hand down her back. She was not wearing anything under the silk outfit, I was certain of that. I was acutely aware of the firmness of her breasts. I could see them in my mind's eye, the day she was on the beach, topless.

It was not possible for her to be unaware of my desire; on the contrary, she was rocking her hips against me, her thighs trembling like a shivering faun's. Fleetingly, I recalled the jet-ski dream and felt it blend with reality.

I could feel conscience and control ebbing. The girl had reduced me to a single passion, a single need which had to be fulfilled. Hang the consequences.

When I was about sixteen, a friend's father had told the both of us, "Remember, lads, a standing prick knows no conscience." Oh, how true, how true!

I brushed across her breast with my thumb, feeling the hard plum stone of nipple beneath the silk. She juddered, bit my lip and fumbled to find the hem of her dress. I knew things were progressing fairly successfully, shall we say, but as she lifted her dress I knew, with a sudden clarity, that it was going to happen. Not a dream. She wanted to do it there, under the trees, standing up.

But, wouldn't you sodding know it? A twig cracked and somebody laughed up by the restaurant. An irritable voice was calling her name. Simone cursed and pulled free from our embrace. She brushed herself down, flicked her hair, looked at me regretfully and turned to rejoin the track.

"Simone! Wait! You must give me your phone number!"

"Non, non! My fahzer is waiting! Mon pere, la bas, regardes-toi! He will be angry if he sees us 'ere. I must go, maintenant. Tomorrow, perhaps. Demain, peut-etre? But, of course, we 'ave to leave very early."

"But we both have to leave tomorrow. Can I meet you somewhere later? Please don't go just yet! Simone!"

She laughed and shook her head. It was too late. She was already at the top of the track; she turned and gave me a sad little wave and then disappeared into the light and laughter of the terrace. The meeting and the embrace occupied no more than two minutes.

I did not ever see her again.

Later, having at least satisfied my bladder's demands, I walked back up to the track, a profound despair settling upon my shoulders. I was heartbroken; as if there had been a proper relationship between us which she had suddenly and irrationally terminated. How could that be? The feeling remained.

Lying awake in the villa that night, the sensations were still tingling on my lips and my finger-tips, not to mention the rest of me. I wondered whether she was also awake, thinking of me? No, I decided, probably not.

For her, it was just a bit of fun. What else could it be? What self-respecting girl would give herself to a complete stranger under the olive trees? And she was going to, no mistake about that. What Spike Milligan refers to as a "knee-trembler" was undeniably on the agenda. The slut! It dawned on me as I lay there, that she was completely in control of the situation. I was a willing participant, no doubt, but she was conducting the score.

Supposing at the last moment, the pulsing, molten-metal moment before the glory of penetration, I had changed my mind? I concede that it's extremely unlikely.

"Look, I say, would you mind terribly if we came back tomorrow? I've just remembered a dental appointment."

No. But just for the sake of the argument, suppose I had cried, "No! Stop! This is so wrong! Unhand me, wench! Get thee to a nunnery, you hussy!" And she had ignored me and pulled me into herself, clamping me to her and riding me like a horse until I needed towelling dry?

"Mon Dieu, m'sieur, c'est fini toute-de-suite? Quel domage! Merde alors!"

Would I have been raped? Who knows. But I think I would have enjoyed the research.

I decided that by Barbara's definition anyway, she was a young tart and I was a bloody old fool to think otherwise. Such a physical, animal encounter is not the prelude to a relationship. It is an end in itself. But wait a minute! Who was looking for a relationship anyway? No, bugger that! I'd have settled for a shag under the trees with a girl less than half my age. You bet your sweet bippy.

Barbara, of course, does not like the word "shag". It is common. But it is correct for these circumstances. For Simone, I think, an illicit sexual encounter with a stranger, would have been what Erica Jong called, 'a zipless fuck'.

I was not important to her as a person; she was simply fascinated by the power she had to pluck me off the beach. Pluck'n'fuck! Make a good game show, presented by Cilla Black.

During the three days between our return from Provence and the beginning of the term, I hardly spoke, hardly ate and, naturally, Barbara correctly divined the reason. From our table at the restaurant on the last night, she had seen Simone appear from the path, followed only a few minutes later by me. Apparently, I was looking flustered and tearful, like, she said, a man who had suffered bereavement. My eyes were darting from one party of diners to another as if my life depended on finding someone among them, she said.

Later, once more fuelled by the wine she had drunk with the meal and the last of the brandy in the villa's pantry, she challenged me, again, about my frequently withdrawn and silent behaviour.

"So you can't make love to your wife, but you can hump some little tart under the trees? Some little tart that, according to you, you've never even spoken to? That you don't even bloody know? No problem getting a hard-on with her, right? And all over in a couple of minutes like dogs in the road! Bastard! Disgusting, shagging bastard!"

"Ssh! You'll wake the girls!" I hissed. "Although if they're still asleep, it'll be a miracle; it's like Vesuvius in here! Don't be ridiculous, Barbara. You're suggesting I screwed her in the open on a public footpath? I've never heard such nonsense!"

Of course, my tone was unconvincing.

I thought I'd try blaming Simone. I said she was predatory and had pounced on me. Well, that was true to a large degree. I suppose I did unzip my fly myself, though. Barbara snorted derisively.

"Ah! Mumsy-wumsy! Poor little victim Mikey, is it? Just minding his own business on his way for a wee-wee and the rapacious French girl-slut jumps on him and pulls his trousers down and gets his little willy out? Don't give me that! If that was the case, then your behaviour would have been one of righteous indignation when you got back to the table, not lovesick loneliness. And there was a damp patch on the front of your trousers. Bastard!"

All common sense and reason told me that Barbara was right. I had behaved very badly and I ought to make amends and stop carrying on like a love-sick teenager. It would have been far better to cut the memory adrift, try to muddle along with Barbara, try to offer her some reassurance.

But I couldn't.

SPIDER'S WEB

Two girls are sitting arm-in-arm on a cloakroom bench. They are friends. It is a few minutes before four in the afternoon and the worst of the scramble to be first out of the building and on to the buses has subsided. Cleaners are beginning to appear with giant brooms and mops which give off a smell of cabbages. A small boy with a tear-stained face is outside the office window, blubbering something about having lost his bus fare. Ellie checks her watch for the umpteenth time.

"Have to go in a minute," she says.

Tracey looks at her sideways.

"D'you want me to wait?"

"Up to you. Might be some time, I suppose."

"You hope! So what are you going to do? Ask him to give you a lift home?"

Tracey giggles uncontrollably at the thought of it.

"I still can't believe that you're going to do this."

"Why not? I told you, I need to talk to someone about it. I trust Doctor Mike. That's all."

"Oh, yeah? That's not all, Ellen Fortune, and you know it. We both know you fancy him like crazy. You always have. You haven't had the courage before. But now, well, you're so hot for it these days! You're really different this year, you know that? Must be since you did it with that lad on holiday."

"Look, I didn't do it with him, alright? Like nothing happened. Not really."

"Not! In your letter you said you were going to do it. So, now you reckon you just lay there and discussed the weather? Yeah? Come on, admit it: there was rumpy-pumpy, wasn't there?"

"Look, Trace, I don't really want to talk about it. Like, it's, well, embarrassing. I wish it had happened, but it didn't. That's all I'm saying."

They have been friends for years. They are close. She does not understand Ellie's reluctance to tell her what happened, or did not happen, in the Isle of Man.

The small boy's blubberings at the office turn to a wail as he comes face to face with the flinty indifference that Miss Hawthorn, the office secretary, has for all small boys. Ellie is grateful for the distraction and calls across the foyer to him.

"Here you are, I'll lend it to you. You can pay me tomorrow."

The boy shuffles towards them. She hands over some coins. He wipes his nose on his sleeve and smiles.

"Thanks," he snuffles and then more confidently, "Cor, I wish you was my sister! I'll bring it tomorrer, promise!"

*

Ellie arrives at Doctor Chadwick's door at precisely one minute past four. Michael cups his hand over the telephone's mouthpiece and signals to her.

"Come in and sit down, Ellie. It's OK, this is not private."

She hopes that it will be private in a minute and that she can manage to talk to him. She hopes he'll understand. He's kind, he's handsome and such a hunk.

Michael hangs up the phone.

"Just some bureaucrat at County Hall ticking me off because we've used one hundred and six too many paperclips this week."

He smiles at her. She looks puzzled.

"It's a joke, Ellie; you know? Ha! Ha! Dear me, what a serious face. Now, what's all this about?"

"Would you mind if I close the door, Sir? It's a bit personal."

"Well, strictly speaking, it should be open, Ellie. You know, male teacher and female student behind a closed door. Not quite the done thing from either of our points of view, if you follow me. But since it's you, I'll make an exception."

"Thank you."

There is a pause.

"Perhaps I can help to get this started, Ellie? I take it this is a personal matter, rather than a school matter?"

"Yes."

"OK. Well, that may make it a little more difficult for me, depending on the subject, but let's give it a try. Let's see; about a boyfriend?"

"No, Sir. I haven't got a boyfriend."

"Really? I find that hard to believe!"

She wonders whether she should add that she's available. And willing.

"Family problem?"

Michael leans his elbows on the arms of his chair and puts his fingertips together. He thinks that when he gets to the bottom of this, he'll wish he hadn't.

Ellie takes a deep breath and rushes headlong into her thoughts before she has time to change her mind.

"It's about my step-father, Brian. I think he's going to, well, he keeps…"

She stops suddenly. It looks as though she's about to cry.

"Take it gently, Ellie. Start from the beginning, eh? You have a step-father. Right. I didn't know that. When did your mother marry Brian?"

"Dad went off when I was eight. Terrible rows with Mum. So bad that Dad used to come and sleep in my room sometimes! He went off with Stephanie. That's his wife now. I see them, but not very often. They live in Scotland. I miss him, you know?"

"Of course. I know."

"Although it's easier at home without him around. Apart from the arguments Dad was always trying to, like, get me on his side against Mum or make me keep secrets from her, so I'd end up in the middle and feel guilty all the time. Then one night there was a really bad row and the next day, he was just gone.

Brian goes to our church. I don't go now, if I can help it. I've known him all my life. After Dad went he seemed to be around at home a lot; one excuse after another, you know, like helping Mum with this heavy job or that trip to town and stuff. I didn't think too much about it and then suddenly one day, like, Mum says they're getting married."

Michael has heard enough to know what's coming. He's been here before. He's also heard enough to know that if his suspicions are correct, he'll have to pass this over to Betty in the morning. It's way outside his field of competence. And she's a girl. But for now, let Ellie unburden herself.

"So were you happy for your Mum?"

"In a way. But I also felt that Brian was pushing into Dad's place, even though he'd gone and it was calmer for me. It was like I was being put to one side. Even more so when Benjamin was born. He's lovely, you know, I love him to bits but they're a family and I'm on the outside of it, especially now Emma's left home."

"So when did the real problem with Brian start, Ellie?"

Ellie shudders as she realises that Doctor Mike is ahead of her.

"Oh, well, about three months ago. I mean, until I was fourteen or so, he didn't take any notice of me at all, except to tell me off about my hair or something. And then, after, well, after I, you know, started to, um, get my woman's shape."

Michael nods. He knows. He can see she's "got her woman's shape". Ellen smiles, blushes again and then takes a deep breath.

"He keeps looking at me, Doctor Chadwick. Leering. Making these remarks about my body. The last three months it's been, like, every day, probably. And twice I've caught him trying to watch me through the window when I'm in the shower. He stands at the bottom of the stairs and watches me go up when I've got a skirt on. On Saturday, he was looking at my underwear on the line and, well, touching it. This morning, as I was on my way out of the door and as I passed him in the hall, he pinched my backside."

Alarm bells are ringing in Michael's head. "Not before time," he thinks to himself, "I've woken up to what's going on here. I've been confronted with this scenario three times before in my career, but never, ever has the girl outlined in such unselfconscious detail the step-father's actions. Not in front of me, anyway. And not without a great deal of crying. It's almost as if she's trying to titillate. Is she? Is she making it up completely? Or is it me that's askew because she's so beautiful and I'm off-balance or whatever I am?"

"It feels like it's getting gradually worse, Sir. To begin with, I thought maybe I was imagining things, but I didn't imagine him pinching me this morning. I'm frightened that he's going to try something on with me, you know?"

"That's as far as it's gone? When he, er, this morning?"

"Yes."

"Have you tried to discuss this with your mother, Ellie?"

"You must be joking, Sir. I couldn't. Be too embarrassed. She wouldn't believe me anyway."

"Do you normally lie to your mother?"

"Of course not. Never."

"Well, you're her daughter. If you are not an habitual liar, she'll be bound to listen and take you seriously."

Ellie looks unconvinced. She doesn't want to discuss it with her mother.

"Do you take me seriously, Sir?"

Ellie swallows hard. It's a daring, forthright question although she doesn't understand just how probing it is. Michael looks surprised. It's a very adult question with a worrying sub-text. He has to be careful. Supposing he fobs her off, sends her away and then tonight her lecherous step-father tries to jump her?

Michael leans forward.

"Ellie, of course I do, but I'm going to have to hand this one over to Mrs Lane tomorrow. She's not in school today; otherwise I could ask her to come in now because it's her field of expertise, so to speak."

"I'd rather you dealt with it, Doctor Chadwick. I trust you."

"Thank you, Ellie, I'm flattered. But I'm afraid it's not an option. Quite simply, I cannot. I am not the expert here and the gender difference between us in any event makes it unwise. For both of us. So here's what we do now."

He finds some paper and, with Ellie's help, constructs a brief précis of what she has told him. He adds his two recommendations: that she should immediately speak to her mother or another trusted female and that he intends to bring the matter to the attention of Mrs Lane early next morning. He asks her to read it. They make a couple of alterations and then they both sign.

He apologises for being so formal, but explains that it is a serious allegation that she makes and therefore, in both their interests, it is best that both agree on exactly what has been said. What he doesn't say is that he thinks he ought to cover his back. Just in case.

She understands. She is grateful and reassured by his calm approach. She wants to hug him and kiss him goodbye. Instead she flutters her eyelids a little and gives him her best smile.

*

By the time Michael sets out for home, it is dark. It has been a busy day. He still has a good deal to do after dinner this evening. A multitude of tasks. He wonders whether he can find the energy. He has no stomach for another three hours of books, essays, timetables and consultation documents. He just wants to sit, perchance to dream.

The car headlights lick tree trunks and bushes as he deftly takes the snaking road through the valley that is his favoured route home.

A rabbit, flicking its tail, hop-scotches illogically from one place to another on the road. It stops. It is too close. There is a soft thudding as the creature is struck by the oil sump and drawn under a wheel. Instinctively, he applies the brakes.

In the rear view mirror, illuminated by the plastic red glow of his lights, he sees the mangled rabbit twitching and convulsing on the tarmac.

CHRYSALIS
1997

When I was about thirteen and a half, I used to spend most of my life, naked, in front of a big mirror in Mum's bedroom. Turn this way; turn that way, very slowly. Like, inspecting myself to see if anything was growing. It never was. Then I'd run back to my room, lock the door and cry.

I had a body like a boy's. Straight up and down. I had boy's legs, all bony and long. I had a boy's bum. It was small and sort of straight down from my back. I must have looked like a walking ladder. But what would I give for that little bum now that things have enlarged and sagged a tad!

I couldn't make it wiggle when I walked. I tried and tried in front of that mirror to make it twitch and roll about like Emma's, but it wouldn't.

The real embarrassment was that I had a boy's flat chest! And all the other girls in my tutor group started their periods before me. I was convinced it was never going to happen. It's true I was the youngest girl in the group, as Mum never tired of reminding me. My birthday is August 20th. But even so, thirteen and a half is quite late to start your periods, isn't it? I had just persuaded Mum to take me to Doctor Martin and then it happened.

It started to get really embarrassing when we got changed for PE. Some of the others were proud of what they had and would show it off a bit; walk around with just their brassieres instead of putting on their blouses straight away. I would try to get changed very quickly in the corner, sort of under my blouse or something so nobody would notice.

That's how it is when you're thirteen. You only see the bad things when you look in the mirror. I was always being told that I had beautiful, big green eyes. Like a cat. But who wants to be told they look like a bloody cat when they're thirteen?

I remember reading about pheromones in one of those teen magazines. Like this chemical kind of smell that you have which is special to you. It's supposed to attract the male of the species. At certain times in your monthly cycle the pheromones go ballistic. That's when you get male interest, it said. I reckoned that because I didn't have my periods yet, that maybe I didn't have any pheromones either, which would explain why I didn't have a boyfriend.

I wanted to have a boyfriend. Well, to be honest, I was desperate for one. But at the same time I was worried that I might not know what to do if one came along. How to kiss. I mean, no one ever teaches you that stuff, do they? I mean you get all that information about erections and condoms and penetration and ejaculation and the seed scorching up the fallopian tube and all that, but they don't tell you how to kiss! In my opinion, it's harder than the main event. Most men, let alone boys, are complete crap at kissing.

I have only found one man in my life so far who really knew how to kiss. Heaven. He kissed me senseless in a meadow. It was our wedding breakfast.

Anyway, there's kissing and snogging. They're not the same, are they? As a kid you get kissed all the time, right? Your Mum, your Aunty; whoever. But that's just affectionate or dutiful, it's not meant to get you going. So when some boy suddenly plants his wet lips on you for the first time or tries to push his tongue down your throat and he's all slobbery and tasting of onions, it's a bit of a shock.

When I was eleven, Carl Summers tried to snog me at the school disco. I suppose that was the first time that a boy kissed me sexually. Like, he thought it was sexual but I certainly didn't. Gross! Everyone else was doing it so I thought, oh well, why not? Got to try it some time.

But neither of us knew what we were doing and he just slopped his loose lips on top of mine. Sort of like a plunger over the plug-hole. I didn't know what to do so I just sat there like, sort of braced, like I was in a dentist's chair until he'd had enough. It tasted horrible, like sour milk or that bloody vile yoghurt drink they sell now in little plastic bottles. There was all this dribble on his chin. I thought I was going to chuck for a minute, what with that and all the pop corn I'd stuffed.

Mum wouldn't have let me have a proper boyfriend anyway. She said I was too young and there would be "plenty of time for all that malarkey". That's how she sees intimate relationships: "malarkey". She reckoned I was better off with the rabbit because they don't get drunk and they don't live so long. Sarcastic cow!

Until I was at least fifteen, no one took much notice of me at all unless you count slobbering Carl Summers. Boys ignored me and so did men. Well, mostly. They didn't look at me as a woman.

Maybe it would have been better if I'd stayed that way. Unattractive to men. It would have saved a load of heartache all round. But you don't know about the sad times until it's too late, do you?

A lot has happened in my life since I was innocent fifteen, let alone thirteen. Well, innocent as in virginal. I wasn't ignorant. There is a difference!

Like the song says, 'Love Hurts'. Physical pain is easy beside emotional pain although you can't really know it until you've had the pain yourself. Or caused someone else the pain, like I have.

Until she left home, I shared a bedroom with Emma. She used to tell me everything about her boyfriends. Because I was so much younger and so behind physically, she probably felt that some of what she was telling me would go over my head. Some of it did because I couldn't fully relate to the physical geography of it all, especially a man's urges and physical reactions. Well, maybe that's not quite true. I kind of knew about it although I couldn't work out why.

So it wasn't that I didn't know about sex before I was sixteen. I read everything I could get my hands on, I heard about it at school and Emma's stories and porno tapes would make your hair curl. It seems I've always known about it. I can't remember a time when I didn't, anyway.

I know I have a very strong sex drive. More like a man's if you see what I mean. Won't be denied. Takes me over completely sometimes; one time in particular.

"Like your father," Mum said once in an unusually candid moment. She didn't mean it as a compliment.

So, I suppose I had that sex drive even at thirteen but it must have been in my head and nowhere else. It was like I was in a parallel universe until that holiday in the Isle of Man just before I was sixteen. I was drowning in pheromones that summer!

So, then men started to look at me. Much older men; I mean guys in their thirties, forties and fifties! And I mean, really look at me. Not just a glance like you might clock a road sign. Assessing me; sizing me. Stripping me. Depending on who it was, I wanted them to or I didn't.

Older men! Well, boys are so bloody immature, aren't they? I fancied older men. I still do. They know how to turn me on. So what? It happens all the time, all over the place. Always has and always will. Just like older men fancy young girls. I've done the reading, so I know what it's about.

Girls whose fathers piss off when they are pre-pubescent often fall for older men: the father figure. Yeah, right.

MANX GULLS
August 1990

All along the shore, there are children playing in the rock pools and running up and down the great expanses of sand temporarily exposed by the long withdrawal of the tide. The sand is clean, a soft yellow and brown, shaped in ripples and ridges by the last waves as they responded to the moon's insistent pull just before dawn.

A small boy, dressed in a red jumpsuit, is tracing the ridges in the sand with his toes and making little marks on them with a piece of stick. His parents watch affectionately from a little way up the beach. Every now and then, the woman makes as if to go to him, fearing he is going to fall down, for he is only two years old and unsteady yet on his feet. The man irritably restrains her, telling her that the boy is fine.

"He's not in any danger. It's low tide, the water is several hundred yards away. He can't come to any harm. Leave him alone, for Goodness' sake!"

As though he can hear his father the boy looks up and jauntily waggles his stick. The mother waves back and smiles. The toddler sees some other children by a rock pool and potters across to watch them. They are prising limpets from the smooth grey rocks and gathering them in a bucket.

Up behind the town, the Albert Tower sits square and indomitable, glowering down on the fripperies of the beach as it has done every day for a hundred years. It sits upon a commanding rise and can survey the whole town and north towards the Point of Ayre. The flanks of the hill are dense with pine trees and thickets of fern, their light green fronds luxuriating now in the moist warm breeze from the south. Gulls circle the tower, their odd, rasping cries echoing round the glens behind and below them.

The father has a pair of binoculars. He pretends to watch sea birds and periodically jots something in a notebook. Sometimes he turns his gaze towards the Tower. It is a favourite retreat for teenagers. The man licks his lips in anticipation of magnified, illicit congress.

Down in Lheaney Road, in the shadow of the tower, an old lady hobbles into her garden, her apron held in front of her, full of broken bread and scraps of bacon. She looks up, makes a cawing noise and the gulls wheel down towards her.

She is worried about her grand-daughter. Ellie is just sixteen and seems greatly changed since last summer.

"How she's filled out in such a short time! Extraordinary. And argumentative too, when she's not mooning about or sitting under the monkey puzzle tree, waiting for the milkman's boy to come by. I hope the girl is not going to go off the rails. We've had one in the family already down that road, we can do without another. The shame of it!"

Down at the harbour, Ellen Fortune is sitting on a wall, watching the fishing boats and waiting. She is pretty, with creamy skin and extraordinary, compelling green eyes. There is a thick tousle of long, dark, curly hair, artfully pulled up off her neck and secured with a grip so that strands fly loose in the breeze. She wears a pair of shorts and a tight, ribbed top, both accentuating her shape. It is a shape she is pleased with, like a new toy, a long-awaited present.

Her step-father is looking at her new shape too, through his binoculars, from his position on the beach.

She is sweet sixteen and only recently been kissed, unless you count Carl Summers, which she doesn't. She hopes to further her progress very soon, very soon indeed. Next week she returns to school to start her 'A' level courses. She is fed up with being a late developer and always the last in the race.

The sounds from the fishing fleet are almost drowned by the gulls and the clatter of a tram as it squeals and screeches to a halt in the station. From the open sides of the first car a boy jumps down and looks towards the harbour wall.

Simon Quale is nineteen, lithe, tall and good-looking with a shock of blond hair. He wears a pair of Levis and a tight white t-shirt, giving him something of the air of an Australian ranch hand rather than a Manx dairyman's assistant.

Ellie sees him straight away and waves a hand excitedly, jumping up and down so that he can see her in the crowd of holidaymakers thronging the kiosks by the harbour. Recognising her, he grins confidently and calls her name.

She waves back and smiles. She wasn't sure whether he'd taken her seriously yesterday. Ellie feels a sudden rush of dizzy excitement. She is meeting this handsome young man not because she loves him forever but because she fancies him and he'll do for what she has in mind. Today, this day of balmy late summer, she proposes to lie with him on the ferns under the Albert Tower and let him take her virginity.

It's urgent and it's time.

CHAMELEON
1997

In the last year of Granfer Benson's life I only saw him once. There was so much crap going on at home with Mum and Dad that we didn't go over to the Isle of Man that summer as usual. When we did go, it was much later in the year. He'd asked to see me and Emma because he knew he was dying. Nobody told me that he was and I think they should have done. He died about two weeks after we got back to Somerset and I cried for days. I think I'd have been able to cope better if I'd known when I had seen him that I wouldn't ever see him again. My bloody family! Dysfunctional, I reckon.

I loved it at their bungalow in Ramsey. Even though we only went once or twice a year, it felt more like home than home itself. Maybe because I associated it with calm and quiet and unconditional love.

By the time I knew them, they were sleeping in separate single beds but in the same room. Weird what happens when you get old! Gran said that he fidgeted and kicked all night and she couldn't sleep next to him. One day, I overheard her talking to her friend Elsie, who used to visit every Thursday afternoon.

"Anyway, Frank doesn't make demands anymore."

She said it sort of hesitantly and almost regretfully, I thought. Elsie snorted.

The day Gran died was just awful. One of the worst days of my life. Mum and Brian had taken little Benjamin down to the beach and I had arranged to meet Simon. The summer I was boiling over with teenage lust. He must have thought bloody Christmas had come early! But it was a disaster. I was so charged up and anxious that when it came to it, I couldn't actually do it. Of course, I suppose some of the shit I'd hidden was making me frightened, but I didn't understand that at the time. I sort of had a spasm down below and like, shut him out! Shame!

It was so upsetting and humiliating that I just grabbed all my stuff and ran off, leaving Simon lying in the ferns, still on full alert! I ran all the way down the hill back to Lheaney Road without stopping, tears of frustration and embarrassment running down my face.

I think it was about three o'clock when I reached the bungalow. If I hadn't been so upset, I might have realised that there was a strange silence about the place. Gran always had the radio on very loudly, on account of her hearing, every afternoon. But it wasn't on. What's more, the back door was wide open and the ironing, a job she always did in the morning, was still on the table, untouched. I kind of knew then that something was wrong.

I found her lying at the bottom of the attic stairs, an old crocheted tablecloth under her crumpled body. There was a dribble of dried blood on her forehead. I called out, I think and bent down to her but, although I had never seen a dead person before, I knew she was dead. Then I screamed.

Later Dr. Phelps told us that it was heart failure and it would have been very sudden and was probably brought on by the exertion of climbing the steep stairs. She would have known very little, he said. Mum and I were just beside ourselves with guilt. I mean, like, how could we have left her for so long? What were we thinking of? Did she fall and then cry out for help, alone, before she died? None of it bore much thinking about but, of course, we couldn't stop thinking about it.

Mum remembered that Grandma had been on about a family heirloom before we went out and we realised that's why she'd gone up to the attic, which she didn't really do at all by then. She'd gone to find it. And obviously, she'd been successful because it was under her body at the bottom of the stairs. We started upsetting ourselves then about whether she'd fallen all the way down or, we hoped, just the last few steps.

When I went up to bed that evening, I started crying all over again. What had already happened that day was bad enough, but upstairs I saw the letter I'd left on the bed when I'd dashed off to meet Simon. I was writing to Tracey about what I was proposing to do with him and I didn't mince my words! I also told her that I saw Brian trying to ogle me through the frosted glass in the bathroom when I was having a shower.

So, it wasn't a letter I would have wanted Gran to read. I don't think she would have done; private correspondence and all that, but I was sure I'd left it in a slightly different place to where I found it.

Surely, she wouldn't have? But if she did read it, then her last thoughts about me would have been so bad. I wondered whether it was shock that brought on the heart attack, not climbing the stairs?

Guilt. How do you live with it?

ROUGH BEAST
October 24th 1990

When Ellie gets home from her meeting with Dr. Mike, she is surprised to find the house empty. Her mother has left a note on the kitchen table explaining that she and Brian have taken little Benjamin to the Church Hall for a surprise birthday party for Abigail, the Pastor's three year old daughter.

"There's some pie in the oven. Make sure you do your homework before you switch on the television! Seems a bit late for a kiddies' party but it's the only time Pastor Jamieson can manage, apparently. Busy at other times with the Lord's work he says! See you at about 7.30. Love Mum. x x."

Ellie looks at her watch. Only five forty. She decides to have a shower; perhaps she was sweating in Doctor Mike's office just now? She hopes not! Doctor Mike! She closes her eyes and his concerned face forms in front of her, smiling.

But first, she will find her old notebook, the one in which she used to write stories about Doctor Mike and write in it again before she forgets a single thing. And this time it's real!

Half an hour later, she steps into the tiled shower cubicle, her mind still engaged with the erotic paragraph she has just composed. She lets the water jet over her hair and down her back. She likes it hot. Her hands slick shower gel over the flat of her stomach, up under her bust and down to her inner thighs. It is as if Doctor Mike's soft, gentle hands are slicking the oil confidently, searchingly over her body! She shudders.

"I wish! Dream on, Ellie!"

The noise of gurgling water and the technicolour fantasies of Ellie's thoughts mean that she does not hear a key in the lock, the opening and closing of the front door, or the soft click of the latch and a bolt being shot.

*

Brian Shepherd is the worst kind of religious fundamentalist. He should be called Wolfe, not Shepherd. He lives his life wearing his Christianity on his sleeve: quoting the Lord's word, insisting on Grace in strangers' houses, attending Church ostentatiously, saying "Amen" a tad too loudly, exhorting neighbours to pray, espousing a rigid, literal adherence to the Ten Commandments and the Old Testament.

He wants to be known in his community as a man of God, a morally unimpeachable citizen, an example to others. There is an almost contemptuous confidence about his Faith: he is doing it right, others have a very long way to go before they can believe as he does. He brandishes his God before him, a righteous staff to ram down the throats of sinners and backsliders, the better to make them aware of their shortcomings.

As is often the way with such zealots, his sermonising pronouncements are the only substance of his Christianity. There is nothing else. Where there should be compassion, in Brian's heart there is only contempt and disdain. Where we might look for generosity of spirit or purse, there is meanness instead. When we seek sympathy and understanding, we shall find naught but self-satisfied condemnation. There is no conciliation, only confrontation; no negotiation, just cold negation.

This evening, Brian has a headache. Or so he has told his wife and Pastor Jamieson, before beating a thankful retreat from the squalling pandemonium of the children's party. He is hurrying home now, his head down against the damp wind, his heels rapping the pavement with steel-tipped blows.

He is hot and he is cold. He has a picture in his mind, something so depraved, so hump-backed and animal that he is hardly able to acknowledge its lip-foaming presence. His conscience, fighting the foul-breathed creature, tells him to keep moving, walk on past the house, keep walking and walking, along the river, up the valley and back again until the thing in his head gives up and goes away.

What darkness drives him tonight only he and his God can know. Whether he has fully-formed and pre-meditated designs on his step-daughter would be for a Crown Court to decide here on Earth and for St. Peter to assess at some later, as yet unspecified juncture, in another place.

Certainly, he has in his mind that the girl will be at home on her own. Undeniably, in recent months, he has found her presence under his roof deeply, physically arousing. Without question, he is agonizingly frustrated for he has slowly discovered what Barry Fortune could have told him years ago, if he had been able to ask. Linda is frigid and unresponsive. She holds to the view that intercourse is for procreation and even then, it is to be executed no more than monthly, with minimum discussion and preamble and with maximum speed in the accepted missionary position under cover of darkness. With her eyes closed.

Ellie's outline to Michael Chadwick two hours ago is in essence correct, except that it is considerably less than half the story. No one except Brian and his omnipotent God will ever know the extent to which the vipers in his mind have multiplied, the extent of the raging nightly torment of his tumescent lust or the frequency of the groaning, splattering, shameful self-abuse behind the locked, garden shed door. He has a photograph of Ellen, in a bikini on Ramsey Beach, fingered and soiled, propped up by the seed trays.

There is no denying either that he has just let himself into the house, quietly and stealthily, even though his conscious mind has no knowledge of any intended action, since it has separated itself now from the more sinister forces beneath. This is a device well known to the religious hypocrite, for only in that way can they continue to pray and worship the Lord.

So what rough beast is this, its hour come round at last, which slouches towards Bethlehem to be born?

*

Ellie has finished her shower and is rubbing moisturising cream into her thighs. She closes her eyes and pretends it is him. She is breathing heavily through her nose.

It was a serious and worrying conversation this afternoon, but it was a conversation with him alone, she had his undivided attention and there was a frisson of something between them. Wasn't there? She smiles to herself.

"Well, if not, there will be next time. What am I thinking? Next time! Where are you trying to take this, Ellie my girl? All the way, of course!"

She laughs as she wraps one hand towel around her head and clutches another, much too small, into a wrap around her upper body. But it doesn't matter; they won't be back for ages yet. Nevertheless, to be on the safe side, she listens briefly before stepping onto the landing. Just the clock ticking in the hall.

She pauses for a moment outside her bedroom door, her back to the staircase. Unseen, a shadow shifts below her, a flicker of blackness. She adjusts the slipping towel and then fumbles with the door knob. She cannot grip it firmly because there is still cream on her hands. She wipes her hand on the towel and tries again.

The house is not empty. Brian is at the bottom of the stairs. His right hand is gripping a stair spindle so hard that his fingernails show pulsing cream moons. There is a half-naked girl on the landing above him. He bites his lip. He can see the voluptuous curve of her rump as the towel flaps; as she leans forward to the door-knob, he sees the generous, swollen firmness of her breasts; a shaft of light from the bathroom draws the contour of her inner thighs.

There is another shifting of blackness and a whispering hiss. Satan is in the house and has wormed a nest in the believer's heart. It wasn't so hard. He just knocked twice, called a name, conjured an image and the heart let him right in.

The Prince of Darkness is overwhelmed with lust. His mouth is dry, his tongue working aimlessly. His hand goes to his groin and finds a pulse, a swelling.

A shape leaps to the top of the stairs, almost in one bound. The girl turns to face it on the landing. The towel slips; she shrieks and tries to cover herself again, but the towel falls to the floor.

She screams in anger and acute embarrassment.

"Go away!"

The shape makes a strange noise in its throat.

"What are you staring at? You leering bastard! Go on, then, have a good look why don't you, you lecherous weirdo! Satisfied now, pervert? Now fuck off! Leave me alone!"

She kicks the door with her heel and tries to get inside and lock it.

The Devil is quick. He pushes her into the room, dart of slippery night, key flicked, door locked, one fluid movement.

She is naked. She pulls the towel down from her hair, trying to hide herself. The beast's eyes are upon her, the tongue flicking red. She yells at the Devil.

"Get the hell out now! What the fuck do you think you're doing, Brian, you filthy pervert?"

The Devil pleads and wheedles a little, smoothing his tail again, wanting to touch and to savour this ripe young fruit. Sink his teeth in, suck the essence within. He clutches at her and she tries to cover her breasts. Tonight, the Devil has luck, has power and phenomenal strength; he pulls the girl's arm behind her back and jerks it up hard.

She screams and tries to kick behind her, tries to bite the free hand which is mauling her breasts, probing her crotch. He is nimble, this incubus, and strong.

The more she struggles, the more its stampeding lust is inflamed. It is aroused by a fight. It is as if it has five hands, for it restrains her and undoes its belt and feels her some more, all in one go. Its tongue is silvered now, foaming with spittle and mucus. Its breath is hot on her back and it bites her neck and whispers vile obscenities in her ears. It jerks the arm again and she yells, for she fears for her life.

"Ellie, Ellie," says the Devil, "stop struggling and it won't hurt so much. Just let me, please let me; you know you want to, you said so just now, you slut!"

"No! No! Brian! Stop it, do you hear, stop it now! I don't want you to; I didn't mean.. You pervert bastard! Help!!" she shrieks and yells again and again.

The Devil thinks it must be quick; the good Christian neighbours will hear through the party walls! They will raise the alarm; let it not be said they would turn up the volume a little louder on their television sets, would cross to the other side.

It strikes her a fierce, vicious blow on the head which stuns her. It throws her face down on the bed and it slaps her again. Protruding eyes clouded by the vipers of desire, it feels for its buttons. It steps smoothly from its disguise; its pointed, steel-hard tail has blue scales and white slime.

Fire and flames. Writhing limbs. Kicking, snarling, ripping, biting, licking. Forcing, prying claws. Tearing at soft flesh.The tail pulsing, pushing, ramming. The Beast has two backs. Screaming and blood. A triumphant, hooting groan of release.

Careering laughter; in a trice the Devil is gone, out of the door the way it came in. A faint odour of sulphur.

Left behind, a devout Christian and Church Elder, a breathless man of the Church, knock-kneed and pigeon-chested, his trousers round his ankles.

Crumpled on the soiled and bloody bedspread, a half-conscious, naked girl, claw marks on her breasts and the Devil's juice in her belly.

OLD DOGS

It takes Ellie no more than a few seconds to regain full consciousness. Although Brian has struck her a bruising, heavy blow, her fury has brought her back to the surface very rapidly. She rolls to cover herself in the bed sheet, aiming a kick at him. He is struggling to put on his trousers and staggers backwards as the kick hits his legs. Ellie screams, and pulls herself away from him to the bed head. She begins to hurl the things on the bedside chest: a book, make-up bottles, a coffee mug; anything that comes to hand.

"Get out of here you bastard! Get out! Get out!"

Her voice rises to a scream.

"Stop that or I'll hit you again!"

"You're a perverted, filthy, rapist bastard! And don't think you're getting away with this! Not fucking likely; I'm calling the Police. Now get out of my room!"

Adjusting his belt, he laughs a bitter, contemptuous laugh.

"Phone who you like, slut. Your word against mine! You consented, you dropped the towel, begged me for it and I reckon you like it rough. What's more, you were ready for it; wet, right? How else could I? You've been asking for it for weeks, parading your body in front of me. You're a whore and a foul-mouthed little slag! You want people to know that? I should keep your mouth shut, if I were you!"

"What!?"

Ellie's voice is shrill, hysterical but somewhere in the back of her mind she is calm enough to recall that this, of course, is the rapist's classic line of defence. Just get him out of the room; don't argue. Don't say anything. Stay calm; he's dangerous. You can phone later. Don't threaten him with exposure, he'll get angrier, remember? Remember? There is something to remember but I don't want...

"I'm not the first, am I? Hey, am I? And I can prove it. Your word against mine!"

She is confused, dizzy, perplexed. She says nothing. What he has just said registers. Prove it? Prove what? She summons strength just enough to stare at him as if he were a brown pastry of dog mess brought in on a shoe. What does he mean? Keep quiet? Keep quiet! Don't tell. Keep it a secret; what? No!

Anyway, there hasn't been anyone. Well, Simon Quale, but how could he know about that? Christ, the binoculars!

"You understand? You're not so innocent. I saw you with that boy in Ramsey! Just now, you heard me come in, you stood on the landing half-naked, you showed me; you enticed me in here and begged me to…"

He coughs, seems to choke, turns on his heel, unlocks the door and slams out of her room. A few moments later, she can hear the shower running.

"No! I didn't consent," yells Ellie at the closed door. "No way. No, no, no! You raped me. You slimy, loathsome bastard! You raped me!"

From somewhere, Ellie remembers some advice about sexual assault. She is surprised to find this coming to her mind; surprised that she is not weeping uncontrollably, not hysterical. Surprised that somehow she is able to start building a wall around this thing already to hold it in, unseen.

The instinct for survival has got her this far: she has been raped but she is still alive. She knows many victims die at the rapist's hands. Her strength of character and determination will take her through the next stage: instinct and the lessons from somewhere tell her she must suppress the desire to run downstairs and douse herself at the kitchen sink. She must preserve the evidence and she must call the Police. Horror! But she must do this now. To delay might be to give weight to the bastard's story. And she might change her mind, or be persuaded to.

"No, I won't change my mind. He has hurt me, really hurt me. I feel dirty. He has taken…I was a virgin, wasn't I? I was, I was! I didn't encourage him, of course not. How could I? Did I? No! I hate him. I won't allow him to get away with this, even though it will be dreadful; God, so awful. And Mum will be hurt too."

She has to get out of the house. She wads her school blouse between her legs and grabs a pair of stretchy jogging pants to hold it in place. It hurts. There seems to be a lot of blood. She scrambles to find shoes, an anorak.

In less than ninety seconds she is down the stairs, through the door, into the street and hammering on the neighbours' door. Kindly Mrs Simpson appears and gathers her in.

"My God, whatever's happened? I thought I could hear screaming but you don't like to interfere, do you? You'd better come in. Dave! Help me with this poor girl, looks like she's been attacked or something."

Only when the Police have been called and she is drinking the hot, sweet tea that Mr. Simpson makes, does she start to react. She is shivering, shaking and wailing like a wounded animal.

The Police and an ambulance arrive before she has drained the cup.

*

Ellie is in the hands of sympathetic but insistent authority.

"Where is her mother, shouldn't she be here?"

When she is sufficiently recovered, they take her to the local station and the special room with the woman officer trained in these things. The Police Doctor carries out an examination, frowns, smiles at the girl, says she'll be alright. Privately, he is appalled. Writes notes on his pad. A kind woman officer says they must photograph her neck, her breasts, between her legs. The bruising; the tearing, evidence, you see. Swabs. Samples. Ellie cries but holds the woman officer's hand and suffers the indignities. It must be done. Promise of expert counselling, later. And a pill, of course, in case, you know, if you want it that is.

"Yes, thank you. It was my step-father, Brian Shepherd. He is the one who did this. He is an animal. I want to press charges. Are those the right words?"

"Alright dear, hold steady. First things first."

" Where is her mother?"

The examining physician reports verbally to the Detective that intercourse has taken place, of a violent and viciously damaging kind. Doubts it was consensual; not normal to see such injuries when the act is consensual but of course that is for the Court to decide, if it goes that far, which he assumes it will. His report will indicate extensive injuries, probable severe internal bruising, commensurate with forcible penetration. Having the girl admitted to St. Bede's for further checks and observation. At least overnight. May be internal bleeding.

"Where is her mother, doesn't the woman care?"

"It was my step-father who raped me. My mother's at Church."

*

Brian Shepherd is cowering, shaking, trembling, whimpering, dog-like, in the garden shed. Cold. He wonders what he did, what happened? Some kind of black-out? What to tell Linda? He tells himself it's the girl's fault: she sits on the

57

sofa with her legs in the air. Tight jeans, tiny sweaters accentuating her breasts, flaunting her body.

"Shows me her body! Asks me for it. Temptation too much. Terribly sorry."

He remembers his God and asks for forgiveness. No answer. God's on another call.

There is a flashing torch; the shed door opens and a policemen steps in. The beam catches a photo of a girl in a bikini.

"Hey, better take a look at this, Sarge; looks like dried spunk on the floor."

"No, you don't understand, it's water absorbent granules for gardening."

"That's right," says the policeman, "and that'll be a picture of a lupin? Come on, let's go."

*

At a quarter to eight Linda Shepherd pushes Benjamin in his buggy round the corner at the end of Church Road. A thin drizzle silvers the space under the street lamp. A dog yaps somewhere over Tinsmead way. She is hurrying to get out of the rain. She sees Brian being ushered into a police car.

"What's going on?"

Brian looks up but says nothing. His eyes are sad and frightened and he cries with his head in his hands.

"What's going on, Brian, tell me what's happened?"

Restraining policeman; balloon on the buggy; child screaming for Daddy.

"It was her," says the Daddy, "she's a little tart, you know. Saw her in Ramsey, up at the Tower, with the boy from the dairy. You didn't know? Not as innocent as she makes out. Made me do it; been tempting me for weeks; asking for it; sunbathing topless; flaunting herself. Sorry, so sorry, forgive me."

"What? Who? What are you talking about?"

Sudden realisation; instinct perhaps. Then doubt, horror, disbelief.

"Where's my daughter? Where are you taking my husband? Let me inside."

"Have to accompany you, Madam, don't touch anything unless we say so, forensic, you know."

All that blood and goo on the bedspread; Christ, he must have given her one!

"Mrs Shepherd, your daughter is accusing your husband of raping her, here in this house. There are samples we must take at the scene of the alleged crime. There may be items we shall wish to remove. We ask that you do not obstruct us in our duty. There will be a form to sign. Your husband has to accompany us to the station to help with enquiries."

"Rape? Rape? What nonsense. My husband is a devout disciple, a servant of God."

*

Dave Simpson in 'The Plough and Sail'. Customary pint with the lads, eight thirty. Rushes in, bursting with news, hardly thinks of his beer.

"Hey lads, guess what? That bloke next door to me, that Holy Joe Shepherd, pompous prick with the hymn sheet? Jumped on his step-daughter and shagged her half senseless! The wife reckons she heard 'em screaming, yelling, you know? Just finished our tea off an' the girl's bangin' on the door!"

So Dave Simpson, horrified and aroused at one and the same time by the girl's blood in his lounge.

"What you on about, Simpo, you daft pillock? He's got no more feeling than a pew-back! Probably got a dick like an earthworm, couldn't punch a hole in a doughnut! Ha! Ha! Ey, lads?"

"No straight up, I tell you, the wife heard him, shouting and groaning; you know, shooting his load!"

Dave Simpson letting his imagination paint the picture he'd like to see.

"Straight up; their window must have been open. There's no mistaking that sound when you hear it, is there? S'like a rutting stag, ain't it? Well, she oughta know, what, ey? Jam sandwich outside, flashing lights and paramedics. Then they took him off to the station."

"Really? Bloody hell! Well, that Ellie's a page three stunner with a body to die for, wouldn't mind it myself. How old is she anyway? Really; you don't say? I thought nearer to twenty; just shows you can't be too careful these days."

"We all seen her about," says a voice, "wigglin' her bloody great tits in a tight sweater. Young girls these days; asking for it, I reckon."

"Brian Shepherd?" says another. "That little prat?"

"Old blokes molesting young girls; bloody disgraceful," says a third, "might be your daughter. If it was mine, I'd be after them stringing the sod up. They all wear tight sweaters – it's the fashion. Don't mean they're askin' for it, does it?"

A few heads nod sagely in agreement. Others not so sure.

By ten o'clock, half the valley knows the story. Or they think they do because, of course, depending upon the who, the where and the why of the telling, the story shifts and changes. At one and the same time it is a heinous violation or a little tart getting her just desserts or simply a prurient fascination with the likely details of a nubile virgin's deflowering.

*

Michael Chadwick enjoys a pint too, some evenings. He finds the cosy, uncomplicated camaraderie of the 'The Plough and Sail' a refreshing contrast with the in-fighting and sniping of the staffroom. He likes the faded, jaded feel of the place; the greasy brown paint, the worn upholstery on the stools and the settle, the dead flowers on the windowsill. The same faces are there every night and usually the same conversations.

Michael will have a beer and perhaps a game of darts. Maybe he'll lever the malodorous old dog to one side, sit in the foetal glow of the inglenook and listen to Nibber ruminating about farming and valley life just before The Great War.

The place relaxes him. Later, especially if he finishes the evening with a shot of Jack Daniels, he'll sleep.

He won't sleep soundly tonight. What Larry tells him as his pint is pulled is a physical shock. It is so sickening that Michael has to sit down for several minutes to regain his composure.

He feels as if it is his own daughter who has been subjected to a brutal, sexual attack. Ellie's frightened face and twisting hands in his office that afternoon swim in front of his eyes. Could he, should he have done more? He would not be human if he did not feel guilt.

But he realises his feelings are not driven so much by professional concerns or even just the normal sympathy that one caring person can feel for another. It is more personal than that. There is revulsion and distaste at such a vile act, that a young woman so beautiful and so gentle, for whom, unaccountably, he feels so responsible, could be violated in such a way; in such a way as she had most feared and imagined in his presence but five or six hours ago. It was him, Michael Chadwick, not his role she had approached. And somehow he has failed her.

Fighting back tears, he pushes his beer to one side. It slops over the table. He stumbles from the pub and into the muddy, puddling wet of the car park. After the fug of the bar, the cold, damp air is like a wet fist. He stands still, swaying slightly, his brow furrowed in confusion.

He knows he has to speak to her. He wants to apologise for somehow not acting to prevent this terrible thing.

And there is something else?

SNARE

Whilst Michael stands in the rain, surprised at his feelings, Linda Shepherd sits by a hospital bed, struggling to understand the events spinning and careering around her mind.

The girl drifts in and out of sleep, sedatives having the run of her veins. She has a pale, clammy pallor, except around her neck where there are bruises, bites and scratches in glowing magenta, blue and charcoal. She has them "in her genital regions too" the nurses say.

Linda doesn't want to think about that.

On her arrival, a Doctor takes her to a private room and says that it would appear that her daughter has suffered forcible sexual penetration of a very violent kind. Stitches were necessary.

Linda purses her lips and shuts her mind.

"There may be further bleeding although tests and X-rays seem to suggest no permanent harm. Otherwise, bruising and lacerations which will mend with time. We're keeping her in at least overnight. The wounds will heal, Mrs Shepherd, but the mind is a funny thing. Could be repercussions. I advise counselling."

Humph! Linda trusts in the succour of the Lord.

"They are saying that Ellie has had sexual intercourse. The very words make me feel sick. She is too young. She's always been too young for... that. But raped? She fought the man but he overcame her, the Police say. Brian, she says. Ridiculous; there must be some mistake."

But she hasn't spoken to Brian yet and outside the house it was clear he was blaming Ellie. So was that tantamount to admitting that they had had intercourse? She supposes so and shudders at the vileness of the thought and wonders where blame is to be placed for this abomination?

"Vengeance shall be mine," sayeth the Lord.

In the snowstorm of emotions in her mind tonight, one thing, but only one, is clear. She cannot believe both her husband and her daughter.

"Did she encourage it, allow it, or was she forced? How could this have come about? Brian is not capable of these things. Not the things they are saying. Although he has seemed a little, inflamed recently. What was it that he said when the Police took him away? She *made* him do this? She led him on and he couldn't help himself. A man, to be sure and they're weak. It's her fault, then? She wanted him to? Disgusting, sordid, lascivious…my youngest daughter? My little girl?

Wilful, like Emma, of course, and forward too in recent months. They've both inherited Barry's waywardness, there's no doubt about that. I thought we'd seen the worst with Emma, but Ellie is much, much more hot-blooded. She has been showing herself off, it's true. That red sweater, so tight. She's grown too fast, she's out of control, can't cope with her own feelings. Hormonal imbalance? That must be it. Or could she have let in some boy and things got out of hand? Now she's turning it on poor Brian to cover up? Oh, dear, it's such a dreadful, embarrassing mess. God will surely send a sign."

Ellie stirs a little in the bed and moans like a ship in fog. She is lost for a while in a miasmic mist of her own swirling, boiling memories, blurred and distorted by sedative drugs. And then suddenly, she is awake, lucid and calling for water.

Hesitantly, Linda bends over the bed, kisses her fleetingly on the forehead, reaches for a tumbler of water and then sits back into the chair. Ellie senses her mother's reserve and confusion, sees the tense set of her shoulders, the taut line of her mouth. It is not what she wants to see; she wants to be enfolded in her mother's arms, protected, comforted, and loved.

"How are you feeling, dear?"

"Like shit."

"Ellie, try not to swear, dear; it's not nice."

"Mum, how do you think I'm feeling? Used. Dirty. Angry. Bloody angry and it hurts like hell. That do for starters?"

"Don't swear, Ellie, please. It hurts? Do you want me to call a nurse?"

"No."

More sobbing and then a long silence. Someone further down the corridor, in another room, is throwing up noisily.

"I left Mrs Simpson looking after Benjamin. Because Brian's at the Police Station, helping with enquiries."

"Helping with enquiries?" Ellie snorts. "Helping with enquiries? Mum, what are you on about? They've arrested him, haven't they?"

"No, dear, I shouldn't think so. You're still in shock, dear. Confused. Just asking him a few questions, I expect, to see if he can shed any light on…you know, about your…about the…about this evening."

Ellie looks incredulously at her mother. She begins to shout, her voice rising to a screech.

"Shed any bloody light? You are joking with me, Mum, aren't you? He raped me, Mum! Are you listening? Raped me!"

"Ssh, dear, people will hear. Try to keep calm."

Linda's eyes dart to the glass of the door, as if she is expecting to see grinning faces pressed against it. Ellie is shouting again.

"So what? I don't care if they do. My step-father's a bastard rapist! Do you hear that? Your creeping, loathsome, bastard husband is a fucking pervert and a rapist!"

Linda, anguished, gets to her feet and wags her finger in Ellie's direction.

"Ellen! Stop it at once, do you hear me? I'm not going to sit here and listen to that kind of talk. I don't know what's come over you these last few months."

"Don't start on that again, Mum. I've heard that one."

Ellie is breathing hard and there are beads of sweat on her forehead and over her mouth. Her hands are trembling, snatching and screwing the starchy sheet.

Linda sits down again, leans towards Ellie and speaks in an almost conspiratorial whisper.

"You're overwrought dear. I understand. Confused. But you shouldn't go shouting accusations like that. I don't know what happened. Not yet. I haven't had a chance to talk to Brian. Let's not get hysterical. I think we should pray together for the Lord's help in showing us a way through this trouble."

Taking a deep breath, Ellie rolls her eyes towards the ceiling and then returns them to her mother's face, to fix her with a stare.

"I know what happened, Mum, I was there. I am not confused. It is quite clear. I got in at five thirty-ish, read your note and had a shower. He must have come in while I was in the bathroom. I didn't hear him. The next thing I know, he's on the landing grabbing at me and then he drags me into my bedroom, looking like…well, I don't know, like a crazy madman. Evil. All spit round his mouth. More than usual, I mean. It was obvious what he had in his mind. He starts leering and pulling at himself and then he grabbed at me again; his hands were all over me, groping at me. I tried to hit him but he overpowered me, hit me and practically knocked me out!"

She pauses, partly to gauge the effect on Linda and partly to take control again of her emotions. Re-telling it is hard, painful, but she knows she must. Linda's lips are pursed again. Her eyes are focused somewhere on the opposite wall. She might just as well be listening to the Shipping Forecast, for all the emotion she is showing.

"He threw me on my face on the bed…and then he…pushed himself inside me…forced me, you understand?"

Her voice tails off, withering to a whine and a sob. There is a long pause. Linda shifts uncomfortably in her chair, reaches into her bag for her handkerchief, snuffles into it and dabs at her eyes.

"Ellie, I want you to listen to me. I want you to stop talking this way. No good can come of it."

"What do you mean?"

"Well, I'm sure we can sort this out ourselves, within the family, with God's help. If you keep talking the way you are, there'll be all sorts. Police, statements, legal costs, a trial. Shame. Newspapers, television. We'd be…"

Now it is Linda's turn to run aground on the jagged rocks of possibilities.

"The Police are already involved, Mum, aren't they? I called them from Mrs Simpson's. He's been arrested. I'm sure he has. Even if I wanted to, which I don't, we can't sort it out ourselves."

"Oh, Ellie!"

"I don't know how this works, Mum. I'm frightened. I need help. I need your help because I've been raped, abused. By your husband, Mum. Mum? Believe me, you have to believe me; it's the truth."

Linda shakes her head and looks at the floor.

"No. I can't believe it. There must be some mistake, some misunderstanding. Did you…have you got a boyfriend that you haven't told us about?"

"What? No, you know I haven't."

"I'm not sure what I know any more, Ellie. Well, maybe just some boy you met at school and invited home who, well, attacked you?"

"What? Mum, like, listen to me, alright? It was Brian. I wish it wasn't and I'm sure you do too, but it was," says Ellie, slowly and quietly as if the strength has suddenly ebbed from her.

"Look, dear, I know you and Brian have had your differences, but he's a good man, a good servant of God."

"A servant of God? Do me a bloody favour, Mum. He's an animal! And whatever I have to do, I'll do. If you won't or can't help, then I'll find someone who will! I think they said the Police will speak to me today and I have to give a statement or something, so that he's, er, charged."

"Ellie, you'll blow our family apart. Please, for all our sake's, just say that it was a mistake, that, you know, things got out of hand with a boyfriend and you're not pressing charges."

"You want me to lie? How fucking Christian is that? It was Brian, Mum. There is no boyfriend. I've been raped. How many more times do I have to say it? He did it and I've made up my mind. I had hoped you would believe me, but perhaps I should have known better."

"Oh, Ellie, it's not as simple as that. There are always two sides to every story."

"Of course it's simple! Two sides? How can there be two sides? He fucked me against my will!"

Ellie's voice rises to a rasp.

"I just cannot believe..."

The two women, mother and daughter, look at each other; so close and yet so far apart.

"Two sides for Christ's sake? He's already poisoned your mind, has he? I asked for it like a slut, right? Is that what he said? The bastard! So if I asked for it, how do you explain this, then?"

In one movement driven by fury, Ellie rips back the sheets and hooks up her hospital gown to reveal her legs and lower body. Her groin is swathed in bandages, front to back, like a nappy. There are blood-stains. Her inner thighs are mottled with blue and yellow bruises, far worse towards the groin area. Above the bandages, in the area of the girl's waist, are other bruises of a smaller kind that look like fingerprints. Linda's hand goes to her mouth; she makes a horrified little squeal.

"Three stitches in the vagina, Mum, he ripped me so badly. I probably wouldn't have had so many if I'd given bloody birth! Two sides? There's two sides, alright. You want me to turn over? You can see even worse on the other side, the nurse says, because that's how he did it to me, Mum, from behind like a dog, so he could hold me down!"

Ellie is yelling, waving her arms about and crying, all at the same time.

Linda has bolted from the room and is leaning against the stark tiles of the corridor wall. Images of blood, bodily fluids, bruising, animal copulation, Barry and her baby daughter's pained and anguished face whirl and turn in front of her eyes, like the worst kind of fairground ride. She is violently sick and a nurse comes running to help.

In the room she has just left, her daughter's shrill, keening cry is slowly bubbling down to the lonesome mewling of a vulnerable creature, torn by the snare.

LEMMINGS

As he blunders out of 'The Plough and Sail', Michael is slapped by the clammy wet of the October night. He can smell smoke from a coal fire somewhere and the ripe stench from the pig farm at East Wingate. The brutal cocktail stops him in his tracks. He looks around him as if the dripping trees, the fag-ends swirling in the gutter or the dead chrysanthemums in the pub window behind him hold the answer to his puzzlement of feeling.

"I shall probably seem very foolish," he thinks. "It is possible. It won't be the first time. To take this step forward will be to topple over the lip of the cliff; there to hang suspended in the ecstasy of the warm uplift, or tumble brokenly to the sharp pebbles below.

I know I should not go. Not for the reason I want to go. After all, it is not right. She would be happy for you to be there; you know she would; the unspoken communication is clear. Not usually wrong about that, are we Michael?

Bloody idiot. She's sixteen and you're forty four. You're married. You're her teacher, for God's sake. Same as Simone under the olives: rampant testosterone. No, not like Simone. Different somehow. All I know is I want to see her. But you can't, fool!

Alright, alright. Go home, then. Act officially in the morning. Have to contact the Police anyway. I imagine they'll want to see the record of the meeting this afternoon. Yes, of course, that's right."

*

Cursing the rain, he dashes for his car. He sits for a while, considering, yearning, doubting, feeling unsure. After ten minutes, he pulls himself upright in the seat, starts the engine and drives off towards the school. He'll make some calls from there, feeling the need for privacy.

He phones the Police, explains his involvement, tells them of the signed record. They want him to bring it to the station right away. He ascertains that Ellie is at St. Bede's. The hospital is initially standard NHS evasive, but he works his charm and eventually manages to establish that Ellie is under light sedation. Her mother has been with her but has now gone home. She is "comfortable". Michael cannot resist a snort of derision. She's been raped by her step-father, no doubt a painful and demeaning experience, and she is said to be "comfortable". How we tidy away horror.

He decides that the best time to make his visit will be very early the next morning.

*

Michael is out of the slumbering, silent house before six and driving slowly, uncertainly, through the streets of Tinsmead village ten minutes later. A man in a blue anorak is walking an obese white dog and a yawning, scratching boy of about twelve is forcing newspapers through letterboxes on the main street.

On the last corner, he sees a woman setting up buckets and pots outside her florist's shop. He winds down his window.

"Are you open?"

"If I'm here, we're open!" comes the reply.

"I'd like some flowers."

St. Bede's is another ten minutes' drive at the head of the valley. The mock-gothic crenellations of the Victorian building cut a toy castle silhouette at the top of the hill, the first of the day's light notching the shape with soft yellow.

The visitors' car park is usually full, a bloated planet with an asteroid belt of orbiting vehicles seeking a landing place. At this time, before the out-patients' clinics are under way, there is plenty of room. Michael pulls into the first available slot and sits, quietly. He takes a deep breath.

He should turn back, for this is folly. He cannot expect Ellie to regard his arrival at six twenty in the morning as conventional behaviour. So she will see it for what it is, for she is not a fool, and will, in all probability, reciprocate. It is the beginning of a slippery slope. It does not need to be approached at all.

He opens, closes and locks the car door decisively. It is less than fifty yards to the marble steps of the grand entrance of the hospital and he sprints all the way.

*

The Sister on duty looks at him suspiciously over her papers, her starched bosom beginning to tremble with affected indignation.

"She has woken up, but she's still very drowsy. It's not even half past six, yet, you know. She really isn't ready for visitors. Are you a relative?"

"No, no, I'm, well, I'm from the school. Dr. Chadwick. It's the only time I can come; busy, you know?"

Michael flounders. The Sister scowls, but notes the man's good suit and educated-sounding voice. She is impressed by "Doctor" and by his smile.

"Very well," she says, softening, "but only ten minutes, mind. She needs her rest. Through there, Brunel Wing, Room C on the right."

The door to Room C is closed but there is glass panel. Michael looks through. Ellie is lying on her back in the bed. Her eyes are closed. Slowly, he turns the door handle and enters the room. He moves across to the side of the bed and looks down at her. He can feel his heartbeat: jelly-beans in the chest.

Ellie opens her eyes. She is still drowsy from the sedatives. There is daylight filtering through the blinds. She decides it must be morning: she can hear a distant clattering of pans in the kitchen and a smell of…what's that? Expecting bacon, or disinfectant, but it's more like aftershave. His aftershave.

Gingerly, she turns her head. Her back hurts. The bruising must be coming out.

"Good morning, Ellie. I hope you don't mind me coming to see you? I just wanted to…it's…well…" The voice tails away.

Ellie squeezes her eyes shut and opens them again. She looks up at him and smiles.

"I've brought you some flowers; well, actually, one flower. Seems a bit mean, doesn't it? Oh, dear! At the time, I thought; well, anyway, here it is!"

There is a chipped plastic beaker on the cabinet. He places the single rose in it. Its extraordinary burgundy hue catches the gleam of morning and suffuses the space around them with a soft pink glow.

"Thank you," she whispers, her voice husky with sleep and strain. "Kind. It's beautiful."

She pauses.

"You have brought me a single red rose."

It is a statement, but the question is there too.

Michael grins and shifts from one foot to the other, embarrassed.

"Um, well, it was all she had. You know, so early."

"Oh, really? She'd sold out of everything else, then?"

She chuckles at his embarrassment and the joke. This is a dream. It must be.

"May I sit on the bed, or perhaps I'd better get the chair?"

"Please, sit on the bed, it's alright."

There is a pause. The end of facile conversation.

"It seems stupid to ask how you're feeling, whether you're alright? I mean, obviously, you're not alright. I'm really very, very sorry. I was extremely upset when I heard about it last night. In fact, upset does not really do justice to the kaleidoscope of feelings..."

He is not quite sure how to finish the sentence, but just looks into the girl's green eyes.

She returns his gaze, unblinking.

"So, Sir didn't bring me any grapes. Sir brought me a single red rose. You know, Sir, I can't believe you did that."

Now it is Ellie's turn to lose her way. This is her teacher sitting on her bed. Doctor Chadwick. Doctor Mike. Sir. The customary distance between pupil and teacher is there and then again, it isn't. He has brought her not just his concern and comfort, but also a token of something?

"Um, you heard last night? When?"

She returns to an easier topic of conversation.

"About ten, I think. In 'The Plough'. You know how it is here. News travels fast. Bad news is a bushfire. I was so concerned, I wanted to come straight away, but, well, you know."

"I wish you had. I needed some…some... something."

Her eyes begin to fill with tears at the recollection of her mother's distance and cool prevarications. Michael sees her distress and pulls his neatly folded handkerchief from the top pocket of his jacket. He flips the folds out of it and proffers it in her direction. Their fingers meet within the soft cotton and link together instinctively, briefly. A pin-prick jolt, like static.

"Ah, yes, so tough times, Ellie. I'll help if I can. When you're ready. I don't know too much about these things, but enough. If you want me to, that is."

His voice is a steady as he can make it, which is not very steady.

"Yes. Please."

"Well, I feel bad about yesterday, you know? Perhaps there was something I could have done then?"

"I nearly didn't come to see you at all," she says softly. "It took some courage. And if I hadn't, he would have attacked me just the same. Been waiting for an opportunity, I guess. Last night it was there and he took it."

"And your mother?"

Ellie's tears come again at the recollections.

"Sorry, I don't mean to upset you."

"It's alright, it's just that, well, she has to come down on one side or the other, I suppose and it looks like I lose. She can't believe us both. Or support us both, can she?"

She begins to sob, this time uncontrollably.

"Well, naturally, she's shocked and confused. Disbelieving too, I expect. So you may have to give her a bit of time, although I must confess the evidence seems overwhelming."

In front of him, the girl begins to cry loudly.

"Ellie, Ellie, it'll be alright. You won't…have to face it on your own."

He puts his arm under her shoulders and she half sits and moves so that her head rests on his chest. He lets her lean there, saying nothing, just feeling her shaking through his arms, smelling the sweetness of her hair and sensing a spinning, dipping sensation somewhere in his stomach.

Neither of them moves for some minutes. The dawn, cautiously, shifts a little further into the room, sidling its tendrils of light surreptitiously around the walls, as if embarrassed to be intruding on a scene of such strange tenderness.

Michael smoothes her hair, intoxicated by its petalled scents.

"Do you want to talk about it?" he asks after several minutes.

"Not yet. Later. I want to tell you about it. I need to tell someone who'll believe me."

"Alright. When you're ready. It's a dark, evil and terrible thing, Ellie, but it's not the end of the world. You will survive, I'm sure."

There is a pause, a silence rich with possibilities. Michael brings his right hand gently under Ellie's chin and lifts her face so that he can look into her eyes. He leans forwards and very gently, almost shyly, he kisses her briefly on the lips. She smiles at him and holds his gaze.

There are no more words. It is not that there is nothing to say, but rather that neither of them can dare to say it.

On the wall above them, the silent hand of the electric clock describes unflustered, smooth circuits of time. Turn, turn, turn. Onward, never backward. Always and in every place and in this room too where a new pivot has just been cast.

BUTTERFLIES

As dying October falls into the maw of famished November, Michael and Ellie are bound ever closer together, just as he had anticipated would be the case. She seeks him out for help, advice and because she cannot stay away; he just as eagerly welcomes her arrival at his door. Nightly, both live in each other's dreams, arm in arm on the silken shores of paradise.

As soon as she is released from hospital she opts to go and stay with Emma. Although her sister lives in a small, one bedroom flat and is preoccupied with a young baby, Ellie is happier to be there than at home. Even after Brian is charged with rape, Linda continues to defend his integrity and therefore, by implication, to damn her daughter's.

At the Magistrates Court hearing some days after his attack on Ellie, Brian Shepherd appears bullish, standing proudly erect in a smart, new grey suit. He cuts the very picture of unjustly maligned professional respectability. It does no good: because of the injuries sustained by his step-daughter, he is deemed a danger to young girls and bail is refused. He is held on remand. Linda is hysterical and outraged, yelling, bawling and finally weeping profusely. She has to be helped from the court by an usher. She refuses to speak to Ellie and is coolly distant with Emma for taking her in.

Although it is difficult for a few days, Ellie responds to Michael's suggestion that she should return to school as soon as possible. She is worried about the gossip and the lascivious interest and staring of the boys, especially after the local paper runs a report following Brian's bail being refused. Although, of course, she cannot be named by the press, it makes no difference because the matter is common knowledge in the valley.

It takes all her courage to come back into the public glare of the school but after a few days, the gossip-mongers move on to consider the case of a girl in the second year, pregnant at twelve. Ellie is then left alone to draw sustenance from the familiarity of the school, from its routines and from the sympathetic concern and understanding of her friends.

Ellie realises that the singular advantage of returning to school is that she will be able to see Dr. Mike. Apart from the trauma of the rape, she thinks of little else. She turns to him daily. She talks through the horror of her ordeal and although he is seething inside with anger and revulsion, he smoothes her a passage, time and time again, through twists and turns, snickets and back alleys as her mind tries to come to terms with what has happened.

Initially, there is a period of self-loathing and doubt. Her step-father's accusatory and defamatory remarks gnaw at her confidence. She realises that the afternoon with Simon Quale will be used against her.

In the dark hours, she wonders whether her desire to lose her virginity that way on that afternoon, does indeed say something bad which she has not acknowledged in herself or does not quite understand. She thinks about her sexuality; it feels as though she has never been truly like the other girls. Perhaps there is something about her, that she cannot recognise in herself, that marks her out for men; arouses their baser instincts even though she does not openly invite attention. Her conviction that she did nothing to provoke the rape wavers for a while.

One dark November evening, Ellie misses the bus which will take her to Emma's. She returns to Michael's office, which she has just left and where she has been seeking comfort. He offers to give her a lift. They both wonder whether the bus has been missed deliberately.

Half an hour later, he pulls into an empty car park behind some industrial units. The car cannot be seen from the road. He switches off the engine and turns to look at her, sitting in the seat beside him.

"Ellie, I've not thought about much else except you for the last few days. I'm going mad, I think! I want you to know how I feel."

She looks at him. This must be the moment of their first, real kiss. They kissed briefly in the hospital, like two butterflies colliding in air, but now; well, things have moved on. She has been anticipating this moment. Savouring it. Now is the right time.

She leans towards him; his senses spin and he feels as though he is floating somewhere above the earth. Her eyelids flutter.

*

They sit together in his car. It is lunch time and they have stolen a private, precious forty minutes together at High Gorge. Of course, she can come to his office, but Michael is recently worried that the increased frequency of these visits is arousing some suspicion. Anyway, both feel the need for time together away from the school and the roles in which that institution casts them.

Hesitantly, she recounts the events at the Albert Tower with Simon Quale and explains why she is worried about them coming out. He responds carefully by assuring her that even if she had had intercourse that day and many other days too, it does not alter the facts with regard to her step-father as she has outlined them to him, although he agrees that the Defence will probably use it to suggest her waywardness.

She talks to him of her father and what she remembers of his marriage to her mother: its breakdown; the arguments; her sense of guilt; the subsequent divorce; what her mother has alluded to as the reasons; her mother's second marriage to Brian and the evangelical work of the church. Michael begins to understand better why Linda is behaving as she is. He explains to Ellie that she is "in denial".

To confront Brian's guilt is also to confront a second marriage in crisis and that may involve having to recognise her own difficulties with physical intimacy. Furthermore, if Brian is guilty she has to face the inevitable repercussions within the Church and the wider community.

There is a silence while Ellie digests what Michael has said.

A stoical walker, head down against the wind, his heavy boots clumping the concrete, comes around the far side of a Rangers' hut, presumably on his way to the top of the hill. He glances in their direction and then seems to look again more carefully, raising a quizzical eyebrow. Michael shifts uncomfortably in his seat, struck again by the now familiar feeling of guilt about what he has allowed to happen.

"Do you know him?" he asks apprehensively. "He seemed very interested."

"Didn't really see him," she says absent-mindedly and then returns to the former topic.

"So I'm being sacrificed on the altar of Mum's respectability and her inability to face her own problems?"

She smiles up at him, pleased with her summary of his analysis.

Michael laughs, thinking it a remark which suggests she is older than her years.

"Looks like it, Ellie. You're not the first and you won't be the last."

"She's a cow. I hate her!"

Sixteen again.

*

74

Barry Fortune travels down from Scotland and spends a few days in a local hotel. He feels he should offer what support he can to his distressed daughter. The Police have been thorough and supportive but he thinks she needs the advice of a solicitor. He makes a few calls and enquiries and eventually arranges for her to see Fiona Perry, the wife of a former school-chum. She is highly regarded and has experience of this kind of thing.

Barry knows, however, that he and his daughter have moved apart. She has hardly seen him since she was eight. They are nervous in one another's company. She is polite and grateful for his help with finding a solicitor and his offer to foot the bill if necessary, but she does not want any more than that and certainly not any attempts on her father's part to revive paternal closeness. She knows and he senses, that there is someone else to whom she would rather cleave to for support. Eventually, he makes an excuse about problems in his office and catches a flight back to Edinburgh.

The matter is committed for trial at the Crown Court. To Ellie's consternation, the Police advise her that the case will not be heard until the following July.

Brian Shepherd's barrister, Piers Sowerby, a thickset man with a fine growth of curling nasal hair, is privately of the view that his client is as guilty as sin. Nevertheless, he commences to do his duty and with Brian's assistance, begins to prepare a strategy which will depend on trying to show Ellie as a consenting partner. He hopes at least to cast doubt in the jury's mind and preferably to persuade them that the girl agreed to intercourse, even if his client's inflamed passions blinded him to the physical hurt he was causing.

Believing that his step-daughter had sexual intercourse on the hill beneath the Albert Tower, Brian advises his counsel of the existence of Simon Quale.

*

Fiona Perry is a forthright young woman whom Ellie finds rather intimidating.

At their first meeting, she advises Ellie that the Defence will in all probability seek to besmirch her reputation and that the physical details of the assault will be drawn out and mulled over in a way which she will be bound to find alarming and very upsetting.

"They'll ask about all the flesh-crawling things, I'm afraid, Ellie. Erections, penetration, ejaculation. They'll probably try to imply that the intercourse was consensual or at least that you encouraged your step-father in some way. You must be ready for that. Can you cope with it, do you think?"

Fiona Perry looks over her half-moon glasses at the poised and pretty young woman in front of her.

"Yes. I have to."

Ellie's voice is firm, controlled.

"They might try to suggest that you are something of a tease."

The solicitor looks shrewdly at Ellie, noting the fashionable, close-cut clothing, the full figure.

Ellie looks defensive.

"You mean they'll suggest I'm, like a bit of a tart?"

"They might, yes. The Law demands that they have to be careful, but it is possible that they will seek to introduce or insinuate matters relating to your relationships up to the point of the attack, perhaps in order to imply that your step-father is part of a pattern of sexual behaviour. Boyfriends; whether you were a virgin before the rape and if not, how many partners you have had. Whether there have been any relationships with older men?"

Fiona Perry has a nose for this kind of thing. She leaves the suggestion trailing in the air and looks carefully at Ellie.

In the ensuing pause, Ellie feels Fiona's understanding but penetrating gaze upon her. She looks down, allowing her eyes to focus on the pink ribbons laced through the tottering stacks of folders on the enormous mahogany desk in front of her. Fiona frowns, almost imperceptibly, and reaches for a pencil and jots something on her notepad.

Suddenly, Ellie feels vulnerable and exposed. She fidgets in her chair and thinks about Michael. Does this woman know? Or is it just a clever guess? Her eyes travel to the window and watch the grey cumulus of the November sky. She is not sure what to say or indeed whether to say anything. Especially about Mike. It could get him into trouble.

"Ellie, whatever passes within these walls is confidential. It goes nowhere. I am on your side, remember? Your father thought it would be helpful. He's right. A barrister will be appointed by the Crown Prosecution Service to present the case against your step-father but you won't have much to do with him or her, if anything. So my role is to help you prepare for what's coming in the trial. If that's what you want. If you think it will help? It's not a requirement, Ellie; so it's up to you."

"Yes, I suppose so."

"Well, then, it would help if you could tell me about the sorts of things I've mentioned so that we can be prepared for what the Defence may try to introduce. Otherwise my help and advice is based on speculation alone which may be misleading for you."

Ellie says nothing but nods again.

"Shall we start by talking about your boyfriends?"

Ellie sits for some time, the solicitor watching her. She is not thinking about boyfriends because there have been none.

She is thinking about the older man with whom she is falling in love.

ON HEAT
(Witness Statement taken 20th November 1990)

My name is Simon Quale. I live at 'Sea View', Douglas Road, Laxey, Isle of Man. I was born on 14th January 1971. I am 19 years old.

I have worked for the Laxey and District Dairy since I left school. We make deliveries to a large part of the east of the island including Ramsey.

I first met Ellen (Ellie) Fortune in August of 1988. She would be thirteen at the time, very nearly fourteen. I was seventeen at that time. I know her birthday is in late August but I am not sure of the exact date.

Ellie does not live on the island. She comes here once or twice a year to visit her Grandmother. Ellie lives on the mainland somewhere but I do not know where. She lives with her mother and her step-father. She told me she does not like her step-father because he looks at her in a funny way. She used the phrase, "He undresses me with his eyes". She also said that she suspected him of trying to watch her through the bathroom window when she was naked in the shower. She used the word "pervert" to refer to him more than once. She did not ever use his name that I can remember. She told me this in August this year (1990). She did not say anything else about him.

Her grandmother lived in a bungalow in Lheaney Road in Ramsey until she died. I believe she died on the same day as the other events referred to in this statement, that is, the 31st August 1990.

*

We delivered milk to Mrs Benson (Ellie's grandmother). If the weather was fine, the first year I knew her, 1988, Ellie would often be in the front garden or down the side where there is a rose garden and a swing.

One day in the summer of 1988 as I was going to the back of the bungalow with the milk, she said hello. She started to talk, jumping from one subject to another; mostly the latest bands and television. She told me her name and how old she was. I thought she was very young for her age and yet she could be quite forward and flirty.

She asked me one day whether I thought she was pretty. I think I said something a bit sarcastic like, "Drop dead gorgeous", although really she was just a skinny kid with braces on her teeth. I remember thinking that for almost fourteen, she was still not developed. I mean, she had no figure at all.

One morning she asked me if I would take her to the cinema. I tried not to hurt her feelings and just said I thought she was a bit young for me. I think I said she should ask me next year.

The next year, in August of 1989, I saw Ellie again at Lheaney Road. She had changed quite a bit. She had started to develop her figure and she seemed more grown-up. I thought she was quite attractive. She remembered what I had said the year before and asked me if I would take her out. She was quite insistent. I was a bit worried that my girlfriend would find out, so I said no. Ellie was obviously disappointed and said I'd promised.

This August (1990) she was on the island again. It must have been just a few days before her sixteenth birthday. I was stunned when I saw her. The change was incredible. Not only did she seem much more adult in her behaviour, she looked really attractive.

Her figure had developed amazingly. I wondered whether she might have had breast implants. She was wearing a very tight top and tight jeans. She was beautiful. I don't mean she was behaving like a tart. She's not like that, but she knew what effect she was having. She wanted me to notice. There is no doubt in my mind about that.

The brace had gone and her face seemed to have changed. We chatted for quite a while that morning because I was in charge of the round by then and I had the time. I could see her Gran watching us through the bay window at the front and at one point she tapped on the window but Ellie said to ignore her.

I saw her two or three times that first week during the day. She said it would be difficult in the evening because of her mother and Gran. That suited me because I generally would see my girlfriend Charlotte in the evenings.

Nothing much happened on those occasions. We hired a rowing boat or walked along the beach, that kind of thing. We kissed a lot, but that's all. I didn't try to touch her or anything. I really wanted to but I thought maybe it was a bit soon and anyway, being daytime, there were people about. I enjoyed being with her. She was good fun. Certainly, I was aroused by her. I wanted to go further and so did she, I could tell. Most girls hide their feelings in the early stages or pretend to be shocked if you try to touch them. Ellie didn't. She was like a boiling kettle. She kissed like her life depended on it.

It was her suggestion to find somewhere more private up by the Tower. At first, I wasn't sure that I had understood her right. Later, I realised that she wanted to go up there for sex, although she didn't actually use that word. She said something like, "I want you to teach me everything you know". If a girl says she wants to go somewhere secluded and then says that, there's only one conclusion to be drawn.

Then she said could I bring whatever was needed and for a moment I didn't catch on that she meant a condom.

Of course I wanted to have sex with her. I suppose I couldn't believe my luck. I wasn't resisting. I was just a bit surprised the way she set it up. It wasn't disgusting or like a prostitute or anything; she is a really nice, affectionate, genuine person. I didn't know at that point, but I assumed she was a virgin. She approached it all in the same way that she might if she'd asked me to teach her to drive a car.

I am not a virgin. I had my first sexual experience when I was fifteen. I had had sexual intercourse with three girls up until that time. I had not discussed this with Ellie before we went up to the Tower.

She suggested we meet at the harbour on the 31st August. It was a Friday and I should have been at work but I got a workmate to cover for me. She was wearing a really sexy pair of shorts. Not loud, vulgar sexy, but very stylish. I couldn't take my eyes off her. She looked much older than she was. She could easily have passed for nineteen, maybe older. I was proud to be with her. I could see other men looking enviously at me. Men a lot older than her too.

We started to walk up towards the Tower. It would have been about one o'clock. She seemed a bit nervous but nothing out of the ordinary. She had a small rug in her shoulder bag and put it on the ground. I remember thinking that she was well prepared. We both sat down and she asked me if I thought she was a "slag" for bringing me up there. I said not.

She asked me if I was sexually experienced and said that she was a virgin. She asked me to treat her sensitively but not like something breakable. She said something like, "Do it to me properly". It seemed a really forward thing for a virgin to say. It all felt strange. With other girls, the first time, I have been the one to take the lead or be persuasive but with Ellie it was the other way round.

She began to kiss me really passionately. She started the intimacy, but I wasn't objecting. We were lying on the rug. She was in a terrific hurry.

I was aroused. I had an erection. I pulled off her top. I couldn't unfasten her brassiere and she took it off. At the same time she pulled off her shorts so all she was wearing were her knickers. I couldn't believe it was happening so fast.

I caressed her breasts. I told her to unzip my jeans which she did. I pulled off the jeans and my boxer shorts. I showed her how to rub my penis. She seemed to know what to do. I showed her how to put on the condom. I did not ejaculate but I was very excited indeed and wanted to penetrate her.

I think perhaps it was too soon for her, even though she was excited. I took off her knickers and got on top of her. I sensed that she suddenly became tense and she looked a bit frightened. Her legs seemed to go rigid and were not far enough apart. I tried to penetrate her but I could not. I asked her to help but she wasn't sure what to do and then she said it was hurting and kind of pushed me off.

We lay there for a while and then she started again. She really was in a hurry; there was no real passion any more. This time she got on top of me. I still had an erection. She tried to put me inside her by pressing down on me but it didn't work. The more she tried, the more tense she got and the worse it seemed to become. She was angry. Not with me, but with herself. She started crying.

I said to just calm down but she wouldn't and tried again. She was on her back again and writhing around, banging her hips against me. She said to push harder. She said it several times. I pushed really hard and she cried out, sort of like a scream but it wasn't a scream of agony. I wasn't sure whether I'd hurt her or not and kind of pulled back. I thought that if I pushed any harder, I might really hurt her so I stopped pushing.

She apologised and all the fire seemed to go out of her. She put her clothes back on. She was crying and sobbing and kept saying she was sorry. I felt bad because maybe I'd not managed to show her to take it gently so that you're ready. After all, I was supposed to be teaching her how to do it and I hadn't!

I wanted her to wait and calm down so that we could try again because I was really frustrated but she didn't want to. She said she'd gone off the idea and felt cheap and she was going. When she was dressed, she went off down the path, still crying. She didn't want me to go with her. I assume she went back to Lheaney Road. After a while, I went home.

I hoped I might see her after that when I was delivering milk but she was never around. I suppose that she was avoiding me or maybe because of her Gran's death, things had changed. Anyway, I have not seen or spoken to Ellie since that day and knew nothing of her until I was contacted by the Police in Douglas about this statement.

Signed

Simon Quale

WORM IN THE BUD

It is late November, dark. The treacle blackness of windows reflects drab office furniture in a fluorescent glare. The door is open. Just. Two heads are in close whisper, shapes entwined in a corner. Michael Chadwick is giving more advice to Ellen Fortune. More advice which justifies him being with her at six thirty. The caretaker is downstairs rattling keys and banging cupboard doors. He wants his tea.

Michael thinks they are otherwise alone. There is a lingering kiss, murmured words of love. He caresses the girl's neck, his fingers under tresses of her hair. She says something softly in his ear. He nods. They kiss again. Ellie smiles and slips through the door, disappearing into the corridor's shadows.

He sighs and turns to pack his briefcase. There is a cough at the doorway. John Sutcliffe peers around the door.

"Ah, Mike! Thought I heard, ah, voices. You dashing off? I'd appreciate a word."

Michael jumps. Realising that his mutterings with Ellie have been overheard, he blushes.

"No, fine."

John Sutcliffe sits down, crosses his legs and jiggles a meticulously polished Oxford brogue. He says nothing for a few seconds, this being part of his new style; a futile attempt to affect gravitas. Only just into the third year of Headship, he is finding it hard going. He is a book man, an accountant, a starchy, beanpole of a figure, devoid of much humour. He is like a ledger on a shelf or, as some cynic in the staffroom observed, a sheet of folded A4 without the charisma.

"There's something I need to pass in front of you, Mike."

Michael recovers composure, senses a crisis and braces himself for the impact.

"Must be important at this time of night? OK, pass it by me," says Michael, attempting flippancy.

"It's not an easy one," says Sutcliffe, coughing and brushing his thinning hair. Michael shivers in his stomach. He raises a quizzical eyebrow, affecting nonchalance.

"Perhaps I had better just come straight to the point."

"Please do."

Michael knows what is coming. Already he can feel the knife's point probing his shirt.

"OK. The Fortune girl seems to be spending a great deal of time in your office, Mike. Not sure that's wise or desirable. Several have noticed. Not just staff either."

He re-crosses his legs and jiggles the other brogue. His nervous fingers tidy his floral tie into his jacket. It has a sunflower design; a present from his wife, to make him more colourful. Failed.

"She's had a rough time, John. You know that. She came to me the night before she was raped. She trusts me; it's a difficult case; it's just extensive pastoral care, that's all."

Michael is as cool as a cucumber it seems, playing a standard return of serve.

"Mmm. I don't think so, Mike. Not just pastoral care a few moments ago as I came up the stairs, was it? It's gone too far, Mike."

Nifty back-hander down the line.

"You've added snooping to your many other attributes?"

Defensive, aggressive sarcasm. Wrong shot, Chadwick. John Sutcliffe surprises himself with his own steely forehand return.

"That remark might be taken as an acknowledgement of the truth of my observation, Mike. I am not a fool, whatever some people here may think. Pastoral care is not your brief. You know as well as I do that you should have handed this matter to Betty ages ago."

"Like most of the girls, Ellie Fortune has a problem with Betty."

Ball in the net.

"One of the House Heads then or the EWO. You know the system. As I say, it's not your brief. But even if it was, Mike, it'd be out of line. The girl is in here practically every day and not just for a few minutes either. And I might as well add that it's been noticed that neither of you is in the building at lunch time at least twice a week."

He adjusts his glasses on the bridge of his nose and wipes his brow with a floral pattern handkerchief which clashes violently with the tie.

"Going home for lunch is not a crime, John."

"True. Sitting with the girl in your car at High Gorge isn't a capital offence either but it's likely to be perceived as professional misconduct. You were seen, Mike. Celia Hawthorn's neighbour was walking up there the other day. He recognised you from school concerts; thought it unusual behaviour and mentioned it to Celia over the garden fence. You know how it is around here.

She came to me with it, very concerned, some days ago. Did you think it would go unnoticed in a small community like this?"

Game and set to John Sutcliffe.

"Any observations?"

Michael is silent.

"I thought as much. You're being a fool, Mike. She's a kid, a young girl. She's a pupil. Taboo stuff, isn't it? You're a good teacher, a bloody good Deputy and if you're not careful, you're going to blow your marriage, your career and your local reputation right out of the water. You may already have done so. I don't know how far it's gone and I don't suppose you're going to tell me?"

"There's nothing to tell," mutters Michael, reluctantly.

"I'll read that as meaning there has been no sexual intimacy and that you're still at the infatuation stage? If that's the case, you may be able to save yourself and I'm giving you the chance to do so, although, God knows, I'm putting my own head on the block. This is a private, off the record conversation. At any later stage, if there has to be a later stage, so far as I'm concerned, this conversation never happened. Understood? As Betty would say, "Read my lips!" So, for Heaven's sake finish the relationship, stop the clandestine meetings and whatever else is going on, now. Pass the counselling to someone else tomorrow morning and make it evident to me and others that things are back to normal and we'll say no more about it. Any alternative will invoke County and national procedures and will be largely out of my hands. It could have only one conclusion."

He ends with a flourish of the floral tie for this is the book man not quite doing it by the book. It is the human face of his new management style.

Michael can feel his hands beginning to shake. Suddenly, the room seems much colder and darker. He manages only a croak.

"Is this a formal warning, or what?"

"No, Mike it isn't anything. It doesn't exist. I just said, it's you and me having a conversation which in five minutes' time I will deem never to have happened."

He pauses and looks at Mike who looks away and says nothing.

"Look, Mike, you've been under stress just lately, we can all see that. It's been a difficult couple of years; you work hard and long hours. Then, you know, your father dying in September and things at home, well, it's perhaps understandable, isn't it? But you've made an error of judgment, Mike. A very serious one. Can't you see? You know as well as I do that a relationship with a pupil is the ultimate in professional misconduct. I'm trying to help you, Mike.

Save you from yourself. It's a disaster waiting to happen but you can't see it, can you? Or maybe you do but you won't acknowledge it?"

Michael still does not answer but stares to one side, at his own reflection in the treacle black of the window.

*

Drives home in the dark, hands shaking on the steering wheel. Very nearly runs down a cyclist on Randall's Lane, even though the bike is clearly and correctly lit. Shouting and gesticulation from the angry cyclist but he doesn't stop.

Key in front door. Evil smell in the cottage of rising damp and sheep. Mutton stew again. Remembers twins are at Youth Club, hence stew. (Hannah currently trying to recruit the family to vegetarianism.) Barbara alone in the house. Lights blazing at all the windows. Pans rattling and banging. Temper blazing too, recognises the signs. Too late now to have a pressing engagement. Nips upstairs, changes into jeans and sweater. Returns straight to drinks cupboard. Fingers trembling, has trouble unscrewing the cap. Whisky fire in the gullet. Tries to keep calm, subdue the shivering.

"I didn't hear you come in," Barbara, tetchy.

"I shouted but you were making so much bloody noise you didn't hear," Michael, defensive.

"What's the matter with you? You look bloody awful. Or do I recognise the look from somewhere? Whisky? On a Wednesday?"

Barbara's opening remarks on a quiet night in; mutton stew for two by candlelight.

"I nearly ran over a sodding cyclist. And I don't need to ask your permission if I want to drink whisky on a fucking Wednesday, thank you."

Michael as before, with aggression.

Snuff the candle – no quiet night in. Barbara snorts. Returns to kitchen. Brings in stew and plates. Bangs them on the table. Throws down a fistful of knives.

"Bon appetit!"

Michael adds irony to the list.

Spooning pieces of meat. Potato and carrot. Greasy wash of gravy. Separates gristle to the side of the plate.

Quietly, almost in a whisper, she speaks.

85

"You don't need my permission to drink whisky, Mike. Agreed," she appears to chew thoughtfully, "but you might need it to carry on with one of your pupils."

Fork half way to his mouth. Stops. Puts fork down, hand shaking all the more. Swallows a mouthful of whisky. Decides to play dumb.

"What's that supposed to mean?"

"Precisely what I say, Mike. Come on; it's clear enough. It's all over the valley, it seems. Very nice situation for me, to have Mrs Bradley draw me to one side in the Post Office this afternoon to report that it is rumoured that my husband is shafting a sixth form girl."

She sniffs.

"I'm sure Gloria Bradley didn't say that, evil old gossip-monger that she certainly is. Anyway, I'm not shafting anyone, Barbara."

"Not yet, is that? Not showing any interest in your wife, that's for sure."

Begins to sob and spills gravy on the tablecloth.

"So you are denying it then, as usual? Girl by the name of Ellen Fortune, I believe. Tall, slim, dark and big-breasted, apparently. So just your type."

"Look, Barbara. Ellie Fortune has come to me for help and advice following a traumatic rape at the hands of her step-father. You know about that. I am giving her that help. That's all; end of story."

"Nice try, Mike, but it won't wash. She says it was rape. He's denying it, I hear. Ellie, is it? I do beg your pardon. And this would be the Ellie who goes with you to High Gorge for lunch-time counselling, would it? The same Ellie that keeps you late in your office? Or causes you to mope about every evening and weekend?"

Michael chews valiantly on a piece of mutton.

"Well, I might just fall for it were it not for the track record. I know how it is with you and busty young girls. Most recent evidence: Titty from Tropez. Simone or whatever the French slut with the bushy arm-pits was called. You lying shit."

Barbara coming adroitly to the point, as is her wont.

Michael is still chewing on the sheep and gesticulates towards his mouth to indicate an inability to respond. Sudden screeching from the other end of the table.

"Well, I've had enough, you hear me? You'll stop this now or it's all over for us, right? I mean it! I forgave you the sordid business with that tart Ann Baxter for the sake of the kids, but not again. Not a-bloody-gain. I'm not going through that misery and humiliation again. No way. I'll file for divorce and screw you for everything I can, including some of the money which your father left you and which you haven't got around to telling me about. Right? And what about the twins? Have you given any thought to the effect this is going to have on them? Call yourself a father? You unfaithful, bollock-obsessed shite!"

A knife flies through the air. Skitters to a halt under the sideboard. Shards of china embedded in the lime plaster. Mutton stew bathing the Laura Ashley print curtains. Some of it in Michael's hair; congealing gobbets of grease.

*

Ellie and Tracey are sitting in Emma's lounge. Emma has taken Baby Wayne to the clinic. Tracey has come for tea. They eat off plates on their laps for there is no horizontal surface in the lounge or the kitchen that is not already strewn with take-away cartons, disposable nappies, coats, pieces of motorbike, CD cassettes, dirty linen and the other detritus of early married life.

Tracey finishes her last mouthful and takes her plate out to the kitchen. She comes back and leans against the doorway, looking at her nails.

"Els, I heard something today. I think I ought to tell you."

Ellie looks up and mumbles interrogatively, her mouth slippery with baked beans.

"Some of the others; well, Mandy, mostly, you know what she's like, they were on about stuff. You know?"

"About the rape, you mean?"

"Well, yeah, a bit. But mostly something else, Els. You and Doctor Mike."

Ellie swallows and flushes a little.

"What do you mean?"

"Oh, come on, Els, you know what I mean. You keep disappearing to go and see him at school. Every day, practically. I mean, you don't hang out with the gang so much now, do you? And you never stop talking about him. And there's this rumour going around that you were seen with him up at High Gorge. I know you've got the hots for him; you have had for years. But you haven't said much about it to me recently, like you always did before, you know, just between us? So?"

"Oh, God!"

Ellie finds a place to put her plate on the floor and leans back on the sofa.

"I suppose it was only a matter of time. I thought it best not to say anything to anyone. Not even you, Trace. I'm sorry, but, well, you know?"

"You mean that it's true? Bloody hell, Ellie!"

Tracey joins her friend almost in one leap across the flotsam.

"What's he like? Are you, well, doing it? You must be mad! I bet he's a ram, isn't he? You little tart! You jammy sod!"

All at once and tumbling out of her.

"No, we're not. It's not like that. It's soft, tender, gentle. He's just such a beautiful, kind, sensitive, handsome man. I can't help myself, Trace."

Ellie's eyes glisten like dewy grapes.

Tracey looks at her friend's radiant face and the lights in her eyes that have switched on at the mention of Dr. Mike's name.

"Yeah, right. Ohmigod! You've fallen for him, haven't you?"

Ellie nods.

"I just can't stop thinking about him. Night and day. It makes me dizzy when I think about him and when I'm with him or he touches me, it's like I'm going to pass out; do you know what I mean?"

Tracey laughs.

"Well, kind of. I suppose I felt like that about Mark for a week or so. But it soon wore off, especially when it became obvious what the horny toad was really interested in. Bloody hell. So does he feel the same? I don't believe this!"

"Yes, he says he feels the same."

Tracey frowns. Ellie gets the words in first.

"Yes, I know what you're going to say. He's far too old, he's already married and he's my teacher. Right?"

Tracey puts an arm around her friend's shoulders.

"Yeah, well something like that, I suppose. I dunno, it seems like it might be a bit dangerous or, well, daft, somehow. But then again, it seems so romantic. You wouldn't be the first to make it with a much older bloke and let's face it, he looks ten years younger than he is. You sneaky little tartlet!"

"That's the downside, Trace. You know, like having to be secretive all the time."

Ellie looks wistful, thinking of how much easier it would be to have a conventional teenage relationship.

Tracey looks serious.

"There's another downside, Els. If it gets out big-time what's going on, he can lose his job, can't he?"

"Yes. He says he doesn't care."

"Bloody hell! Really?"

*

Linda is in the Post Office too that day, although not at the same time as Barbara Chadwick. Gloria Bradley is still there, having taken up a more-or-less permanent station on the stool by the greetings cards stand. She is enjoying passing on to any who will listen, and a number who don't, the salacious tidbit she heard this morning from her neighbour, who in turn had heard it from that nice Mr. Chalmers who goes walking up through the Reserve and all over the hills, whatever the weather.

Linda listens to Gloria's information in silence, her head to one side and her lips pursed as if she is sipping vinegar. When she returns home, she immediately goes up to Ellie's room and begins to turn out drawers and cupboards, strewing their contents across the floor and the bed. She is not quite sure what she is looking for or indeed if there is anything to be found, but she knows her daughter's tendency to keep a diary and horde letters. What that ghastly Mrs Bradley told her was embarrassing to say the least, but if it's true then the probability is that Ellie has written something down. She ought to know about it if so and anyway, it might help Brian's situation.

She is on the point of deciding that she is on a wild goose chase when she remembers the attic cupboard. It is full of all sorts of junk: she looks at the tangle of dusty items and, with a sigh, decides that she really hasn't the time or inclination to search through them. As her hand goes to switch off the light, her fingers find the riffled pages of the notebook, just where Ellie had wedged it, before going to have her shower on the night of the rape.

WHITE HERON'S WINGS
1938

There is a wet mist sliding down the valley. Michael pulls up his collar and feels in his pocket for the car keys. They are still in the house, on the hall table where he threw them earlier this evening. No matter, he thinks, the chill night air will slap my face for me. He decides to walk across the fields to 'The Plough and Sail' and have a pint or two, or maybe even three or four. The welcoming drabness of the place will calm his nerves.

The earlier drizzle and now the cloying mist have turned the footpath at the edge of the field into a churned ribbon of grass and slime. The former village pond, once no doubt chuckling full with ducks, moorhens, newts and sticklebacks under a festooning fringe of willow, is now a mire of filth, old mattresses, pieces of a rusting bicycle and a supermarket trolley. On a branch of scrub elm, he notices that someone has tied two used condoms, one a virulent lime green. Cheeky trophies of some young man's conquests, they bob pendulous and globular in the damp night. As he negotiates a dog's rancid coils in the middle of the path, he ruminates on the delights of the rural idyll.

Michael takes in the public bar. In the glow of the inglenook, Old Nibber sits on the settle, chewing the stem of his clay pipe and occasionally fondling the ears of Larry's geriatric spaniel which snuffles contentedly in the ashes of the fire. Nibber looks up and lifts his hand to Michael in welcome.

"Evening, Mike. Usual?" says Larry.

Michael is surprised by the polite and conventional greeting, which is not really Larry's style.

"Evening, Larry. Yes, please. Really very cold out there; nasty drizzle in a biting wind."

Michael delivers his weather forecast a little tongue-in-cheek.

Larry grunts as he pulls on the pump.

"Bloody November, isn't it? Soon be friggin' Christmas. Bound to be cold. I don't know why people keep remarking on it."

"The festive season, Larry? Your favourite time of year."

"Fuck the Festive Season. It's all commercial bollocks!"

Michael laughs, reassured. For a moment he had thought that Larry's customary gruffness had deserted him.

"We know what to expect when we come in here, though, Larry, don't we?" Michael counters. "A bright convivial atmosphere and the alluring and enduring bonhomie of mein host!"

Larry grunts again.

"Well, people can always piss off down to 'The Bear'."

"True, Larry, indeed they do have that choice. But 'The Bear' is five miles away! You have a monopoly on local charm and aplomb. Might need to refer matters to that nice Mr. Major; see whether, in the rush of his success, he can drum up some private funding for some competition for you. Another pub over the road, for example. Then the consumer would undoubtedly benefit from the advantageous effects of true market forces."

"The consumer can go fuck himself," responds Larry. "And don't start on about the bloody Tories in here; you'll upset the regulars and I rely on the trade!"

He laughs uproariously at his own irony.

"Mike! Over 'ere, me lovely!" Nibber lifts an arthritic arm and wiggles a couple of fingers.

Michael had thought to sit on his own and stare into his beer but Old Nibber is already shuffling his bony bottom along the settle to make room. He nudges the spaniel with his toe and it reluctantly twitches to one side, allowing him space for his feet.

"Evening, Nibber. How's tricks?"

The old man sucks in his cheeks as if pondering a weighty question.

"I hears you's havin' a spot of bother."

Michael raises an eyebrow.

"Well, you could call it a spot of bother, I suppose," Michael replies cautiously.

"Mmm," mumbles Nibber. "Got it bad, ave 'ee?"

Michael slumps back in the settle.

"Yes, I have," he mumbles hesitantly and then, as if a plug had been released from a blockage, "I'm appalled and compelled at the same time; love-struck and guilt-stricken. I can't think straight, I can't work. I'm off my food; I hear her voice in the wind in the trees and in the songs of the birds. I walk with her all night in my dreams, suffused with the pink hues of love and the thundering drums of desire. Desire, Nibber, for a girl of sixteen. So, how's that for a kick-off?"

Nibber laughs a thick, liquid laugh from somewhere deep in his chest, his Adam's apple leaping like the bobbing head of a chicken.

"You should have been a bloody poet, Mike," he says. "Listen, you's not the first to go crazy after a young girl and you won't be the last. Makes a study of it, see. She's a beautiful young girl, I'll give 'ee that."

"She is, inside and outside."

"So, you's guilty on account of being married and her being only a young'un, an' a pupil of yours too? Forbidden Fruit, see?"

Nibber sucks noisily at his pipe.

"Just before the last war, I were Head Gardener for old Colonel Wiseman up at Chase House. My wife Edie was a chamber maid. Colonel let us have this little cottage in the grounds. Ar, we was set up 'andsome until I bust a gurt hole in it."

Nibber stops to suck at his beer.

"Lily Spencer, her name was. New kitchen maid. Late summer of 1938 I'm talkin' about. She was fifteen an' I was forty one. Ha! First afternoon she's there, Cook sends her out to the kitchen garden to fetch in some runner beans. I sees her standing in the doorway in the old stone wall.

'You Charlie Marshall, as they calls Nibber?' she asks. 'I've heard about you, so 'andsome!' Her voice is all rich and warbly, like a gurt pigeon. She got pretty yellow curls under her cap. Little pink rosebud mouth. She's got a white apron on an' I can see her shape and curves under it, you know, an' it makes me mouth go dry. I mean, she's a woman in that way, you know, not a girl."

Michael laughs in recognition of his own feelings.

"She may be a girl but she's also a mature female?"

The old man looks at him and grins a toothless, hollow grin.

"Ar, right enough," he says. "Any road up, she starts rippin' and tearin' at they beans. 'Ers 'opeless. She's pulling all the flowers off and all sorts. 'Hold up', says I and steps forward to pull her hand away and show her proper.

Then everything 'appened fast. It was like the world stopped turning. I could hear the bees buzzin' an' there's an aircraft droning over the fields up the valley a-ways. Jimmy Gurney was on the other side of the wall, snip-snipping at the box hedge. The perfume o' that box was very strong. Ever since that day, whenever I smell 'ee, it takes I right back to that afternoon in the kitchen garden with beautiful Lily.

I've taken 'er hand but I don't let go. She turns to face I and that kind of wraps me arm round 'er waist. With 'er free hand she pulls off her cap. There's a great waterfall of blonde hair. I can smell soap or one o' they scents on 'er: lily o' the valley 'twas. She looks straight in me eyes and I knows what she wants from I. She tilts her chin back a fraction and I kiss her!

Just like that! I mean, can you imagine? No more'n two minutes since I seed 'er. That'd never 'appened to me that way before. Weeks before I kissed Edie when we was courtin'.

I'm drowning in sweet elderberry juice; I don't know how else to describe it. I never tasted lips like hers before. Nor not after, neither. Never. Well, that's it; I'm drugged by her and there's all'n there is about it. It seemed to last forever that kiss. Me knees buckle an' I think I's goin' to fall over.

She's makin' little whimpering noises. Then she runs her hand round me neck and into me shirt front. I'm sort of swooning into her. Everything starts to spin; spinnin' at a gurt speed."

Old Nibber pauses almost breathless from the revived memory.

"Mmm, sounds familiar!" says Michael. "Love at first sight, then, Nibber?"

"Ar, boy, 'twas an' all. But let's not forget the other thing, now! I'm kissin' her an' by and by I'm fondlin' her breasts, you know? She's big for her age, mind and very firm. So my old man is straining to get out of me pants! She knows it 'an all, 'cos it's like a withy in the wind, proddin' at her!

But she just suddenly froze and said, 'Not here!' grabbed the beans she'd yanked from the wall and ran. Later she told I she wanted to 'ave I but thought I might think she was a bit, you know, fast with it bein' like that. 'Twouldn't a been 'er first time, either, she says. I don't know! But I wish't I'd 'ad 'er right there, rolling and thrashin' among the beans and the marrows. Lovely, eh? Might 'ave been better if I 'ad, too. Put an end to it there'n'then, like, maybe. But it wasn't to be.

When an older man's chasin' a young girl, 'ee's after the sex. First rule, that is. Maybe she's old fer 'er years an' that but I doesn't care what anyone says, a big part of it's the sex. Best sex I ever 'ad in me life was with Lily, when eventually we got to it. 'An' I've had some women, I can tell 'ee, out on the land, during the harvests, durin' the War, under the 'edges, up against the trees! Lovely!

Well, this that I'm tellin' you about would have been September 1938. War clouds was gathering all over Europe. Hitler was tryin' to wipe out the Jews an' on about a pure blood race an' I was delirious about a fifteen year old kitchen maid! Makes you think, dunnit? Who was more out of 'is mind: 'im or me?

Well, we manage a couple of minutes one afternoon in the copse by the river. Just enough to kiss and cuddle and for her to stoke me fires again. Then she has to dash back in case she's missed. 'Fore she goes, she gives I this little bitsy hanky to dab me finger, see? I'd cut mesself earlier an' it were bleedin' so she gives I her little hanky. Fresh white with lace at the edges and little dog roses embroidered in one corner. An' smellin' o' that lily o' the valley. Still got that hanky, Mike, you know. Not quite so white now, but precious that is.

Well, o'course we gets rumbled. Mrs Wiseman doesn't want any trouble or scandal with her servants, so easiest thing to do is to send Lily packing. She does, the same day. I don't know where she's gone. I can't find out.

Months go by. I'm miserable, cold inside, crying inside like, stumbling through each day like part of me's been cut out. After a while, I think she must have found somebody else. So I try to forget her and make it up with Edie. It's 'ard. Bloody daft, eh? After all, I hardly knows the girl, but she's got I in 'er spell, alright. 'S like that sometimes.

Months after, I gets a message from 'er. Be 'twards end o' March nineteen thirty nine. She's over Peasebury way. I don't hesitate more 'an a second. That evening, I throws some things in an old bag and leave Chase House. I never say a word to no one and I never went back. Didn't come back at all here for over forty years.

It takes me the best part of the next day to find her. When I do, she falls into me arms and it's like I've been re-born. She's found a job at the local mill and 'as lodgings in the town. We go back there and get straight in the bed; 'ardly time to get our clothes off. I don't think we got out again for about three days! We was greedy fer each other, see?

Like I say, never known sex like it. Well, something dazzlin', kind of, for a man of forty odd to be makin' love to a beautiful, willin' young girl. Lifted up onto the gurt smooth, white wings of they herons that swoops and dips over the lake, that's how it was."

Michael laughs.

"Now who's the bloody poet, Nibber? Sounds wonderful, but I get the feeling it didn't stay that way; there's a storm coming?"

"Oh, ar, always is, Mike. Last rule. It doesn't last; it can't."

"What, never?"

Michael cannot conceal his disappointment at the change in Nibber's tone.

"Well, I won't say never. Rarely, then. We was alright, all through the war. That was somethin' I suppose, 'cos there was lots that wasn't. You know, went off and suffered bloody hell somewhere an' then came back to a different hell:

no wife. No, we was fine until about 'forty eight, 'forty nine. She's about twenty five by then an' I'm well into my fifties, of course.

It's bloody odd, in a way. It works alright when she's sixteen, seventeen and you's forty. You can keep up with 'er. An' Lily took some keepin' up with, I can tell 'ee! But add ten or twelve years to your ages and you's out of step. 'Appens to some men. The Old Man takes a nap more often. You's not itching for it every minute of the day. At least, I wasn't. I'd cooled down, you know? But she hadn't. In her prime but I's past my best. A man has to satisfy a woman, Mike. So, well, you can guess the rest. She meets someone else. Before I know what's happening, she's gone. Just like I did ten years before. I come home one afternoon to a Dear John wedged behind the hall mirror."

The old man brushes away a tear. Michael is touched to see that after all these years, the hurt is still there.

"I heard that the bloke upped and left her after a few years. Be about nineteen fifty four, I suppose. I wrote to where I thought she was. I didn't get no reply. Never. Sent messages with people, you know. Sent a birthday card every year, with a little message and me address, just in case. Maybe I should 'ave gone to find her. Maybe I was too frightened, in case 'er runs away again. Bloody daft. I dunno. Huh! Maybe, maybe.

So, I just kind of sits there, thinkin' about her and 'ow it used to be. Wishin' she'd come back, with her rosebud mouth and tangle o' curls. But it doesn't 'appen. Maybe I'm an old fool, not makin' any sense, Mike. I dunno. Thirty five years we both just sits in our different spaces; bloody stupid, eh? I never forgets 'er. Never.

Anyway, one day, out of the blue, I hears she's dead. Nineteen eighty. Riddled with cancer. An' then, the strangest thing happens. A packet comes in the post two days later. Inside there's a flower, very old, preserved in some sort of perspex or summat. There's a scrap of paper inside as well an' I can just make out her writing, 'Charlie's beans 1938. First kiss'.

Well, you can imagine. Cry? I'm an old man but I wept like a babby. Still got it, 'o course, that flower. There's a letter from a neighbour tellin' I what happened an' about the funeral arrangements. 'Bout two weeks after the funeral, another parcel arrives. Says they're clearing Lily's place and they find an old shoe box stuffed with birthday cards. My name on 'em. Perhaps I'd like to 'ave 'em? She'd kept every one, none missing, all tied up with a red ribbon."

Nibber pauses, swallows hard and wipes his eyes again.

"So she got what you posted but didn't ever respond? Why not?"

"Who knows, boy? I ask mesself every day fer ten years an' I still ain't got an answer. An' she ain't around no more to say. So that's it, son. Old Nibber's story. Mark, learn and inwardly digest as my ol' mam used to say."

"Christ, Nibber, how sad."

"It was sad. Still is. Rips me ol' guts to shreds even today and it was bloody nearly fifty years ago. So, there 'ee is."

There is another long pause.

"The odds is heavily against you, son. An' I know that whatever I say is not goin' to stop you, 'cos, well, whatever will be, will be."

Both men sit silently, staring into the fire, the one considering what was, the other contemplating what might be, despite the tragic story laid before him. Nibber coughs.

"Like a bloody gyroscope, what happens. While you's not looking, Cupid, or one 'o they, gives a gurt tug and you's spinnin' and whirlin'. People are shoutin' at you from out there, but you can't really make out what they're saying. Only clear thing is the girl.

You have to cling to each other, keep her in focus, otherwise you get thrown off. It slows down a bit after a while but you still have to hang on. Then, it slows a bit more; maybe a bit of a wobble. And then, one day, that wheel you's been standin' on all this time hits somethin' hard. There's a nasty screeching sound, the 'scope wobbles off the pivot and jumps off the bloody table onto the floor. Momentum gone. You's finished, sprawled on your face, nursing your bruises."

Michael watches as the old man rushes his last words, his voice getting shriller and shriller. His cap spins on the end of his crooked finger and then, as Nibber falls silent, it drops off into the grey ash and dying embers of the fire at his feet.

EYE OF THE TIGER

Five minutes later the taxi sounds its horn outside the pub. Michael covers his head with his jacket, bids Larry goodnight and stumbles through the angular ribbons of freezing rain to the unwashed-shirt-fug of the car.

" 'Riverview Lodge', Edgemouth. Can't remember the name of the road; down by the harbour?"

The taxi driver grunts as he kicks the vehicle into first gear.

"I know it. Not where you live, though, Doctor Mike!"

The figure turns and Michael recognises the face of Anthony Southwell, a former pupil.

"Hello. Anthony, isn't it? "

Anthony grunts again.

"Tony. Tone.Thought you lived up Watery Lane?"

"You can't do anything in this bloody valley without everybody knowing your business, it seems," snaps Michael, allowing his irritation to come to the surface.

"Sorry," says Tone. "Just making conversation."

"I have an aunt who lives at Riverview. She has an elderly, flatulent Pekinese which has managed to wedge itself in the chimney whilst searching for Santa. Aunty's drapes are being damaged by puffs of soot and methane gas. I'm the only one likely to be able to coax the creature down again because I speak Mandarin, the language of the farting, dwarf pug-dog. Alright?"

Tone gives a nervous little cough, Michael's savage sarcasm recalling the peonage of his schooldays.

"Whatever you say, Doctor."

He shifts the vehicle aggressively through the gears as the valley road unravels ahead of them, a glistening, shimmering black filament in a swirl of water and leaves. Michael slumps into the greasiness of the plastic 'leather' of the back seat, watching giant foam dice attached to the rear-view mirror, bouncing a game of chance.

Images from Nibber's romantic and tragic story conjure themselves in his inward eye: the middle-aged gardener swooning for the alluring, rampant young kitchen maid; the ecstasy of the togetherness and then the lachrymose, waning days. Lily chewing a pencil, writing her valedictory note; Nibber alone again through the long, weeping nights and finally Lily dying slowly of cancer somewhere, perhaps alone and in pain, too stubborn to contact the man who waited for her.

Michael wrestles with the story, balancing its essential vigour and sparkle with what Nibber himself saw as an inevitable decline and loss.

" 'Riverview Lodge'," announces Tone bluntly, pulling the car to a splashing, juddering halt.

Michael is jolted from his musings.

"Right. Thanks."

"You'll find Ellie Fortune at number twelve, Doc. Second door over there, up the stairs, third landing," Tone smiles wickedly, showing yellowing teeth and a woolly-looking tongue.

"What? How do you..?"

"Gary Green is one of my mates. In the same tutor group, weren't we? He's married to her sister, Emma, right? Lucky sod. Big bird, yeah?"

He guffaws crudely and makes a cupping movement with his hands.

"Like two bleedin' canteloupes!"

Michael decides to ignore the deliberately provocative remark.

"How much do I owe you?"

"Four quid, Doc, since it's you. Looks like little Ellie's going to be the same. Nice pert arse, too."

Michael snorts indignantly.

"I engaged you to drive me here, that's all. Making vulgar remarks was not part of the implicit contract. Here's your money. You just blew any chance of a tip."

He gets out, slamming the door, stepping up to his ankles in a puddle. He sees that there are no others within several yards; Tone has deliberately stopped by this one.

Tone's window comes down and his grinning face appears.

"No good coming the high and mighty, Doc. Everyone knows what you're up to. Mind you, I tried to get in there myself, so I don't blame you. Good luck to you, Doc. Give her a long, stiff one for me."

He pauses and then looks contemptuously at Michael.

"That's if you can get it up, of course. Old enough to be her father, eh, Doc? Bit of a dirty old man, is it?"

The words have no sooner left his spittled lips than Tone toes the throttle and the car shoots forward, its rear wheels sending another wave of oily water into Michael's shoes.

"Merry Shaggin' Christmas, Doc!"

"You egregious little shit!" Michael yells at the tail lights.

Tone makes a two fingered gesture as he slews the car round a corner and disappears from view.

"Wanker!" he yodels.

Once the sound of the car's engine has died away, Michael is aware of the silence around him. Apart from the mournful hoot of a boat somewhere out on the Sands, there is only the pattering and sluicing of rainwater. There are no human sounds at all, not even a television in the apartment block behind him or the usual drunks kicking bottles and hurling oaths on their way back from the town. Perhaps it is later than he thinks.

He looks down at himself and sees that he is a sorry sight. His trousers are sodden wet from the knees down, his shirt and coat are almost as bad; he can feel water running from a floor-mop of hair and his shoes are larded with mud. He splashes across the pavement and into the doorway indicated by the loathsome Tone. It is dry, but daubed with offensive graffiti and smelling sharply of urine.

Suddenly, he feels ashamed and sees himself as others might do; as Tone as already implied. A middle-aged man, the worse for drink and the weather, wandering a seedy block of flats, looking for a teenage girl with whom he is hopelessly infatuated, when he should be at home with his wife and children.

"Oh, Christ! What am I doing?"

For several minutes, Michael stands motionless in the doorway, staring unseeing at the chipped tiles and the scraps of plastic litter temporarily glued there by the slimy rain.

Suddenly, he turns to the doorway, opens it decisively and leaps the echoing concrete steps to the third floor, two at a time.

*

He works out by a process of elimination which must be number twelve and stands in front of it, temporarily immobilised by apprehension. He sees that there is a small label stuck to the door which says, "Gar 'n' Em's place" and another one under the bell push with the exhortation, "Not working. Knock loudly!"

He curses silently. He lifts a hand and raps his knuckles smartly on the wood. There is no response. He leans forward and opens the letter flap with one hand and raps again, harder.

"Ellie! Ellie! It's me!" he stage whispers.

He bangs on the door a third time, using the flat of his hand, yelling through the letter box.

"Ellie! Ellie! Are you there? It's Mike!"

But still there is no response, although someone switches on a light in number thirteen. He is about to give up, when he senses rather than sees or hears, a movement behind the door. He is sure someone is standing inside.

"Ellie?" he whispers, "Let me in! It's me, Mike."

"Mike?" comes a voice. "Is that you?"

"Yes, open the bloody door! How many Mikes do you know?"

The door opens on a security chain, a pale face appears, the door closes, there is a rattle as the chain is released and then Ellie is standing in front of him, her hair tangled and her eyes heavy with sleep.

"What are you doing here? What time is it? Are you alright? You're soaked! Come in, quickly. Look at you! Like, what are you about?"

She takes his hand and drags him in.

"Oh, nothing much really; just doing a spot of Christmas shopping at the supermarket round the corner. You know, turkey, plum duff, figgy pudding, that kind of thing. Well, I got pissed off by the plastic mistletoe and the 'Silent Night' muzak, so I thought I'd drop by and see if I could serenade the building with my rendition of 'O Come all ye Faithful'. More 'come' than 'faithful' this Christmas, by the look of it. No, sorry, forget I said that. We three Queens of Orient are; one in a boat and one in a car!"

He trills and minces.

"No? Let's see: couple of mince pies, a glug of brandy, ravish any buxom wenches who may be about; alright, just the one wench then, as long as she's buxom; ah, yes, those'll do nicely and I'll be on my way," Michael says, grinning like a demented gargoyle and squeezing water out of his hair and wiping it from the lenses of his glasses.

"Shit, sorry, I've had a few beers."

Ellie looks at him and giggles.

"I can't believe some of the stuff you come out with!" she says.

"All part of my charm, my sweet," he slurs.

"So how did you know where to find me?" she asks prosaically.

"You said 'Riverview Lodge' was where you lived. I had the questionable good luck to hire a taxi driven by one Anthony Southwell, or Tone as he prefers to be known, as if he was a sweet musical note rather than a loathsome, grubby guttersnipe, wrist-dragging gibbon and mottled turd on two legs. Seems he is best buddies with your brother-in-law, he who is designated 'Gar' on the door, although one might have thought his bloody name was short enough already. Why do young people have to keep shortening everybody's sodding name? Um, anyway, Tone very kindly brought me right to the door."

"Oh, God."

"Well, it doesn't matter much now, Ellie. Everyone knows. The whole valley, it seems."

"It's gone midnight, Mike. I was asleep! Give me a minute to wake up."

Michael stops flicking water and looks at her.

"Sorry, Ellie. Look, I came to see you because, well, I can't stop thinking about you. I've fallen in love with you; damn it and I've come to take you away for a year and a day, to sea, in a beautiful pea-green boat. You're the pussycat, in case you were wondering. Green eyes, right? I'm the owl. They used to call me that at my last school; the kids. Must be the glasses, I suppose."

"Mike, like, you're pissed as a fart! How many beers was it, did you say?" says Ellie, giggling.

"Well, one or two. Or five. Nine? I don't know. Dutch courage. I wouldn't be here otherwise. Where's your sister?"

He suddenly lowers his voice to the level of a conspiratorial whisper.

Ellie whispers back, "She's staying at Mum's. Wayne wasn't very well, so they put him to bed and didn't want to disturb him again."

"Oh. And Gary Glitter?"

"Not here. Drinking and porno video session with his mates somewhere. That's Gary. Harmless, but animal," Ellie smiles wickedly. "So, we're all alone. Did you get a vibe about it?"

"No, no, I didn't, well, I don't know really. I had a row with Barbara and went down to the 'Plough' and sank a few pints, er, then I got a taxi over here. Impetuous, not inch...ooo...intuitive."

He smiles, rather sheepishly, as his mouth stumbles at the words.

Ellie laughs.

"Come on, we'd better get your clothes off, you're soaked through. You can borrow Gar's dressing gown and I'll hang your stuff on the radiators."

"Aren't you going to invite me in properly before you start tearing my clothes off?"

"You might not want to come in when you see it. It's a tip. Look, nip in the bathroom and get your things off. The dressing gown's on the back of the door. While you're doing that, I'll try to clear a space so we can at least sit down."

"OK."

"That's the bathroom. Green door with fish stickers."

"Really? Funny, I thought it might be an aquarium."

Inside the bathroom, he splashes his face furiously with water, hoping to rinse away the muddling effects of the beer. He manages to remove his wet clothing in the tiny, cramped space. The dressing gown is too small and smells of cigarettes and cheap deodorant. Michael wrinkles his nose and unconsciously checks the pockets. There are a couple of crumpled tissues, what look like small pieces of burnt toast and a condom in its foil. Unbelievable, thinks Michael. Is Fate trying to tell me something here?

"Mike? Are you alright? What are you doing in there? Gone to sleep in the bath?"

"No, no. Just powdering my nose," he says and opens the door.

He his amazed at the transformation in the flat. It looks altogether tidier, cleaner, and bigger. And Ellie too; she's pulled a comb through her hair and splashed water on her face. The sleepy look has gone.

"Good Heavens!" he says. "How did you do that?"

As she picks up his wet clothes and drapes them across radiators, she says, "No choice, living here. If you want a thing done, you do it yourself. I've had plenty of practice."

Michael watches her as she flits around the room. Her movements are swift, darting, almost nervous, like a young gazelle in the presence of a tiger. He wonders, briefly, whether he is indeed predatory. Older man; young, impressionable girl. An old tiger on the prowl, his pudenda swinging low in the long grass. Dingly-dangly tiger's stripy codpiece.

Her legs skip and turn as she hangs the clothes, the smooth nakedness of her thighs appearing occasionally from within the patterned silk kimono she is wearing. He perches on the arm of the weathered sofa and watches her.

"I've never seen your naked feet before," he offers.

She stops and stares down at them, as if seeing them for the first time. She smiles. "Turn you on, do they, naked feet?"

"Generally, no. But in your case, yes. All of you turns me on, actually."

102

"I'm not too sure I'm attracted to you in Gar's grubby old dressing gown!" she laughs.

She pushes the sleeves of his coat down the back of the radiator and turns to face him. They look at one another for a moment and she steps towards him.

"Just a joke, Mike. You wouldn't believe how much I fancy you. More than fancy!"

"It started with a kiss," he sings, "in the back row of the classroom... You remember that?"

"Technically, it was the hospital bed, I think, but the real clincher was in the car park at the back of the industrial estate. So romantic," she replies, grinning. "You never kissed me in the classroom. Interesting idea, though."

"Don't tempt me," he says.

There is a long pause. Neither of them quite knows what to do or say next. Somewhere in the distance, a clock chimes just once.

Ellie takes a deep breath.

"I love you, Mike. You know that. I think I've always loved you. It's so powerful this feeling, you know, sometimes it frightens me," she whispers. "I want to, so much, and then again I don't."

"Frightened?" he queries, dropping down to sit beside her.

"Well, I want us to make love, Mike, I really do, but, well, I'm really scared it's going to hurt. You know, I'm still not fully healed after; well, it was only five weeks ago."

"No one's rushing anything, Ellie. Least of all me," Michael gives her fingers a little squeeze.

"Well, not too much, anyway," he grins, looking at his watch.

"And I'm frightened that when it comes to it, that I might not be able to do it anyway; you know, what the counsellor was on about? Mental scarring and stuff."

"Ah, yes," says Michael, preparing to make light of what he knows she is likely to have been told, "your formative sexual imprint being a damaging one and all that."

"Yes," she says quietly. "But it wasn't the first experience, was it? I dunno. Well, it was, but it wasn't, if you see what I mean. You know, the time with Simon Quale last summer. I told you."

She knows she's not making much sense, least of all to herself.

He strokes her hair, for some minutes saying nothing, just making soothing noises. Eventually, she sits up, apologises and in a rush of sentences, describes the essence of the events with Simon all over again, but this time using less euphemistic language. When she has finished, he kisses her nose and laughs.

"Ellie, come on, don't upset yourself. Look, how did you feel about him? Were you in love with him?"

"No, 'course not. Not like this, with you. Like, I fancied him, yeah, in the way that girls fancy the singer in the band. Or the hunky guy in the magazine advert, you know? But that was it."

"So before you went up the hill with him and when he started kissing and cuddling you, what were your thoughts? How did you feel about it?"

"Well, I just wanted to do it. To fuck him. Oh, sorry! I mean, I just wanted to lose my virginity, I suppose. Kind of get rid of it, if that makes sense. I know that you're supposed to be proud of it and hold onto it for Mr. Right and all that, but to me it seems like I haven't grown up or something. I want to be like the other girls for once, instead of always being two or three years behind. Like, time to get your ears pierced; you're thirteen. Does that sound terrible?"

"Understandable."

"I was aroused, no doubt about that! You know, he's a good looking guy and he knows which buttons to push. But it wasn't going to be making love with an orchestra in the background. I don't know, it just wouldn't work. I couldn't do it and it was so humiliating!"

She looks tearful.

"Perhaps you were too consciously aware of the mechanics of the business, so preoccupied with the physical requirements of intercourse, that you forgot to relax and trust to instinct? Too busy worrying about how the projector works, instead of being swept along by the movie?"

"Yeah, could be. Wow, Mike, how do you come up with all that stuff?"

"I'm older than you, or hadn't you noticed? They call it experience."

"Yeah, like, I noticed. And I like it. And it doesn't matter."

"You hope!" says Mike, an image of sad Nibber flickering in the back of his mind.

"Some things we don't really need to be shown in too much detail. The human race got where it is without sex education. But with Simon it wasn't about making love and it was only about fucking in so far as you wanted the t-shirt. Fair summary?"

"Yes. It sounds funny when you say the f-word. Like it's far worse than if someone else says it."

"You'd better get used to it. I regret to announce it is part of my lexicon. It's probably the most common expression in most secondary school staff-rooms, as in 'Fucking Monday' or 'The fucking Headmaster.' Dreadful, but true."

Ellie laughs her deep laugh.

"Anyway, some people can just do it with almost anyone and for them it's just like swallowing or urinating. A simple, physical process. Those porn stars you watch? Pumping away all day in front of the cameras; the girls squealing and the guys looking all nonchalant, like all they're doing is rodding a drain! For the rest of us, it's a bit more complicated and involves the heart too. I am pleased to report, Miss Fortune, that you are in the latter category."

"Thank you."

"Look, I need a pee and then I'd love a cup of coffee. Any chance?"

"As long as you don't mind a chipped mug with no handle," she says, the worried expression lining her face.

"Divine!" he says and makes his way to the bathroom.

Ellie goes into the kitchen, finds two mugs, fills the kettle and then returns to the lounge and stands by the window. The lights of the town flicker dismally in the rain. A plastic carrier bag lifts, parascending in the eddies of wind around the building before snaring on a tree branch. The flashing navigation lights of an aircraft track a path across the night sky. Ellie wonders idly whether any of the women on board have ever sat after midnight, alone with their handsome English teacher, calmly discussing how they want to fuck each other.

Except, she thinks, he hasn't actually said that. It was me that said it. Maybe I am a forward tart? God, what a thing to say to anyone, especially him!

"That's better!" says Michael, coming back into the room.

"I'll get the coffee," says Ellie.

She makes it in silence, Michael leaning against the door frame, watching her. She carries the two mugs on a tray into the lounge and sits down on the sofa again, beckoning Michael to join her.

"So, what happened this evening?" she asks.

"After you left my office, John Sutcliffe comes in and says he knows what's going on. Remember the rabbitty-looking bloke up at High Gorge a few days ago? Neighbour of one of the secretaries or something. Recognises me. Blows the whistle. So, Sutcliffe warns me of the consequences with my job and so on."

"Oh, Mike, no! Oh, bloody hell! I knew it."

" 'Fraid so. I drive home, nearly run over a wandering cyclist and then have a plate-throwing competition with Barbara. Well, she threw the plates, I was fielding. She accuses me of having an affair with you and says the whole valley knows. We're headline news."

"I know. Tracey told me all the kids are on about it," Ellie begins to look tearful.

"Looks like I've blown my local standing; my wife is threatening divorce; no doubt the twins will suffer nightmares and die of grief and embarrassment; I'm about to lose my job, maybe, and a sad old man at the pub says don't do it anyway. Apart from that, no problem. Happy days are here again. And you, how's your day been, darling?"

Ellie frowns.

"It's not really funny, Mike. Things are getting serious. You make everything into a joke, it seems."

"Not really. It's the beer and a defence mechanism. I've always been the same. Otherwise we'd have to slit one another's throats. Sorry. I know it's serious. That's why I'm here."

"OK. Well, Mum's being a cow, of course. Still not speaking. I suppose she won't now. That's really hard for me, right? She's telling everyone there's been this big mistake and The Pervert is not really a pervert at all. I don't think she's actually coming out and saying I'm a slut, but she might just as well. That reminds me: when I went to see that solicitor, Fiona Perry, like, the one that Dad arranged for me?"

Michael nods.

"Well, she was on about how Brian's side will try to make out that I'm a right slag? She made some remark about had there been any relationships with older men?"

"Christ! So now it's out, they could demonstrate that there is and leave the jury to draw a conclusion about your implied sexual behaviour and preferences."

Ellie smiles ruefully.

"I don't think I would have said it so cleverly, but yeah, something like that."

"Rabbit-face or even Tone the two-legged turd would make ideal witnesses, of course."

"Actually," says Ellie hesitantly, "it's worse than that."

"Is that possible?"

"Simon Quale has been contacted by the Police to make a witness statement or something about what happened at the Albert Tower," Ellie says, her voice cracking with emotion.

"How do you know?"

"I keep in touch with a girl on the island. Helen James. Known her since we were kids. Lives in the same road as my Gran used to. She knows Simon. He told her. She told me. Got a letter yesterday."

"But how would your step-father know about that anyway?"

"He's a bloody pervert, right? He's got a pair of binoculars, pretends to be bird-watching. He must have been watching us from the beach. Well, he said as much, sort of. It's the kind of thing he does. I'd seen him peering up at the Tower loads of times before. It's the only explanation."

Ellie almost spits the words in her contempt.

"The sneaky, filthy bastard. I hate him. But it won't look good, will it? Like, I set it up and made it clear what I wanted from Simon. He said he was surprised. As if it was a driving lesson, he said," Ellie looks embarrassed.

"Oh, dear."

"Can you take one more?" Ellie smiles a weak smile.

"Oh, no," screeches Michael in theatrical mock horror, "not the black lagoon!"

"This one is adolescent, OK, so you don't need to say so," begins Ellie defensively. "I've had a crush on you for years and I've kept a little notebook, a sort of diary and story book with stuff about you in it. Stories about us being together. You know? And I wrote in it on the night of the rape, before The Pervert came in, about when I came to see you and the things I felt. Well, we both felt, as it happens. Yeah? Well, I hid it in a special place in the eaves cupboard in my bedroom. And now it's gone."

"How do you know?"

"I asked Emma to fetch it for me this morning. When she phoned this evening to say she wasn't coming back, she told me it was missing."

Michael frowns.

"Could she have been looking in the wrong place?"

"No. She knows the place. She used to keep condoms there when she started going out with Gary. We shared that bedroom then."

"You mean they used to do it in the cupboard?" Michael looks surprised.

"Don't be daft!"

"Bloody Norah! So, you're assuming that your mother has found it and will allow it to be presented as evidence for the defence, if that's what they want?"

"I don't know, Mike. I suppose so. Is that how it works? How could she do such a thing? It's private. She's no right to go poking through my stuff like that."

Michael nods his head.

"Of course not. But from her point of view, whatever she does she loses: either a husband or a daughter. I guess she's going for damage limitation. She might feel it's better to have an estranged daughter than a husband in prison."

"I hate her 'n all."

"I'm not surprised."

They are silent for a moment while Ellie twists at her sleeve, her mouth set in a hard line.

"It's all a bit of a mess, then," she says, eventually.

"Yes, but we caused it. We can't blame anyone else," says Michael. "I suppose we should have been more careful. Or not got involved in the first place. But somehow, you throw caution to the wind when it's like this. Well, we seem to have done, anyway."

"So, what are we going to do? Are you saying it's over?" Ellie asks tremulously.

"What makes you think that?"

"I don't know. You might lose your job. Like, we shouldn't have got involved in the first place, you said," she replies.

"OK. Tough talking. Do you want to back off now, before any more shit hits the fan? I mean, there might just be time?"

Michael looks straight into her eyes.

She grabs his hand and brings his fingers to her lips, kissing them.

"No, I don't. I love you Mike, I want to be with you," she says in a clear voice. "You know that. If I have to suffer, then I have to suffer if that's what it takes. But what about you? I don't want you to lose your job, Mike. You're a brilliant teacher."

"You'll be an adulteress and they'll call you a slag; a tart," he probes.

"You'll be an adulterer too. So what? Happens all over the place these days. You'll be an absent father and a dirty old man as well," she counters, "and disgraced and jobless."

"Tone the Turdlike already called me a dirty old man earlier, so don't you start! And when you're forty, I'll be sixty eight. Past it, probably. How about that?"

"Mike, we've talked about this before. I'll do whatever it takes. Anyway, at sixty eight you could be fitter than me. Like, I might have cancer, or that bone-crumbling disease; you know, osteothingy, at thirty five. Or I could get run over when I'm twenty. No one knows."

Ellie's tone is clipped and not for the first time, Michael is surprised by her steely resolve.

"How can you think that way when you're only sixteen, Ellie? Amazing! But all our lives, people will think you're my daughter and give us critical looks. It'll always be an uphill struggle. People are quick to condemn," continues Michael.

"So what? I don't care about other people. It's not illegal, is it? And we won't be the first. What is this, anyway, a test? What about you? I've said what I think. Your turn."

"I know. OK. All sorts of things. Confusion. Surprise. It's all happened so fast. Guilt, a lot of the time, about Barbara and the kids. Ashamed of myself, I suppose, too. Because you're a pupil. It flies completely in the face of everything my profession is supposed to be about. It's called professional misconduct. Gross misconduct, actually. So all that. Am I off my head? Concerned that I'm leading you into something you'll come to regret when you're older. Or I might regret."

"That's a lot of negative stuff, Mike," Ellie says sadly.

"Yes, but there's a great deal more, Ellie. Don't be hasty! If it was only those things, then I wouldn't be here tonight, would I? Taking absurd risks just to be with you now; see you just for a few moments, perhaps, because I assumed your sister would be here."

"I suppose so," she responds, a little reassured.

"I am driven by something larger than those negatives, Ellie. I am consumed by my need for you, despite all of those worries. I look into those green eyes and fall headlong from the top of a high building. I smell your skin or your hair and I lose my being, my sense of place, of time itself, so I'm floating like thistledown over the meadows. When we are together, whatever the fears, we are one and I breathe freely the honeyed sweetness of life. Apart, I walk shards of glass and gasp for air."

Ellie is watching his eyes, bathing in his words, her lips apart in wonderment at his beautiful language.

Michael whispers, "Or put more simply, I love you. Desperately."

She leans forward and kisses him very slowly and gently, so softly that her mouth on his is the merest dust of pollen on a petal.

"Mike. Make love to me. Please. Now."

In one movement, she wriggles free of the kimono. Under its own silken weight, it slithers to the floor.

II TIME PIECE

CLOCK WATCHING

It's half past two but he's not back. Where the hell is he? I suppose he's alright? Phone the Police? Maybe give it until three. Too soon anyway: they'll only laugh at me, won't they? Bloody policemen; patronising women in the way that men in uniform do.

I feel rejected. I haven't done anything to deserve this. And what about the girls? He hasn't thought about them. My back hurts again. Stress of all this. He won't be thinking about me. Too busy with his own feelings; urges, more like. Urges for teenage girls. It's disgusting, at his age. It's not respectable.

He doesn't find me attractive any more. Doesn't actually say so, but I can see it in his eyes. Keeps his distance; barely touches me; pecks my cheek. Distaste, really.

He's with that girl, Ellen, the bitch. Slim, dark hair, large bosom; young, nubile. A bloody child! The type he looks at these days. Other men's daughters. And they smile back at him, the sluts. Lifting their skirts to show more leg and pushing their breasts out. Leading him on. No shame. They respond, for crying out loud.

He's screwing the little bitch-slut somewhere; pushing himself into her, I know it. I feel sick. Am I going to be sick? No, no, breathe deeply. That's it. Breathe. My back is really painful. Stabbing pain; think about that, not him and the bitch. Physical pain is easier.

Two forty five. I must do something. At three o'clock, then.

That night at Gassin? Not time for them to do it, surely? Well, how long does it take? Takes him ages now, if ever it happens. If he can get it up at all. His eyes closed and his face all screwed up as if he's in pain or trying to imagine someone else is under him, of course. That's how the joke goes, doesn't it? Except in my case, it's not a joke, it's real.

When we were young and he was so desperate for me, he sometimes would finish in just a few seconds. So, there was time for him to screw that girl at Gassin. But he wouldn't do that, would he? Like a dog, out in the open with some stranger? He would, the bastard; I think he would!

Shit! Damn him! Bastard, bastard, bastard! Unfaithful, fornicating, lecherous bastard! I hate him! No, no, calm. How could he be with her at this time of night? She'd be at home with her parents, surely, a girl of that age? Oh, well, just her mother, I suppose, because of the rape. Alleged rape.

Phone and find out! Well...

Phone book; work it out! OK, Mike, you bastard. Let's start the counter-offensive by seeing whether the girl's mother knows what's going on, shall we?

Time's up!

AT THE THIRD STROKE

Linda Shepherd sits up. There is a handset by the bed. She picks it up gingerly. Unless it's a wrong number, someone calling at three thirty in the morning can be the bearer of nothing but bad news.

"Hello?"

"Ah, is that Linda Shepherd?"

Barbara's voice is hesitant, clotted with emotion and anxiety.

"Yes, who is this, please?"

"The Linda Shepherd who has a daughter called Ellen at the Comprehensive?"

"Yes. Look, who is this, please? Have you any idea what the time is?"

"I know, Mrs Shepherd, forgive me. My name is Barbara Chadwick. My husband is Doctor Chadwick. I don't think we've ever met, Mrs Shepherd but, obviously, you know who my husband is."

Linda's response is cautious. Of course she knows who Doctor Chadwick is; he is the teacher featured in her younger daughter's notebook, a notebook presently in the hands of Piers Sowerby, counsel for the defence. What does this woman want?

"Yes, Mrs Chadwick, I know who your husband is. I assume this is important for you to be phoning me at this hour of the morning?"

"I'm sorry, Mrs Shepherd, I really am. Do you mind if I ask you whether your daughter Ellen is at home?"

In other circumstances, Linda might have told this intrusive questioner to take a running jump, but these are not other circumstances. They are extraordinary circumstances and although she is in part irritated and in part muddled by sleep, her instincts tell her to answer the question.

"Well, no, she's staying with her sister at the moment. Why?"

Barbara is uncomfortable, not sure whether her worst fears about an embarrassing telephone call are about to be realised. Nevertheless, her instincts drive her on too.

"Right. Look, I'm sorry to seem so persistent, I really am. Is your other daughter with Ellen now?"

Linda, the miasma of sleep and worry beginning to clear from her head, suddenly begins to understand the reason for this quavering voice's questioning about her younger daughter. But she must be careful.

"As it happens, Mrs Chadwick, no. My other daughter, Emma, is here with me and my grandson. My son-in-law is…well, to be honest, I don't know where he is, but he's not at their flat. So Ellen is alone. I assume. Why?"

Barbara swallows hard.

"I see. Mrs Shepherd, I believe that your daughter Ellen and my husband are carrying on some sort of affair. Were you aware of that?"

Linda is evasive.

"Well, perhaps a schoolgirl crush."

Barbara snorts.

"I think you'll find it's more than a crush. My husband is not here, Mrs Shepherd."

There is a catch in Barbara's voice. She barely manages to articulate her last sentence. "I believe that he is with Ellen right now."

*

In Church Road, Linda Shepherd helps Emma to settle Wayne back to sleep, telling her that the phone call was a wrong number. She does not want Emma phoning Ellen to warn her. She knows the sisters are close. No, she needs time to think, to decide what, if anything, she is going to do with the news she has just heard.

If what Barbara Chadwick suspects is true, then it is a disgrace and puts her younger daughter beyond the pale. Beyond redemption, even. If it is true, and it seems likely in the light of the notebook and rumours she's heard, then perhaps it does bear out Brian's contention that Ellen is sexually over-charged and precocious? That she is attracted to older men and they to her and that she in some way enticed Brian into her bedroom and his terrible, sordid deed?

For Linda has had time to think about that night, over and over. Time to talk to her husband who has remained steadfast in his story (lie or otherwise, she thinks) that, yes, intercourse took place but he couldn't help himself because Ellen appeared naked at the top of the stairs, stood with her legs apart and beckoned him into her room. Satan saw his moment of weakness and entered his soul, so, he couldn't help himself and didn't know what he was doing; didn't know he was hurting the girl so badly. Satan saw that he still has a strong sex drive and is often frustrated because, well, you're not so keen on that side of the marriage, are you my dear? I'm terribly sorry. No, not your fault, of course not.

No, she thinks, I am not so keen on that side of the marriage and so maybe I drove him to this, through my failure to satisfy his conjugal needs. Therefore I must help him now, although it means I have to disbelieve my daughter. Take sides. So terribly difficult. But this gives Brian's account much more credibility, doesn't it? She is behaving like a young whore. We have evidence. Better than some adolescent account from the boy in the Isle of Man.

Do we have evidence? No, she'll deny it. And so will he, of course. There will be no proof in the morning. I must go there now!

She is out of bed and beginning to look for her clothes when another thought occurs, for Linda Shepherd is a clever woman. She picks up the telephone and asks for the Police.

*

"With respect, madam, we can't go running around after every young girl who's gone to the disco and taken some young lad back to her flat."

"Officer, you're missing the point. Ellen did not go anywhere, so far as I know. She was alone at my other daughter's flat. And this is not a young lad. This man, if I am right, is in his forties. We are talking about an abuse of power and position here, Officer. Perhaps he forced his way in? Maybe he overpowered my daughter? Maybe he has seduced her against her will? I find it hard to believe my daughter would willingly entertain the advances of a middle-aged man."

There is a pause.

"You'd be surprised, Madam. How old is she, did you say?"

Linda draws breath to play her trump card.

"Just sixteen, Officer."

She closes her eyes at the little white lie, mentally asking for forgiveness.

"Perhaps it is a relationship which has been going on for some time; since before her sixteenth birthday. I have found evidence in my daughter's handwriting to suggest this may be the case. Furthermore, Officer, the man is her school teacher."

"Do you have the address, please, Madam? We'll get it checked out straight away."

"Yes. Thank you."

*

In an apartment block down by the harbour in Edgemouth, two lovers are again riding the speedboat of desire. It is a curling, boiling swell that tosses and twists them in its delicious grip. They are barely in control of their craft but it matters not for they are exhilarated by its bucking, heaving motions. They cling to one another, screaming, as the bow lifts and plunges once more into the salt froth and foam of the trough.

Somewhere else, maybe far out at sea, at some impossible distance beyond the horizon, there is a hammering sound.

Michael regains balance and pulls to shore. He wonders if the neighbours have heard the sounds of their passion. Ellen tenses.

There is the noise again. Bang, bang, bang.

"Christ! What's that?"

Michael staggers to his feet.

"There's someone banging on the door," wails Ellie, terrified.

Bang! Bang! Bang! Louder, followed by a voice.

"Open the door, please. This is the Police!"

"Oh, no!" squeals Ellie.

The two stare at one another, disbelieving, hearts beating overtime. The voice is louder this time, coming through the letter flap.

"Miss Ellen Fortune? This is the Police. Open the door, please."

"Oh, my God! What are we going to do?" Ellie whispers, frantically clutching the kimono to her breasts. "You'd better hide!"

"Don't be daft, Ellie. Where am I going to hide in this rabbit hutch? I'll stay in here. Open the door. Pray. It may not be what we think," but as Michael says this, he knows in his heart that his optimism is entirely misplaced.

NIGHT DUTY

Ellie pulls back the security chain and opens the door. Outside are two uniformed police constables, one a woman.

"Good evening, miss," says the Constable, evenly. "Miss Ellen Fortune?"

"Yes?"

"Perhaps it would be better if we came in for a moment, if you don't mind? Rather than standing here on the doorstep. Nothing to worry about, we just need to ask you a few questions. More private inside, I'm sure you'll agree," he says, flicking his head backwards at the other doors on the landing.

Ellie has sufficient presence of mind to try to act as if disturbed from sleep.

"What's this about? Is something wrong? My family, or something? I was asleep. It's the middle of the night."

The Constable smiles reassuringly.

"No, nothing like that. Nothing wrong, unless you tell us otherwise?"

WPC Elisabeth L. Harding gives her colleague a nudge in the back. She invariably passes the long, quiet hours fornicating in the back of various patrol cars and thus she is a popular pairing with the constables on night duty. She knows a thing or two about coitus interruptus, of course, for duty has a habit of calling at the most inopportune moments. If she's not mistaken, she sees it now. The girl's eyes are dilated, her lips are flushed a deep pink and there are new bites on her neck. She reeks of sex, she's dripping with it. Asleep, my arse. Horizontal, maybe, but not asleep.

"Come on, love, we'd better have a look, if you don't mind? Just to make sure you're all right. We had a call from your Mum. She's pretty worried about you," says Harding as she takes Ellie's elbow and moves through the doorway.

"My Mum? You had a call from my Mum?"

Ellen is momentarily confused, unable to piece together this strange jigsaw. The notebook? But, even so, how could Mum know that Mike is here tonight? It wasn't planned. Not even Emma knows. No one knows, do they? Tone the taxi driver?! No, he wouldn't bother, surely?

"Is there anyone else here, Ellen?" asks the Constable, not really needing an answer. "Come on, love, it's pretty obvious, isn't it?"

"Well, I..."

The constable glances down the hall and takes in the open door of the empty kitchen.

"Would you mind waiting in the kitchen there with my colleague? Thank you."

"Aren't you supposed to have a search warrant or something?" she says bravely.

The policeman chuckles.

"Quite an assertive young lady, aren't we? Well, it's up to you. I can get one organised if you insist, while WPC Harding waits with you here. Take about half an hour. Bit of a waste of time, if you don't mind me saying so. We're not going to turn the place over, Miss, just checking to see you're safe, at your mother's request."

Realising that her token objection is so expertly pushed aside, Ellie allows herself to be propelled into the kitchen by WPC Harding.

In the lounge, Michael has grabbed some clothes from the radiator and struggled into them, although they are still wet. His bare feet make contact with the sticky wetness of discarded paper tissues: the plentiful evidence of their night of love. He bends to pick them up as the door opens.

"Just leave those, Sir," snaps Constable Lewis, as he moves into the room. With a practised eye and nose, he takes in the scene in a split second. A mess of tissues, wet patches on the bed settee, an animal, salty smell of considerable sexual activity, a bedraggled and unshaven middle-aged man standing guiltily in front of him, his apparently wet shirt incorrectly buttoned and his fly unzipped.

Lewis has seen it before. An old guy caught flagrante delicto, more or less, after shagging a young girl. A gorgeous little thing too, the lucky sod.

"Don't I know you, Sir?" says Constable Lewis, barely able to conceal his amusement.

"I expect so, Constable, most people seem to recognise me these days. But you have the advantage over me, I'm afraid," Michael says bitterly.

"Constable Mark Lewis. Left the school about eight years ago, Doctor Chadwick."

"Right," says Michael disinterestedly. This isn't the time for a reunion conversation, he thinks.

"Look, er...I suppose I should call you Constable? There's nothing untoward here, I can assure you. Ellen and I are; well, we have a relationship. She's over sixteen."

"I see, Sir. She's a pupil at the school?"

Michael sighs.

"She is. But, like I say, she's over sixteen."

Constable Lewis allows a smirk to flicker around the corner of his mouth.

"So you're being a bit of a naughty boy, then, Sir? Big trouble for you if this gets out, I should think?"

"As I say, Constable, she's over sixteen and a consenting party in the relationship. The school thing; well, you're right. It's my intention to address that later today," Michael replies, automatically looking at the electric wall clock he noticed earlier, seeing its minute hand at a quarter past the hour. "But even so, there is nothing illegal or criminal here, is there?"

Constable Lewis does not answer the question.

"Presumably, the young lady can verify her age. How did you get in here, Sir?"

"In the usual manner, Constable. I knocked on the door and she let me in. Why, are you suggesting something else?"

Michael knows he is sounding defensive, but his irritation at the smirking young constable is getting the better of him.

"I'm not suggesting anything, Doctor. Just trying to establish the exact circumstances here. My colleague will be doing the same with the young lady. Independently, you see."

"OK, I'm sorry. I had an argument with my wife earlier this evening. She accused me of having an affair. I went down to the pub, probably drank too much beer and emboldened by that, got a taxi here. Ellen did not know I was going to turn up. I did not know she was alone. I assumed her sister would be here. One thing lead to another. You know," says Michael, realising that he needs to give as much information as possible and hopes that Ellie is doing the same.

"You got lucky, then, Sir," Constable Lewis says.

" 'No comment', I believe is the traditional response to some questions," says Michael.

"The answer is fairly obvious," says the young policeman, waving his hand at the settee and the tissues, "but I have to ask you all the same. Sexual intercourse has taken place?"

Michael wonders whether to object, but realises there is no point.

"Yes," he says. "But, to repeat once more, she's over sixteen."

"So you keep saying, Sir. It may not be as simple as that. There are laws pertaining to men taking young girls under eighteen without their parent's consent. And we've had a call from her mother, expressing concern. She didn't know about this, it seems. When did the relationship start, Doctor Chadwick?"

"Er, late October, I suppose. About five weeks ago. And before you ask, this is the first time we have made love and her birthday is in August and no, there was no relationship, sexual or otherwise, when she was only fifteen. And I didn't 'take' her anywhere. I have explained how I came to be here."

"Ah, yes; you made love," says the Constable, sarcastically.

"This is our first night together," says Michael, rather lamely, feeling that the night is suddenly turning sour.

"Congratulations, then, Sir," says the Constable, unable to resist the riposte. "Of course, you might be well advised to think about whether you can prove that if you have to, Doctor. That's just a bit of friendly advice, from an ex-pupil. Sir."

Constable Lewis smiles broadly, revealing a cluster of mildewed teeth.

Michael is open-mouthed in astonishment.

"Now, if you wouldn't mind," continues the Constable, "I'd be grateful if you could stay in here while I have a quick conflab with my colleague."

Constable Lewis leaves the room, closing the door behind him, and nods to WPC Harding to join him. They stand just outside the front door, within sight, but out of earshot, of Ellen. It takes them only a few moments to confirm what they had already deduced: the stories tally; the man and the girl are telling the truth. Harding adds that the girl had a passport and other papers with her in her bag in the bedroom and her age is as stated.

While WPC Harding positions herself between the doorways in the flat, PC Lewis remains on the landing and contacts the station.

"Sarge? PC Lewis, down at 'Riverview Lodge'. Girl in the flat, Ellen Fortune, aged sixteen. Seen her passport; birthday last August. Also there Doctor Michael Chadwick, aged about forty five. I know him, as it happens. Married school teacher. Her teacher. Says they've been seeing each other for about five weeks. No sign of forced entry or coercion; stories tally. Intercourse taken place. Almost caught them at it. You know; standard stuff. Middle-aged bloke shafting a young girlie. Cut and dried, really. Well, not dry, actually, Sarge. Pretty wet. They must have been at it for hours like a couple of mechanised rabbits."

The Sergeant laughs at his young constable's vulgarity.

"What d'you want me to do, Sarge? Bring 'em in, or what? Or shall we just leave them to it? There's plenty of time before dawn and I don't think they've finished yet!"

"Stay with them, Lewis. I'll check it out."

As he puts the phone down, he makes the connection he should have made some time ago: Ellen Fortune is a name that he has seen before.

*

"Mrs Shepherd? It's Sergeant Box at Tinsmead Police Station."

"Yes?"

"I have had two officers visit your daughter's flat. Ellen is there with someone named Michael Chadwick who, as you suspected, is a much older man; her school teacher. Ah, the scene suggests that intercourse has taken place but both parties independently state that the relationship is consensual. No sign of force or coercion, Mrs Shepherd. I'm sorry. This may not be want you wanted to hear."

"I see," says Linda evenly.

"It is possible that the relationship has been going on for some time, since before your daughter's sixteenth birthday, but my officers doubt it from what answers they have had to their questions. Two months at the outside, they say. Of course, even if you wanted to press charges in that regard, I'm sure Chadwick and your daughter would deny it."

"No, no, I don't wish to press any charges. I just wanted to be sure she was OK. Not hurt or being forced to do anything against her will."

"It would appear she is a fully consenting party."

Linda allows herself a smile.

"This incident is recorded somewhere, Sergeant, I assume? In your officers' reports or log-books or whatever you call them?"

"Yes, Madam."

"Would you please ensure that your officers record full details? This may have a bearing on another case, involving my husband, which is set for trial on 10th July next year."

At the end of the conversation, Sergeant Box turns to radio his officers, ruminating on the cunning of some women as he does so.

Linda Shepherd sits tapping her fingers on the bedside cabinet, calculating her next move.

THE DARKEST HOUR IS JUST BEFORE DAWN

Behind the chipped blue door of number twelve, Michael and Ellie have returned to the lounge and huddle together under a blanket, shivering more from shock than cold. Ellie has been crying.

"I don't understand how Mum can have known you were here. Like, no one knew. It doesn't make sense."

"Work it out. Tone Southwell? He knows; he brought me here in his toss-pot of a taxi. You know him better than I do. Would he phone your mother? Surely not?"

"No, I don't think so. Unless he has a grudge against you?" asks Ellie.

"Not me. Never taught the greasy slob. Maybe he has a grudge against you? He told me he tried to get his oily fingernails inside your panties. Jealousy does funny things."

Ellen looks embarrassed.

"He told you that? The toad. Well, yes, he tried it on a few weeks ago but no big deal. No, I don't think it's him."

"OK. Larry or Old Nibber at the pub? No, I don't think so. The one person who knows for sure that I am not where I'm supposed to be is Barbara," he says.

"OhmiGod, yes. So? You think she phoned my Mum? Do they know each other?"

"I haven't the vaguest idea. Maybe. Is your Mum in the phone book?"

"Yes. Well, under the name Shepherd."

"Mmm, I reckon she could track it down, then. Your step-father's name has been in the papers quite a bit. I'm not especially surprised that she's done the detective work. What does surprise me is that she had the courage to make the call at three in the morning or whenever it was. But that must be it. It's the only logical possibility. You realise what the motivation might be for your mother phoning the Police? I don't imagine, incidentally, that Barbara, if we're right about all this, was expecting her to do that. Well, she won't even know, perhaps. No, she'd be assuming that your Mum would come running round here, catch us at it, go berserk and take you away, telling me never to darken your door again, or else, etcetera, etcetera," Michael says.

"Yes, Mike, I've worked it out; I'm not stupid! There will be a Police record to say we are an item. A sexually involved item, now!"

Ellie cannot suppress a grin.

"Right? So they can call on those Constables to give evidence at The Pervert's trial. To make me look like a slag. A slag who is turned on by middle-aged men. Yeah?"

"You got it in one, Watson. Looks like it, I'm afraid."

There is a pause. Michael watches the second hand of the clock, slowly tracing long circles through the winter night. Ellie dabs at her eyes with her sleeve.

"So what are we going to do now that the world's falling apart around us?"

"We need to take some control back if we can," he begins again.

"How do you mean?"

"Maybe we need to try to lie low for a bit. Until after the trial, anyway. Although it's months away. After it's over, well, we could just jump in the car; I don't know?"

"Go off together?"

Ellie's eyes sparkle with excitement at the sheer audacity of it.

"The pea-green boat or whatever it was you said earlier?"

"Something like that. I want to be with you, Ellie."

"And I love you, Mike, you must know that by now?"

"But we can't be together here, not in a thousand years," he continues, "so it follows it would have to be somewhere else."

"Oh, Mike, yes! Ace!"

She jumps out of the settee and bounces around the room, a child again.

"But what about your job? Your wife? Your kids? Money?" she wails, coming down to a hard landing.

"I didn't say it would be easy. It won't. It'll be bloody hard and it won't just be hard for us. And because it's not just us that'll be affected, it'll be all the harder for us, if you see what I mean," he smiles apologetically for his clumsy explanation.

"Harder for you than me, Mike," she replies.

"Maybe. You want to make it the plan?"

"Yes, definitely," Ellie says firmly. "You?"

"I'm in. OK. It's the plan. Say nothing to anyone. Not Emma, not Tracey, no one. Right?"

"Of course not," she replies, a little hurt that he should think she might.

"Right, so first, I have to deal with Barbara and then John Sutcliffe."

"Yeah, like runaway!" she giggles, wriggling back under the blanket again.

Carefully, Michael begins to explain to her how he intends to spend the early part of the morning, surprised again that his unconscious mind has already put together a plan of action.

AN' THE TIMES, THEY ARE A-CHANGIN'

30/11/90

Michael,

For very obvious reasons, I leave off the 'dear'. You are no longer dear to me and this makes me very sad.

I know where you were last night. I know who you were with and I know what you were doing. It doesn't really matter now, but for the record, I phoned Linda Shepherd who, apparently, contacted the Police. That was her idea, not mine; she didn't say that's what she was going to do. But any trouble it causes you is entirely your own fault.

She phoned me back to tell me what they told her. Thank you so much for that.

Also for the record, if you had been truthful with me last night instead of being evasive and if you had apologised, I might have forgiven you. Again. But it is too late now. Now that you have laughed in my face and had your way with that child.

She is just a child. Think about this: when she grows up and gets fat and loses her nubile girl's shape, you'll tire of her. Then what? Another one? You'll end up a very sad old man, all alone.

We have gone to Mum's. At the moment, I have told them that Nanny is feeling unwell and needs our help. It will be your responsibility to tell them what's really happened.

If you can spare some thoughts for people other than yourself, think about Hannah and Lucy's Christmas.

I shall contact a solicitor in the morning and do whatever is necessary to get a divorce under way. Naturally, I intend to name the child as co-respondent. It begins to look as though that poor Brian Shepherd was right. No doubt all this will aid his case. I hope so.

Please do not contact me at Mum's. It will be necessary to speak only if I want to speak in which case, I will call you.

There is nothing else to say, except that I am desperately disappointed, unhappy and sad. No doubt the twins will echo those feelings in due course.

Perhaps there is something else to say. It will not surprise you. Once, centuries ago it seems, I loved you and you loved me and I thought it would stay that way forever. Why? Because I trusted my own feelings and, furthermore, you told me that's how it would be.

It has not stayed that way forever. You have changed everything. You have treated me and the girls abominably.

The root cause of this? You are a devious, superficial, selfish, unfeeling bastard.

Barbara

*

At seven forty five, Michael pulls into the school car park, noting with satisfaction that, as he expected, John Sutcliffe's car is already there. Minutes later, he is at Sutcliffe's door.

"John! Morning. I need to speak to you urgently, privately," he blurts as he comes into the room.

John Sutcliffe looks up from his diary. He takes in his Deputy's appearance and notes a certain wild-eyed look, an uncharacteristic untidiness about his shirt, normally so neatly pressed and his empty hands. Mike is always clutching timetables, folders, pens, rulers.

"Alright, Mike. Sit down. What's the matter?" he asks, already beginning mentally to answer his own question, hoping he's got the wrong answer.

Michael switches the sign to 'Meeting in Progress' closes the door firmly and sits down.

"John, I want to tender my resignation with immediate effect."

John Sutcliffe's curling eyebrows attempt to join his receding hairline.

"What? You must be joking, Mike, you know you can't do that. You know the rules. You have to give..."

"Hear me out, John, please," interrupts Mike.

John looks at Michael, beginning to hear the strain in his voice, to attune to the tensions emanating from his every movement.

"Sorry, I'm sure. Go on then," he says, perhaps a little coldly, for he knows there can be only one issue which has brought this on.

"I spent the night with Ellie Fortune. Barbara phoned Ellie's mother, who in turn phoned the Police. The Police almost beat the door down and gave us the Spanish Inquisition at four in the morning. No charges are to be brought, thank God, not that I can see how they could be, but of course there'll be a police record. Who knows, maybe some sharp-nosed reporter will pick it up? Or it'll hit the rumour mill. Nothing stays secret for long round here. In any event, it'll get dragged into Brian Shepherd's trial next year. Bound to. His defence counsel will think it's his birthday. Barbara's pushed off to her mother's with the girls and is going to divorce me, she says. So, I think it would be better if I resigned now before the crap really starts flying. Just like Mrs Thatcher, only for different reasons. One assumes."

John opens his mouth in amazement, begins to speak, stops, coughs and starts again.

"You're telling me you spent the night having sexual intercourse with a sixth form girl? And somehow the Police are involved?"

"Yes, John, that's the essence, seen from your point of view, I suppose," Michael replies.

"Well, of all the idiotic bloody…Evidently, you took no notice of what I said to you last night. Really, I think..."

"Look, John, I didn't come in here for a lecture. I actually don't give a toss what you think. Maybe I am an idiot, I don't know. Quite possibly. All I know is that I am insanely in love with her and I have to be with her and that's that. We intend to make our lives together. One day, we shall be married. Definite," Michael sits back, folding his arms defiantly.

John Sutcliffe looks carefully at Michael, rapidly trying to take in what he has just heard and to make sense of it, coming as it does from the mouth of a man normally so reliable, dependable, measured. Who's he trying to convince, he thinks, me or himself?

"I don't think you can possibly have thought this through, Mike. She's only sixteen, for Heaven's sake. Come on, you know what sixteen year old girls are like. They change their affections as often as they change their lipstick."

"Not this one," Michael responds sharply. "Not Ellie. Believe me, you'll see."

"Mike, you're not thinking straight. Stress or grief or whatever it is has clouded your usually sound judgment. You're wrong. She's not a mature woman; she's a girl. This is absolute madness."

Michael looks at the man opposite him.

"It's love, John. Simple as that."

"No, Mike, it's lust. Don't you see? You're blowing your career, your marriage, and your reputation; for what? A sixteen year old kid? I had thought better of you, Mike," snaps John, losing patience with his colleague's patently absurd infatuation.

"OK, OK. You'll have to think what you bloody like, John. Anyway, the issue I'm trying to address is not my relationship but my position here. Presumably we both agree it is now untenable? So I am handing in my resignation - here you are, it's in writing - so that it can be dealt with swiftly and painlessly as far as the school is concerned. No 'suspended from duty' or County enquiries; I just disappear into the night. For a while, you can say I'm off sick or I've gone doolally if that's what you think. I don't care; say whatever you like."

"It may already be too late for that, Mike," mutters John.

"It makes it easier for everyone, John, don't you see? Easier for you and County Hall if questions come. You just say that I am no longer employed by the County. Full stop. Easier for me too frankly."

"I don't know. Maybe."

"Look, if I go into my office for a normal day's work right now, knowing what you know, you can't ignore me and just let me get on as usual, can you? You have to follow me in there and suspend me from duty, pending a County enquiry, right? Unprofessional conduct."

"True. You've blown it sky high, Mike," says John.

"You'll probably have Mrs bloody, holier-than-thou Shepherd on the phone any minute, anyway, registering her complaint. News gets out about that and it becomes a story worth following for as long as all that takes. Weeks, maybe. Reporters phoning up, television cameras at the gates. You know how it is. If I resign now, I'm an ex-member of staff. Maybe there'll be one story in the press, but probably not. Quick kill, John."

John Sutcliffe draws in a long breath and then releases it in a whistling, hissing sigh.

"OK, Mike, I'll try and run with it. Leave it with me and I'll contact Sheila Lovegrove in Staffing at nine o'clock and see what I can do. I'm not sure what their attitude will be. I'll phone you later at home. That's it? There's nothing else to say, is there?" John says with an air of cold finality, getting up from his desk and crossing the room towards the door.

Michael stands up too, suddenly feeling his position, experience, career and credibility fall away from him like a loose beach towel, leaving him vulnerable and somehow rather pathetic.

Outside in the car park, a few early pupils are gossiping idly. They are surprised to see Doctor Mike, usually so brisk and efficient at this time of day, wandering rather aimlessly towards his car and then standing and staring around him as if he has suffered sudden memory loss and knows not where he is.

TURNING BACK THE CLOCK

Michael swings out of the school car park, scattering bemused children in all directions and points the vehicle towards Edgemouth.

He drives recklessly with one hand, the other scrabbling in the glove box for a cassette tape. He glances at the label, inserts it in the dashboard slot and turns the volume knob. He decides the valley would like to hear too, and winds down the window as Johnny Kidd and the Pirates slam into the metallic chords of, 'Shakin' All Over'.

He yanks at his tie, undoes it and then throws it through the window. There is a folder of school papers on the passenger seat beside him. He clutches a few sheets at a time and hurls them through the open window too, watching them in the rear view mirror as they dance in the car's slipstream and then fall into the ditch.

"You made me shake it an' I like it, baby!" he yells as he turns the corner into Harbour Road and pulls up in front of 'Riverview Lodge'.

He is nearly at Ellie's floor, when he comes face to face with a woman dressed in an old-fashioned mackintosh. She is coming down the stairs as he is bounding up them. They very nearly collide under the momentum of Michael's upward rush. He moves to one side to let her pass.

"Sorry," he apologises.

"Well, that's something, I suppose," she says with tight lips, adjusting a brown headscarf.

"I beg your pardon?'

"You don't know me, do you Doctor Chadwick? I'm Linda Shepherd. Ellie's mother," she adds rather superfluously.

Michael freezes and looks at her, his hands hanging limp at his sides.

"Oh. Er, how do you do?" he says rather lamely. For the moment, he is off his guard and not quite sure how to deal with this unexpected, forced encounter.

"If this wasn't a serious situation, that would be quite funny," she snaps. "Since you ask, I'm boiling with anger at what you have done to my daughter. How could you? She's no more than a child. I placed her in your care, as a teacher. In loco parentis, I think the phrase is. You should know better than me. You're supposed to be the educated one. You have abused your power, Doctor Chadwick, in the worst possible way."

Michael looks the woman in the eyes. Something tells him he is listening to a rehearsed speech, rather than a genuine outpouring of anger.

"Mrs Shepherd, I am aware of my personal failings. And I think the Bible says something about letting he who is without sin cast the first stone," Michael retorts.

Linda opens her mouth as if to reply but thinks better of it and remains silent.

"No, I'm not pretending to be an angel," says Michael. "Far from it. But let me remind you, it takes two to tango and your daughter has been to dancing lessons."

"What do you mean by that?"

"I mean that Ellie knows her own mind. She wasn't seduced, Mrs Shepherd. If anything," Michael stops suddenly realising his intended comment will play into her hands.

"If anything is wrong," continues Michael, deftly switching the course of his original sentence, "then I am sure she would have told you just now. But she didn't, did she?"

Linda lowers her head and looks at the floor for a moment. She draws in breath and speaks in a tense monotone.

"I'd like you to stay away from Ellie, Doctor Chadwick. I mean, I suppose you'll go and see her now and she can explain what I mean. Then, you must keep away. That's all," and with that she flicks at her coat, puts her nose in the air and is gone. Michael looks at her back with surprise as she disappears down the stairwell.

*

"Quite extraordinary," he says to Ellie a few minutes later in the lounge of the flat. "Practically everything she said felt like a speech. It wasn't coming from the heart at all. What did she want, anyway? She says you'll explain?"

Michael looks at Ellie, realising that she has hardly spoken at all since he came through the door.

"What's wrong?" he says, putting an arm around her shoulders.

Ellie sniffs and swallows hard.

"She's a cow. A fucking cow," she wails. "She says she's sending me away until the trial, so as to be away from you and your influence. She's arranged for me to go and stay with Aunty Brenda in the Lake District. She says I can go to the school there. Either I do as she wants or she'll call the Police again and try to get charges brought against you."

"What? How?"

"Really, Mike. She's got the bloody notebook. I said, didn't I? There's stuff in it about you going back years. So maybe she thinks we were doing it when I was under age. Well, she didn't put it quite like that, but that's what she meant," Ellie snorts contemptuously. "I wrote loads when I was in the second and third years. Beginning of the fourth year too, I think. Not so much after that, not until last month, you know. I'm sorry, Mike, I'm sorry!"

She leans into him, sobbing.

"It's alright, Ellie, it's alright. Look, it's done. You can't change it. Is there anything in the notebook which might be taken to be incriminating?"

Ellie looks at him, her lip quivering as if she will burst into tears again.

"Mike, I'm so sorry. I was going to tell you, really I was, last night, but we kind of got diverted," she says.

"Best diversion I've been down for years. They're usually a real pain in the arse," he laughs. "So, what did you write?"

"About two years ago, when I was fourteen, I wrote this story about us in it. There's no doubt it's you because I use your name. You're like a Prince, you know and I'm the princess in the tower. You climb up the wall at night to rescue me, but, well, I want you to get into bed with me first. So you do. And I've got nothing on. And you ask me how old I am and I say fourteen but I'm big for my age. Bit of wishful thinking there at the time, you see. And then we do it. Six times!"

"Bloody hellfire, Ellie! You're joking? Tell me you're joking?"

She shakes her head. Michael whistles through his teeth.

"It explains last night, anyway! But, look, how did you write it? I mean, was it all cosy metaphors and heaving bodices and flickering starlight? Or was it filth?"

Ellie takes another deep breath.

"I didn't have a bosom then. I did in the story, of course. No, Mike, it's physically detailed stuff. Very, very detailed. Really. Everything, in graphic detail. You and me."

"Jesus! But how would you be able to write it like that if you were a flat-chested virgin of fourteen?"

"I told you: Emma. We shared a room. Porno videos. And we shared her boyfriends, if you see what I mean. Everything they did, she described to me. I used to lay awake waiting for her to come home on a Friday and Saturday night, so she could tell me what had happened. And anyway, I just seem to have known for ever."

"I'm speechless," says Michael, scratching his head.

"I knew more about oral sex at the age of twelve than most married women might learn in a lifetime, if they learned it at all. Emma got around a bit. Probably still would, if she wasn't saddled with Wayne."

"I need to get this straight in my mind. So, in the notebook, there is a story; just one?"

She shakes her head again.

"No? Good God! Right, there are stories, plural, featuring you at fourteen or whatever? You give your age? Yes? Christ! Stories featuring you and me, by name? Yes? By name, in which there are detailed, physical, accurate, no-holds-barred descriptions of us having sexual intercourse?"

"Yes," she says, "and fellatio and cunnilingus. And I know how to spell them, before you ask."

"Jesus, Mary and Joseph!" he whistles. "And are these things dated? I mean, could they reasonably be said to have been written last week?"

"No chance. They are under a date, Mike. I said, it's like a diary. Anyway, my handwriting's changed quite a lot in the last two years. They are obviously musings from my juvenile period," she chuckles, remembering a phrase he had once used in a lesson.

"I see. If someone wanted to make it look that way, then, these stories might be used to suggest that we have had a sexual relationship for years. That means I could be charged with having sex with a minor."

Ellie looks at him and sees the concern in his eyes and senses panic welling up inside her.

"Not really though, Mike, surely? Because Emma would be able to say, or Tracey, because she read them all at the time, that they were just..." Ellie doesn't complete the sentence.

"Yes, that they were just stories. But, Ellie, a skilled barrister could then suggest that a child of twelve, thirteen or fourteen would be unlikely to have such knowledge for a story, even in our sick society, unless she had had the experiences herself, at the hands of an older man. And then he would suggest I had managed to silence you from telling the truth, even to your friend or your sister. That's what child molesters and abusers do, you know? Do you see? It could be suggested that the events in the stories really happened and that your notebook is your way of getting the trauma out of your system."

Michael's explanation is frightening both of them.

"But I'm not, like, traumatised in the stories. I'm loving it!" Ellie declares.

Michael winces.

"That probably doesn't make it better, Ellie!"

"Oh, God, I'm sorry. What can I say?" she whispers.

"Listen, Ellie. I'm not cross about it or blaming you, right?" insists Michael. "You weren't to know at the time that your ghastly mother would try to use them against you. Well, against me, I suppose."

"Will she do it, do you think, if I refuse to go? Why do you think she's so keen to pack me off to Aunty Brenda's?" asks Ellie.

"Well, as a matter of fact, I don't think she would do it, actually. Having one trial she's involved in is bad enough, surely? I don't know, though. I'm afraid to say that I don't think I'm too keen to take the risk, sweetheart. No, I think there's more to it than that, relating to Brian's trial."

Michael's brow furrows as he considers the situation, tries to think himself into the mind of Ellie's mother.

"It makes her look better, doesn't it? At the trial, if asked, she can say that as soon as she found out the terrible facts about her daughter's seduction by a grizzled, horny old schoolmaster, she packed the unfortunate, deflowered virgin off to a safer place," Ellie smiles.

Michael laughs loudly.

"Hey, I do the sarcastic long sentences around here, you know! Sending you away makes her look like a caring, honest, Christian wife? Right. And her rapacious husband benefits in a way from bathing in the reflected, unctuous glory! I think you're right. Cunning, eh?"

"Yes, that's what she is. She's not caring, that's for sure. So you think I have to do as she says?" asks Ellie, the resentment barely disguised in her voice.

"Well, as I say, there is risk if you don't. I don't know; I mean, this is all a foreign country to me, Ellie. Who knows? Innocent men have been hung on a murder charge. The wrong verdict can happen. A clever barrister could make it sound very, very likely that we'd been at it for years. And there'll be a Police record of last night's wet tissues."

"OK. No sweat then. I'll go and spend every day wandering the bloody Lakes pining for you like a character from Emily Bronte."

"Wrong county," Michael says. "So what kind of a jailer is your Aunty Brenda?"

"Well, she was quite strict with my cousins Paula and Jamie, but she's not that bad," says Ellie.

"So if you were a good girl for a couple of weeks, she'd relax a bit and you could go out on your own?" asks Michael.

"Oh, yes, I should think so."

"I have a cousin who lives in Ambleside. I could always pay him a visit or two," Michael announces with a boyish grin.

NOW'S THE SEASON TO BE JOLLY, TRA-LA-LA, TRA-LA-LA, TRA LA LA!

Two days before Christmas Eve, Barbara telephones Michael.

"Ellie? Is it you?"

"It's me. Your wife, not your child-slut."

"Oh. What do you want, Barbara?" he says coldly. "You've woken me up. And she is not a child."

"For Christ's sake, Michael. Drunken stupor again, is it? It's gone ten o'clock, you know. And she is barely sixteen, Michael and she is still at school, as you very well know, so as far as I am concerned, and most other people too, I should think, she is a child. And that is what I shall call her. I refuse to use the little slut's name."

God rest you merry gentlemen, let nothing you dismay.

Michael is about to refute that term too, but stops himself, realising that Barbara is being deliberately, albeit understandably, peevish and contentious.

He fumbles for his wristwatch and sees that she is right.

"What do you want?"

"We need to talk. I've been at Mum's a month. Things can't go on like this," she says mechanically.

Michael freezes, thinking that she is about to suggest moving back to the cottage and trying some kind of reconciliation.

"The girls would like to see you, although God knows why. Fascination with pond life, I suppose. This afternoon? You know, if it's not too much trouble and you can drag yourself out of bed. Then when you bring them back we can have a few words," she says as if they were arranging a trip to the supermarket.

"What, at your mother's?"

"Hardly, Michael. No, I'll come out to the car and say what I have to say there. It won't take long, I can assure you."

"Er, OK. I'll pick them up at two o'clock. I'll be the one wearing the trout mask; make sure the kids don't confuse me with your mother."

Laughing, he puts down the phone without waiting for her reply.

*

He showers, shaves and finds some clean clothes. At two o'clock, he pulls up slowly outside his mother-in-law's house in Combe Down. Jowls of grey clouds are flopping on the damp rooftops.

Then a poor man came in sight, gathering winter fuel.

Michael turns off the engine and waits. A curtain flicks in the front room and a few moments later the front door opens and the twins appear on the path. Lucy turns back to look at someone inside, says something and then takes Hannah's hand and the two of them walk towards the gate. The front door closes.

Inside the car, Michael takes a deep breath. He jumps out and throws his arm around the two little girls, the three of them a tight, weeping bundle on the pavement. The curtain flicks again.

"How are my two lovely girls?" he says, swallowing back the second wave of tears.

In a tiny, tight voice, Hannah says, "OK, 'spose."

She pulls away from Michael and turns towards his car.

A few minutes later, as they drive down Entry Hill towards the city, Michael says, "So, shall we go and gorge on ice cream and then find you both some presents?"

Deck the halls with sprigs of holly.

"Yeah!" replies Lucy with what feels to Michael like forced enthusiasm.

"Huh! Too cold for ice cream," snaps Hannah.

They compromise and find a surprisingly quiet little café in one of the arcades where those who want ice cream can have it and those who want to be resentful can sulk and then eventually weaken and ask for a rum baba. Michael leads them to a relatively private corner table where, he thinks, they may be able to talk more comfortably.

He has failed to be sufficiently sensitive to the circumstances. The girls are used to communicating with their father in fits and starts as the day progresses at home. This is an odd, new game. They do not understand the rules. They feel unhappy. Their mother is angry with Daddy. He looks scruffy and this feels awkward and false. What to do in this strange new world?

Lucy swallows the last of her Knickerbocker Glory, smacks her lips and drops her long spoon with a loud clatter. She looks at Michael to see what this transgression of normal table manners will produce. He looks at her balefully and frowns.

"I'm freezing to pigging death," she announces shrilly.

138

"Lucy, I don't know where you've heard that but it's not very nice in the mouth of a little girl," Michael says sternly.

"If you're cold, it's your fault for having ice cream, div," says Hannah, sarcastically, through a mouthful of sticky rum baba.

"That'll do, Hannah," interposes Michael quickly. He is not in the mood for squabbling and can sense the early signs. The twins are being fractious and rebellious.

"She is a div," responds Hannah.

"I said, that'll do," says Michael.

Hannah gives a long sigh and mutters something under her breath.

"Hannah," remonstrates Michael, "if you have something to say, let's all hear it. Don't mumble into your beard."

Lucy laughs and Hannah looks frosty.

"We're fed up at Nanny's," blurts Hannah, "and we want to come home."

"Yeah, like before," agrees Lucy.

"Look, girls," sighs Michael, "you're not little babies. You know what the score is here, although I'm sure my version and Mummy's will be entirely different."

"And Nanny's," says Lucy. "She says that time will tell and stuff like that, on and on."

"I've always thought that "Time will tell" is one of your grandmother's most over-worked and fatuous remarks," snaps Michael.

Lucy looks puzzled.

"What's fatuous?"

"It means silly or stupid. Of course time will tell; time will tell every bloody thing, won't it? Or it already has, if you subscribe completely to Einstein's Theory of Relativity."

"Language, Daddy!" says Hannah.

Michael looks rueful and tells himself to calm down. He realises that the tensions of the situation are making him short-tempered, but who is to blame for that? He has caused the tensions. Whatever has happened, it is not the twins' fault.

"I don't think we know what you're talking about, Daddy and anyway, you're not answering the question," Lucy complains. "When can we come home?"

"Like before?" asks Michael. "I'm sorry but it's not going to be like before, girls. I'm very, very sorry because I know it's making you sad and angry with me; fair enough; but that's the brutal truth."

Hannah's bottom lip quivers for a moment and it looks as though she's going to burst into tears, but she manages to recover herself.

"There's stuff at home we want to get, then," she says petulantly.

"Yeah," chimes in Lucy, "if we can't come home then I want my drawing things. Can you bring them for me?"

"If you let me know what you want," begins Michael, "oh, but no, I might not be able to bring them just yet. I may be away."

There is a silence whilst the twins digest this information and then, as if their father was not there, Lucy turns to Hannah and says matter-of-factly, "I expect he's going to see that little tart. I expect they're going to f... do it, you know."

Hannah nods at her sister in agreement.

"Keswick tart!" she splutters and they both dissolve into peals of hysterical laughter.

Michael coughs loudly.

"Girls! That's enough! Now, what do you want for your Christmas presents?"

Lucy looks at Hannah who frowns but Lucy is going to say it anyway. She has decided that she's not going to let the matter drop.

"The best present in the whole wide world? Stop all this messing about that you're doing," she announces in the clear, piping voice that she reserves for her considered pronouncements and occasional State functions.

Of all the trees that are in the wood, the holly bears the crown.

Michael raises an admonishing eyebrow, conscious of a curious, critical glance from the haggard waitress behind the counter. Lucy, however, is not to be silenced by a mere expression on her father's face.

"Stop behaving like a hormoned teenager and make it up with Mummy. And then we can all go home."

"It's hormonal, not hormoned, you divvy," whispers Hannah, pompously.

Lucy sniffs.

"Whatever," she says, aggressively.

"I think we just dealt with all that. Is that what your mother says?" asks Michael. "And keep your voice down, Lucy. We don't want the whole place listening in."

"Embarrassing," adds Hannah.

"OK," says Lucy, almost as loudly as before. "Yeah, I s'pose so; what Mum says. So what? It's true, isn't it?"

"Do you know what it means?" asks Michael, rather obviously avoiding the issue.

"We know what it means, Dad. We're not babies any more, like you said. And we know what shagging means too. We overheard Mummy saying it about you to Nanny," counters Lucy.

"Is it what you think too, H?" asks Michael.

"Yes, Daddy, of course it is. You're making us very unhappy," she says and begins to snivel into her napkin.

"When are we all going home? Together. Like before?" says Lucy firmly. She is not going to let this moment dissolve into pools of tears like her sister. "We're fed up with being at Nanny's. She makes us eat porridge every morning and we can't even say bum."

"Well," says Michael.

"Mummy says when you've shagged it out of your system, you'll want to come home again. With your tail between your legs," blurts Lucy.

Gloria in excelsis Deo.

"Lucy!" says Hannah, scandalised.

"So! So! She did. You heard her too," mutters Lucy, beginning to realise that she may have over-stepped the mark.

There is another uncomfortable pause. Michael sips at his coffee.

"So when, then?" insists Lucy.

He puts down his coffee cup.

"I've told you, girls; look, things have not been too good for Mummy and me just lately," he begins. "It's probably more my fault than hers, but..."

The twins both study the design on the tablecloth intently.

Lucy looks up briefly.

"We know what's going on. But she's one of the kids in the sixth form, Dad. Gross, isn't it?"

"OK," says Michael, "we'll use her name, then. Ellie; Ellen. I'm sorry if you think it's gross. I don't, of course."

"We see her about, Dad," confirms Hannah.

"Mum says you're not in love with her, it's just infa...infantile...no," struggles Lucy.

"Infatuation," Hannah supplies the word.

"Yeah, that's it. And shagging."

"I expect she does," says Michael lamely.

"She says you're infatooted or whatever it is because she's got long legs, a flat belly and big boobies," says Lucy, employing the piping voice again. "Well, actually, she said tits."

"I am not in the least bit surprised she says that. It sounds like the kind of thing she would say. Is she saying it in front of you?"

Lucy shoots a glance in Hannah's direction.

"Well, not, not exactly," says Hannah.

Michael looks at them expectantly, waiting an explanation.

"We were on the landing," says Hannah, "and we heard them talking in the kitchen."

"And Nanny didn't tell Mummy off when she said tits or shagged," offers Lucy, "but she tells us off even if we only say bum or willy or something. It's not fair."

"I see," says Michael, ignoring Lucy's last remark. "Some might call that eavesdropping."

The girls look at each other but surmise that their father is not really angry. Lucy shrugs her shoulders.

"And just for the record," he adds, "life invariably is unfair. Sorry, but it is. And already I can hear your Mum telling me to stop introducing pessimistic analyses in front of you."

"Dad, sometimes we don't know what you mean," Hannah remarks plaintively.

"Are you and Mummy going to get a divorce?" says Lucy bluntly.

Hannah makes a clicking noise and rolls her eyes towards the ceiling.

"What's the matter?" says Lucy sharply. "That's what we want to know, isn't it?"

"Alright, girls," says Michael, intervening, "don't start squabbling. The answer, Lucy, is that I don't know yet. It does largely depend on Mummy but, well, yes, probably."

Both girls are silent, examining the table cloth again.

"But even if we do, it doesn't mean we've stopped loving you two. It just means that we have decided to live separately," he adds.

"Will you go and live with Ellie?" asks Hannah, quietly.

"It's too soon for that, Hannah. I mean, too soon for that decision," replies Michael. He realises that his daughters have already moved the relationship to at least the next phase before he has had time to talk to Ellie about it.

"But I suppose that in the fullness of time we shall."

The girls look at each other. Hannah's lip begins to tremble. Suddenly, Lucy's bravado deserts her and she begins to wail and then to bang her fists on the table.

"I hate her, I hate her," she blubbers, "she's a horrid cow and a slag and a tart!"

All the heads in the café turn in their direction.

Silent night; holy night.

*

An hour later, he sits in the car waiting for Barbara to come out of her mother's house as arranged. She keeps him waiting for nearly ten minutes and even though the engine is running, his feet are going numb. Eventually, she appears at the front door and stumps purposefully towards him. She is wearing a large red coat and some sort of flat, felt hat. Michael smiles to himself, despite the situation, for he thinks she looks not unlike a pillar box.

She flings open the front passenger door and collapses onto the seat. Michael has already decided to try to snatch the initiative, rather than to allow himself to be wrong-footed. He starts talking before she has even shut the door.

"I won't say good afternoon," he begins, "because I have no doubt you will respond with some savagely caustic remark. So may I ask straight away what you have been saying about me and Ellie to the twins?"

Barbara looks a little surprised by the aggression in Michael's tone.

"What do you mean?"

"Well, they obviously know she's up in Cumbria. How? Why? And they have referred to her this afternoon as a tart and although Lucy didn't actually use the f-word, I think she was about to," he replies curtly, "in order to describe my relationship with Ellie."

"Does it matter if they know where she is? What's the problem? And I can assure you, Michael, that I have done my best to keep all discussions factual and non-emotional. It hasn't been easy. Obviously. They are very, very distressed and disturbed. I have not used the word tart in their hearing."

"I think you may find they're hearing more than you think they are," he says. "I suggest you keep the kitchen door closed when you're ranting on about it with your sodding mother."

"Leave my mother out of it. She's been very kind, especially to the girls. I don't know what I'd have done without her."

"Ask your father. He's got a comprehensive plan on it."

"I'll ignore that. And I don't rant. Look, Mike, we both did the child psychology. You know what happens to kids in this situation as well as I do. If they are unsettling you or needling you, it's no surprise, is it? I expect they're doing it deliberately. Their way of hurting you a little by way of return for what they sense you've done to them. Their way of showing you their dismay, anger, disgust and revulsion at what their father is doing. Not to mention the humiliation they are likely to feel when they get back to school after Christmas. Have you thought about that? It's all over the valley, so you can imagine some of the stuff they'll be subjected to in the playground. You may not have thought about it, but they have. I was up half the night with Hannah last night, crying her eyes out with worry about the first day of term."

Michael feels a stab of pain, just as Barbara intended. He realises that already he has lost the initiative of the conversation, if ever he had it.

"You haven't given it a bloody single thought, have you? You're so wrapped up in your own selfish, lustful affairs that you can't even consider what effect all this might be having on your kids. If all they did was call her a tart and imply that what's uppermost in your mind is your next fuck, then I'd say you got off lightly," Barbara glares at him.

Michael lowers his head and studies his knees.

"OK, OK," he mumbles. "What did you want to talk to me about? Let's get it over with; I'm freezing to bloody death out here."

"Just try to think about them, instead of yourself. I know you couldn't give a shit about me anymore, but at least give some thought to what effect you're having on them. They're still young."

"Alright, Barbara, alright!" Michael shouts. "You've made your sodding point. I'm the complete, selfish, fornicating bastard. Message received and understood."

He pauses; she sniffles. Then, more calmly, he speaks again.

"Look; for what it's worth, I'm sorry. I didn't plan to hurt them. Or you, come to that. I don't know; it just…"

"It just sort of happened? Huh! Don't give me that crud, Mike. What happened to free will? You chose to do what you did. It wasn't forced on you," she snaps."You're making a big mistake, Mike. In time, you'll see that I'm right."

"I can hear your mother's favourite phrase coming on," he replies. "I don't believe I am making a mistake but time will tell."

"Quite so. I give it no more than a year, at the outside. She'll tire of it long before you will. She's a kid and she's a user. She's just playing with you. Finding out what power she has over men. She must be very pleased with herself at the moment. You need to think about it. You're going to look like a bloody fool."

Michael looks puzzled.

"What do you mean, power over men?"

"Christ, you can be so blind, sometimes. Like all men when some young slut's sucking their dick. Isn't it obvious? No, I suppose it isn't to you, is it? That's the whole point. Look at it this way. What has she caught? Snared might be a better word. Not a spotty youth like her friends, some immature gibbon with his knuckles grazing the floor and smelling of B.O. and fried food. Not a bum-fluff, gangling oik wearing an oily, ripped jacket with Iron Maiden scrawled on it. Still exchanging smutty jokes behind his hand about hard-ons and jerk-offs with his equally simian mates. Jumping up and down at the school disco like a bloody pogo stick, ignoring all the pretty girls in the corner who've made an effort before coming out and had a shower and got changed? An inarticulate, greasy slob who is about as sensitive and romantic as a baboon? If he pays a girl any attention it'll only be to smooth talk her so he can lift her skirt up in the side alley and shoot his packet into her before she's had time to check her lipstick!

No, no! Oh, no, none of that for your precious, precocious Miss Effing Fortune. A child she may be but she has netted handsome, debonair, Deputy Head Dr. Chadwick, hasn't she? Look what I got, girls! Quite a catch. And what's more, she can let it be known that he's really good in bed and that he's leaving his wife and children for her; the bitch!"

Barbara's analysis dissolves into sobs and tears as she arrives at the final, painful sentence.

Michael cannot resist a grin, for it was Barbara's caustic and vulgar sense of humour which had attracted him to her all those years ago in the student bar.

"Very amusing. Shoot his packet! Very good; very drole. Have you been working on that or was it entirely spontaneous?"

"Oh, piss off," she hisses.

"Anyway, I don't agree. You are ascribing a degree of guile and pre-meditated cunning to Ellie which, frankly, she could never possess. She's not like that at all," says Michael, defensively.

"I didn't expect you to agree," she says. "You're still at the blind stage. But you'll see."

"So you keep saying. Well, this discussion just going round in circles, isn't it? Obviously, we are looking at the thing from entirely different perspectives and so we're never going to agree. By definition," he replies assertively. "So is that it? You wanted to see me to tell me that she's the cat and I'm the mouse?"

"No, actually, I didn't plan to say any of that; although I'm glad I've said it. It needed saying, even if, predictably, you don't want to listen, or can't listen, at the moment."

She pauses and takes a breath.

"No, I want to talk to you about what happens now, given that you've done what you have and are clearly hell-bent on continuing on the same course. I've been doing a lot of thinking over the last month, Michael and I've made a number of decisions. All of them, I hope, with the girls' interests uppermost. We cannot pretend to be a married couple any more. I've had enough, given that this is not the first time that you have dipped your wick. Maybe I still love you, maybe I don't. To be honest, I don't know. Contempt is getting in the way. But I can't live with you any more, that's a certainty. What you have done to me and our marriage is unforgivable. You are treating me like shit. I meant what I said in the letter I wrote to you a month ago. I've seen a solicitor, as I said I would and you should be getting the divorce papers any day now. Please don't bugger about with it or start delaying or something. Let's just get it over with. Finito. Goodnight, Vienna, to use your favourite phrase. Yes?"

She looks at him.

He studies his knees again for a while and then looks up, although he finds it difficult to look at his wife, instead staring ahead at the fog gathering around them.

"Yes, alright. I agree, I suppose," he says.

"You suppose?"

"I mean, I agree it has to happen but I haven't thought about how. I haven't seen a solicitor. I suppose I should."

"Yes. Obviously, we have to decide on the practicalities: the house, money, possessions and so on. My solicitor will be writing to you and I think you would be best advised to take his letter, with its proposals, to your solicitor."

Michael doesn't reply straight away, but chews his lip, considering this sudden turn of events. Of course, he thinks, I should have thought about this; she's right, there has been time enough.

"Proposals?" he asks.

"About the cottage mainly. I don't want it sold, not now anyway; I think that for the foreseeable future, I should be there with the girls so that the disruption in their lives is minimised. So we have to get it valued and then agree how to proceed from there. Basically, I may have to buy you out; maybe eventually, not now but at an agreed figure; a figure to take account of everything else of value, including your inheritance and, well, everything that's happened. And there have to be arrangements for the twins. It's not going to be easy, or cheap. So be prepared."

"You mean that you're about to take me to the cleaners?" Michael says.

Barbara snorts.

"Please don't take that tone, Michael. If we can agree things between ourselves it will be easier, quicker and cheaper than having the solicitors wrack up costs over it. Remember what happened with Jane and Paul?"

Michael grunts his agreement and smiles to himself. He remembers what happened to them alright. Paul had told him about it, in detail, several times. Apparently Jane had awoken in the middle of the night, and found herself alone in the bed. When, after thirty minutes, Paul had not returned from what she presumed to be a visit to the bathroom, she went to investigate. Hearing muffled moaning noises from the guest bedroom, she gently opened its door and saw her husband taking the seventeen year old babysitter from behind.

"She arrived for the finale,'" Paul had said. "Impeccable timing, Jane. She'd have been none the wiser; we'd managed it two or three times before, but little Mandy is a bit of a squealer. Delicious, firm little body," he had sighed, "and unquestionably the best sex I've had for years. You should try it, Mike. Unbelievable."

"I could take you to the cleaners as you put it. Maybe I should," Barbara is saying. "Mum certainly thinks so. But, perhaps surprisingly, I find myself of the view that we should arrive at a sensible solution. I won't say amicable, because, well, that's not how I feel, but I don't want years of antagonism and protracted arguments and bitterness because that will have an effect on the twins and, as I say, they are uppermost in my mind. I just hope that you will be prepared to see that what you have done and what you intend to do, I assume, comes at a cost."

"Alright, I'll think about it. And see a solicitor, I suppose," he says.

"Good. And I'd like you to move out of the cottage now, so that the twins and I can go back there before the start of term," she announces with a note of finality. "Mum's been kind but, well, we can't stay here forever."

"That's one thing we can agree on. No one should have to stay with your mother forever. And that includes your father," Michael says, enjoying the opportunity for further insult. "And what am I supposed to do, then? Sleep in the shed?"

"That's your problem. You should have thought about that before you started humping the child. No, not the shed, don't be stupid. I think it would be best if you were some way away from the valley. I want us to be able to move back there at the weekend."

She looks across at him defiantly.

"That only gives me three days, for Christ's sake!" he complains.

"So? You've got a lot on, have you? Get it organised, Michael. Rent somewhere."

Michael opens his mouth to object, but changes his mind. A revelatory thought has suddenly occurred to him and he wonders why it has not done so before. Perhaps Barbara has unwittingly presented him with the answer to his current depression and malaise. Of course! Being at the cottage is part of the problem. It is the past, not the future. He could indeed move out: it would give him plenty to do and the process of making a fresh start in a new place would surely make him feel better?

Barbara looks at him, both sadness and contempt in her eyes.

"You are a cruel, thoughtless bastard," she says. She levers herself out of the car and slams the door as hard as she can.

Michael sits for a minute, reflecting on what has just occurred. It does not make him feel any better about himself to acknowledge the accuracy of Barbara's parting remark. She is right and, not for the first time in recent weeks, he feels ashamed.

Instead of returning to Watery Lane and the lonely gloom of the cottage, he starts the car and drives back through Bear Flat to the city. He knows of a letting agent in George Street, once recommended by a colleague. The rather suave young man there takes him to see an immediately available flat. It is furnished, clean and tidy and has a parking space at the rear. The road is noisy, but that's reflected in the rent. It'll do for six months.

The following day, he withdraws money from his own account at the bank and pays the suave young man six months' rent and the necessary fees in advance, in cash, to expedite matters. He can collect the keys on Saturday morning, the young man says.

TOO LONG WE HAVE TARRIED

They are sitting huddled together under a travel rug on the back seat of Michael's car, parked in a remote spot off the road on Derwent Fells. Michael drove up from Bath in the early hours and Ellie has taken advantage of a gap in her new school's timetable.

"How do you know this place? It's beautiful. Remote too: ideal."

"Horse riding," she says. "I come up here quite often. I like the view and there's a good gallop going back that way."

"I've brought something for you," he says, breaking an ensuing silence.

She sits up and looks at him.

"A present?"

"Well, yes, in a manner of speaking."

He reaches forward across the seat in front and fumbles in the glove box for a package. Ellie looks intrigued and giggles.

"Mike?"

He hands her the little, gift-wrapped box and smiles.

"For you. I hope you like it."

She looks at him again and then begins, slowly, to remove the paper. Within is a dark blue presentation box and a heart-shaped ring case. Before opening it, she looks up at him again; the green in her eyes catching what is left of the pale afternoon light.

"You have to open it, Ellie. The case is incidental," he says jokingly.

"I know. I'm just enjoying the moment because I think I know…"

She lifts the ring from the case and looks at it in wonderment. The diamonds flicker and wink at her.

"For me? Oh, Mike, it's beautiful. I've never had anything like this before," she whispers, tears beginning to come to her eyes.

"You like it? I wasn't sure what you'd like, you know, I mean, we've never actually talked about jewellery."

"Of course I like it. It's enormous. It must have cost a fortune, Mike!"

"You're worth it. I can get it re-sized if it's too small. Or big."

He pauses, swallows and then says, "Ellie, you know how I feel about you. Like the Jeff Lynne song says, you have blown me away. I cannot conceive of being without you; I love you into eternity, I want to be with you for the rest of my life and, well, when we can, will you marry me? O let us be married, too long we have tarried and here's what we do for a ring. Apologies to Edward Lear."

She looks at him, bursts into tears, throws her arms around his neck and kisses him over and over again, on the cheek, the chin, the nose and the mouth.

"Of course, oh, Mike, of course I will, I love you too!"

"I take it that was a yes, then?"

She laughs.

"When do you think we might be able to?"

"Not sure yet. I mean, maybe we should leave it for a few months. You know, like everything else! But I got some divorce papers through yesterday. Barbara means business."

"Good."

"I'll check on what you're supposed to do to get married. I mean, I think you have to apply or register your intent or something with the Superintendent Registrar in the district where you live even if you are hoping to get married somewhere else. You know; regulations; paperwork."

"Sounds fine to me, Mike. You know how I feel - just go ahead and do whatever needs to be done. I can't wait."

As the last faint glimmer of the sun falls under the snow on the ridges of the hills in the distance, Ellie slips the ring onto her finger. It is a perfect fit.

*

The return journey is difficult. It is not so easy to find his way in the dark and several times he takes a wrong turning. He curses to himself as he joins the M6 and it begins to rain heavily again. He wonders why he didn't call his cousin in Ambleside and stay there for the night. Stupid. But, on the other hand, if he had he would now be involved in small talk, family gossip and the like. He's not in the mood for that.

The radio is still tuned to his morning's station but the reception is not so good. Eventually, he finds Radio 4. Someone is talking about stealth bombers and surgical strikes. There is sound track of missiles, explosions, gunfire, the tearing of metal. Baghdad is being attacked; the allied forces led by America have launched operation Desert Storm to liberate Kuwait.

Michael has never heard anything like it on the radio before. The howling sound of the missiles, the screech of the jets and the screaming of people under fire sends a terrified chill through him.

It is a profoundly distressing drive back to the empty flat in Bath. His mind has retained that final glimpse of Ellie brushing away tears; the radio is conjuring images of apocalyptic firepower, of innocent children blown away in small pieces, ordinary men and women never able to see the sun or live and love again.

He cries until he can barely see the road ahead.

THIS DAY TOO SHALL PASS

As the weeks go by and the days become warmer and longer, the little girls look at their Mummy in her summer dresses. They seem bigger than before. Their Mummy is losing weight. At night, the little girls whisper together about how their Mummy is getting thinner and thinner. They think that it is because she is worried about things and because she is upset at what Daddy has done.

Sometimes Nanny takes them quietly to one side and says that they are not to worry too much and that Mummy will be alright soon.

"This day too shall pass. Time is a great healer," she says, but they do not really understand what she's on about.

They know that their Mummy wants to divorce their Daddy and this means that they will never all be together in the same house again like before. Before the girl. They will never all go on holiday to France again. This makes them sad. Sometimes it makes them angry as well. At night, out of Mummy's earshot, they talk about how they could poison the girl, cut up her body and throw it in the lake. And then Daddy would come home.

They know enough to know that Daddy has been having sexual intercourse with the girl and that because she was a pupil at Daddy's school, he is no longer a teacher. Nanny says if that was not bad enough, he has also broken his marriage vows. That he has brought shame on them and himself.

They think they know what sexual intercourse is and what it's for. But they are confused about the mechanics. They know what a car is for as well but they don't understand how that works either. Grown-ups talk about the man putting his seeds in the woman. "Putting? Is that like putting coins in a money box? I reckon there's something that grown-ups aren't telling us," Lucy says, "I bet you."

At school, Mrs Lane showed them diagrams, but it was hard to see from the back and anyway they couldn't really work out what all the lines and squiggles were supposed to be. Diagrams and props are not real bodies. All the girls giggled. They wondered whether it was some sort of joke.

"Get real; people don't do that, do they? They do? How funny. Well, I don't care what anyone says, I'm not doing that with a boy, baby or no baby. It sounds yukky and disgusting."

The boys talk about it all the time. Some of the older boys say that they can make the seed come out of their penises.

"Wanking, innit; you wanna see?"

Hannah is embarrassed and says that she has to go to hockey practice although secretly she thinks she would quite like to see how sunflower seeds or something like them could come out of a boy's penis. The dirty boys are laughing and say you have to get a boner first and Hannah mumbles something and runs away. She wonders what a boner is and where you can buy them.

Lucy goes to watch the boys behind the gardener's hut on the top field and discovers, with amazement, what a boner is. Later, she reports to Hannah that the boys can make a bone go in it.

"Carl Smithers must have a very big bone because it was ginormous and sticking right up like a ruler and they sort of rub it a bit and then they go all funny and start shouting and grunting and then it spurts this white stuff. It was all over the place. Yukky disgusting! Really gross! The white stuff is the seed, Hannah, it must be! And while they were boning or whatever it's called Carl Smithers was telling the others about this girl from Grange School on the bus and they were alone on the top deck, right, and the girl put his hand in her knickers and the boy said it was all wet and he friggled about and made her go or something and then she had to blow something, but it wasn't a kiss, I don't think, I can't remember and the boy said it took about ten seconds and she spat some splunk all over the window and then all the boys said tell us again, Carl and so he started on about it again and they starting boning some more so I came away. Something like that, anyway. I didn't know what they were on about half the time, but the bone is real, Hannah, I saw it. God's truth."

Hannah does not want to believe a word her sister tells her.

Lucy thinks about the boner and the spurting and some sort of truth begins to emerge in her mind.

They know that you are supposed to be in love and married before the man can plant the seed. That's what Mrs Lane said anyway. But they know that lots of people don't worry about that. It must be fun because all grown ups and some of the older kids and the telly and magazines and pop songs go on and on about it all the time. And the boys were definitely enjoying the boner.

Daddy is doing it with the girl for fun. But they know that they are not having fun and neither is Mummy.

One day, Lucy sees a picture of the girl in an old school magazine in Daddy's study. It says that Ellen Fortune, Tutor Group 5J, is to receive the Carter Trophy for all-round academic performance. In the picture, the girl is smiling in a sort of smug way. Lucy can see that she has very big bosoms and surely she must be deliberately pushing them forward? Lucy cuts the picture out and sticks it on the little notice board in her bedroom. She has a box of pins which have bright, blood-red heads. Sometimes, as she is passing the board, she pushes a pin deep into the girl's face. Or one of the big bosoms.

If she listens carefully, she can hear the girl screaming. It makes her feel better.

FORTY YEARS IN THE HALL

Brian Shepherd is on remand. He is counting the days. Through the clawing sharp nights of winter through to the humid stench of summer, he numbers each day, a day at a time. He has to share a cell with three other men. It is loud, coarse and vulgar. There is a permanent smell of urine, faeces and body odour. He is afraid to go to sleep in case they attack him or hurt him in some way. They know what he is supposed to have done. There are very few secrets here. They are interested in what he has done. Not from a legal point of view, but from a physical point of view. They read 'The Sun'. It shows them young girls' bodies every day. Maybe not sixteen, but seventeen and eighteen. If it's in the paper, it must be alright and anyway, what difference do a few months make?

If Shepherd had raped a much younger girl, a little kid, then they would certainly mark him. He'd be a paedophile, wouldn't he? Scum. But the girl was older. Sixteen, well, it's not so clear-cut, is it? Old enough to bleed, old enough to breed; that's what they say, isn't it? We all know what sixteen year olds can be like. Some of us have been there too. And those of us who haven't, well, we've seen their smooth young bodies in the paper, spied on the neighbour's teenage daughter sunbathing topless in the back garden and been to our mate's place to watch the porno. Some of the stuff you can get now!

Shepherd says she was a temptress. Odd, churchy, stuck-up word, but they know what he means. All wiggling tits and arse and cock-sucker lips. Up for it. Lots of them are, these days; even quite young ones will do it. One man, Sinclair, wants to know all the details. Wakes Shepherd up in the middle of the night with a kick and goes back to pleasuring himself on the top bunk.

"Tell us, then, Shepherd, what was she like? How did you do it to her? Did she scream? Did she come? Ey, ey? Come on, tell us, you little fucker."

Lascivious Sinclair. Wanting to know, wanting to see the picture in his mind. On and on, all night, every night, questioning, wheedling, rubbing, groaning.

Shepherd, refusing to give more than brief details. Convincing himself that Ellie had tempted him. Yes, asking for it. She did. Yes, I did have intercourse with her, your Honour, but she wanted me to, I know it. I'm so sorry your Honour, but I couldn't stop myself once I had begun; I got carried away. Her body, your Honour...

The Lord is my Shepherd. Every night, silently praying that God will believe, will understand, will forgive and will deliver him safely from this Hell. And it would be even better, he thinks, if the jury could do the same.

*

There is a damp cottage up at Valleys' Head. It squats in the lee of a craggy outcrop and has a wonderful view as far as the Polden Hills.

In one corner, standing where it was placed over thirty years before, is an old clock. It has not been moved since. So delicate is its mechanism, it was thought that to disturb it would do untold harm. There is a clotted skein of cobwebs and the husks of dead beetles between it and the wall. Its tick is slow and deep in tone like someone tapping a penny on an empty rosewood box.

This afternoon, in May, the old flagstones are littered with books, magazines, clothing, old tins, boxes and chests, ancient tools, official papers and bundles of letters and cards. An old man shuffles slowly and painfully between the piles, rearranging here, sorting there and periodically sinking into a broken, horse-hair armchair to recover his energy. When he moves, it seems he does so in time with the sonorous ticking of the clock.

Old Nibber is putting his affairs in order and getting ready to die. He has been unwell for several weeks, silently and without complaint nursing a gnawing pain in his bowels. Two days ago he noticed blood in the toilet bowl and that night the pain was much worse and sharper. It was so bad it made him cry out in the darkness, his bony fingers clutching the rusted iron bed-frame until dawn. He knows, in the way that animals and some people do, that his time has come. And there are things he must do before it's too late.

He has told no one of his illness. He does not want the interfering hand of science; the kindly but intrusive help of social services; the throttling starched sheets of hospital. He wants to die quietly, peacefully he hopes, at home. He will die alone, for that is his destiny.

He has managed his nightly walk to the comfort of the inglenook at 'The Plough' until three weeks ago. Since then, he has been less often. He has explained his absence, when Larry has asked, by saying that his arthritis is playing him up and he's finding it difficult to walk.

It takes him the better part of two days to go through his possessions. Those things which are of no use are burnt. He washes and irons all his clothes and puts them into neat piles in his rickety wardrobe. Magazines and old newspapers are stacked and tied in bundles. As best he can, he cleans the cottage from top to bottom. Finally, he sits down at the old oak table in the kitchen to write those letters which must be written and to check that he owes no one anything. He puts forty pence in an envelope for the milkman. He leaves the papers and envelopes on the table.

At last, satisfied with his efforts, he has a bath, folds his clothes neatly and puts them on a chair, pulls on his night gown and drags himself up the twisting staircase for the last time.

In the small, dark hours he calls out just once, in pain. Then he breathes out a long, whispering sigh.

"Lily, I see 'ee now. My Lily, oh, Lily, you've come for I at last," he rasps.

A few moments later the cottage is completely silent. The old man is motionless and the clock on the cold flagstones downstairs has stopped.

Old Nibber used to sing, years ago, to his neighbour's children, "And the clock stopped, never to go again, when the old man died..."

The old man is indeed dead in his bed. He is lying on his back with the sheet and counterpane neatly folded under his elbows. His arms lie across his chest and his hands are together in prayer. His eyes are closed and it appears that his remaining strands of hair have been recently combed and parted. On the bedside table there are neat bundles of old letters and cards, each tied together with a new piece of red velvet.

So that his mouth should not fall open in death, the old man has placed under his chin a rolled, white handkerchief. It looks very old and it has some sort of rose design embroidered in one corner.

Concerned that he hasn't seen the old man for days, Larry the publican lets himself into Nibber's cottage one afternoon and discovers what he had suspected. The old man has been dead for some time and yet the bedroom smells of lily of the valley.

REPEATED SEQUENCES

Those six months or so up in Cumbria with Aunty B were really weird. On the one hand, I was living this normal, sixth form school-girl life of lessons, more lessons, essays, washing my uniform, reading girlie magazines when I should have been doing my homework, shopping, worrying about my hair; all the usual stuff.

Mum was being such a cow to me that I didn't want to be back in Somerset, so it was OK. Aunty Brenda was great: she could be like a Mum when you needed it but because she wasn't actually my Mum, she was a bit like a sister as well. For the first few days she was edgy as hell; God knows what Mum must have said to her about me or Mike but when she realised that like, I wasn't actually going to freak or anything, she calmed down and left me alone. Just as well.

I missed Mike, I really did. I yearned for him somewhere in my loins. I read that in one of those novels you buy on station platforms.

So, just a normal schoolgirl but on the other hand I was an older man's lover. His fiancé, I suppose you'd say, because he asked me to marry him, didn't he? And I was meeting him in secret and loving it. I really wanted to tell some of the new friends that I made at the school about him, but I didn't dare. It was difficult, because girls always talk about that sort of stuff and so when I was asked about my boyfriend I just used to say that he was in The West Country waiting for me and make it sound like a really weepy story. They lapped it up. But they'd have lapped up the truth even faster!

Thinking about it now, it's amazing that for the whole of that time, no one sussed what we were doing. Or if they did, they chose to keep quiet about it. I mean, sometimes I'd get back to Aunty B's really flushed after making love with Mike maybe half a hour before - it seems to take me ages to calm down afterwards - but nobody said anything even though I was like a belisha beacon and probably reeking of it.

Some of the boys at the school tried it on. One lad in particular, Ian, who was in my English group, wouldn't take no for an answer. He was really dishy and I quite fancied him. I kept on saying that I was already spoken for and he'd make some comment about how my boyfriend was miles away and he wouldn't know if I didn't tell him. I was tempted; I mean, you know, just for a laugh. I wouldn't have actually done anything with him, would I? A snog, maybe, but there's no harm in that if it doesn't lead anywhere, is there?

But then I remembered about being engaged. Like, I knew I was engaged, but the word, the concept hadn't registered. Doesn't make sense does it? Makes me sound like an uncaring tart? I didn't wear the ring in case I forgot to take it off and Aunty B saw it. Anyway, I told Ian I was engaged and that headed him off for a while.

Of course, Mike picked up on it and it was the cause of our first argument.

Most weeks he'd come up on a Thursday and because we hadn't seen each other for a few days, we'd both be, like, desperate for it, you know and we'd go straight to the cottage he rented and spend the afternoon in bed. God, the sex on those Thursday afternoons that summer! Amazing. We were making love but it was animal lust too. Rutting was a good word for it, Mike said. He kept telling me it was the best sex he'd ever had and he couldn't seem to get enough of me. He was always gentle, caressing, arousing. I mean, he wasn't clumsy or a squeezer or a groper. God, some days we'd do it four or five times in the afternoon before I had to go. It used to make me feel like jelly and one time I actually kind of passed out while we were doing it I was so sexually aroused. No wonder I arrived at Aunty B's like I did!

Anyway, as I say, Mike picked up on the Ian thing one Thursday afternoon when we were lying together after a marathon session. He just suddenly asked about it. It would have been better to lie, probably, but I didn't.

"Ellie," he said, "you really do have the most beautiful, amazing, erotic and arousing body. You know that?"

"So you say. Have I?" I said, although of course I knew what he meant. I mean, I got wolf whistles like I was on a permanent railway siding.

"Lots of young girls are pretty. Attractive, you know. But there are some who have an extraordinary sexual magnetism."

"You mean I've got big tits, a tiny waist and a pneumatic little arse?" I interrupted him. I felt like teasing him a bit. "I think that's how you put it last week."

"Well, yes, but not just that. It's not just the physical attributes, you know. There's some other indefinable quality too. A kind of sexual aura. And you know, some young women possess it for only a short time, like a flower's intense perfume that fades after its work is done," he said.

"So you mean that one day I'm going to be like falling blossom? All withered and brown at the edges and smelling slightly off?" I asked.

159

He gave me a very searching look but didn't answer. I had the feeling he didn't really want to answer or that I'd asked him about something too difficult for him to talk about. I suppose in fact I had touched on something very significant but I didn't really appreciate that at the time. It wasn't for some months that the topic came up again.

He went very quiet for a few moments and his expression changed as though something had just occurred to him which he had never thought about before. I thought he was going to answer my observation, but he didn't; he wanted to go back to the Ian thing.

"And I don't suppose I'm the only one who thinks that you are beautiful, am I?"

"Mike, it's you that I love. You know that," I replied, kissing him. I meant it, I really did. I could see the danger signals and I was trying to head him off but it didn't work.

"What about the boys at school? Any of them showing any interest? Come on, Ellie, I'm not a bloody fool. I bet they're round you like wasps at a jam-pot."

Well, you can imagine, it went on from there. He can be very jealous. He kept on and on, so in the end, in irritation really, I told him about Ian. Just as well I didn't mention any of the others. He went a bit mental for a while and started stomping about. He made me promise not to lead him on or go out with him. I said it was natural for boys to ask girls out and he had to trust me. He couldn't put me in a cage; all the stuff.

He said maybe I didn't know when I was leading boys on, that I might be doing it without realising it. So then it was my turn to get pissy because I felt he was suggesting I was a born tart.

We both sat there sulking for a bit. He'd obviously calmed down and apologised and said that I should realise that the age gap was bound to make him jealous sometimes and that he couldn't help feeling threatened by younger males. I should put it down to his anxiety about his age and a recurrent fear that I would tire of him and go looking for someone younger.

I said again that he had to trust me and that he was making himself sound like a bloody lion. He laughed like a loony at that, for some reason. I said that he should remember that I had said I loved him and wanted to marry him.

He apologised some more and we both relaxed and then we made love again, even more passionately than before, if that's possible. But afterwards, when I was back at Aunty Brenda's and in bed, I felt really quite pissed off about it. I mean, I felt like I'd been told off and that he didn't actually trust me at all. But I

160

hadn't done anything wrong, had I? Well, maybe I had in my head, but that's allowed isn't it? Sexual fantasy they call that.

We're all allowed to dream about fucking someone else, aren't we? Everyone does it.

TIME SERVERS

Brian Shepherd is dressed immaculately in a light grey suit. He stands upright in the dock, looking confidently towards the judge, Mr. Justice Brownsmith. He has his hands together in front of him, a suitably respectful and humble pose, he hopes, which will add to the air of quiet respectability which he has tried to create.

This is the same Brian Shepherd who likes to spy on courting couples through binoculars; the same Brian Shepherd, the Church Elder, who has been known to masturbate in his garden shed, a picture of his buxom teenage step-daughter in a bikini on the shelf in front of him; it is the same Brian Shepherd, the respectable citizen, who tried to look at this naked girl in the shower; undeniably the same Brian Shepherd, the man of God, who last year forced sexual intercourse with his step-daughter, intercourse so violent that it caused her physical injury and required stitches.

It is the same Brian Shepherd who has convinced both himself and his wife that it was The Devil who made him do it. Satan had him in his power for a while and presented him with a vile temptation, which slithered from the mouth of the precocious girl and which he was unable to resist. He does not intend to tell the court this, of course, because they may put him down as a religious nut, a zealot who might be better off behind bars. No, he will put it in more prosaic terms.

He alone knows what was going through his mind that evening as he hurried home, certain that Ellie would be the only one in the house. But whatever it was he was thinking and feeling, it has been pushed so far down in his sub-conscious, so thoroughly cemented down by the presence of the Devil in the events, that it is unlikely to surface again. He believes his own story so implicitly that it is now no longer a story, it is fact.

"Brian Shepherd," says the Clerk, "you are accused of Rape, contrary to section 1 (i) of The Sexual Offences Act 1956 in that on the 24th day of October 1990 you did rape Ellen Amanda Fortune. How do you plead?"

Brian Shepherd looks mildly surprised. It is a look he has been practising to suggest that he is dismayed that it should even be necessary to ask him such an absurd question.

"Not guilty," he replies immediately and confidently. He would have liked to add, "of course" but Piers Sowerby, QC, has warned him against any diversion from court routine or doing anything which the Court might think is trying to be clever.

The Leading Counsel for the Prosecution, Charles Wingate, QC, is rather slow and ponderous in opening his case. Sowerby is pleased to see Wingate leading the Prosecution because he thinks it gives him no small advantage: the man has no real flair, no real sense of the Court as Theatre and is saddled with a rather pompous voice. Sowerby has seen judges and juries bored to tears (and slumber) by Wingate in the past.

The Prosecution's case will rest upon evidence and statements to be presented by the police who were called to the scene, forensic information from the scenes of crime officers, the medical report of the Police Surgeon, Ellie's neighbour Mrs Simpson and, of course, Ellie herself.

Initially, Sowerby holds his fire, allowing Wingate to blunder along, lose his place in his papers, trip over his own feet and laboriously work his way through the statements given by the various Police officers. He toys with the idea of seeking to undermine the forensic evidence by challenging the officer about the methods which were employed but thinks better of it on the grounds that the Jury may view this as bloody-mindedness or straw-clutching. In any event, that intercourse took place is obviously not disputed by anyone.

When the Police Surgeon is in the witness box, however, he decides to create the first of what he hopes will be many doubts in the Jury's mind.

"In your experience, Dr. Freeman, would you say that the injuries sustained by the Complainant could only have occurred if intercourse was non-consensual?"

"What I said," replies the doctor with a trace of irritation in his voice, "was that penetration on this occasion, to have caused these kinds of injuries, would have been quite sudden and violent and would therefore be commensurate with a very considerable degree of force being used."

"Yes," says Sowerby, "I think we understand that. Let me put the question another way, in the hope that it may assist you. Are these kinds of injuries, in your experience, possible where the sex is consensual?"

"Very unlikely," says Freeman. "Not impossible, but very unlikely."

Sowerby smiles to himself. Those are the words he has been waiting for.

"Not impossible; maybe unlikely, but not impossible. Thank you, Doctor Freeman. That is all, thank you."

*

Wingate has Mrs Simpson called to the witness box and it is during his patient questioning of this rather slow and over-awed woman that Sowerby notices something about her responses which he could not have known before this moment, but which he thinks he will be able to exploit during his cross-examination.

"Mrs Simpson," says Sowerby, perfectly audibly, but with his head down a little, "what were you doing on the evening in question, just before Miss Fortune came beating on your door in the manner you have already described in your answers to my learned friend?"

Mrs Simpson is leaning forward, a strained expression on her face.

"Pardon?" she says. "I didn't quite catch all that."

Sowerby repeats the question.

"Oh, well, my husband was washing up the tea things and I was watching the telly. Television," she replies.

"Is the kitchen close to the room where you watch the television, Mrs Simpson?"

"I beg your pardon? Can you speak up a bit, please?"

Sowerby repeats the question.

"Oh, yes," comes the reply, "it's one o' they l-shaped open plan arrangements, so the kitchen is open to the dining area and the lounge area."

"I see," says Sowerby, pausing for effect. "So you had the television on and your husband was washing dishes?"

"Yes."

"Is your husband quiet when he does this?"

"Pardon?" says Mrs Simpson and again Sowerby repeats the question.

"Oh, no, not at all. He makes a dickens of a racket, 'cos he doesn't really want to do it, see?"

"Mrs Simpson," says Sowerby, smiling, "tell me, are you a little hard of hearing? Forgive the personal question, but I do think it may have a bearing here. I have noticed you asking both myself and my learned friend to repeat ourselves this afternoon."

Mrs Simpson looks a little embarrassed.

"Well, yes, I am a bit."

"Do you need to wear a hearing aid, Mrs Simpson?"

"I do sometimes. But I don't like to. They're such ugly things."

"Do you remember whether you were wearing your hearing aid on the evening in question, Mrs Simpson?" Sowerby offers up a silent prayer.

"No. Well, I don't usually at home. Not unless we've got guests," she says.

"You were not wearing your hearing aid on the evening in question. Thank you. May I ask further, Mrs Simpson, what difficulties you experience as a result of your hearing deficiency? For example, are you able to hear clearly in social situations?"

"No," says Mrs Simpson, "that's when I need the aid."

"And without the aid, are you sometimes confused as to which direction a sound is coming from?"

"Oh, yes, it does happen sometimes," says Mrs Simpson, a bemused expression on her face.

"Tell me, Mrs Simpson, without your hearing aid, it's no doubt necessary for you to have the volume on the TV set turned up quite high?"

"Well, yes," says Mrs Simpson, puzzled as to where the barrister's questions are leading. "Me husband says it's too loud for him."

"Indeed. And this screaming which you say you heard, Mrs Simpson. Did your husband hear it too?"

"No, he didn't. Well, the kitchen's on the other side, like, next to the other neighbours at number thirty."

"Yes, I see. It's a terraced house?"

"Yes."

"So let me just re-acquaint myself with the scene in your house on that evening, just before you opened the door to Miss Fortune. Your husband is washing the dishes, quite noisily, you said. You have the television on in the adjoining open-plan room with the volume turned up high, you say, to a level which your husband generally regards as too loud. And you are not wearing your hearing aid, although you do have one prescribed. Is that correct?"

"Well, yes, I suppose so," says Mrs Simpson sheepishly.

"Mrs Simpson, I am only repeating back to you what you have said to me. You suppose so? Is it or is it not a correct description of the scene?"

"Yes, that's correct."

"Your husband does not hear any screaming but you, despite being hard of hearing and despite the sound of the dishes being clattered and the loud television set and despite occasionally being confused about where a sound is coming from, you were able "distinctly" - that's the word you used to my learned friend just now - you were able to hear distinctly the sound of screaming coming from next door, from the Fortune's house at number twenty six?" Sowerby fixes Mrs Simpson with a penetrating stare.

"Well, yes, I heard screaming; coming from somewhere."

Sowerby smiles to himself.

"From somewhere? I see. You heard screaming. From somewhere. What kind of screaming, Mrs Simpson?"

"I don't understand," says Mrs Simpson. "Screaming. Screaming is screaming, isn't it?"

Sowerby answers in a rather patronising tone.

"With all due respect, Mrs Simpson, no. Little girls chasing each other up and down the beach or being tickled unmercifully by their fathers will scream, shall we say, in delight or excitement. Someone who has had a limb severed will scream in agony; an entirely different noise. Which was it here?"

"Well, I'm not sure," she says. "Screaming is all I can say, really."

Sowerby pauses. He has been about to take Mrs Simpson further but now there is no need.

"You heard screaming coming from somewhere," he repeats, deliberately accenting the last word. "From whence it came, you could not be sure and, I put it to you, you did not necessarily hear very clearly or accurately. And you were unable to determine whether this screaming sound was indicative of delight or pain?"

"If you say so," says Mrs Simpson, petulantly.

"No, Mrs Simpson, I don't say so. You do. I have merely repeated what you said. That will be all. Thank you."

*

As Ellen makes her way to the witness box, she feels a wave of nausea wash over her and wonders, just for a fraction of a second, whether she is going to faint. The day which she has dreaded for months but which she knew would come as a result of her insistences last October, has finally arrived. The courtroom is stuffy and hot and as Ellen takes her place in the box, it seems that the panelled walls are pulsating and that the room is contracting and squeezing the life out of her. She clutches the rail around the box, closes her eyes and takes a very deep breath.

Michael's assessment for Ellie of how things will unfold is more or less correct where Wingate's questioning is concerned. He takes her through the early stages of what he wants to show as Brian's growing lust and then, eventually, leads her quite gently but thoroughly through the fine details and mechanics of what she says happened that evening. She copes with it calmly and as matter-of-factly as she can. She finds that by imagining herself watching the scene rather than being a victim of it, she is able to recount the details in a way which seems to satisfy Wingate. Afterwards, she wonders whether a display of emotion, tears or hysterics would have been a better tactic.

Throughout, Ellie is keenly aware of the Jury members watching her, especially the men and particularly two middle-aged men in the front row. She is conscious of the need to play down her feminine body language; those things which she knows from experience can excite men of all ages. At Mike's suggestion, she has bought and is wearing a trim two piece suit, the skirt fairly loose so as not to cling to her bottom and the jacket full cut and buttoned. She has put on a bra which flattens, rather than the under-wired type which she usually prefers. She wears her hair un-styled; loose in a long pony tail and she has only a hint of make-up.

Whilst she undergoes questioning by Wingate, Sowerby makes frequent notes on his pad, watches her intently and pulls on his fine crop of nasal hair. And then, quite suddenly and abruptly it seems, Wingate has finished. Ellie looks across nervously to Sowerby.

He rises quickly to his feet, adjusts his gown with a flourish and then stands with his hands clasping the front edges of the garment, looking at her.

"Miss Fortune," he says, "I'm sure that my learned friend and members of the Jury will agree that you have thus far acquitted yourself most impressively in what are obviously trying circumstances for you."

Sowerby gives a little nod and a smile towards her. Bastard, she thinks, I'm not fooled by that.

"So I won't detain you too much longer this afternoon. I just need to clarify one or two points and ask you for some additional information. Miss Fortune, I think that you intimated to the Police in your statement on October 25th last year that at the time of the alleged offence, you were a virgin?"

"Yes, I was," Ellie replies nervously.

"So that during the course of the alleged offence, you say that your virginity was taken from you by the defendant without your consent? That is your position?"

"Yes."

"Is the loss of your virginity a source of great sadness and anger to you, Miss Fortune?"

Wingate looks up and at Mr. Justice Brownsmith.

"Mr. Sowerby," says the Judge sternly, "I don't need to remind you of the restrictions on questioning of which we need to be mindful here?"

"Your Honour, the Defence will later seek to introduce evidence to show that the Complainant's attitude to her sexuality and virginity is not as it has been presented by my learned friend for the Prosecution. It is challenged by the Defence, thus the Defendant's not guilty plea. I can assure the Court that it is this attitude rather than any extensive specifics of the Complainant's sexual history which the Defence seeks to lay before the Court," wheedles Sowerby.

"Very well, Mr. Sowerby. Continue."

Sowerby turns back to Ellie. The slight delay has given her sufficient time to see where the questions are leading. She feels like an animal caught in a trap from which there is no escape.

"So prior to the events of October 24th last, you were proud of your virginity, pleased to have retained it?"

Ellie considers the question briefly and recalls how she and Mike have discussed this particular issue. There is no point, she thinks, in suggesting that she was proud of her virginity only then to have Sowerby introduce the Quale episode to demolish the suggestion. He's going to introduce it anyway, she reasons, so he might as well get it over with.

"I wasn't particularly proud of it, no," she says tentatively.

"I put it to you, Miss Fortune, that not only were you not especially proud of it, but that you had, not many weeks before this alleged offence, set out to lose your virginity. To get rid of it; be shot of it, we might say. You planned to do so, in fact?"

Ellie sighs resignedly.

"Yes."

Sowerby looks expectantly at Ellie but she says no more.

"Perhaps I can help the Court here," says Sowerby. "And I hope that the witness will co-operate with me in saving the Court's time and, perhaps, her own extended discomfort in acknowledging what I am about to lay before the Court?

In essence, Miss Fortune, on the afternoon of August 31st last year, you arranged to lose your virginity with a Mr. Simon Quale at a location in Ramsey, on the Isle of Man, where you are an occasional holiday visitor, that place having been until recently, the home of your grandmother. You had pursued Mr. Quale each year, during your annual holidays there, for two or three years and last August you stepped up your pressure on him to take you out. He did so and then some few days later you suggested meeting at a lonely spot for sex. You told him what it was you wanted and why and made all the arrangements, including bringing a rug to lie on and reminding Mr. Quale of the need for contraceptives. Is that a fair summary?"

"Yes," says Ellie quietly, her eyes looking down at the floor.

"I realise that this very embarrassing for you, Miss Fortune, but I must ask you to speak up so that the whole Court can hear. Is what I have just outlined a correct summary of events on August 31st last year?"

"Yes," says Ellie in a clearer voice, her shoulders slumping with resignation. "Yes, it is."

"Thank you. But in the event," continues Sowerby, "you were frustrated in your desire. Although you commenced to try to have intercourse with Mr. Quale, several times, it was not in the end possible for you to do so because you were too tense and he was unable to penetrate you?"

"Yes."

"Thank you. So, a few days later in early September last year, you returned to school and the sixth form still technically a virgin?"

"Yes."

Sowerby pauses and wipes his forehead with a spotted, red handkerchief. Ellie can feel all the muscles in the back of her neck tightening, for she knows that Sowerby is not finished yet. She glances quickly towards the dock and can see that Brian Shepherd is sitting there impassively, watching her carefully.

"Miss Fortune, in your answers to my learned friend's questions, you said that you had not, prior to the alleged offence, ever had a proper boyfriend and thus you had no extensive direct experience of the physical side of relationships. Is that so?"

"Yes," says Ellie.

"Are you in a relationship at the present time?" asks Sowerby, his eyes seeming to bore into her skull.

"Mr. Sowerby," intervenes the Judge, "I have difficulty in seeing what relevance this can have..."

"Your Honour, I have to ask for the Court's indulgence again. As I have explained to the Court, the Defence is not interested in the physical nature of this or any other relationship per se and does not intend to seek extensive information from the Complainant about that. Rather, the Defence is interested in the date of the commencement of this relationship, insofar as it has a bearing on the date of the alleged offence, and the age of the complainant's partner."

The Judge nods. "Very well."

"Are you in a relationship at the present time, Miss Fortune?"

Ellie swallows hard and can feel the blood rushing to her cheeks. Her hands are clammy and she can feel beads of sweat in the small of her back. She is acutely aware of the eyes of the jury upon her, particularly the middle-aged man dressed in a check suit who is licking his lips. She is also aware of The Perv's cold, penetrating stare from the other side of the Court and her mother in the public gallery, her mouth a hard, thin line.

"Yes, I am," she almost whispers.

"Again, I must ask you to speak up so that the Jury can hear, please, Miss Fortune," says Sowerby.

A little louder, "Yes."

"Your partner is a Michael Chadwick, Dr. Michael Chadwick who is forty four years old. Is that correct?"

"Yes."

"Are you more attracted to older men than young men closer to your own age?"

"No," says Ellie. She's not going to let Sowerby lead her down that avenue too easily. She hopes.

"You find them no more or no less attractive than younger men?" Sowerby tries again.

"That's right. It depends on the personality and the looks, not the age," she says confidently, speaking lines that she and Mike have already rehearsed.

"How long have you known Michael Chadwick?" asks Sowerby, deciding to move on. He leans forward to find a paper on his desk.

"Since I was about eleven, I suppose," Ellie replies.

The Court is suddenly very attentive.

"Yes, in the sense that you were a pupil at Combe Valley Comprehensive School where Dr. Chadwick was an English teacher and Deputy Head teacher until recently?"

"Yes."

Ellie looks up and is aware that all eyes are now on her. There is a silence broken only by the faint squeak coming from one of the ceiling fans. Previously there had been shuffling, coughing, chairs creaking; but now, silence.

"So initially your relationship, if that's even the right word, was simply that of pupil and teacher? Nothing out of the ordinary?"

"Yes."

"Did you have a crush on Dr. Chadwick, Miss Fortune?"

Oh, Christ, thinks Ellie, now we're on to the stories in the book.

"Yes."

"And from about the time you were fourteen, you kept a diary, a book of explicit, detailed stories featuring yourself and Dr. Chadwick in which a full sexual relationship was taking place?"

Ellie feels acutely embarrassed and ashamed.

"Well, yes, but they were just stories. You know, a schoolgirl's fantasy," she says with a pained expression.

"So they were just a fiction? At what point, then, did the relationship become real, personal and not just a crush or the product of your literary imagination?"

"Well," says Ellie cautiously, "I'm not sure..."

"Miss Fortune," snaps Sowerby, "I must ask you to reconsider the question. When did the relationship move from the usual teacher-pupil one to something more personal and intimate between you? To the kind of relationship, in fact, which you had fantasised about for some time?"

Ellie takes a deep breath again, deciding again that the best course of action is to give Sowerby what he wants to hear; what everyone wants to hear and get it over with.

"I went to see Dr. Chadwick on the same afternoon of the day of the rape because I wanted to confide in him about my fears about what was going to happen. I was worried sick about the way Brian was behaving towards me and I thought he could help," she says. "And at that time, in his office, there seemed to be, well, I don't know; a sort of feeling between us, although I did wonder whether it was my imagination again at first."

"Miss Fortune, most lovers can pin-point with some accuracy the exact date and time that their romance began. All I am asking you to do is the same. Was it that afternoon? Or another later time?"

"Dr. Chadwick came to see me in the hospital, the day after the rape. He brought me a red rose and we kind of kissed."

Shit! Thinks Ellie, I shouldn't have told him that. No one else knows about that. Or do they? I must concentrate but I'm getting flustered and it's so hot in here. Let's get on with it; let me out of here.

If Sowerby is surprised by this revelation, he does not show it. Some members of the Jury, however, are clearly dumbstruck. Mr. Check-suit is still licking his lips and attempting to undress Ellie with his eyes.

"Dr Chadwick came to see you in the hospital? At what time?"

"I don't know for sure," says Ellie. "Early. They were making breakfast, I think."

"Let us be clear about this, Miss Fortune. You are telling the Court that probably not much more than twelve hours after the alleged offence, whilst you are in a hospital bed recovering from your injuries, you commenced a relationship with your forty four year old teacher who came to see you bearing a red rose?"

"Well, you make it sound..." Ellie begins, plaintively.

"I am merely repeating, for the Court's benefit, what you have already told us. I am not making it sound like anything, Miss Fortune. Is that, in essence, what happened?"

"Yes."

"Thank you."

Unusually, Sowerby pauses for a few moments and turns over the sheets in a loose-leaf file. Ellie begins to hope that he has finished with her so that she can escape from the publicity of the witness box: the stares of the jury ranging from surprise to pity to contempt to lust; the snickering smiles of the young journalists chewing on their pens and whispering to their colleagues; the smug expression on her mother's face and the Pervert's holier-than-thou, righteous, self-assurance.

"Finally, Miss Fortune, I must ask you to cast your mind back again to one particular point on the evening of October 24th last year," begins Sowerby again. "In your testimony, you indicated that having had a shower, you opened the bathroom door, listened briefly for a moment to check that you were alone before proceeding across the landing to your bedroom, the door of which was closed?"

"Yes," says Ellie once more, this time her heart racing.

"You checked because, I think you said, you had left your dressing gown in the bedroom and therefore you were able to cover yourself with only a quite small hand towel. One towel was wrapped around your wet hair and the other around your body, as best you could?"

"Yes."

"You said you were unable easily to open the door because there was moisturising cream on your hands. Was it at this point that you became aware of the Defendant's presence on the landing?" asks Sowerby.

"Yes, that's right," says Ellen.

"He was behind you?"

"Yes. I had my back to the stairs as I was struggling with the door and he must have come up the stairs behind me," she replies.

"If you were concentrating on the door and keeping the towel in place and you believed yourself to be alone in the house anyway, what happened to make you aware of the Defendant's presence?"

"Well, he made a noise, I suppose."

"A noise? What sort of noise? You mean he grunted? Or he spoke?" asks Sowerby insistently.

"Both. He was grunting and pulling at himself," Ellie sighs and corrects herself before she's asked to. "Pulling at his genital area, I mean. Like I said before, his trousers were unbuttoned and he was masturbating."

Sowerby looks at her, waiting.

"And what did he say, Miss Fortune? You said he spoke."

"He said something like, "Ellie, please, let me...", " she mutters.

"Is that all? "Ellie, please let me..." It was a question or statement unfinished?"

"Yes. I think so."

Sowerby pauses and strokes his chin reflectively.

"So he used your name and he asked you to let him...what? What did you understand by his question?"

"Well, I knew he'd been trying for ages to watch me in the shower. He tried to at Gran's on the Isle of Man. So perhaps he meant let me see you...I don't know!"

Suddenly, Ellie is overcome and begins to cry.

Sowerby thinks the witness is being deliberately evasive but he waits a respectful second or so.

"Miss Fortune, I know this is all very distressing for you but I have to press you on this point. So you thought he might have meant that he wanted to see you completely naked?"

"Yes," snuffles Ellie.

"Did you think he might have meant anything else?"

"I suppose so. I don't know. I mean, I was frightened. He looked so weird. And I was embarrassed and angry. It was difficult to tell what he meant. He's a really weird guy," Ellie tries to recover herself.

"I see. Again, I have to press you. What else might he have meant, did you think?" Sowerby says.

"He'd been trying to feel me, touch my buttocks or my breasts; grope me whenever I walked past him. For days, weeks. I don't know. Maybe he meant, "Let me touch you"."

"I see. So you think he might have meant, "Let me see you naked or let me touch you." Would you regard it as possible, Miss Fortune, that the defendant was asking whether he could have intercourse with you?"

Ellie looks aghast.

"What? Well, no I don't think so," she stutters.

"How can you be so sure?" insists Sowerby. "You agree that he didn't finish his question?"

"Yes."

"You also agree, I ask again, that he might have meant that he wanted to see you naked or that he wanted to touch you?"

"Yes."

"So, given that, and the fact that he did not complete the question, I suggest to you that he may also have been asking for intercourse with you. Is that not possible?"

Ellie seems unable to speak for some time but is frozen, rigid with apprehension.

"I don't know. I suppose so," says Ellie, flatly.

"Whatever he meant, Miss Fortune, what did you say and do at this point?" Sowerby stops fiddling with his gown and his papers and looks at the girl in the witness box.

Ellie looks helpless and glances across to Mr. Justice Brownsmith, as if appealing to him for help.

"Answer the question, please, Miss Fortune," says the Judge.

Ellie closes her eyes and seems to shrug her shoulders.

"It's hard to remember. I mean, I told him to eff off."

"That's all?"

Ellie can tell from Sowerby's tone that Brian has clearly told him that there is more. She whimpers a little and chokes back the emotion which is rising in her throat.

"Well," she says, "I was angry with him and I wanted to sort of shock him I suppose so I..."

"You were angry with him, yes and so what did you do to show that anger and to try to shock him? Miss Fortune?"

Ellie takes a shuddering breath.

"I pulled the towel off my body; well, it was hardly covering it anyway and I said, I said something like, "Here you are then, you effing pervert, have a good look! Are you satisfied now? Now eff off and leave me alone!". "

Sowerby smiles to himself. Shepherd was right about this, then.

"Let's be absolutely clear here, Miss Fortune. As well as telling the Defendant to leave you alone you say, you also said something like, "Here you are, have a good look"?"

"Yes," says Ellie, realising that this admission is critical.

"And at this point, Miss Fortune, you were completely naked and you were facing the defendant?"

"Yes."

"So the Court is to understand that although you say you were suspicious of your step-father's motives because for some time he had been behaving suggestively towards you and trying to touch you inappropriately and despite the fact that he had suddenly appeared on the landing behind you, was masturbating, and he had asked you to let him do something; we are not sure what this might be but you agree that it would be something of a sexual nature; despite all this you expose yourself completely and invite him to take a look?"

"Well, yes, but I was shouting at him and telling him to get out of my sight and stuff like that."

Sowerby stands impassively for a moment, as if he has forgotten what he wants to say, although Ellie realises it is for effect and for what she has just said to rest for a moment with the Jury.

"Miss Fortune, how long were you standing this way, completely naked, so that the Defendant could see you?"

"I don't know! I wasn't timing it. No more than a few seconds."

"Miss Fortune, would you please explain to us, to the members of the Jury, why you exposed yourself and invited the Defendant to look at you?" Sowerby asks insistently.

"I said. I wanted to shock him, you know, like slapping someone's face. To try to make him see that he's a disgusting pervert," she says loudly.

"And did your action have the desired effect?" asks Sowerby, as if the answer was not yet already in the public domain.

"No, obviously not. He lunged towards me and tried to touch my breasts. I kicked the bedroom door open with my heel and tried to get inside to lock it but he overpowered me," she almost wails.

"So your ruse of exposing yourself did not have the effect which you say you intended. Did it occur to you then, or has it occurred to you since, that removing the towel and inviting the Defendant to take a look at you, might have been seen as an invitation to take matters further sexually?" Sowerby asks. "Might have been seen as your way of saying "Yes" to the Defendant's unfinished question?"

"No! No," says Ellie. "That's not what I meant at all."

"So you say, Miss Fortune," smiles Sowerby. "But that's not the question I asked you. I asked you whether you agree that whatever you thought *you* meant, the Defendant might reasonably have concluded from your action and invitation to him that you were agreeing to him furthering the sexual advances already explicit through his masturbation and his question to you?"

"No, I don't agree. I was screaming at him to eff off. My expression and, well, my body language would have made it clear that I was rejecting his advances," she says.

"But, Miss Fortune," says Sowerby, "you have just explained to the Court that your body language included exposing yourself to the Defendant."

*

That evening, Sowerby allows himself a brandy after dinner as he goes to his study to prepare for the next day of the trial. He is pleased with the way things have gone. He has managed to demonstrate that matters in this case are not quite as cut and dried as has been suggested by Wingate. He could see from the changing expressions on some of the faces in the Jury, whilst the flighty girl was undergoing cross-examination, that genuine doubts were growing in the minds of at least some of them.

He is pleased that he has managed to elicit from her as much information as he has. He wonders now whether anything much more is to be gained from calling Dr. Chadwick and the dairyman Quale to the witness box.

In the event he does so but only briefly in order to confirm what the girl has already said in cross-examination and to put a little more meat on those bones. He also calls Constable Mark Lewis to outline for the Court what he found at Riverview Lodge on the night of 29th November; again, not to dwell solely on the complainant's sexual behaviour alone, but to show that only five weeks after an allegedly traumatic rape she is enthusiastically consummating a relationship with a middle-aged man, something which a traumatised victim of rape - at the hands of another middle-aged man - might not be expected to do.

By the time the moment arrives for him to sum up the Defence case, he is confident that he can present a sound and persuasive argument.

*

"Ladies and gentlemen of the Jury," he begins, "there is one thing and one thing only in this case upon which we can all agree. Everyone in this courtroom who has attended properly to the proceedings here in recent days will agree that sexual intercourse took place on October 24th last year at approximately six thirty in the evening between the Defendant Brian Shepherd and his step-daughter, the Complainant in this case, Miss Ellen Amanda Fortune. Beyond that one fact, opinions diverge.

The Prosecution bases its case on the evidence of the Police officers at the scene, including the arresting officers and the scene of crime officers, charged, you will recall, with responsibility for forensic evidence. Further, they asked us to listen to the evidence of the Police Surgeon, the complainant's neighbour Mrs Simpson and then, finally, the complainant herself.

The forensic evidence demonstrates that DNA samples taken at the scene from semen found there link the Defendant to the alleged crime. That is not denied because of course, it is agreed that sexual intercourse took place. The scene of crime officers also reported a considerable amount of blood on the bed linen in the complainant's bedroom.

The arresting officer, you will remember, commented on the quantity of blood at the scene but it was later shown that the Complainant was menstruating at the time that intercourse took place. Further, the Complainant asserts that she was a virgin up until that point and had not ever used tampons for sanitary protection, preferring the pad type for that purpose. Dr. Freeman, the Police surgeon, confirmed that a virgin girl's hymen, when ruptured, can produce a significant quantity of blood. His examination of the Complainant concluded that it was possible that some of the blood at the scene might have been the result of this happening, although you will recall that Dr. Freeman was unable to confirm with certainty that the Complainant was a virgin, as she says, before the alleged offence occurred.

In any event, Ladies and Gentlemen, the presence of blood, even a shockingly considerable quantity of it, does not of itself necessarily mean that a rape has occurred or gives us sufficient reason to convict.

The forensic evidence showed that there was also blood resulting from injuries sustained by the Complainant during intercourse. Dr Freeman said that in his opinion these injuries would be commensurate with violent and forceful penetration and although this was unlikely during consensual sex, it was not impossible.

It was not impossible, Ladies and Gentlemen. Not impossible. Police Constable Lewis, called to Riverview Lodge in the early hours of Friday 30th November last year, gave evidence to show that the Complainant and her current partner, Dr. Michael Chadwick, had clearly spent a night of frequent love-making on the sofa. Dr Chadwick was elusive on this next point, you will recall, but did eventually concede that the complainant is a vigorous and enthusiastic participant in sexual intercourse. I ask you to bear that in mind when considering the evidence of the Police Surgeon.

Ladies and Gentlemen, I ask you to regard a part - the important part - of the evidence of Mrs Simpson, the complainant's neighbour, with some scepticism. By her own admission, she is hard of hearing and can be confused about where sounds are coming from. She believes she heard screaming and the Prosecution would have us believe that it was the complainant's pained screams which she heard coming through the party wall. But we do not know, because the witness is unable to tell us, what kind of screaming she heard, if indeed she heard screaming at all. The Defence suggests that this issue is far from clear and therefore cannot be relied upon.

In some respects, Ladies and Gentlemen and as is so often the case where rape is alleged, it is a question of who to believe, the Complainant or the Defendant.

The Defence asserts that the Complainant is a sexually highly charged young woman who, through inexperience and youth, has yet fully to realise the effect on men of her sexuality.

This is a young woman who, from the age of about fourteen, began to write detailed and sexually explicit stories featuring herself and her teacher and now lover, Dr. Chadwick indulging in fellatio, cunnilingus and sexual intercourse in all manner of positions and places. You have some of these accounts in the papers presented to you and it is clear that the 'I' of the story, the narrator, the

Complainant, Miss Ellen Fortune, is enjoying the sex. Initiating it, in most cases. She is not a terrified or manipulated victim.

You have had referred to you one particular story in which quite violent intercourse takes place where the Complainant imagines herself lying over a barrel of some sort and being penetrated from behind by Dr. Chadwick where she writes, "He rammed his giant penis into me time and time again and it hurt so I cried out but I screamed with pleasure too and he did it even harder."

Ladies and Gentlemen, it has already been suggested that you might find the essence of this story - a rape fantasy, in effect - most significant in the context of this trial. It might be argued that the Complainant has long nurtured a rape fantasy involving a middle-aged man. Of course, we might all ask how such a young girl could think in that way or have such detailed knowledge, how such a young mind could be so corrupted. But, urgent though such questions might be, they are not for this Court to pursue today.

The complainant is a young woman who last August set about importuning a young man so that she could dispense with her virginity. She made, you recall, all the running and all the arrangements. Mr. Quale in his evidence and his written statement, says that she told him to "push harder" when he was unable to penetrate her during their final attempt at intercourse. In effect, she asks him to behave in a more violent way.

Further, Ladies and Gentlemen of the Jury, we have seen that this is a young woman whose fantasy about her teacher has now become reality: her passion for a much older man realised perhaps beyond her wildest dreams. This relationship commenced properly about twelve hours after the alleged rape and then, five weeks after the complainant had sustained injuries as a result of that alleged rape, she spent several hours making love, several times, to Dr. Chadwick on a sofa in her sister's flat. Hardly time, one would think, for the physical wounds to heal sufficiently, let alone the emotional wounds that one might expect if indeed she was raped as she alleges.

The Defendant himself, in his evidence, told us that he believed that the complainant had been teasing him and leading him on for some months. He cited occasions when she had walked about the house, after showering, in only her underwear; an occasion when she had sunbathed topless in the garden when she knew for certain that he was at home and many occasions when she had worn very tight jeans and tops which accentuated her full figure. He said that his wife had spoken to the girl about this but it had made no difference to her behaviour and, in fact, she had on one occasion taunted him and asked him whether he was "turned on" by her figure.

Ladies and gentlemen, you heard on Friday, during my cross-examination of the Complainant, that just before the alleged offence took place she removed a small towel from herself and invited the Defendant to look at her naked body. The Defendant believes that she consented to intercourse at this point, that the act of revealing herself in that manner, after he had pleaded with her, was tantamount to consent.

The Defendant has told us that he does not recall the complainant saying "No" or asking him to stop or to leave at any time during what followed. He has told us that he was certainly very aroused by her presence in the house, the way that he believes she teased and taunted him with her body over several months and on that evening, he was especially aroused at her nakedness.

Consequently, the Defendant does not deny that intercourse was very vigorous; violent even, but the Defence asserts that, as we have shown in other related contexts, this is what the Complainant had fantasised about through her middle teens, what she now wants as the norm in her relationship with a much older man and what at the time she believed was necessary in order for penetration to occur on the first occasion that she would have intercourse. It might have been frantic or even violent but, Ladies and gentlemen of the Jury, the Defence puts it to you that this was not rape.

If as the Defence asserts, this was consensual sex, then the question arises as to why the complainant contacted the Police so rapidly to accuse her step-father of raping her. Only the complainant knows. We may only surmise that, as often in these situations, a feeling of anger or self-disgust emerged. Perhaps the complainant was frightened of what she had unleashed in herself and did not want to believe that it was of her own volition but rather something forced upon her. There might be a thousand answers and we shall have to leave the question hanging in the air.

Ladies and gentlemen of the Jury, you are charged with a heavy responsibility here today because it is your duty to decide whether the Defendant is guilty of rape, as the Prosecution alleges. Rape carries serious penalties and a custodial sentence would almost certainly follow conviction.

Ladies and Gentlemen, to send a man to prison you have to be certain. If, as the Defence has sought to show, sexual intercourse here was consensual, there are serious reasons to doubt that Ellen Fortune was raped on October 24th last year. If you share those doubts, even if only some of them, then it is your responsibility to acquit the accused, Brian Shepherd."

*

Cramped in their airless room, the Jury is unable to agree.

The younger women jurors incline to the notion that the Defence has raised all manner of irrelevance. Even if the Complainant does prefer older men, likes rough sex and is something of a manipulator, as the Defence seems to be claiming, it does not alter the fact that she says she told the Defendant to stop at the crucial time. She was quite clear about that and these jurors believe her. They recognise that she probably is a girl with a high sexual charge, but they have also sensed something of Ellie's essential honesty. Further, the injuries sustained seem to go far beyond what a virgin girl would willingly endure during her first consensual sexual experience.

"It just does not sound like consensual sex," says one. "It sounds like a male rape fantasy being played out; by the Defendant. No girl will willingly be hurt and injured that way during sex; it happens only in the fantasies written and read or filmed by men. The evidence in front of us, what the Judge said we had to look at, says force and coercion. Look at those medical reports. They hold the key. She told him to stop; that's that. It's rape. No doubt. The Defendant is twisting the truth."

The middle-aged men from the front row of the Jury are not so sure. Mr. Check-suit has been persuaded by the Defence's suggestion that the girl is a bit frisky and that she started something without fully realising what she was doing and it got out of hand.

"But she started it alright," he says, "and gave the Defendant the come-on by dropping the towel to expose herself. What's that supposed to mean if she's alone in the house with him and he's masturbating in front of her? What's that supposed to mean to a guy except come and get it? She agreed. OK, he was rough with her, but she agreed."

"Even if she did, and I don't think she did, she changed her mind straight away or very soon afterwards. Maybe when he started to hurt her. She told him to stop and she started screaming," says the younger woman.

"Well," says Check-suit, "she says she told him to stop. But he has no memory of that. And some screaming of some kind might have been heard by a half-deaf woman but we don't know for sure that it was the girl's."

"I agree," says the first young juror. "But I don't think she wanted him to in the first place. I think that's what we have to focus on here. She didn't say yes in the way that we need to be sure she said it, if you see what I mean. OK, she drops the towel and tells Shepherd to have a good look, but isn't that the kind of stupid thing an angry, naive girl might do in that situation? She goes to see Chadwick and tells him that she's worried that she is going to be sexually assaulted. Do you do that if you want to have sexual intercourse with the person in question?"

"You might," says Check-suit, "if you're a prick-teaser. A manipulator."

"Male terminology superimposed by men on female behaviour to which they would like to ascribe some sort of covert or deviant sexual motive," announces a bookish young woman in bright red.

"Come again?" says Check-suit, snickering.

"But she isn't a manipulator, in my opinion," says the young one again. "She's a very pretty girl overwhelmed by the force of her own exploding sexuality and its obvious effect on men. She's a bit confused, basically. But I don't think that the Defence has shown abundantly clearly that she categorically and unequivocally agreed to intercourse with her step-father. Like I say, the business with the towel is probably as she described it. Hasty; silly; not thought through. Designed to shock, maybe, like teenagers like to shock before they discover that actually they've made a grave error. She didn't agree. No way, he raped her."

"I agree," says another young, mousey woman.

"But if you were raped, you know, injured and violated as is suggested, would you be canoodling with another much older man the next day?" says Check-suit's companion, a man with bulging eyes like a toad. "Methinks she doth protest too much. She's a good-time girl who bit off a bit more than she could chew and felt cheap when it was over and she realised just what she'd done."

And in this vein, on and on for hours at a time on the first lengthy afternoon and then again all the next day.

The Judge calls them into the Court to ask whether they are close to any verdict. Their Chairman says that there seems to be an impasse and they cannot agree. The Defendant smiles quietly to himself and thanks his God. Sowerby is a little more cautious and wise. He knows that an undecided Jury does not necessarily mean an acquittal at this stage. It simply means that he has marshalled a good case. But it might not be good enough.

The Judge sends the Jury away again saying that he would still prefer a unanimous decision but if that is really not possible, then a majority verdict of 10:2 will be acceptable.

Finally, the next afternoon, after five more hours of circuitous deliberation, the Jury returns to the Court announcing that it has reached a majority decision.

*

Fifteen minutes later, Brian Shepherd, his complexion pale and clammy and his hands trembling like a man with Parkinson's Disease, is led from the dock to commence a custodial sentence; found guilty, as charged.

Fifteen minutes after that, Check-suit and Toad are comfortably ensconced in a city pub, a pint of beer in front of each of them. Their preferred topics of conversation are the probable size of Ellen Fortune's breasts and whether she's really too young to be as good in bed as she looks as if she ought to be. They agree she'd knock them dead on page three.

*

In the corridors outside the Court, Ellen Fortune is trying to escape a gaggle of newspaper reporters. They press against her and hold microphones to her face, asking how she feels now, will she be going home to her mother's and will she be seeing her boyfriend again?

"Ellen! Ellen! What's it like for you being in love with your forty-four year old teacher?" calls one voice. A camera flashes and then another.

"This way, love!" yells another photographer. "Give us a smile and a bit of a wiggle, you know!"

"Ellie!" shouts a louder voice and this time one she recognises.

"Mike!" she cries with relief. "Help!"

He pushes his way through the throng towards her, elbowing and deliberately treading on toes and nudging cameras in order to make a passage. He grabs her hand and pulls her towards him. With his arm around her waist, he propels her down the rest of the corridor towards the glare of summer light out in the street.

Suddenly, they are on the pavement. Mike's car is bumped up on the kerb, its engine running and the doors open. A traffic warden is already bearing down on the scene.

"Sorry! Emergency!" he shouts. "Just delivering some runcible spoons to number one court!"

The Warden looks puzzled but assumes legal folk must know about these things.

Within minutes, they are out of the confines of the city and on the road south, heading for open country. Sellotaped in the rear window is a large, hand-drawn sign.

The pea-green boat
(Temporary substitute during repairs)

III PENUMBRAL ZONES

SEAGULL ON THE BEACH

It's over! The sun is high in the sky, she is with the man she loves and they are heading into tomorrow.

"Phew!" she says, slumping back into the seat, "time to relax!"

"So what was the verdict?" says Mike.

"Guilty," she replies.

"Thank God for that. I was beginning to wonder for a while, when it became clear a quick decision wasn't on the cards. Are you alright, you know? What sentence did he get?"

"I don't know. He'll be sentenced next week, apparently. Mike, let's not talk about it. He got what he deserved. That's it. I don't want to think about it anymore, especially some of the stuff that Sowerby said about me," she says with a pained expression.

Michael looks across at her, deciding whether to press the subject or to leave it as she has suggested.

"Worse than we expected?" he asks tentatively.

"Yes," she replies, "in his summing up or whatever they call it."

"But he's just doing a job; you know, trying to get his client off the hook. Anyway, the jury didn't believe him, did they?" Michael says reassuringly, giving her hand a squeeze.

"Depends how you look at it. Took them long enough to make up their bloody minds."

She says nothing more and Michael keeps quiet in case she wants to continue.

"You want to talk about it? What he said? It might help you to share the burden."

"Mike, I know you're trying to be helpful and all that. Thanks; I mean, it's really kind and loving of you but I really don't want to have to think about it or go through it all again." She stops and looks through the window, seeing the fields flash by but with her inward eye, still picturing Sowerby addressing the jury.

"You know, it's been like so awful; humiliating for me," she starts again. "And it's been hanging over both of us for nine months; given us sleepless nights and got in the way of our relationship. Let's just leave it; it's a long way behind us already," she says, raising a thumb to point over her right shoulder.

Michael simply nods.

"OK. I just thought you might feel better if it's out rather than in."

"No, Mike, really. Maybe later. At the moment, I just want to forget about it. It doesn't exist."

She turns in the seat, reaches for her large shoulder bag and begins rummaging in its deeper recesses.

"I got so hot and sticky in that court. I want a clean t-shirt."

As she finds what she is looking for, she notices his sign in the back window.

"Hey, what's that?" she laughs. "Just married or something?"

She screws her face up in an effort of concentration to read the lettering backwards.

"A little early," he says, "but it can now be arranged."

"This is the pea-green boat? Temporary version? Fantastic; oh, Mike, you don't know how much that bloody silly notice means to me. I love you so much, you know that?"

"Thank you," he smiles, taking his eyes off the road for a moment to glance at her.

"Where are we going anyway?" she asks, giggling. "Not Bath or bloody Keswick, I hope?"

"Correct. I'd like to say, in order to maintain the child-like fantasy which currently amuses us both, that we are going to the land where the bong tree grows."

"Aha! I looked all that up, because I just knew you would slip it back into the conversation and now I know what you're on about!" she announces triumphantly. "So, Owl, where's the honey, the money and the five pound note?"

"Well, lovely pussy, Oh, pussy my love, what a beautiful pussy you are, er, no, best not to talk about pussy if I'm driving! The honey is in the boot. Well, one jar of supermarket own."

"Really? You're having me on?"

She starts laughing all over again.

"Not yet, but there's time later. Money? Well, I have some in the wallet and loads in the bank. Plenty enough, anyway. The five pound note was more of a problem; or at least, the type that Lear was on about in 1870. They were like a newspaper in size in those days."

"Really?" she says, looking very surprised.

"Well, maybe not a newspaper, but they were pretty large."

"No, I'm on about the loads of money in the bank," she laughs.

"Well, as I say, there's enough. Let's put it like that. And you can have some if you play your cards right. I'll think of something you can do," he leers suggestively.

"I can imagine!"

"Not unless you can see into the darkest, lust-crazed recesses of my mind, you can't!" he retorts.

"You haven't answered my question. Where are we going?"

"Devon coast initially. Then we'll see. Proper, quality time on our own, don't you think? You know, no pressure, no secrecy, and no trial hanging over our heads. I've organised something for three weeks down there and that should give us enough time to decide what we want to do and where we want to be. Is that OK?"

It occurs to him as he speaks that he has set his plan in motion without consulting her at all.

"Mike, it sounds like heaven. I don't care where it is as long as it's not here or Keswick. Take me to it," she replies.

For some time, there is silence and Ellie relaxes back into the seat, closes her eyes and lets the sun on her face and the thrum of the engine caress her nerves. They have left the city far behind and are in open undulating country, its lush fields full of grazing cattle. Suddenly, Ellie sits upright again and turns back to Mike.

"What did you say, just then? I mean earlier? I mean about it being possible to arrange marriage?"

"Ah, yes, that," he replies. "I am now a free man. Decree absolute also in the boot. In a folder with other papers, I mean."

*

The sun is slipping down the sky by the time he turns off the busy coast road and into the much narrower lane that will take them to their destination. There are a few wispy cirrus clouds on the western horizon and already the sun is starting to suffuse them with a pale, pink and orange tint. He hopes they will be able to enjoy a sunset from the beach a little later.

He concentrates on the narrow road as it slips down into a wooded combe, looping through tight bends as it does so. At one point they pass through a dark tunnel of fern-draped, high stone walls with a canopy of trees overhead. What light penetrates here is filtered green.

At the end of the tunnel, the car emerges into a world enclosed by the combe behind them, the cliffs to either side and the glinting sea ahead. A pebbled beach is approached over a little stone bridge which spans a river which has run down the valley with them on its tumbling passage to the sea. As the car crests the hump of the bridge, Michael can hear the gurgling waters below and then he catches a brief glimpse of the rocks and stones in the riverbed.

He turns a final sharp bend in the road and then they are in an open area of grass in front of a low white-washed building. He decides to go and announce his arrival and collect the chalet key, rather than shaking Ellie awake, for she seems to be in a deep sleep. He gets out of the car, closes the door as quietly as he can and makes his way over the crunching gravel to the café where he knows there is also a little office which deals with the chalets and the occasional campers who pitch their tents on the field behind him.

*

"Ours is called 'Seagull'. Round the corner to the right there, under the cliff, on the beach. Our home for the next three weeks. Our love nest on the beach."

He starts the engine, reverses a little and then begins to drive around the front of the café.

"Look, see, over there," he points with one hand as the car moves onto a sand and gravel track leading along the highest part of the beach, under the cliffs. As they drive slowly away from the café, the track rises over a ridge of pebbles. Now the shimmering green sea and the beach can be seen clearly. Ellie gasps appreciatively.

"Oh, wow, Mike! It's beautiful!"

Several hundred yards further along, at the end of the track, there are four or five chalets; small wooden bungalows each with its own parking space and small area of grass in front. They are each painted a different colour: one is light blue, another a sea green and the one at the far end is a soft grey.

"This one is 'Cormorant'," says Mike, peering at the sign over the first chalet's door. "That one is 'Tern', so I reckon that ours must be at the end?"

"It'll be the last one! Let it be the last one, Mike! It must be, look, it's seagull colour; there, the grey one. Yes, it is! Mike, they're so sweet! Just look at the little balconies and each one's got matching colour, check curtains! Oh, I love it!"

Ellie is so excited she is bouncing up and down in her seat.

"Yes, this is the one," says Mike as he parks the car at the far side of the last chalet. "When I booked it, the bloke said it was separated more than the others from its neighbours and it looks as if it is. About twice the distance, I should say, and nothing on this side anyway, since it's the last one in the line. That's good. Must be the one they use for honeymoon couples so that other people can't hear the squeals of orgasmic delight. Probably built on stronger foundations too, to withstand the hammering it gets."

"Mike, you are just so romantic!"

She throws her arms around him and kisses him endlessly.

Once inside, they inspect the galley kitchen, the lounge with its bench seats, bookshelves and television set. On the walls are faded sepia prints of old photographs of the area, one showing the beach with clinker-built fishing boats winched up on the pebbles, all surrounded by grizzled, bearded men in oilskins and sou'westers.

The main bedroom has a window facing the beach. It is more like a ship's cabin than a conventional room since the bed is built into almost the entire space available, leaving just enough room to open the door and for a bedside cabinet and small wardrobe.

"It's, like, fitted. You can't walk round it. Which of us is going to sleep on the inside and climb over the other one to get out?"

"I can't get over a girl like you so you'll have to get out and make the tea yourself!" he says in a Goon voice. "Well, the cast-iron bladder of youth wins the inside place. I'm up and down like a fiddler's elbow, especially after a few beers."

She turns to face him.

"Mike, this place is just so lovely. Look, come and see."

"I know. Why do you think I brought you here? We can see better from the little balcony," he says, taking her by the hand and leading her into the lounge again. There he unlocks the large doors and slides them apart so that they can walk out onto the timber deck of the balcony. Here, the sound of the surf is louder and the clean, salt smell of the sea fills their nostrils. They lean together on the rail, for several minutes silently surveying the scene.

The bay is about three or four miles long and describes a gentle curve under the high cliffs behind them and beyond. The cliffs are topped by green fields and copses of trees. The occasional stunted trunk clings precariously to any ledge affording sufficient toe-hold. Ellie notes that the cliff faces are evidently eroding, for in places there are bare white and yellowish wounds where great chunks have sheared away, forming tumbles of boulders, earth and ripped shrubs at the base of the cliffs.

The ridges at the top of the beach are high enough to prevent them seeing the water's edge, even at high tide. An indication, Michael says, of the way the beach plunges rapidly into cold, green depths only a few yards off-shore.

The chalets are located about a half mile from one end of the bay's gradual curve. To the left, they can see no further than the field with the tent because of a high headland. Its hard, rock face looks defiantly out to sea, as if challenging the waves to pull its legs away. On its summit, they can just about make out two people standing, gazing out to sea.

At the other end of the bay, about a mile or more to the west where the sun is hanging above the sea, there is another high headland and then many miles beyond and above that there appears to be an area of much higher, flatter ground. It seems darker than its surroundings, Ellie thinks, perhaps because the highest points of the land mass appear to have been sucked up into the underbelly of cloud which hangs there.

"Dartmoor," Michael says, following Ellie's gaze.

"Really?" Ellie says, trying to recall to her mind a map of the south west of the country, but without much success.

"It's like in that film about the lost world," says Ellie. "You know, cut off from everywhere else. You can see out to sea and the cliffs and that's about it."

"Precisely. Timeless, in a way. Look, don't you just love the way that the afternoon light silvers the surface of the waves?" says Michael. "Constantly shifting, flickering, one moment reflecting a patch of sky, the next a fragment of cloud. No two days or seconds, come to that, can ever be the same, you see? There are an infinite number of possibilities; always different and yet always the same. Timeless."

Ellie looks at him admiringly.

"And I love your way with words, Doc," she says softly, kissing his cheek.

*

It takes only about an hour to unload the car, empty the various boxes, cases and bags and to organise satisfactory stowage places for their possessions.

"Well," says Michael, "now that we've set up the nest, how about something to eat?"

"You know, I felt hungry and was wondering what the time was and I've discovered I haven't got my watch." She holds up her arm to show him. "I think I've left the bloody thing on the shelf in Emma's bathroom."

"Oh, dear. Well, I suppose she'll hang on to it for you. Maybe we can get you another one," he says.

"Maybe. It's no big deal; it's only a cheapo. Anyway, I don't need one, do I? Not now. Not here."

"I suppose not. Steak and chips OK?" he asks. "With a bit of green salad?"

Ellie grins.

"Ace! My favourite. You've got some here?"

"I know it's your favourite. Surprisingly, that's why I bought it. In the cool box," he says, pointing to a blue polystyrene box which she had not previously noticed. "Organised it at lunch time. Oven chips, but they're not too bad. Red wine or white?"

"I'm not sure I like red wine," she says, artfully.

"Have the white then. It's sweeter. I like the red. Developed a real taste for it during all those holidays in Provence. Eons ago, in another life."

He takes two wine glasses from the cool box and a bottle opener and opens both bottles, pouring the white first, handing Ellie the glass before pouring a red for himself.

"Here's to us, then," he says. "The Idyll; our world and no one else's!"

She laughs, repeats the toast and they touch glasses and drink. Ellie thinks to herself that she cannot recall a moment when she has been happier.

Despite her desire to help, Michael insists that he should prepare the meal because she looks so exhausted.

"I didn't know you could cook," she says after watching him for a while.

"We never talked about it, did we?" he replies. "I mean, we've conducted our relationship thus far in my office, the back of my car, over the phone or during snatched hours in the holiday cottage in Applethwaite. Not in our own home, as it were, you know, proper domestic circumstances without a clock ticking in the background."

"Mmm, true. This wine's really nice," she says, licking her lips like a cat.

"Good. Anyway, I don't know whether frying a bit of steak and heating up oven chips constitutes proper cooking. What about you?" he asks.

"It smells pretty good to me. Yeah, I can cook. I quite like it. Enjoyed Domestic Science. Well, I did when we had Miss Forrester. Had old Mrs Watson in the fifth though, when Miss Forrester got pregnant. Fortunately, she was alright with me because I did as I was told and was quite good at her subject, but she could be a real cow, you know?"

"She was a real cow in the staffroom too, if it's any consolation," laughs Michael.

"I'm not surprised. What was the real story with Miss Forrester? I mean, she was really a miss and not married, wasn't she? And she did leave in a bit of an unexpected way, didn't she? The rumours were really flying. Spill the beans, Sir; go on, you can tell me now. We're both a long way from that place," she urges.

"I'm surprised you haven't asked before, given your nose for the salacious, lip-smacking stuff."

"Thanks, Mike! Well, it was years ago, wasn't it? I'd forgotten about it until now," she says, taking another sip of the Chardonnay.

"Yes, she was pregnant alright. And no, she wasn't married," replies Mike, chopping tomatoes into thin slices.

"Well? Who was the father? Come on, you tease, you know that's what I want to know!"

"Simon Dixon, Lower Sixth. As I suspect you suspected?"

"I knew it! That's what everybody said but none of the teachers would say, not even those you could normally get stuff out of like Mr. Hamley," she laughs, slapping her hand on the table. "What happened, exactly? There was this rumour about them being caught in the medical room."

"They were. It was very late and Ralph was locking up and he heard noises; you know, those kinds of noises, coming from the medical room. He opens the door and there they were: the lad with his trousers round his ankles and her on her back, gripping his buttocks as he was stuffing his little giblet into her roast turkey. All very embarrassing for everybody, I expect. Crawler Ralph goes running to the Head in the morning. Eric Staines then, of course, it was before Mr. Shit-Sutcliffe arrived. Staines tries to suppress it but he's worried about old Ralph blabbing when he's had a few at 'The Lion'. Then, a while later, she announces she's pregnant and that Dixon is the father and they intend to make a go of it together. So that was it. She left. Was encouraged to leave. Quickly. And leave the area, which I believe she did."

"Just as a matter of interest, how do you know it was a small giblet?! A giblet indeed!!"

She howls with laughter.

"I don't. Probably wasn't actually, knowing Sarah Forrester. Reputed to prefer them hung like a shire horse."

"You! You're so crude! Shame about Miss Forrester, though," says Ellie, "she was a good teacher, even if she was shagging the sixth form boys."

Mike puts down his spatula and turns to look at her, a look of surprise on his face.

"Boys? Plural?"

"That was the rumour. I was only in the third year though, so I was hardly tuned in to sixth form gossip then. You know what third year girls are like: it's all eye shadow and rivers of quim juice."

He snorts with amusement.

"Now who's being crude? That's the crudest thing from the mouth of one so young that I've heard for ages."

"It's true, though," she giggles, taking another gulp of the wine.

"Even though I was in the profession for more than two decades, Ellie, I didn't know that. Really? Well, you learn something every day. Is this all the girls or just you?"

"Like, girls do it too, you know. Between fifty and eighty percent of girls over the age of puberty. At least every week, apparently. I looked it up once," she says. "Bit of a wide range isn't it? Girls won't admit to it, I suppose. I'd say the eighty percent is more accurate. There's always a bunch of prissy girls."

"Ah! I see you're in that mood, then?" he asks playfully.

"What mood?"

"Blunt language! We're talking dirty this evening, are we? OK, then. It's certainly true that prissy is not a word I would think of applying to Miss Fortune! Anyway, I wouldn't be surprised if Sarah Forrester was shafting half the Lower Sixth. We thought we'd done a pretty good job at keeping the Dixon business hushed up. You know, big staff meeting; Eric and the Chair of Governors both threatening hellfire if anyone said anything; need to protect the school's image, blah-blah; can't have parents thinking that their callow sons are going to be seduced, have their dicks sucked, lose their virginity and give the rampant little cookery teacher a cream bun in her gas-fired oven. Here's one I prepared earlier, so to speak. Obviously it wasn't as hushed up as we thought. But then you never can hush things completely. Someone always blabs. Especially with stuff like that. Like they are, or were, about us."

"Was she rampant, then?" asks Ellie, giggling.

"Jesus, I should say so. You know that lighting technician's platform at the back of the stage? She was up there with Paul Smedley after the staff Christmas dinner one year. They were humping away like a couple of rabbits."

"Mr. Smedley?!" shrieks Ellie, beginning to laugh uncontrollably with disbelief. "But he's, well, he's old; I mean, he's going bald!"

"He's probably at least five years younger than I am, my sweet, and anyway, it's the knob that counts in that situation, not whether you are a barber's delight," says Mike, washing the lettuce in a colander. "The other blokes in the P.E. Department used to reckon that he might not be the sharpest javelin on the rack, but he was indeed the shire horse to which I alluded earlier. To whit, he has an enormous donger. No doubt she was aware of that reputation; hence the attraction. He was giving her a seeing to, no doubt."

Ellie is practically doubled over on the seat, laughing, the tears streaming down her face.

"You're joking! I don't believe it! Mr. Smedley! Anyway, how do you know?"

"No one else does apart from them and you now. Promise me on your word of honour you won't say a word," he chuckles, holding two fingers to his forehead like a wolf cub. "Dib, dib, or whatever it is."

"Your sordid secret is safe with me," she laughs.

"Thank God for that," he says sardonically, pouring himself another glass of Merlot. "The nation's moral security depends upon it. It might get out that sometimes teachers shag each other on school premises. Oh, yes, they do, you know. And by the nature of things, it's generally pretty hurried. Between lessons, breaks; and always with the imminent fear of bells or discovery. The bells, the bells! Adds a certain piquancy if you like that kind of thing. You'll find them grunting away, standing up in broom cupboards in the dark, bathed in that distinctive smell of floor polish. In fact, it's so dark that our frisky Miss knows not whether it's a mop handle she's grabbed or a dick. Excuse me, is this Cockfosters? No it's just my umbrella!"

Ellie is clutching at herself, her shoulders convulsed with mirth, as Michael gets into his stride.

"Or you'll find them fornicating in chemmy prep rooms, a shuddering, chalky passion dislodging their mortar boards and rattling the bottles of H_2SO_4; on the sweaty mats in the P.E. store, break-time coitus flavoured with the odour of sock and jock-strap; behind the hedge on the top field, in a ditch with old crisp packets and desiccated dog turds; in empty classrooms after the kids have gone, Miss on the teacher's table and Sir bracing his heels against the map cabinet or, as we have seen, on lighting towers at the back of the stage. Stores and cupboards are favourite, of course, but you'd be surprised at the ingenuity. And, as I say, speed is of the essence. A twenty minute morning break: a vigorous, five minute knee-trembler with Miss Fox in the book store; a couple of minutes cleaning up; two minutes to the staff room; five minutes for a cup of tea and you've still got plenty of time for a pee and to mark a couple of books. Yes, it must be kept secret; if it ever becomes public knowledge, there'll be questions asked in Parliament."

"Mike, for God's sake, stop it! I'm going to wet myself in a minute."

Michael smiles.

"It's being cooped up all day with horny teenagers that does it. Hormones in the atmosphere. Ten minutes in the place, breathing that air and all you can think about is how long it is to break time when you can press Miss Fox up against the dexion shelving and slip her an eye-popping crippler. Such a tension reliever; much better than paracetomol or stewed tea from the staffroom urn, you know."

Ellie is helpless with laughter, waving her hands feebly in the air.

"Anyway, back to Donger Smedley, squeezing his gargantuan icing bag and Fanny Forrester with her cherry-topped little rock cakes. Well, you see, I'd left something in my office and went the long way round for some reason. I don't know why. Anyway, I wouldn't have known they were there but for the fact that she was making so much noise. So I went to investigate. Well, you do, don't you? I could see her feet protruding over the edge of the platform above me. His too, of course. He still had his shoes on. High romance, eat your heart out. I knew it was her because of those ghastly lime green socks she used to wear. Well, her voice too, I suppose; she was squealing, "Oh, Paul, Paul, you're making me come!"."

"You're pulling my leg, right?" splutters Ellie, wiping tears from her eyes with the back of her hand.

"No, no word of a lie. It's not just sixth formers who feel each other up and orgasm, you know! Or third formers, according to your thesis. Anyway, I knew it was Smedley with her because there was only one person in the place called Paul and what's more I recognised his sarcastic voice. It was as much as I could do not to laugh!"

Michael chortles at the recollection.

"Well? Come on, what?"

"When she said she was coming he said something like, "Thank Christ for that, my knees are through to the bloody bone on this concrete!" and then the pair of them, well, you know, emitted sounds which gave me to understand that

197

their congress was mutually pleasurable and that matters had come to a head, so to speak. More wine?"

Ellie explodes with laughter, fanning herself with her hands again and going a bright red with the exertion of it all. Michael lifts the neck of the bottle and raises his eyebrows and she manages to nod. He refills her glass and then turns the steak and pours on some more pepper sauce.

"You just crease me up, you know that? My insides ache with laughing. God, what a turn-on, though, don't you think? Doing it on the lighting tower! Fantastic! Don't fancy the broom cupboard though. Hey, is that ready? It smells delicious."

"It is. In that drawer there is a table cloth and some napkins. Candles and candle sticks on the bookshelf. Will you do the honours? Be nice to have a bit of style, don't you think?"

"OK, boss," she says and quickly finds the things he has referred to and sets them on the table.

Although it is by no means dark, the candles give the meal a romance it might not otherwise have had. It is memorable for both of them. It is not the first meal they have eaten together, although there have been very few in conventional surroundings, but it is the first where they know that they have the rest of the evening, the night and the rest of their lives together.

Later, the meal complete and the dishes washed and put away, they walk hand in hand along the shore. They sit down on the pebbles, Michael putting his arm around her. She leans into him, once more kissing the nape of his neck and running her hand through his hair. He shudders with pleasure.

In the west, the setting sun suddenly finds a dream hole at the base of the bellies of cloud which have been slumped over the moor all afternoon. Shafts of orange and yellow light laser out across the sea and the bay. The breakers' spray is minute droplets of juice breaking the fruit's pith; individual pebbles cluster like oranges on a stall, glowing on one side and umbered on the other. The girl turns to look at the wonder of the scene, exclaims in delight and turns to share her excitement with the man at her side. Soft yellow light plays around the tresses of her hair and glints in the green of her eyes, giving her an ethereal quality which seems to mesmerise him.

"Ellie," he murmurs, "there's an almost surreal beauty about you out here tonight. Quite stunning. I'm not sure whether I'm awake or dreaming."

She lifts her eyes to his and says nothing but simply smiles, touches her forefinger to her lips and then places it on his.

"Ssh!"

He smiles back, understanding that she just wants to sit with him and hold the magic of these minutes, to try to make them forever, for such a scene of beauty is not granted as a commonplace every day. Indeed, the flare of sunset lasts only a minute or two before the clouds swallow the sun into their darkness again. As they do, a cold wind blusters suddenly from the sea. Michael pulls Ellie to her feet.

"Come on. Time to get inside," he says. "It'll be really cold out here in a minute."

*

In the early hours of the morning, Ellie mutters, stirs and then awakens. Moonlight is filtering through the gap between the cotton curtains and she can see the outline of the room and Michael's sleeping form beside her. He is lying on his back. She looks at him for a moment and then puts her hand out to place it on his chest, gently stroking him and beginning to run her hand over the edge of his ribcage and down to his belly. His eyelids move, imperceptibly.

"Mike," she whispers in his ear, flicking the tip of her tongue across his ear-lobe.

"Ellie? You were asleep earlier?"

"Ssh. I know. I was dreaming, Mike," she murmurs, her voice like the wind through dry reeds. "I was dreaming about the lighting platform!"

"What?"

"It was us; the two of us, not them up there. You know?"

She giggles and kisses his neck.

"Were we?"

She whispers, "I've been dreaming about it; we're up there, Mike. You pulled me up there. It's dark and a bit dusty, but we don't care. There's other people about; kids, but they can't see us. We're kissing, Mike and you undo my blouse. It's my school blouse, Mike and you can feel my breasts, yeah? And they're much bigger than you thought; much bigger! Because I've got on this flattening bra because otherwise the boys make remarks; you unfasten it and you pull off my panties..."

Michael grins to himself.

"Doc, make me come!"

And they both laugh.

*

Whatever noise the lovers will make, it will be drowned by the breakers thundering onto the beach. Whipped into a creamy spume by the wind, the surf crashes onto the shoreline, flecks of foam flying up the strand. It drags and swirls the shingle and pebbles, ceaselessly pitching one stone against another, endlessly, back and forth, round and round, long after the lovers have finished.

And it will do the same long after all the dreams and passions of generations of lovers not yet born are likewise spent; back and forth, endlessly, until all are ground to mere grains of sand.

SHIFTING SANDS

"Fancy that barbecue later?" says Michael, appearing from the bathroom with a towel around his waist.

"Yeah, why not?"

She looks out of the window. It frames a picture of horizontals: the bubbly line of the first ridge of pebbles, a strip of glittering blue sea and then the misted horizon under a duck-egg sky.

"It looks beautiful out there."

"Something wrong?"

She looks at him and smiles but doesn't say anything for a while. Eventually she puts down her piece of toast and speaks.

"Mike, this is like a fairy tale for me, you know? It's just wonderful being here with you and not being back there. Out of time, like, not even thinking about all that."

"I agree," he says quietly. "So?"

"Well, I don't want it ever to stop or ever to change and I don't want anything to ruin it and I'm worried that something might. Or someone. And I'm really pissed off that the worry is there. You know, the past coming back," she says, looking at him. "Do you see what I mean? Of course you do! Stupid question."

He smiles back at her.

"Not arrived in Lethe yet, then?"

"What?"

"Legendary river supposed to cause people to forget the past. Well, the past has a habit of sticking its nose into the present. History is the thing that is dead but which won't lie down. William Golding. Anyway, who do you mean? Your mother, I suppose?"

"I wish I was as educated as you!"

"I wish I was as young as you. You can acquire education; you can't acquire youth."

"Ha! Anyway, yes, Mum said she would make trouble for us, didn't she? We spent months under cover worrying that she might. Maybe now she has a reason to spoil it for us?"

"Revenge, you mean?" Michael asks.

"Yeah, I suppose. She can be really mean. But I really don't know whether she would and it's bugging me something rotten. So I've got to find out," she replies, her tone increasingly determined. "I think I'm going to phone her from the box by the café. She'll definitely be at home at this time. She never goes out until Benjamin's had his morning sleep. Are you OK with that? If I phone?"

"Of course. And for what it's worth, I don't think she will. Spoil it I mean. I don't know why because I don't really know her at all, but it just doesn't seem likely, somehow," he says. "Not now."

"I hope you're right! Anyway, it's time to find out and there's no time like the present," she says.

*

The telephone box smells strongly of urine, despite the fact that at least three panes have been vandalised so that sea air can enter the confined space. She heels the door open to try to let in more air, finds her coins and dials the number in Church Road. As the number connects, she wonders whether she is phoning home or whether she is merely phoning the place where her mother lives.

"Hello?"

Her mother's voice sounds strained.

Despite the stench, Ellie takes a deep breath. Her hand is shaking where it rests. "Mum, it's me, Ellie."

There is a pause during which she can hear her mother's breathing.

"Mum?"

"Yes," says Linda. "Ellie, where are you? Are you alright?"

Ellie is surprised by what seems to be a tone of relief or even pleasure in her mother's voice. This is not what she was expecting. An argument might have been easier to handle. She closes her eyes and can feel tears squeezing their way through the lids.

"I'm alright. Mum, this is hard," she begins.

"You're telling me," Linda says, her tone a little sharper. "But I'm glad you've made contact after all this time. Why are you phoning now?"

Ellie is having difficulty in reading her mother's attitude. She seems pleased, resentful and suspicious all at the same time.

"How's Benjamin?" Ellie asks. "I miss him, you know."

"Regrets already then, is it? Well, you made your bed of sin. Now you must lie upon it, " says Linda and then, in a slightly softer tone, "He's alright. Just had his breakfast. Growing fast now."

"I suppose he must be. Look, Mum, I'm in a call box and I haven't got much change so, well, I'm just going to say it and if it makes you hang up, then that's too bad."

Ellie sets her jaw, feeling that old need to assert herself with her mother.

"I'm not hanging up."

There is a long pause during which Ellie thinks she can hear her mother sniffling.

"You are my daughter, whatever's happened and whatever you've done," says Linda, her tone suddenly more conciliatory.

"I haven't done anything. Nothing I'm ashamed of or regret, anyway, whatever you want to think. How's..?"

"How do you think he is, Ellie? He's wretched, frightened and very depressed. The conditions are indescribable; degrading for any human being; awful."

The sniffling gets louder.

"Mum, I had to do what I had to do. I know it's hard for you and I'm really, really sorry for you because it's not your fault. But I know what happened that evening. I wasn't prepared to just say nothing, like you wanted. That would have been wrong. Maybe he'd have done it again; to me, or some other poor girl. But anyway, in the end the Jury saw the truth."

"I know."

Ellie opens her mouth to speak and then registers fully what her mother has said, or seems to have said.

"What?"

"Brian confessed to me, two days ago, when I visited. That what you said is substantially true. He did what you said. He admits it. To me anyway. Ellie, I..."

Linda can go no further and starts to cry.

"Oh, my God. Mum, Mum, don't cry, please!"

"Let me finish, Ellie," says Linda, recovering her composure. "I've spent the most awful two days and nights since he told me. Terrible. I have to apologise to you. I should have believed what you said. Maybe I believed it all along but I didn't want to hear it. The Devil works in a devious way. Brian said that he heard the voice of the Lord, telling him not to live a lie. Only the Lord knows why he has sent us this test but we must bear with it and pray."

Ellie rolls her eyes.

"Yeah, OK. I'm glad that the truth is out. So what will you do?"

"What can I do? I have to wait. It's hard; you know, people talking behind their hands, avoiding me in the street but, as I say, if this is God's Will, then it must be done. He has admitted his sin and asks for forgiveness. I must help him."

"But he raped me, Mum. I'm your daughter. Doesn't that count for something?"

"Of course it does. I apologise again, Ellie. I was wrong and I must ask your forgiveness too. He is my husband; you are my daughter. I cannot turn my back on him now he is repentant, Ellie."

"OK, OK. It won't be easy, Mum, I'm sure," Ellie says, still reeling from the news that her mother has imparted.

"Ellie, won't you come home? I need your support here; we can overcome this together; I'm sorry for what happened."

Linda's voice trails off into more crying at the other end of the line.

"Mum, I'm not coming home. Back, I mean. Not to live. Not after what's happened and even after what you're saying. I'm sorry, but I can't. Maybe I'll visit. I don't know at the moment," Ellie says quickly.

There is another long pause before Linda speaks.

"Where are you?"

Ellie, startled, realises that she doesn't know the name of the place. Mike went off at a tangent when she asked him. Somewhere in Devon; this is ridiculous, isn't it? Dartmoor! She looks across at the café but there is no clue in the lettering on its walls; she looks down at the telephone and at the panels on the wall of the box but identification marks have been scratched out, daubed with paint or otherwise vandalised.

"It doesn't matter where I am, Mum. I'm OK. I'm making a new life, away from all that. I'm happy," she says.

"How can you be happy, Ellie? Living in a state of sin. You're with him, I presume? Chadwick?"

"Get used to it, Mum please. This is how it is. His name is Mike. Michael if you want. He's a good man, Mum. We're in love, we want to be together. So we're happy. Simple, really. And we're going to get married," she says with a note of absolute finality.

"Don't be ridiculous, Ellie," her mother snaps.

This is more like it, thinks Ellie. This is the Mum I know of old. Had me worried there for a minute.

Linda continues, "It's disgusting. How can you, I hardly like to say it; with a man old enough to be your father? Well, I suppose…and what about his children? And his wife, poor woman. You're living in sin; I can't see it any other way."

"Oh, for Heaven's sake! Age has nothing to do with it. They're divorced now and I don't agree that it's sinful. We love each other. Period."

"You're only sixteen, Ellie, of course age has something to do with it," Linda says.

"I'm seventeen next month, Mum. I know what I'm doing. And so does Mike," she replies.

"I doubt it. But you've always been stubborn. There's not much I can do about that, I suppose, but I think you're making a very big mistake," says Linda.

"Mum, listen, my money will run out in a minute. I need to ask you something. Months ago you threatened to make trouble for Mike and me, remember?"

"Yes."

"You made it very difficult for us, sending me up to Cumbria, but we're still together. That should tell you something. Right? So, like, are you going to cause trouble? Before you answer, I want to say that I told you the truth about Brian and I'm telling you the truth now, right? My relationship with Mike began in October last year. Not before I was sixteen," Ellie blurts it all out in one go, conscious that her time must be running out.

"What you read in my notebook, which you stole, really, didn't you? They were stories. Fantasies. Not diary entries. Right?"

"I've got enough trouble of my own to contend with Ellie. I don't know how I'm going to manage for all these years. I was angry with you then. I thought you were making it up. Now I know you weren't. That's hard. Really hard. My husband lied to me. My husband did something unspeakably vile to you. I have to accept that, but he's still my husband and, as I say, I have to stand by him. He says he wants forgiveness and that he wants to repent. Thanks be to God. So we must pray. All of us. But you say you won't come home and maybe I have only myself to blame for that. I am between the rock and a very hard place. Why has God sent me this suffering if not that I should learn how to love Him more by praying for His guidance?" says Linda.

"I don't know how to answer those questions, Mum, you know that. I just need to know whether you're going to the Police about me and Mike. Whether you believe me this time. And whether you're going to try to stop us marrying. That's it really."

"Alright. I believe what you say about when your relationship, as you call it, started. I'm not going to cause trouble. It's time for healing. I cannot condone what you are doing in any way but, well, there it is. Better married than co-habiting, I suppose. At least promise me that you'll phone or write occasionally?"

Ellie hears her mother take a shuddering breath and she just has time to say, "I'll think about it, OK?" before the line goes dead.

*

"So that's about it," says Ellie as they walk along the beach. "She'll leave us alone. That's quite a weight off my mind. I couldn't seem to blot it out. I've managed to kind of forget everything else, but not that."

"It's a great relief, Ellie. Well done for finding out," he says.

"And as for the rest of it, well, I was gob-smacked. The bastard Perv actually admits it. To Mum, anyway, which is all that matters to me."

"Good," replies Michael, adjusting the bag on his shoulder. "Does it help to take some of the sting out of what you said Sowerby said in his summing-up?"

"Yes. I think so. Oh, I don't know."

"And it also means that any future communication between you and your mother will be easier. Now she knows you were telling the truth and her husband wasn't."

They walk on in silence for a while. Michael reflects on this turn of events and sees that it is bound to make Ellie feel calmer and it should surely help to restore her self-esteem after the battering it has taken.

For her part, Ellie wants to hope that her step-father's confession must undermine the foundations of Sowerby's argument although even now she supposes that there was an element of truth in some of what he said. But she decides, again, to push that particular matter out of her mind. It is a technique which she acknowledges in herself and one which she knows she learnt many years ago.

"How about this spot?" says Mike, breaking their silence. "No one for miles and it's reasonably flat just here and there's something to lean against."

206

He points at a large rock protruding from the pebbles.

"Yes, it looks great. I'm not sure I want to let the outside world, especially Mum, in to spoil this," she describes a wide half circle with one hand.

"No, I know what you mean," nods Mike, beginning to take plastic containers of food out of the bag.

"I didn't want to lie to her and say that I would phone every week or something when at the moment that's definitely not what I want to do. Have you made any contact with, you know, your kids?" Ellie looks at him.

"Do you mind if I do?"

"No, no, not at all. I'm just curious. It's not their fault that suddenly their Daddy is not at home because he's run off with a sixth form girl and everybody's whispering about it? Or they were. Like you say, I expect it's calmed down now," she says quietly. "I remember how I felt when my Dad buggered off. He didn't contact me for months and months. I don't know; awful. Don't punish them, Mike."

Mike stops and gazes out to sea. He notices a large container ship pushing east up The Channel. It is many miles off-shore and seems suspended in haze.

"No, it's not their fault, you're right and I feel really bad about it. I mean, I feel guilty. I suppose I ought to phone. Or write, at least. But, like you, I don't want to break the spell. We're being very selfish, doing what we want to please ourselves. Causing other people a lot of pain in the process, aren't we? My kids; your mother, just for starters."

"So it makes you feel so bad that we have to stop?" she asks.

"I didn't say that. I just said it makes me feel guilty sometimes. And you can't really deny that we are being self-indulgent."

Ellie sets her mouth in a firm line.

"Mike, I'm just not going to think about that, OK?"

"OK. We'll have to one day, though."

"Maybe. One day, then. Not today; let's not spoil today. It's just so perfect here today. The sound of the sea, the sun. And us, together. It's all I ever wanted, Mike, you know?"

Ellie looks at him and smiles radiantly.

"It is perfect. You're right," he replies looking up and down the beach.

There is a heat haze beginning to rise from the pebbles as they absorb the sun's rays.

"You know what? This is really weird," says Ellie, rolling up the legs of her already brief shorts and taking off her blouse to reveal a skimpy bikini top.

"Mum asked me where I was and I realised I don't know where I am. The name of this place. Like, how daft can you get? I haven't a bloody clue where we are and we've been here more than a week! I mean, I know we're in Devon because I remember you saying that on the way here and I know that's Dartmoor way down the coast, but apart from that, I'm out on that sea. Like, adrift in an open boat. What would I do if we got lost and separated and I had to find my way back alone?"

She laughs at the thought of it and looks around at their surroundings.

"Oh, well, yes, er, point me to the beach with pebbles under the cliff and, er, the rock that sticks up. It's got a white bit on the top that looks like fossilised snow! Some chance. They'd think I'd escaped from an asylum."

Michael, laughing, leans on the rock next to her and takes her hand.

"It does look like fossilised snow, now you come to mention it. If you got lost, there wouldn't be any shortage of helpers, if you were dressed like that," he says, indicating the bikini top. "Stunning! So, you don't want to know the name of this place, then?"

"It's going to sound stupid, but no. It might shatter that spell. I mean, I'm sure I'll see it written up somewhere sooner or later, but for now, no. I'm happy to be living in limbo. Or the land where the bong tree grows. Lethe or whatever you called it? You, me, the beach, the sea and the cliffs. Paradise."

She closes her eyes and stretches out her arms, enjoying the sun on her face and body.

"Well, you'll be pleased to hear that Paradise has been extended. While you were in the phone box, I nipped down to see Mr. Butler at the caff and managed to book 'Seagull' for another month. Until the end of August. He had to juggle some other bookings around but he managed it. I hope that's OK?"

She throws her arms around him.

"Alright? Mike, you are the most wonderful man. Of course! Bliss! I could stay here forever. Just like this."

"And we can have it longer than that, if we tell him soon, he says. You know, if we want."

"Yes," says Ellie, "forever."

He slips his arm around her waist and they sit looking at the lazy surf, indolently shuffling stones and strips of kelp at the waterline. Further out, the horizon has all but disappeared in the heat haze; the container ship is a whispery grey smudge and the only clouds in the sky are those still resolutely clutching at the moor.

"What about this barbecue, then?" she says, nudging him in the ribs after they've been sitting in contented silence for some minutes.

"I feel so lethargic! Not like me at all. Must be the sea air, do you think?" he says.

"More likely to be sex at two, three and four in the morning," she giggles. "You're not getting enough sleep, poor old man!"

"Mmm. Could be. I'm just so horny in the early hours."

Ellie laughs.

"Yes, I had noticed."

While he is starting the fire and beginning to unwrap the chicken, she wanders off to the water's edge and stands looking out to sea, one hand shading her eyes from the glare beginning to bounce off the water as the sun approaches its zenith, the other hand resting on her hip. After he has successfully lit the fire and placed some twigs on the charcoal, Michael looks down the beach to the girl. She is just so beautiful, he thinks. Let me be with this delightful, affectionate, intelligent and warm woman forever. I know it's impossible, but, please, just this once.

He has joined her at the water's edge and puts his arm around her waist.

"Look!" he says suddenly. "Seals! Can you see them?

"Yes! Look at their little snouts! They're so sweet!"

"You wouldn't say that if you were a mackerel, just about to have your head ripped off to make an hors d'oeuvre! There, that one, see? He's looking at you!"

"Is he?" she says, surprised.

"You know what that Big Daddy seal is saying, don't you?"

She looks at him and grins.

"I'm getting used to your sense of humour now, so I can probably guess."

"He says he didn't know that melons could grow by the sea!"

She slaps him on the shoulder and turns to run back up the beach. He grabs at her arm, slides on the pebbles and topples into the surf, soaking himself from the waist down.

"Shit!"

"Serves you right, lech!" she squeals.

He recovers himself remarkably quickly and scrambles up the pebbles behind her. With a supreme effort, he throws himself forward in a kind of rugby tackle and manages to grab her heel as she too begins to slide on the stones. He pulls her back towards him and envelops her in his arms. She resists in only a token fashion. They kiss and he runs his hand down her back and onto her bottom.

"Mike! Stop it! We can't do it here! You'll get us arrested," she laughs. "Although I must admit, the idea appeals. Outdoors, you know!"

"Alright. I'll see what I can do," he laughs.

An hour later, they are both leaning against the white-capped rock again, contentedly chewing on the barbecued chicken, the tomatoes and some garlic bread which Mike has been keeping hidden in the bag as a surprise.

"You know that old photo in the chalet?" she says, licking her fingers. "Like, all the fishing boats and all those hairy fishermen?"

"Mmm?"

"I reckon it was taken up there, by the café, you know? It looks the same as the picture, except that the building wasn't a café then, by the look of it. But everything else is the same. The cliffs, the beach, the sea. When do you reckon that picture was taken?"

"Turn of the century. 1890's even."

"As long ago as that?"

"I should think so. They'll all be all dead now, some drowned out there, I expect," he points out to sea with a half-chewed chicken leg.

"When those men were standing there that morning, the photographer froze that second of their lives and no doubt they noted it; talked about it for a moment or two, but it went. They returned to their own lives and concerns: you know, would they get back alright from their trip, would they catch enough so that they had enough to eat tonight, would their children survive disease into adulthood, would their house stand another storm. Earthly cares. And now? What was all that worrying and fretting for? It doesn't matter anymore, as the man once sang."

"Yeah. Like we're all just specks in the plastic dust-pan of time."

He laughs.

"Where did that come from?"

"I made it up."

"I like it. And those fishermen in the picture, as they looked along the beach towards Dartmoor, what do you reckon they saw?"

Ellie picks up another piece of chicken and studies it for a minute and then turns her head to the right to look along the beach.

"Well, the same as us. It hasn't changed, has it? OK, some rocks have fallen down and trees have got bigger or got blown over in a storm, but it's actually still the same view, isn't it? I 'spose."

She looks at him as she sinks her teeth into the chicken leg.

"Actually, there's lots more trees in the picture than now. On the cliff top. But even so, it's still the same. You can see that it's the same place even though ninety years have gone by."

"That's right. As we were saying the other day about the light on the sea, it's the same but minutely different. You couldn't say the same about any town or city scape, probably, after ninety or more years."

"Funny places, aren't they, beaches? I mean, they're kind of land but they also belong to the sea sometimes. They are like they are because of the sea so they're kind of sea too but they're not permanently under water. Depending on the tide and stuff, they can be one or the other. Or both. Or neither. Do you see what I mean? I was thinking about it yesterday. Sad, aren't I?"

"No, not at all. The penumbral zone. Nothing's clear; everything's shifting."

"Yeah, I know. J.G.Ballard. You mentioned him in the first lesson last year, remember? I went and read some."

"I am suitably impressed."

"Good. Anyway, on the beach, like, you're in a place which exists but doesn't exist, isn't that right?"

She looks at him for confirmation.

"Could be. Your thesis; expand on it," he grins.

"Yes, Doc. Well, there are boundaries, like the water's edge or the cliff or these banks of pebbles? But they keep moving. But you can't actually see them move, in a way. Well, the tide, maybe, but it's a bit like watching paint dry. So you can't, like, measure the space precisely. And like, it's then and now and tomorrow as well. The same but different."

Ellie stops and takes another bite of chicken.

"Does this make sense or is it just, well, crap? So people, like the fishermen, move across it but nothing really changes. Although they do themselves, of course and eventually they die, like you say. But the beach doesn't and yet it's always changing because it can't be permanent either. It just can't be. It has to change all the time. But you can't really see it changing. A mystery. Do you see?"

Mike looks at her and nods.

"Well, they call it the Jurassic Coast, you know. So it's been around a while. Maybe it is the land where the bong tree grows," he laughs. "A place that sounds like we ought to recognise it, but it eludes us somehow."

She looks at him and smiles and then leans across and gives him a chicken-greasy kiss on the cheek.

"Bloody hell! This is getting a bit deep, isn't it? Feels like an English lesson. Did you bring any beer?"

"Yes, I did. So you're drinking now as well as swearing and living in sin with an older man?"

"That's right and I love it!" she cries.

"I don't know; you'll stop going to church next."

He turns to reach into the bag for the beers and as he does so, out of the corner of his eye, he can see that the clouds over the moor are a brooding, ominous slate-grey.

It is with some surprise that he recognises that a storm is brewing.

BUTTERFLY IN THE MEADOW

I can't remember how many weeks we had been there before it was my birthday. When I was seventeen, I mean. I suppose it must have been four or five but it was difficult to tell at the time. Like, you know, we lost all track of what day it was. No, we didn't; we knew if we cared to think about it. But we didn't need to know and we didn't want to know either. There was lots of stuff we didn't think about. We lived self-indulgently inside our heads. Inside each other's heads. That was the limit of our world; a timeless world on the pebbles.

Anyway, of all the days during that time, I think maybe my seventeenth birthday stands out most clearly in my mind. It was a fantastic day. After you've been living like, on the beach for so long, you can tell from the smell of the sea and the feel of the air at night what's coming the next day. The sea air there has almost got a texture. You sort of get tuned in to the natural signs like the colour of the water or the shape of the waves or the type of cloud over to the west. It's not always the same.

On that morning I woke up really early, about six and I just pulled one curtain to the side a bit because Mike was still asleep and I didn't want to wake him. I was kneeling on the end of the bed and just looking out at the beach and the sea and it was perfect. The light was beautiful that day. Mike taught me to think about the light; to notice what it was doing. There had been no wind for some time and the sea was almost still and silent. Quite unusual there. There were just a few gulls over near where they winch in the boats. They were sliding about on the air currents, kind of like hang-gliding over the beach and then across the sea. White scythes with a blue background, Mike used to say when we saw that. He could always find the words to describe something so beautifully. I think maybe I've learnt some of that stuff from him. I hope so.

After I'd been looking out of the window for a few minutes, I climbed over Mike, because I always slept on the inside. He was still fast asleep so I put a full kettle on the gas and went to have a shower.

I was only in the bathroom about five minutes so I was surprised to find him sitting in the kitchen, the coffee made, when I came out.

"Good morning, beautiful," he said and gave me that smile that he used to do with his mouth a bit lop-sided. He didn't always do it and he said he didn't know when he was doing it or when he wasn't. But I was! It used to send shivers down me and it had done since I was about fourteen and he did it in assembly one day. What a turn on! Whenever he had that smile you knew there was something up his sleeve.

"Happy birthday," he said and reached under the table and brought out this package all wrapped up with gold paper and a red ribbon.

I didn't know quite what to say because it was so unexpected. I mean, not just him being in the kitchen when I thought he was still asleep, or the fact that he'd obviously bought whatever it was on his last trip to Bere and concealed it from me, but I suppose the truth was I had kind of forgotten it was my birthday anyway.

He didn't say anything else but just sat there, looking at me and smiling that smile and occasionally running his fingers through his hair.

I said something silly like, "Oh, Mike, thank you, it's really sweet of you. You didn't have to, you know."

"But I did," he said. "So are you going to open it or shall we spend the day looking at it on the table?"

I think it must have been then that my suspicions were aroused that something was going on because he seemed really excited, like a child. More excited than I was. And he'd gone from deep sleep to coffee-made to creating a little moment in less than five minutes.

I sat down on the opposite side of the table and looked at him again and then down at the package.

"What's going on?" I said.

"Like the man said, open the bloody box!"

I usually tear wrapping paper to shreds but I removed this very carefully. There was a long narrow box inside. It had a hinged lid and a tiny, delicate gold catch. I flipped the catch and lifted the lid and saw the most gorgeous diamond necklace you have ever seen in your entire life. He knew his jewellery, did Mike. It had been beautifully made, not stamped out by a machine. I took it out of the box and just sat there with it in my hands, the diamonds twinkling in the morning light. It felt as though I'd been staring at it for ages before I looked up at him looking at me.

"Mike, it's beautiful. Really, really special. Thank you. I love you; not just because of this itself but because you care enough to give it to me," I finally managed to mumble rather inadequately, I thought.

I shall never forget what he said then. Well, there's a lot about that day I will never forget but some of it is sharper in my memory than other bits. He leaned towards me, kissed me very gently on the mouth, took my hand and looked right into my eyes.

"It's special because you're special to me, Ellie," he said softly. "The last month or so has been the most wonderful thing. I know we laugh and joke about, well, the physical side of things and, you know, that is incredible for me, the best, but it's not just about that. I'm entranced by the whole package, not simply the body."

I felt as if I was going to cry and couldn't say anything because my throat seemed to have closed over. Finally, I managed to get some words out.

"Mike, you know I feel the same. Thank you so much. But where am I going to wear it?" I said, laughing. "On the beach when we barbecue the mackerel?"

"Well, I may be able to help there. That's one surprise," he said quietly. "There's another one, if you're up for it?"

I just looked at him quizzically. From his pocket he took a plain, white gold wedding band to match the engagement ring I already had and which I had not taken off my finger since the trial and our freedom from surveillance.

"I've put everything in place for us to be married later this morning, if you'd like. Hooken Registry Office. Twelve o'clock. What do you think?"

I felt my mouth open and close about six times. I remember feeling icy hot and my legs started shaking. A large bee had come in through the door. It was blundering about by the window trying to find a way out. Weird, the things you remember, sometimes. I can still hear that bee's low-throttle noise and the way it thudded softly against the glass while Mike looked at me, waiting for my reply. I picked up the wedding ring and looked at it.

My reply wasn't long in coming. I'm not sure there were words to start with, it was more a scream of utter jubilation before the words came tumbling out. I expect the people in 'Tern' must have thought we were having sex for breakfast again, I was yelling and jumping about so much.

I've often thought about that morning over the years. I mean, you can see why I reacted as I did. I was, after all, a young girl desperately in love and to be swept along like that was just so romantic. That's how I felt at the time, there is no doubt. Some people would say that Mike had a bloody nerve just setting things up without telling me. Control freakery they call that kind of thing now, don't they? I suppose I might see it that way, if it happened now. I don't know. Maybe it would be nice to have the chance to find out! But when you're young and crazy with love, you do crazy things. That's how it's supposed to be, isn't it?

Of course, I had said to him that afternoon, months before, in the car in Cumbria, when he gave me the engagement ring, that he should get a wedding organised. So he had! It's just that he kind of forgot to tell me!

Anyway, he'd thought of everything, I had to hand it to him. When I started, after about ten minutes, to panic and worry about what I was going to wear, he led me to the spare bedroom and opened the wardrobe door. He'd bought me a really lovely blue outfit: a little high cut jacket and a pencil sheath skirt which flattered my figure. I liked to think I was fashionable but actually I was rather conservative in my tastes. I'd seen it in a shop in Keswick months previously and he'd gone back without me and bought one in my size. And then kept it hidden. Ditto shoes, blouses, little gloves: the works. Now what kind of man does that? Yes, I know, it depends on how you want to see it.

Well, I wanted to see it as I suppose many seventeen year olds in that situation would see it on their birthday morning, living in a little wooden chalet by the sea with their handsome older man. Like the pages of a novel, wasn't it? I don't mean that Mike was manipulative: he wasn't. He wasn't manoeuvring me into a corner. He wasn't like that. No. That's clear to me now although there did come a time when it seemed that way. No, he was nuts about me and he liked to get things organised and, yes, alright, sometimes the age-gap thing meant that he'd go ahead and do stuff without involving me, as he might if I was his daughter. Maybe that was inevitable but he wasn't deliberately and schemingly trying to trap me in marriage.

What's more, I was a spirited enough person at sixteen, seventeen to have told him where to get off if I had wanted to. Definitely. I didn't want a white wedding in church with all that hype. I never had. I had more or less severed links with my mother and my father had more or less severed links with me. I wasn't going to have a big family wedding, no matter what. Like Mum said, I'd made the bed, etcetera. Part of lying on it meant that my wedding to Mike would be a small affair; just the two of us, whatever. So I was I happy. Like ecstatic, in fact. It was what I wanted and it was the most wonderful birthday present to go with that divine necklace.

I remember in every detail that breakfast time and the hours that followed, as we rushed about getting ourselves ready and going to Hooken; and also I remember the walk back along the cliff top from Bere and where we stopped in the meadow. Clear as that August morning's light on the sea. But I don't really remember the wedding itself very clearly at all!

The room where we got married was pokey and painted dark green. It was grubby. It smelt vaguely of cats and I wondered how that could be. I remember that the Registrar looked me up and down and then looked at Mike. Gave him that knowing look that men give each other sometimes. Same with the bloody witnesses. I mean, we didn't have any, did we, and it seemed to be the one thing that Mike had forgotten. We all make mistakes!

So he went up to this guy from the previous wedding! They were all standing about taking pictures when we arrived and Mike asked if he and his wife would mind doing the honours. The wife looked at me and didn't quite sniff, but bloody nearly. Her husband looked at me, stripped me with his gaze and then turned to Mike and said he'd be pleased to help. And I could tell what he was thinking, too. Something like, "You lucky bastard! Look at the tits on her! And I'll bet she fucks!" You know, the sort of things men say to each other when they think women can't hear.

So we went in, the words were said, and we came out. All over. We were Man and Wife.

"May I offer my congratulations?" our leering witness said, not very subtlely trying to peer down my cleavage.

"Bloody hell," said Mike as we stood outside. "I've spent more time queuing up to get through the checkout at Tesco's!"

We both laughed. Mike asked someone from the next wedding party to take a picture for us because the leering guy said he had to shoot off. This woman had a bit of trouble with it and the photo is wonky and out of focus. I've still got it. It's the only photo of that day and when I look at it, it makes me cry.

You can see how proud I was from the way I'm standing. And that's how I felt. I was really proud to be his wife. The necklace is very clear. And the ring! And you can see my figure in that outfit too. It surprises me now when I look at pictures of myself in my teens. I mean, I've still got quite a good figure now, I suppose, but you know how it is when you're in your teens. And, the other thing, of course, is that I do look very young. Seventeen, but only just! Fourteen years ago.

I don't think Mike can have a copy of that photo. We had only the one developed at the time and I've got the negative as well. It seems a shame. Maybe he wouldn't want one.

"Congratulations, Mrs Chadwick," Mike said to me and we had this terrific snog right there on the pavement with people all staring and clapping. Awesome.

Then we went to this little French restaurant in a side street somewhere and had a wedding breakfast of French sea food and wine. It probably wouldn't have mattered if it was a burger and chips. Sometimes what you eat is, like, eclipsed by the occasion and anything would taste amazing. This was amazing anyway so we were in heaven. We sat there staring into one another's eyes dreamily and chewing on moules and swigging wine. It seemed like hours but it can't have been because the sun was still quite high in the sky and hot when we came out.

Then we did this really amazing thing. Just before we left the restaurant, Mike asked if I'd like to change into my jeans and a clean t-shirt. Er, right, I thought. Now what? He had a change of clothing for both of us in his shoulder bag. After we'd changed he asked the restaurant guy to get a taxi and we went to Bere, not back to the beach. The taxi dropped us right at the bottom of the High Street by the harbour. Just for a few minutes, I thought we were going to take a boat ride but that wasn't what Mike had in mind.

"I thought a stroll along the cliff top back to the chalet would be good," he said. "Beautiful views, we can walk off the wine too."

Walking just for pleasure wasn't something I was much into before I was with Mike. Well, teenagers don't much do they? But Mike got me into it and of course walking around there was fantastic. We'd walked to and from Bere before so it wasn't new, but that afternoon it turned out to be very, very special.

The beginning isn't all that because you have to go past this caravan site. Whenever we did, Mike said it was an abortion despoiling the Heritage Coast. He used to lead off a bit about that kind of thing sometimes. Anyway, after you get past the caravan site, the path sort of climbs up a bit and you can look back at Bere harbour. Really pretty. But the best bit is another half mile along as you come round Bere Cap and you're up above the sea on top of the cliff, like, on the same level as the seagulls and the cormorants. You see the world the way they see it.

We looked back towards the town and the path that goes round the harbour and looked at the little figures there.

"Small figures dwarfed by a dramatic landscape," Mike said. "Like us; a big day in the bigger landscape". Or something similar.

"So did you arrange the weather as well as everything else?" I asked Mike as we strolled over the grass on the Cap.

"Ordered especially," he laughed and squeezed my hand. "I know you like big fluffy clouds as you call them so I organised for some to be swanning about over the sea. Galleons with billowing white sails."

As you walk over the Cap, the next bit of the cliffs is fenced off to stop you going too close. Great chunks of it keep falling away and it's not really very safe. Sometimes I dream that I'm standing on a cliff like that and then I can spread my arms and jump out and fly around the cliff face and over the waves with the birds. I mean, I can sense the currents of air under me and feel how I have to move my arms to change direction or like, flop my legs down to come in to land and stuff. It feels real and yet I've never actually flown, have I, so how does my brain know how to make the dream feel real? Weird.

After a while you get past the bit where it's all collapsing and you come to this really wide, flat area of grass. We'd walked past it about three or four hundred yards and Mike started to veer off to the right, away from the cliffs.

"Where are you going?" I said. "The path's this way, isn't it?"

"Trust me," he said and smiled, holding out his hand for me to join him.

Well, I trusted him, of course, so I followed. We went down another path which sloped away from the big grassy area. We came to one of those, like, kissing gate type styles and then the path split and we went to the left. The right fork was the one that was used. You could see from the way it was worn to the earth. To the left, it wasn't. It was obvious that people didn't go that way because the grass was high and hadn't been trodden down at all.

"Hey! Where are you taking me?" I said.

The path, if you could call it that, was so narrow and overgrown that he was in front of me. He turned and looked at me and gave me that lop-sided grin again.

"You'll love it, I promise. Not far; just through there."

He was pointing to a hedge in which there was a small gap. Again, it was clear that the only things going through the space were rabbits. We squeezed through to the other side. We were in a small meadow. It wasn't very big really; I mean more the size of a pony paddock or even a large garden. It was completely surrounded by hedges, elder trees, hawthorn bushes and scrub elm. You couldn't see in any direction at all, not even back the way we had come in. It was like a forgotten world; I don't know, as though the farmers around there had thrown up fences or whatever and were tending the other sides but somehow this funny patch had escaped their notice. No one had been in there for years.

The grass was about knee high and was full of all sorts of wild flowers. I'm not too sure what they were but the ones I remember best were a very bright blue. I think Mike said they were either cranesbill or scabious but he wasn't sure either. "I'm not a bloody botanist!" There were splashes of red and yellow too.

There was a breeze which caused ripples and waves in the grass as it blew across the meadow. You could still smell the sea and you could hear the gulls too but although the sounds were not coming from that far away, they seemed very distant and slightly unreal.

"Oh, Mike," I said, "it's magical. How did you find it?"

"Pure chance. You remember a few days ago I walked to Bere from the chalet? Well, I saw the path back there and wondered if it was a shortcut that would take out the corner by the Cap. I came to the fork and something made me explore down here."

"Amazing!"

"I knew you'd like it," he smiled.

I walked into the meadow a bit further and then sat down in the grass. I took off my shoes and then stretched out on my back, looking up at the sky. I remember that there were two vapour trails, sort of high up in the blue which crossed each other. For a few moments I thought about all those people five miles up, going wherever they were going, oblivious to the newly married couple lying side by side in the meadow. Aircraft fascinate me that way. Little worlds in the sky.

Mike had joined me down in the grass. I have a very clear recollection of two butterflies, red admirals, I think, which danced into our little clearing. They both alighted on blades of grass and seemed to look at us for a while before the two of them lifted off together. Mike said they were dancing an airborne sardana; a Spanish dance, that is.

We just lay there for some time, looking up. The butterflies disappeared from view. It was a beautiful few minutes of quiet. As I looked at the grass rising on either side of me, it seemed that the individual blades were much higher than they were in fact: as if they were soaring tens of feet into the sky and I was lying in like, a flickering green building with blue lamps in the ceiling. I began to wonder whether I was hallucinating or whether the waiter at the restaurant had slipped something in my wine!

"It's like a church," I said after a while. I hadn't explained what I meant or anything but Mike knew what I was on about. It was like that sometimes, especially with those highly charged moments.

"Makes up for the Registry Office, you mean?"

"Better than a real church," I said.

Mike sat up, took his shirt off and then bent his head towards me. He kissed me as I'm sure he had never kissed me before. That sounds just so slushy and stupid now, like the words of that old sixties song, but I'm sure it's true. Really. I remember that he put his hand under my neck and lifted me towards him so that it felt like he was carrying me or I was floating in a green boat.

We kissed for a long time and then, very slowly, he began to undress me. I say it was slowly because that was the thing that kind of surprised me for two reasons. Usually, we were so frantic for it that the clothes came off in seconds, if they were on in the first place. I mean, he always slept naked and I would have only a little top or something. But if it was during the day, and it often was, then we'd almost be tearing at the clothing in our hunger for each other.

The other thing is, well, I found then and I still do that I usually get most aroused if it is a bit frantic. I mean, I like foreplay and all that but I like the man to show his urgent desire, if you see what I mean! I come on quite strong then. It puts some guys off, though. They can't handle it.

But that afternoon in the meadow, our wedding afternoon, was more highly charged than any other occasion I'd experienced before. Or since, come to that. And we were going slowly. And the incredible thing is that Mike knew what I was feeling and behaved accordingly. I mean, after our clothes were off, we just lay there kissing and caressing and kissing for ages and ages and I began to feel really dizzy with it. If you've not experienced that, you've never loved. I don't mean horny or desperate for it or aching for the sensation of penetration. I mean dizzy. Like, light headed. And it wasn't the wine. It was kissing the man I loved beyond all sense or reason. Sometimes that's what love is. I haven't felt like that ever again. It was so special.

So, that afternoon in the meadow, after what seemed like days of kissing so that I thought I was going to lose consciousness altogether, we made love. Slowly, agonisingly and excruciatingly pleasurably for hours. Or so it seemed. Who knows? We lay there, gently rocking in the tender green arms of the grass until we were spent.

We made love in the meadow with the butterflies overhead and the grass swaying with us. It wasn't having sex or rutting; not just fucking. Oh, yes, we had done all of those things. Many times but not that afternoon. No, we consummated our marriage by making gentle love in the meadow and it was the most beautiful, serene and ecstatic afternoon of my life.

And thinking about it now makes me cry even more than looking at that ghastly photo!

I don't know how long we lay there. It was a long time, because the sun dropped under the cliff and suddenly we felt cold. I suppose the light was going to dusk by the time we'd dressed and found our way back to the cliff path. It was almost dark when we arrived back at the chalet.

We sat in the little kitchen for a while. Mike lit a candle. He'd do that sometimes and we'd just sit in the quiet of the evening, maybe watching the reflection of the moon on the sea. He opened a bottle of wine and although we'd already had more than enough for one day, it felt like the right thing to do. After a while of silence, he just touched my hand. I turned from the window to look at him. I realised that he had been watching me and not the moonlight.

"Thank you, Ellie," he whispered. Just that. Nothing else. But I knew that he meant thank you for marrying me, thank you for loving me, thank you for making love to me. All that. I knew it then and I knew it later; a lot later, and I know it now. I didn't feel I needed to say anything. I just leaned over and kissed him again, like before in the meadow.

Then he took my hand and led me outside onto the beach. The day had been perfect and so was the evening. The sea had been calm and flat all day. It still was. The moon was above and below: two yellow discs, one held rigid in the sky and the other shifting very gently on the surface of the sea.

We walked along the pebbles for a while, almost to the flat spot where we had the barbecue. Mike stopped, turned to me, put his arms around me and began to hum a tune, very quietly, as we began to move together under the stars.

"And hand in hand, on the edge of the sand," he started to sing, "they danced by the light of the moon, the moon, the moon..."

I laughed for the utter joy of it and kissed his chin so as not to stop him singing.

"...they danced by the light of the moon."

And we did, for ages. I wish I could go back to that night again.

Later, he couldn't sleep and he got up in the early hours and sat down at the kitchen table and wrote me a long love letter. I'm not really sure why he didn't give it to me the next day; perhaps he intended to write more. Maybe he felt that some of it struck the wrong note. I don't know. But I didn't know about it then or actually read it until many months later.

Maybe that changed everything.

SQUIRRELS UNDER THE ELMS

Sometime during the week following our wedding, we decided to go for a long walk up the West Cliff above us, to the top end of the village to 'The King's Head' pub. You have to go the opposite way to walking over the Cap to Bere.

The path starts just behind the café and it rises incredibly steeply to the top of the West Cliff. Just before you get to the top of the path there is a vantage point where the view is simply amazing. It was one of our favourite places. There's one of those seats that you find in spots like that: half a log nailed onto two shorter bits of log that are the legs. We must have spent hours sitting there in the morning sun during the weeks we were living in the chalet.

It's right on the edge of the cliff and, surprisingly, there was no fence or safety rail at all. I could indulge my flying fantasy for hours there! Sitting on that seat you could see the whole world. Well, our world anyway and that was enough: the curve of the bay right back to Dartmoor with millions of wet pebbles by the water's edge; the fields of The Cap because West Cliff is higher than The Cap; sometimes you could even see rabbits nibbling away over there, their little tails bobbing about in the sunlight. You could see back up the combe about a mile, a couple of thatched roofs half hidden in the trees and, of course, you could see miles out to sea.

We liked to watch the ships in the far distance. I think they intrigued us both. They always were a long way out and so they were always, like, fuzzy because of the heat haze or the mist or something. I mean, you could see they were ships but somehow you couldn't quite make out their exact outline and if the sea and the sky had rubbed out the horizon, the ships appeared to be suspended in a kind of milky space.

Mike liked walking behind me on the climb up. He liked to watch my backside!

"What a magnificent, tight little bottom you have," he'd say. Or, "There's nothing quite like a pert young rump!" That kind of stuff. He was always saying that kind of thing. He was a very physical sort of guy, I suppose. And then he'd give it a little slap or a squeeze.

"What makes a rump pert, then? I mean, what is pert?"

He laughed.

"Well, firm, I suppose. Quite high off the thigh, rounded and small. Not flat to the back. Not slack and wobbly. Like the haunches of a filly. Almost by definition, only to be found on young women and girls," he explained, smiling his seductive smile.

"I see. So now I'm being compared to a horse?"

"Just to illuminate the definition for you, that's all."

"Oh, well, that's alright, then," I said with mock sarcasm.

"Interestingly, I believe that there are not only age criteria here but also ones of ethnicity. So, for example, young African women are rarely pert since they tend to be quite large in the buttock department; southern Mediterranean girls are pretty good; I'm especially inclined towards the girls of Provence; but Asian girls are probably the best. My brother spent some time in the Far East and he reckoned that teenage Filipina and Thai rumps are world-beaters; small, round and tight," Mike said, adopting the same tone I had been used to hearing in the classroom. He was swinging my arm with his hand and kicking idly at pieces of twig and sticks on the path.

"You're unbelievable. A dirty old man, some would say."

"I'm sure. Let them say it; they're probably right. Who gives a tuppeny?"

"You shameless old lech!"

"Probably. Now, would you care to hear my full exposition on the delights of the rock solid, flat belly?" he enquired.

Men! What can you do with them?

We didn't generally linger over much going along that path because it could be quite chilly. The trees are close together and they cut out most of the sun, so it's a bit gloomy and dark too. We liked it later that year, in the Autumn, when some of the leaves had gone so there was more light. The leaves smelt nice too. Well, I thought so. Mike didn't like it; didn't like anything to do with Autumn very much. He found it depressing.

"The season of piss-wet mists," he called it.

Then you cross a couple of fields before the path splits in about six directions under several enormous elm trees. Elm Corner, we started to call it. Sometimes, we'd stop there and watch for the squirrels. There must have been a nut tree around somewhere because they were always busy nibbling.

'The King's Head' is a very old building; one of those places you come across in the West Country that's at least four hundred years old, is made of stone and the people who built it didn't have a plumb line or a spirit level and were permanently pissed. Or all three. We got there at about one o'clock and it was quite busy. It could get very crowded, especially at the weekends and during holidays because the tourists and local hoorays had found it. The building is sideways to the road and at the front are some rustic type tables. The car park is at the back and to get to it, people have to drive their bloody four-by-fours across the front, right by these tables, which spoils it all a bit.

Through the open door, I spotted a small table vacant by the inglenook so I nabbed it while Mike went to get the drinks and order some sandwiches. Of course, I wasn't eighteen but lots of pubs didn't seem to worry too much about the law on underage drinking, especially in the country. I think it's stricter now. Anyway, I looked a lot older than seventeen.

There was quite a crowd at the bar and Mike had to elbow his way to the front to get served. After a while, I couldn't see him properly. He was lost in the scrum. I just sat there, like, twiddling my thumbs and pretending to be fascinated in the ceiling or the pictures on the wall or something.

I could sense people looking at me which made me feel a bit uneasy. As we'd arrived at the pub, we were holding hands. We got the usual quizzical or critical glances. Mike said he wasn't going to pretend that we weren't an item when we were.

"People can think what they like," he said. "Anyway, we're married now. Flash your ring and give the old biddies the finger."

Of course, men looked at me anyway, not just because I was with Mike. I took to examining the grain on the table top and began re-arranging the beer mats.

I first noticed the two guys after I'd been waiting for Mike about five minutes. They were sitting on the other side near the door. They looked like locals: they seemed very relaxed and they had cow-shit on their boots. One of them was quite short and he had a spotty face and ginger hair. He was constantly fidgeting about and his boots were dropping crap and slime on the flagstones.

The other guy was much better looking, taller and slimmer. He had dark curly hair down to his shoulders. Actually, if I'm honest, I'd have to say he was very good-looking. And he knew it. He had that cocky manner about him. And I mean cocky. He was leaning back in his chair with his legs wide apart. He was watching me and when he saw me glance in their direction, he winked at me and smiled. He had very good, even white teeth.

I could feel myself blush straight away.

That wasn't really like me, to blush so easily. I don't know why I did. Something to do with the way that Curly looked at me. I was wearing just a white, v-necked t-shirt and a pair of tight jeans. What was I supposed to do?

Wear a bloody veil? Have them cut off? Why do guys have to watch you and leer like that just because of the size of your breasts?

I felt that he could see right through what I was wearing. I could almost feel his hot, beery breath against the skin between my breasts. Very sort of physical. Don't know. I can't explain it.

Curly said something to his spotty friend, adjusted his crotch openly and Ginger laughed a sort of smutty laugh. Then Curly lifted his glass and tipped it up and towards me and raised his eyebrows, miming, "Want a drink?"

I was quite annoyed about it. I mean, they must have seen me come in with Mike, so what were they playing at? I decided they must have thought he was my father and that it was OK to make a pass, especially while he was out of sight.

I frowned and shook my head, lifted my left hand, pointed at my rings and then pointed in the direction of the bar. For some reason, Curly seemed to find this very amusing. He threw his head back and laughed loudly. As I turned my head away from them, I saw out of the corner of my eye that he looked at me again and made a kissing movement with his mouth. Ginger guffawed like a donkey.

I just sat there, avoiding their gaze, fuming and going hot and cold. Stupid. I wouldn't let two shit-covered farmhands make me squirm like that these days.

"Christ," said Mike as he put down two beers and some crisps on the table, "I'm sorry to have been so long. There's only one bloody barman who is a useless little tosser. Cheers!"

I picked up my glass and took a sip.

"Cheers," I said.

"What's the matter? You look like thunder."

In a fraction of a second I decided to say nothing of the little incident with Curly and Ginger. I didn't want to spoil our day and I knew Mike would get excited if I told him.

"Oh, it's alright," I said. "Some woman built like a tractor trod on my foot on her way out just now."

"Ah! On her way to get the harvest in," he said, drawing deeply on his glass again. "What do you reckon to the beer? It's a local brew called Happy Jack, apparently."

I forced myself to return to our previous light-hearted mood. I took another sip of the beer.

"Well, I'm still in training where beer is concerned, aren't I? But, yeah, it's not bad. Quite sort of fruity? Why is it called Happy Jack, I wonder?"

After about half an hour, we began to form a theory about that. We noticed that everyone in the bar was laughing. I mean, there were all sorts of chuckles, shrieks, guffaws, gurgles and giggles beyond what you might normally expect to find in a pub which is collectively enjoying itself. We were laughing too in that silly, back of the classroom way that you do sometimes for no particular reason. And you can't seem to stop.

"Either it's a very high alcohol content or they've put magic mushrooms in it or something," Mike slurred.

A girl appeared through the throng, carrying a tray with our lunches on it. She paused in the middle of the room, looked round expectantly and then emitted a squealing noise.

"Two 'am'n'cheese sallids!"

Mike put his hand in the air, as if he was about to ask to be excused.

"Please Miss, over here, Miss!" he chortled.

It wasn't particularly funny, but I couldn't stop laughing. The tears were rolling down my face. As I was wiping my eyes, I happened to see through a gap in the throng that the guy with curly hair was still looking in my direction.

"Tell me, Hayley," Mike was talking to the girl as she unloaded the tray. She had a name badge on her chest. Mike was staring at it; or maybe he was just clocking her boobs.

"What do they put in this beer? Do you know?"

"Do what?" she squeaked.

"The beer. It seems to be having a strange effect on everyone. What do they put in it?"

Hayley looked at him as if he'd just asked her to describe the basics of jet propulsion or something.

"Ay? I dunno. It's me uncle's pub, innit? I'm not from rahnd 'ere. I'm on me hollidees, like, workin' in the kitchen," she said and turned on her heel. Mike and I looked at each other and laughed much louder than the remark justified.

"Don't you just love the local Devonian accent?" Mike said and we started chortling and hooting all over again.

There was a bit of a lull at the bar and so Mike shot over and bought two more pints and two glasses of wine! He said he thought it wise to stock up. We ate the ham salads and carried on drinking and giggling. I did my best not to look in the direction of the door, hoping that the two guys would drink up and go.

"This beer is sliding down very acceptably," said Mike, pushing an empty glass to one side and starting on his third pint. I was going a little more slowly but even so I wasn't that far behind him.

"You'll be drunk," I said.

"And if you drink too much beer, you'll get fat," he retorted.

"And then you won't find me so attractive?"

"With nearly three pints of this on board, everything and everyone looks attractive," he said, but I knew he was avoiding my question and not for the first time either! He only ever looked at young women. Or girls. So what would happen when I was thirty and slightly over-weight, I wondered?

"I need a pee," he announced. "Won't be a minute."

The toilets were in an adjoining building so you had to go outside to get to them.

Curly watched as Mike got up, pushed his way through the crowd and disappeared through the door. Then he looked at me and smiled. I felt trapped because I knew what was going to happen and I was powerless to stop it. He got out of his seat and came over to our table. I could see from the way he was walking that he'd probably had one too many. Very deliberately he sat down in Mike's chair and looked at me. It was the kind of look that said he wanted to strip me and have me.

"Look," I started to say, "that..."

"...seat's taken," he said quietly. He had a very gentle voice and he smiled as he spoke. "I know. I saw your Dad. I've been watching you, you know."

"I had noticed," I said and then immediately wished I hadn't acknowledged that I knew what he'd been doing. I had tried to sound pissy but it came out wrong somehow.

"I'd rather you didn't. And he's not my father. Please go back to your friend before my husband comes back. Otherwise there'll be a scene."

I tried to emphasise the word "husband".

"Just trying to be friendly. No harm in that, is there? Your husband, ey? He's a very lucky man, then, with such a beautiful young wife," he said, his eyes flicking deliberately to my cleavage.

"We're both lucky," I said rather feebly.

He seemed to consider this for a moment.

"Mmm. Maybe one of you's luckier than the other? You visitors? Or just moved in around here?"

"No," I said, that way not giving a satisfactory answer to any of his questions. I was still trying to sound annoyed but my voice seemed to be coming out in this strange, little girl way. I was starting to feel really uncomfortable because I knew Mike would be back any moment. Afterwards, I realised I should just have got up and gone outside to find Mike, but I didn't. I just sat there. Worse.

"How old are you? Quite a bit younger than you look, I reckon," he grinned. "I bet you're not even old enough to be in here drinking that beer. Yeah?"

I tried to give him one of Tracey's really scathing looks. It obviously didn't work because he burst out laughing.

"Sugar and spice and all things nice, kisses sweeter than wine," he sang, pursing his lips into a kind of kiss again like before.

"My name's Dave, by the way. How do you do?"

He put his hand towards me. Like a complete bloody idiot, I shook it. I mean, it was kind of instinctive, wasn't it? I should just have ignored him and looked the other way but I didn't. I shook his bloody hand instead. And then I did something even more stupid.

I told him my name and then I started giggling. It was because he'd started singing; I mean, can you imagine? In a crowded pub like that? And I suppose I'd decided that he didn't actually mean any harm. You know, he was just like the boys at school, wanting to chat me up. Like, yeah, so what? He was just a bit merry with the beer. He looked at me cheekily and he knew that I thought he was good looking and he knew that he was being really forward and a bit out of order and that there wasn't too much I could do about it. Like, it was so out of order it wasn't out of order at all. And, I don't know, maybe I was flattered or something, even though I didn't want to be. Hard to explain.

It goes without saying that it was at that precise moment that Mike came back from the loo. And found his wife giggling and holding some guy's hand. Oh, shit!

He stood completely still, as if he'd been freeze dried, in the doorway. Then he crashed through the people between us and almost landed on our table. He had this really weird expression on his face; I'd never seen him look so angry before. Dave looked a bit startled because, of course, he had his back to the door and didn't see Mike coming. Mike grabbed the front of his t-shirt and hauled him upright.

"What the hell are you playing at? Leave my wife alone!" he yelled.

He was really red in the face and sort of spitting. I'd never seen him like that and I didn't like it.

"Hey, man, calm down!" Dave spluttered.

I put my hand on Mike's arm, kind of, to restrain him, I suppose.

"Mike, it's alright, he was only..."

"Calm down? Listen, you long-haired spunk-rag, this *is* calm, right?"

Mike had Dave's face pulled to his own and was snarling at him.

"But if you don't fuck the hell off and leave my wife alone, you'll see really angry and then you'll feel a sharp pain as my knee hammers into your stinking, over-active scrotum! Got it?"

By this time one or two men were moving towards Mike to haul him off Dave and the publican was shouting something from the other end of the bar.

"So now fuck a long way off!" shouted Mike, giving Dave a push and a shove which sent him tumbling onto the floor, almost knocking over the three people nearest us.

"Mike! Leave him alone, please! Someone'll get hurt," I screamed.

"Oi! That's enough!" shouted the publican, arriving as Dave was trying to stand up. On account of the drink he'd had, he was having some trouble. His face was looking really thunderous. Ginger was holding on to him. I suppose he felt humiliated being pushed over by someone older than him and in his own local as well. I could see there was going to be trouble.

"Mike! Leave it, let's go," I said.

I thought Mike was going to ignore me, but he paused, looked at me and dropped his arms to his sides.

"OK, right, come on," he said, grabbing my hand and pulling me towards the door. "Please accept my apologies, Landlord. Although the fault lies with Hairy Tampon there."

Within only a few moments, Mike was striding up the path we'd come down earlier. I could tell that he was still fuming by the way he was carrying his shoulders .

"Mike!" I said several times, "please wait for me! Slow down, I can't keep up at this pace."

But he didn't slow down at all until he got to Elm Corner. Quite some way from the pub. I'd fallen a long way behind him and it took several minutes before I caught up with him. He was standing in the middle of the path, his back to me, his hands on his hips, like, panting with the exertion of the climb.

I slumped down on the grass under the trees, clutching my side. I had a stitch. I wasn't sure what to say or do. I could see Mike was still angry and I didn't know whether to say anything or keep quiet. We'd not been in that situation before. I decided to say nothing until I could see that he'd calmed down. It was very quiet, except for the leaves in the elms, whispering to each other. One of the squirrels appeared and sat on a log, watching us. After what must have been at least five minutes, Mike turned and faced me.

"Why did he come over to our table?" he said, surprisingly quietly.

"I don't know, Mike," I whined, probably rather petulantly. "He just did. I couldn't stop him."

"Why didn't you tell him to piss off?"

"I did. And I made it clear I was married and that you were my husband. Twice. He didn't seem to take any notice. I'm sorry, I suppose I didn't handle it very well at all. But it's not that big a deal is it? I mean, I thought you were going to kill him!"

He turned and looked up the path for a while as if thinking about that. Then he turned to face me again.

"Look, Ellie, I'm not stupid. I know men are turned on by you. Your body. They're bound to be. I've seen the way they look at you. Some of them are going to try it on. Inevitable. I suppose I have to expect that and learn to live with it, although it's hard. It sometimes feels threatening. Maybe I didn't handle it too well either. I don't usually get myself into brawls, you know. Sorry. It must be the beer."

"Mmm," I mumbled. I couldn't think of anything sensible to say or that wouldn't be likely to make him angry again.

"But answer me this and then I'll try to forget it," he said. "Why were you holding his hand and why were you laughing like that?"

"Mike, it really isn't such a big deal as you are making it. He was just some half-drunk guy who staggered over to try to chat me up when he saw you'd gone out. You know how it is. He held out his hand to introduce himself and, like a fool, I shook it. I mean, instinctive, you know how you do? Stupid, I suppose, was it? Sorry," I replied, looking down at my shoes. I did think he was over-reacting, to put it mildly.

"Laughing like what?" I added.

"Giggling. Simpering. Fluttering the eyelids, Ellie. Like you were enjoying the attention," he looked at me searchingly. "Not at all like you were telling him to piss off."

I didn't quite know what to say. Well, I had been giggling. Perhaps I had been enjoying the guy's silly flattery. Maybe I am a tart, I thought; back to the stuff they said about me at the trial. I could feel tears in my eyes.

Mike must have seen the tears too because I saw his face soften. And I knew that he knew why I was about to cry. If I'd wanted to, I could have manipulated the situation then by bursting into tears but I held them back because I didn't think it was right to do that and Mike deserved an answer. It was an understandable question, after all, although I did feel a bit confused about why he was going off on one so much.

A squirrel was sitting on the log with its tail in a big question mark. It was waiting for my answer too.

"Mike, I'm sorry, truly I am. I wasn't leading him on. He was staring at me earlier when you were at the bar and when we were eating. I tried to make sure I didn't look in his direction in case, like, he would think I was returning his grins and winks and everything. When you went outside he just got up and parked himself in your chair. I did ask him to go away, really, Mike. He's persistent. I suppose he did flatter me; well, like you say, he would, wouldn't he? I was going to get up and come outside but I didn't. I don't know why," I said, the words tumbling out of me between sniffs.

"OK," he said. "But you seemed to be enjoying the attention."

"Mike, sometimes you forget that I'm a teenager. I'm seventeen. Just. You know, like I'm a silly girl. I try not to be and to be grown up and a responsible married woman and stuff and I think I manage that quite well but I can't always do it. So I'm flattered, maybe, by cheeky young lads. Most girls are, even though they might be resisting it or feeling that someone is taking liberties. So, I giggle when I shouldn't? Embarrassment, maybe. Apprehension in this case, probably because I knew you were coming in any minute! I'm a bloody kid, aren't I?"

Mike didn't say anything but just kind of paced about under the trees, kicking at the earth and twigs. One of the twigs flew off when he kicked it, making quite a noise which startled the squirrel.

Mike was obviously thinking about what I'd said.

"Are you jealous, Mike?" I said to him softly.

He came over to me and sat down beside me.

"Ellie, of course I'm bloody jealous. But more than that. I'm frightened of losing you. Sometimes I'm really frightened. Like just now, I think."

He looked at me and I could see wetness in the corners of his lovely eyes.

I think that was the closest he ever came to telling me what was bugging him.

"Mike, you idiot. We've been married less than a week. I haven't stopped loving you since last Tuesday, have I? Tuesday, was it?" I kissed him on the cheek. "He was just a cocky lad who'd had too much Happy Jack. Let's not make it into a big deal, please?"

"No, alright. I'm sorry. Sometimes I think I love you too much," he said.

I decided not to ask him what he meant by that. Instead, I smiled as he took my hand and we stood up to go. I thought it was best if we just forgot about it all. Pushing stuff away was what we both did best then.

I looked up into the branches of the tree and saw that the first squirrel had been joined by its mate. They sat together on a curving branch, watching us walk arm in arm down the path.

It made me feel better.

SHADOWS

I wish Dad could have met Ellie. He'd have been bowled over by her. Not just her looks; he'd also have loved her directness and her enthusiastic, spirited approach to life. What they now insist on calling "feisty" if you look in the Women Seeking Men columns of the local and national papers. Every woman over a certain age; about twenty three, reckons she's bloody "feisty". Men, of course, would call it "arsey".

People are like linguistic sheep these days, all following along using the same words as everyone else. "Cool," for example. Bloody pathetic.

Ellie was seventeen when we got married at Hooken and I was forty four. But it didn't feel like that kind of difference. Not to us, anyway, not at the time. She was overjoyed. It took only about twelve minutes but even so, it was a romantic ideal; for both of us, probably. It was a strange, unreal time.

When Barbara and I got married in 1973, it was months in the planning and every fiddling detail was of supreme importance. She wanted us to be married because she was twenty four and time was, "Getting On". She had to, "Settle Down" and I had to, "Make An Honest Woman Of Her," and then, "Put Our Future In Bricks And Mortar". I shouldn't blame Barbara, really. Our generation operated in accordance with accepted markers like that. You work your way through the various stages for forty years and then collect a pension and a truss, "potter" for a while before becoming "frail" and finally you shuffle off this mortal coil. Jesus, what a life sentence!

Ellie's attitudes were different. Ceremony and ritual suck. Today is more important than tomorrow. Bugger yesterday, that's for has-beens. Pleasure without conscience, even. Hedonistic, I suppose but immensely liberating suddenly to find yourself swimming naked instead of being pulled under by the weight of the water in your boots.

Ellie didn't care that she had no part in the arrangement of the wedding, such as it was. She didn't care that there was no fanfare of trumpets, confetti, bouquets, ribbon cutting, speeches and the statutory disco with Whitney Houston's, "I will always love you". What she cared about was that I loved her enough to make the commitment. I think that for Ellie, the trappings were always immaterial.

What happened in the pub that afternoon shook me and made me really worry about us as a couple. It made me realise that I felt threatened whenever other men showed any interest in her. That I was, in effect, on the defensive, feeling that I had to repel boarders. Not relaxed and confident, but on my guard. Maybe it was that fear that was behind my decision to bring her to the beach in the first place: trying to find security by stepping outside time.

I'm sure now that there was nothing of any great significance in what happened in the pub that day. I was angry. Mostly, I was angry with the tosser for trying it on in that bloody underhand way as soon as I'd left the bar. As they say, I just saw red.

I was angry with Ellie too, although I don't think that she deliberately set out to flirt with the bastard. But her generation saw things differently. They didn't conceive so much of "possession" in a relationship, as my generation did, or does. A girl or a wife can go out with her girlfriends and flirt idly with other men and it doesn't mean that she's going to cheat on the boyfriend or the husband. It's what they do; part of their social milieu. It's not a deal-breaker, as Ellie once said.

I was also angry with myself: angry because I lost my temper, angry because I had seen things out of all proportion and angry that the incident threw this element of our relationship into very sharp relief. Much of what Old Nibber had said to me months previously went through my mind in the hours and days that followed and, if I'm honest, some of the things which Barbara and even Sutcliffe had said. Young men would always challenge me for her affections. Like that pride of lions!

In reacting as I had, I was as good as saying that I didn't trust her completely. Maybe I was showing that I didn't properly understand her and that I was not confident about her love for me. And she knew that. I think the whole thing underscored my own lack of confidence about whether a marriage with such an age gap and therefore with such different attitudes to these sorts of things was really viable.

But if I'm honest, there was more to it than any of that because I had begun to harbour niggling doubts about Ellie herself.

She once asked me, on another occasion, what men thought sex was for. I said that in my opinion most men didn't indulge in sex to make babies; that's a side effect. For most men it's probably about pursuit, penetration, possession and ejaculation – release. Love too, one might hope, or something sanctified by marriage but that is probably less of a pre-requisite than it is for women, especially as the years go by and the old social mores about how women are supposed to behave sexually are eroded.

She thought about that for quite a while.

"Love is really great and sex wouldn't be as good without it, probably, but I'm not at all interested in babies. I expect that will change. Am I a bit of a slag, then, to want to be penetrated and to achieve orgasm? As priorities?" she asked. "Women are not really supposed to *want* sex or enjoy the animal side of it, are they? It's alright for lads but if a girl wants it and shows that she does, then she's a whore. Yeah, I know that nowadays that attitude is being questioned, but I still feel that I'm a tart sometimes."

I made some remark about Victorian attitudes and the controlling influence of the Church over the centuries but she was only half listening.

"Or that I could become a promiscuous tart quite easily."

I was a bit taken aback by that and I didn't want to talk about it. I'm not even sure that she did, really. Obviously, we should have done. But we didn't really talk about lots of things, including the incident in the pub. We were too frightened to allow the emotions some space. They just festered below the surface, for both of us. What we set in motion later that afternoon was a further attempt to create a timeless dream-world. It was probably about as far removed from what we ought to have done as you could get.

Hindsight! What a wonderful thing.

LOOKING OVER THE CLIFF EDGE

We walked together, our arms around one another for some time before either one of us spoke. It was as though we just needed that physical presence to reassure ourselves and to soothe the grazes we had given each other. Grazes, I think, not wounds.

"Let's explore, Mike, shall we? Maybe there's another way back to the beach; you know, another path along the cliff top closer than this one where we can see the sea again?" She was grinning at me, tugging at my hand and bouncing up and down on her toes with excitement. She looked so beautiful.

"I love you," I said. "And I'm sorry for doubting you."

"It's OK," she said quietly. "And I love you too. And I can see the lust in your eyes, Mike, and no, I don't think this is the place! That beer is powerful stuff! Isn't it supposed to have the opposite effect?" she laughed, pulling at my hand again. "I seem to remember something about that in 'Macbeth' in the third year but you kind of skated over it."

"Come on, then," I said, "let's see if we can cut a swathe through the jungle. The cliff and then the beach must be in this direction. Yes, there is something about that in 'Macbeth'. The porter at the castle says that drink inflames the desire but takes away the performance. You remember? The brewer's droop speech, they call it at Cambridge."

"Well, I remember that I thought I knew what it meant but I wasn't sure and you seemed in a hurry to skip over that bit! Not that I would have asked of course. My mousey period, wasn't it?"

I laughed.

"I probably was trying to skip it. Older school editions of Shakespeare had all that kind of stuff edited out, you know, because explaining the likely effects of too much beer on the achievement of a boner, as you lot used call it, could be a challenge with year three."

I think that's how we dealt with tension sometimes in those days. There'd be a period of silence, one of us would say sorry, we'd kiss or make love or get into the sexually explicit banter which we both enjoyed.

The track we had found didn't get any easier to negotiate, but it didn't get more impenetrable either. Evidently, it was used occasionally. After about ten or fifteen minutes of disentangling ourselves from brambles, we came to a small clearing. Here the dense, snaring undergrowth was replaced by a mass of ferns, their gentle fronds moving imperceptibly in what little breeze managed to find its way down into the place.

"Do you think someone lives down here?" asked Ellie, sounding apprehensive.

"Maybe not someone, but something," I said in my best Hammer Horror voice. "The wolf man of West Cliff, who feeds on the ripe, swollen breasts and pert buttocks of nubile girls."

I squeezed her backside as she was bending down to pull away another bramble.

She squealed and slapped my hand.

"Stop it, you're frightening me, going on about werewolves. And don't you ever think of anything else except nubile girls?"

"No. When I do stop, you'll know I'm dead."

We pushed ahead. The going was now more difficult and for some yards we had to bend double to get through. I began to wonder whether we were going to have to retrace our steps when the track suddenly arrived at another clearing, this time much larger, where it formed a t-junction with a second, slightly wider track. We stood in the filtered sunlight, looking to the left and the right.

"Which way now?" said Ellie.

"Well, the sun's ahead of us to the south so presumably we need to go to the left so that we end up somewhere near where we want to be," I said. "I wonder whether this path actually gradually picks its way down the cliff to the beach somewhere? You know, maybe down into that gulley we've seen from the beach, further along from the fossilised snow rock."

It seemed to me that the track was descending off to the left and we surely couldn't be far from the top of the cliff. We couldn't see it, but we could smell and hear the sea and somehow one sensed that the cliff edge was very close. It was unnerving.

"Mike, look!"

Ellie's voice was an excited whisper. Ahead of her, partly obscured by a curtain of ivy, was a small gate in a high fence made of branches, rotting pieces of plywood and rusting tin. At one point, just to the right of the gate, what looked like the bottom of a dinghy had been wedged into place to form a rudimentary fence panel.

"Wow," said Ellie, "do you think someone lives there?"

"Doesn't look like it."

This shack was obviously completely abandoned and had been for some time. About half of the flat area around the shack was at least knee-high in grass, brambles and nettles. The window facing us was hanging open. We stood looking at it for a little while.

"I'm going to look inside, if I can," said Ellie.

"Maybe the owner's dead in there."

"Bloody hell, Mike!" she squealed. "Don't say that kind of thing!"

She hesitated momentarily but then the excitement of the moment overcame any fear that my facetious remark may have engendered. She was at the broken window, peering into the gloom of the shack. I looked too but it was difficult to make out much of the interior. The window we were craning through was obviously at the back of the building. There appeared to be at least two other windows on the front but they had heavy cloth hanging over them. I moved away from the window and could see that there was some evidence of a path going around to the other side, presumably the front, of the building.

I followed it and came to the other side of the shack where there was a verandah arrangement and a door. The verandah was set at right angles to the cliff face which I thought was odd until I realised that it probably wouldn't be a good idea to have the door facing the winter's blasts. The verandah was on the opposite side to the overgrown track leading from the cliff path and so one had a sense of complete privacy there. It would be possible to sit by the door, look to the side to the sea and also admire one's little garden. Delightful.

I leaned on the door. It opened after a bit of a shove, the rusty lock giving way immediately.

It looked as though the structure was formed from a large shed or agricultural building. Surprisingly, it seemed basically sound, presumably because it had at some several times in the past been liberally coated with tar and creosote and the like. One could only think that someone must have dismantled the original building and then hauled it here in pieces before re-assembling it.

There were two rooms: the largest was an all-purpose living room and the smaller of the two was a bedroom. Whoever had lived here had left without making the bed, such as it was. It was strewn with some crumpled, grey sheets and a couple of those rough, abrasive blankets that I remember from my post-war childhood. The whole thing was covered with filth and cobwebs suggesting that it had been abandoned for some considerable time.

"Spooky," said Ellie, looking into the bedroom. "But I like it."

"So do I," I agreed. "Why, though? I mean, it's a hovel, isn't it? You'd use it as a dog kennel or a tool shed if it was in your garden at home."

"Maybe. It'd clean up quite easily, though. A few hours of soapy water and a broom. Where is home, anyway?"

She looked up at me from her kneeling position on the floor where she was inspecting an old range or stove at one end of the living room.

"You could cook on this, I reckon."

"I suppose so. Imagine someone heaving that bloody thing down here. Or up here. Maybe they used a wheelbarrow. The floors are concrete! They must have had a barrow or a trolley of some sort, surely? Or borrowed a helicopter, maybe."

"It's really cute, Mike. Just think what it would be like if you cleaned it, did a few repairs and then painted it. I don't think it's a hovel at all. Or at least it needn't be," she said. "I mean, what a place to live."

"You mean you approve or not?" I asked.

"Oh, yeah! Fantastic! What a view! And so peaceful. Just the birds and the sound of the sea. Oh, but what would you do about, well, you know, a toilet? Or fresh water?"

"I don't know. Maybe you have to piddle and poop over the cliff. Hang your arse out into the void and hope for an offshore breeze."

"You say the sweetest things," she chuckled.

"You'd have to carry water in. For drinking anyway. Perhaps you could collect rainwater. There's a big tank or butt thing at the side. Did you notice?"

"No" she said.

"You'd definitely need to be resourceful."

"I quite like the idea, though," she said. "I suppose it's like the chalet, only more so."

"Much more so," I laughed. "There's running water, sewerage and electricity down there!"

We went outside again. The area around the shack was less approximately fifty feet square. To the front, there was a small picket fence and then the cliff fell away very steeply, although not vertically, two or three hundred feet to the beach below. We stood, hand in hand, just breathing in the sea air and floating in the view.

As we stood there, a cormorant rose from beneath us on the currents, as if it was riding one of those glass lifts you see on the outside of buildings these days. It sat on the up-draught for some moments, so perfectly in control of its environment that its wing feathers were barely disturbed. You might have thought that it was suspended on wire or standing on some invisible perch. Then, as suddenly as it had appeared in our field of vision, it wobbled, tried to regain equilibrium and then slewed away to the right, disappearing under the edge of the cliff.

"Amazing," said Ellie. "Just absolutely perfect. Who could ask for more?"

There was a bench by the fence, made of some stout pieces of timber; sawn railway sleepers, perhaps, nailed together rather clumsily.

"It's facing in, not out," said Ellie. "Strange. You'd want to sit facing the sea, wouldn't you?"

"Yes. Maybe the owner liked to look at his garden. After all, you could sit on the verandah to watch the water. There must have been a garden: you can see some hydrangea, for example, buried in there."

I gave the bench a shove with my foot but it seemed secure enough so we sat on it back to front, leaning with our arms on the back rail, watching the waves, the clouds and what we decided was a family of cormorants putting on a spectacular air show for our sole benefit.

It was difficult to drag ourselves away but eventually we did, pulling what remained of the gate behind us. As we turned to go, Ellie noticed that someone had painted a name on the side of the shack. The sea air had peeled and pitted the paint but it was still possible to make out the words. It said, 'The Crows' Nest'.

"I didn't see any crows," said Ellie.

"I expect it refers to the look-out position. You know, like on a mast. Or maybe not; I seem to remember from somewhere that the cormorant is also known as the sea crow," I said.

"In that case I think it should be called 'Cormorants' Nest'," she replied.

I was right about the path. After a while it started to drop quite steeply and tumbled out into the side of the gulley we had seen from the beach several times. Later, as we started crunching our way along the pebbles by the shoreline, we looked back to the gulley and the cliff. It was not possible to see any part of the paths we had trodden or the shack we had seen. To the casual visitor to this shoreline, they did not exist. You had to know they were there or, as we had done, be somewhat intrepid in your choice of route and stumble upon them inadvertently.

All the way back to the chalet, Ellie was eulogising about the shack. It had caught her imagination. I suppose because I had been so doubting of her earlier in the day, I wanted to please her. I decided that I would try to find out who owned it.

Later that evening, after we had eaten our meal, I went along to the café to find Paul Butler. In the preceding weeks we had become quite friendly and developed something of a rapport. When I arrived at the café, he was wiping down tables and stacking chairs.

"Busy day?" I said.

"Not half. Hundreds of bloody kids dropping ice cream everywhere," he grumbled. "Why don't parents watch what their children are doing these days or discipline the little bleeders occasionally?"

"I used to know a cheerful publican like you once," I said.

"Well, serving the great British public when it's having a day out is a pretty embittering experience," he growled. "More and more bloody people seem to be finding their way down here now. It didn't used to be like that, you know."

"No, I know," I said. "But it's all money in your pocket, isn't it?"

"I suppose so. Anyway, I hope you're not after an ice cream or a cup of tea because we're closed," he said, throwing his wet cloth into a bucket. "I'm almost done here and then I'm off to the 'Carpenters Arms' for several pints. Join me?"

"Thanks, Paul, but..."

"Don't tell me. You've something far more interesting back at the chalet," he winked.

"Something like that," I said. "You might be able to help me with something, though. We walked back from 'The King's Head' this afternoon across the top of the West Cliff. Quite a difficult path, you know where I mean?"

"Of course. Used to chase the girls up there when I was a lad. Shag Lane, we called it. On a warm summer's evening, there wouldn't be a horizontal space available. I don't think youngsters can be bothered these days. Too far for them to walk and there's no disco up there. They just do it in the car parks now," he laughed.

"We saw an abandoned shack up there. 'The Crows' Nest', it's called. Do you know who owns it?" I thought I might as well come straight to the point.

"There's more than one actually. And there are some tucked under the bottom of the cliff at the back of the beach. But, as it happens, I know the one you're talking about. It was my Uncle Jim's place. He lived there for thirty or more years, all on his own. Happy as Larry. I used to go up there when I was a kid and spend all day with him, watching the birds and the sea. Or helping him with his garden or his woodwork. He used to carve little model ships and sell them to the tourist shops in Lyme. He died a couple of years ago, poor old sod. Cancer got him in the finish. Why do you ask? Not that you're the first one."

"Well, I don't know. We rather like it, I suppose. Quite like to live up there. Back to Nature and all that. Would the owner sell it, do you think?"

"Christ, Mike, you're joking aren't you? I mean, it's alright for a holiday home or a weekend retreat but you wouldn't want to live there all year round, would you? It blows like a bastard on that cliff in the winter, you know; cold as charity. And everything you want, you have to carry up there," he looked at me, frowning.

"I know."

"I get asked about four of five times a year, I suppose. Usually day-trippers. Romantics, though, not realists."

"Well, I suppose that's us! It's obvious that being up there is not a picnic, Paul. I mean, you'd have to work hard and be resourceful and be prepared to compromise and all that. No hot showers in the morning!"

"It could be done, Mike. There is a water tank of sorts up there collecting rainwater. I suppose you'd need to think about a wind pump or a generator. It's feasible," said Paul, picking up his bucket. "Uncle Jim could never be bothered with refinements, but it could be done."

"You know who owns it now, Paul? I'd like to talk to them."

"You already are," he said, smiling.

"You mean..?"

"Yes, it's mine. Uncle Jim said I could have it when I was just a kid. He was as good as his word."

"Are you interested in selling it?"

"Well, I don't want to go up there anymore. I've no use for it. You're the first person to ask me about it who I think might just make a go of it, so why not?"

Half an hour later we had agreed a very modest cash price, shaken hands on it and Paul had kindly said that we could take possession as soon as we wanted. I had set out twenty minutes before to make a casual enquiry and within that short time, I had become the new owner, more or less. It seemed too good to be true. But then, my experience has been that genuine West Country folk are much more trusting than people round here.

"The lawyers will tit about for weeks," he said. "You'll need to get it sorted next month if you're daft enough to be proposing to spend the winter there. And you can have 'Seagull' down here until you're ready. And just for the record, I think you're a very lucky man; you know; and I also think the pair of you are barking mad!"

"You may be right, but if so, you've just made a madman's day," I said, heading for the door. "Enjoy your beer!"

I ran back to the chalet so fast, I could hardly speak when I arrived. I practically fell through the door.

"Whatever's the matter?" said Ellie. "What's happened? Hey, you've got that grin again. What's going on?"

"You're not going to believe what I've just done," I gasped.

"What? Mike, tell me!"

"I thought I'd go and see if Paul Butler had any idea who owned that shack," I said.

"You found out? Really? Excellent! So what are you thinking, Mike? We could go and see them and find out if..?"

"I've done better than that! Paul is the owner and I've just bought the bugger! He says we must be mad," I wheezed. "Maybe we are. Hardly given it considered thought, have we? But what the hell! Incredible bit of luck that he should be the owner, although not surprising in a way, I suppose. He's lived here all his life. Anyway, I've done the deal, we can move in when we want."

Ellie just stood there looking at me, her eyes blinking and her mouth trying to form words which just wouldn't come out.

IN THE BUBBLE

"Really," I said. "I'm not joking. It's ours. The first home that we own together is an ancient, tiny wooden shed hidden on a cliff face. With no electricity, water or sanitation. I hope I do not disappoint you, my dear?"

Ellie let out a terrific whoop, grabbed me by the hand and started dancing me around the chalet.

"Amazing, Mike. Thank you so much! Oh, I can't believe it!"

"It's true," I said. "Do we have to go and choose curtain material tomorrow?"

"Could be! Mike, I want to go there now! Come on," she laughed, pulling at my hands. "Let's go back up there now! Yeah?"

"Now? It's quite late, though. Soon be dark!"

"So what? You've got an important appointment in the morning? We'll take the torch. It's warm tonight. Grab a blanket. We'll sleep up there. Oh, come on, Mike, it'll be exciting!" Ellie was already pulling blankets off the bed.

As ever, Ellie's enthusiasm for the moment was infectious. I could have raised all manner of staid objections to her impetuous plan but I didn't. No small part of Ellie's attractiveness to me was her youthful verve and ability to throw caution to the wind. You can spend your whole life holding back.

Of course, what we ought to have done that evening was calmly to have discussed the events in the pub and examined our feelings about them. Instead, I went and bought an isolated shack on an exposed cliff without any real consideration of the practicalities of living in it.

Half an hour later, we were stumbling back up the gulley, loaded with blankets, water and a plastic carrier bag of food we grabbed indiscriminately from the fridge.

When we eventually arrived at the shack again, it must have been approaching midnight. Standing in the garden space, we could feel the cool breeze pulling in off the sea. The sky was pretty clear. A long way out, we could see the lights of a ship moving down the Channel.

"So, shall we sleep inside there or light a fire out here? Can't say I fancy that ramshackle, filthy bed," I said. Despite my desire to match Ellie's enthusiasm, I was aware I was sounding a dour note.

"Stop rushing and organising! We could just sit for a bit, couldn't we? Listen to the waves, watch the stars and the ships out at sea," she whispered, kneeling on the bench we had sat on earlier in the day.

"OK, in a minute. I think I should get a fire going. I think we might be glad of it later. We could sleep on the verandah, look, and feel the warmth of the fire if I light it about here," I said, directing the flickering torch beam to a reasonably clear spot about ten feet from the verandah itself.

"What is it with your generation? Forever organising bloody things? OK, OK, but if you set light to the place, I'll never forgive you," she laughed.

Rather than grovelling about collecting sticks, I went inside the shack. It had occurred to me that there might be things inside, like the bed, which we could burn. I directed the rather feeble torch beam around and decided that underneath the sink arrangement was the most likely place to find what I was looking for. A moment later, I saw that my assumption was correct, for thrown there I found a battered wood axe.

In addition to the rotting bed, there were a number of old orange boxes, which must have served as occasional tables and two split, broken chairs. I threw all these items out through the door.

"Hey!" Ellie shouted. "We've only been married a week! Is it the drink? Something I said? Or sexual frustration?"

I laughed and then stood in the doorway, the axe in my hand.

"There's only one thing I can do in the circumstances to assuage my consuming sexual needs," I cried. "I must destroy the marriage bed!" I leapt off the verandah and began setting about the bed timbers with the axe.

Ellie giggled to herself from her position on the bench.

"Mmm! I've always admired your chopper, Doc."

"Thank you for that inevitable double entendre," I chuckled, arranging small pieces of wood and cardboard and offering a lighted match to them.

"It's true," she said.

Smoke was issuing from the pile of tinder and flames began to flicker from the edges of the cardboard.

"There, look at that," I said, leaning back on my heels and admiring the fire which was now taking proper hold. I placed some larger pieces of timber on the crackling flames.

"A man and his trusty chopper," I said.

"Please, Sir, when you taught me in the third year, I used to look at your trousers, you know, wondering how big you were. God, isn't that awful? Now I've embarrassed myself! But girls do, you know!"

Ellie used to come out with stuff like that sometimes. It could be quite startling. Or threatening, depending on your mood.

"You're joking? No, you're not joking. Just as well I didn't know at the time. Still, I suppose men are no different, are they?"

"True. But I was only fourteen, Mike! Not very nice, is it? I should have been playing with my dolls, shouldn't I?"

"When I was fourteen, I wasn't playing with my train set any more either."

"So what were you doing, then?"

"Same as most fourteen year old boys, I expect. Riding my bike on the pavement, giving v-signs to old ladies who complained about it, throwing stones at chickens, farting, belching, swearing, smoking and wondering about girls. You know, talking dirty with the other boys. Looking at rude magazines if we could get them. They weren't so readily available then and porn films and the like were beyond our ken or reach."

I went over to the bench, standing behind her with my hand on her shoulder.

"Not doing your homework, then? Like you told us we had to?"

"I did, actually, but I made sure there was time for all the other things too."

We were silent for a while. As we watched the stars and moonlight reflected in the sea, I caressed her neck and ran my fingers through the tumble of her hair.

"And what about, well, you know, that thing that boys do?"

I knew Ellie well enough by then to know what kind of thing she wanted to talk about and what the likely conclusion would be. Talking dirty was one of her favourite methods of getting herself aroused. I suppose it must have dated from the days when she and her sister had talked through the various things that Emma had been doing with her boyfriend.

"What?" I said blankly, pretending not to know.

"Masturbating," she whispered suggestively.

"Oh, that! Boring!"

I yawned loudly.

"Well, yes, plenty of that. Like most fourteen year old boys. And about seventy percent of girls, according to you," I said.

"And?"

She began to wiggle her backside against my trouser front.

"Sometimes, a few of us would go down to the beach on a summer's evening and sit between the beach huts and the sea wall. Without the fear of discovery you had at home. I had a friend who was so horny, he used to do it in class, regularly! Double physics; seventy minutes of acute tedium and he'd jerk himself off two or three times when the master nipped into the prep room or was writing on the board. Really, I'm not making it up! Boys' grammar school, you see. Unnatural hothouse of adolescent sexual frustrations. Spunky Williams we called him, for obvious reasons."

Ellie chuckled.

"He was amazingly fast," I continued. "Three or four strokes and he was there. The floor around his stool would be awash with it by the end of the lesson!"

Ellie breathed out fiercely and wiggled against me some more, this time with more urgency.

That was the amazing thing about Ellie. Under certain circumstances, she could go from nowhere to that state of sexual arousal and readiness in what seemed like seconds. It didn't always happen that way by any means but when it did, she had an animal passion which always took my breath away; surprising me with its ferocity.

That night up at the shack was something else. The fire was crackling and spitting behind us; the sea was rattling the pebbles below; the breeze was rubbing at the tree branches while we, under the moon and stars, were convulsed with tumultuous desire and making so much noise that I am sure it must have carried over the water to the ships far out at sea.

Perhaps it was the unexpectedness of the evening's events which gave our love-making such abandon; maybe it was the shadows and the firelight; perhaps because we were outside on the cliff top that we were consumed with such excitement and lust; perhaps it was just the simple fact of the height of the bench which facilitated so perfectly our favourite position: who knows?

But the occasion is cast in my memory as a time of one of the most, if not the most intense sexual experiences of my life.

HIGH TIDE

They are fortunate that September and October are largely fine months, without prolonged periods of heavy rain or low temperatures, for it enables them to devote many hours each day to the renovation and cleaning of 'The Crows' Nest'.

On the first day, they spend hours emptying the shack of old Jim's remaining possessions, most of which are burnt. Michael scrapes soot and spiders from the old stove, hits the smoke pipe coming from its top to test for soundness and inspects the section above roof level by climbing up a reasonably sturdy sapling near the verandah. Satisfied, he throws in some dry sticks and sets light to them. They are both delighted to find that the stove draws well and soon the two hotplates are too hot to touch.

There is a sink of sorts in the main room with an old tap above it. Michael is surprised to find that it has not rusted and turns after a little pressure is applied. The water that gushes out is a lurid green and smells vile.

"Stagnant rain water in that tank," he says. "I'll let it run to empty it and then we'll have to see about cleaning the tank or replacing it altogether."

"What do we do about washing?" asks Ellie.

"I imagine that old Jim washed infrequently. It's only recently that people have started showering morning, noon and night, you know. Even when I was a kid, a bath once a week on Sunday evening ready for school the next week was considered adequate."

"Yuk! Disgusting! I hope you're not expecting us to do the same? Especially if you want me to continue with the intimacies!"

"I may have to give you a regular blanket bath," he mutters lewdly.

"You old reprobate."

"If it doesn't rain, there'll be problems. Water will be the greatest challenge. I mean, we'll have to carry in drinking water in any event, won't we? But otherwise, we shall be relying on the Almighty to send it to us from the skies. And you know how reliable He is."

"That's because you don't pray to him," she says.

"Crap; I tried it once and it didn't work," Michael retorts, dismissively. "Maybe we need a bigger tank. Or more tanks. Have to think about that. At least cooking isn't going to be a problem now that we know that thing's working and it'll also heat the place in the winter."

"How far is the pub?" asks Ellie. "We could get drinking water there. I mean, they'd sell it to us, surely? Or they would have done until you nearly caused a riot!"

"About half an hour's walk? Maybe less. It's true it is all downhill. I think we should explore the possibility of a little hand cart."

Exhausted with just thinking about the Herculean task before them, they flop onto the floor and sit in silence for some minutes, Michael idly examining the spiders traversing the timbers above his head and Ellie mentally furnishing the space.

"Are we mad?" says Ellie after a while, laughing.

"Probably. Paul Butler thinks so anyway. Do you think so, then, now that grim reality is before us?"

Ellie moves across the shack and stands in the doorway for several moments before walking out onto the verandah.

"Come out here, Mike," she says. He joins her and puts his arm around her waist.

"Look at that view. Just the sea. Beautiful. And the cliffs. No houses. No roads. Clean air. And silence. Just us. Now; no past; kind of no future. And we're mad?" Ellie says.

"It is beautiful. But no anything means no facilities. No people means no social life, doesn't it? I mean, isn't that going to bother you?" Michael asks.

"Just because we live up here doesn't mean we have to be, what's the word? Recluses, does it? We can still go down to the village or Bere or wherever we want, can't we?"

In the days that follow, their doubts about what they are doing occasionally re-surface, but on the other hand, they have a considerable sense of joint achievement when the construction of a small outhouse is complete. Likewise when Michael's extensive enquiries about solar panels conclude, after several weeks, with the satisfactory installation of a unit which, coupled with a small wind turbine on an aluminium mast, will charge a battery to provide some power for lights and which should at least warm water, if not heat it.

Michael realises at an early stage that hoping that they can, between them, achieve all that needs to be achieved before an early winter might set in is futile. Further, it might hinder their ability to live in the renovated and improved shack until the following Spring if certain basics are not attended to straight away.

He asks around in the village and in Bere and finds two reliable and knowledgeable men who are happy to be employed on a casual basis to assist with construction work and who are also strong enough to manhandle materials and new equipment, like a large fibre glass water tank, up the track from the beach.

Paul Butler introduces Michael and Ellie to Ben Fielding who lives in a shanty property at the foot of the cliff, just past the gulley going west. He encourages them. "Returning to a simple life of self-reliance, right? Delighting in the natural environment," says Ben, adjusting the piece of string in his pony tail. "Alternative society, man."

They discover that Ben is not so alternative as to have turned his back on the combustion engine, for he has a beach buggy with a trailer which, at low tide, he uses to travel back to the village to pick up supplies.

"I reckon we could use one of those," says Michael. "Only problem is, I can't get it up the cliff to the shack. Care to rent me a parking space at the side of your place, Ben?"

"Can't see why not, man," says Ben.

Later, the two men realise that having two beach buggies, both for relatively infrequent use, is an unnecessary duplication and so Michael buys a half share in Ben's machine. It is an arrangement that works well.

"Worth its weight in gold, this thing," says Michael one late October afternoon as they head back along the beach from the village in the buggy. The trailer bounces along behind them, loaded with boxes and packages bearing testimony to what they hope to be their last shopping trip.

"I hope we can get all this stuff up there before it gets too dark," says Ellie, shading her eyes against the reflection in the sea of the sun's almost horizontal light. "Let's put those curtains up tonight. They'll look excellent!"

"OK. And then we're done, aren't we? Surely, please? No more! My wallet's had such a hammering this last two months, I'm not sure it'll ever recover!"

"I can't think of anything else at the moment. So tomorrow we actually move in? I mean, we don't use the chalet anymore? I can't believe that we've actually done it. Finished! Hurrah!" Ellie lifts her arms in the air and whoops loudly. Ahead of them an old man walking his dog turns and looks at them in surprise.

"We could have moved ourselves up there a couple of weeks ago but you wanted every last thing sorted out, if you remember! I've paid Paul for the chalet until Thursday, the end of the month. But yes, tomorrow is the big day."

"I know, but I just thought it would be good to move in with everything done," she laughs, still waving her arms in the air, enjoying the sensation of the salt air on her face.

"Do we have a house warming?"

"Of course. We're not recluses, remember?"

"OK. Well, I'll make a few calls later."

*

The following morning, they carry the remainder of their possessions up the track to 'The Crows' Nest', having given Paul back the key for the chalet. Ellie puts everything away and then begins to prepare some snacks for the little celebration they propose that afternoon.

At about three o'clock, there is a knock at the door and on opening it, they find Paul and Mary Butler standing on the verandah, a bottle of bubbly wine in Paul's hands.

"Congratulations on the new home!" says Paul. "We still think you're stark raving mad, but we both hope you'll be very happy here on the cliff."

"Thanks," says Michael, taking the wine from Paul's outstretched hand, "that's very kind of you. Come on in and see what we've done."

"Good Heavens," murmurs Mary, admiringly. "I hardly recognise the place."

Ellie smiles, pleased that Mary is making this friendly approach.

"Well," she says, "most of the time and money was spent with the roof, the insulation, the inside walls and the toilet."

"Not to mention the cess pit construction which involved the hire of a pneumatic drill and generator; what fun that was; and the water tanks, solar panels, wind turbine and plumbing and wiring," Mike says, waving a dismissive hand in jest.

"But the biggest problem was the spiders!" Ellie squeals. "There were hundreds of them everywhere and some as big as mice! They were just so gross!"

She shivers involuntarily at the memory.

"But it was all worth it, wasn't it?" replies Mary, laughing. "You'll always have spiders although maybe not so many now you have a ceiling and if you keep flicking the broom!"

Mary smiles and takes Ellie's hand.

"Not just a pretty face, is she?" Paul says, winking at Ellie. "She rolled her sleeves up and got sawing and lifting and digging along with the boys, didn't you?"

"Of course," smiles Ellie. "The colour scheme is mine. I thought the pale lemon in here would make it always seem sunny, even on winter days and in the bedroom, we've got a nice sage green. Restful on the eyes, it says in the book I've got."

Michael looks at his wife admiringly. She looks radiant and confident as she leads Paul and Mary across the room to look at the little kitchen area. Paul is impressed by the neat wall cupboards which have been hand-made. Mary enthuses about the bedroom with its warm, cork floor and the pretty pine bed.

"The whole place seems bigger," she says.

"No," says Mike. "Same size. Well, except for the loo. An outside facility, but better than nothing. No, it's just that we've kept it clutter free."

The conversation is interrupted by the arrival of Ben who has put on a clean pair of trousers for the occasion; he is followed almost immediately by the helpers Stan Harden and Pete Bush and their wives and children and, finally, Patrick Davies, the publican at 'The King's Head' with whom Mike has made his peace.

The little shack is full with the sound of laughter and admiring voices. The consensus is that Mike and Ellie have worked a miracle in transforming a tired old shed into a very attractive home.

"I think it's so sweet, my dear," says Mrs Harden, her fingers stroking the beige and cream check curtains in the main room. "And a carpet as well! My, my."

"Not so sweet carryin' 'ee up that path, was it Pete?" chuckles her husband and everybody laughs.

"You've got 'ee done just in time," pipes up Pete in his reedy voice. "They'm sayins likely to be a hard winter."

"Well," says Patrick, raising his glass, "we should propose a toast to the pair of you. Here's to Mike and Ellie and their new home!"

Everyone raises a glass to their lips and the toast is drunk

"Thank you," says Ellie. "It's excellent to see you all here. Thank you. And especially thank you to Stan and Pete. We couldn't have done it without you."

"So," says Mary," what will the two of you do now it's finished? I mean, how are you going to spend your days now that you've stepped off the edge of the known world?"

Everyone looks at Michael and Ellie, but neither of them speaks. Michael looks at Ellie and sees that she has a puzzled expression on her face.

"It was great that people made the effort," says Ellie, flopping onto the little sofa later that evening, "but I'm glad it's over and they've gone!"

"Yes, I'm knackered," grunts Michael. "Two months of frenzied activity taking their toll now it's all over, I suppose."

"You're just getting old," giggles Ellie, prodding him in the stomach.

"Tonight, I think you may be right," he replies, yawning.

"So, what are we going to do, now that it's finished?" Ellie says after a few minutes. "For two months we haven't stopped and every day has been busy. If we've not actually been up here or hauling stuff up the path, we've been down at the chalet planning what to haul the next day. Now all that's over."

"So you reckon we'll have time on our hands?"

"Yes," she says. "I suppose so. Like you say, we've been so busy that the thought of what we do now just hasn't entered my head. I mean, it hasn't anyway, has it, since we got here in July? But you must admit, it's a good question."

"The honeymoon is over, then?" Michael says bluntly.

"Come on, Mike, there's no need to be pissy. Mary's question this afternoon got me thinking that's all. It's a fair point. What are we going to do for the rest of our lives? Outside the known world, she said."

"Just being here will take more time and effort than living conventionally, won't it?" Mike says. "We'll still have to spend time fetching supplies and water, chopping wood, washing by hand and so on. And if, as you say, I'm getting old then I regret to say that most of the work will devolve upon younger shoulders."

"Oh, yeah? Well, obviously there'll be chores and I agree that they'll be time-consuming but even so they won't take all day, every day, will they?"

"No, I suppose not," Mike grunts. "I thought you were happy to watch the sea and the birds and listen to the silence?"

"At the moment, I am. But if that's all that's going to happen in my life for the next sixty years, then maybe not. I could go crazy."

Ellie looks at Mike, her mouth suddenly set in a petulant mould.

Mike looks surprised at her tone. This is not like Ellie.

"Alright, alright! Calm down! What's got into you tonight? Is it the fizzy wine?" Mike pulls himself up from his slouch on the sofa and looks at Ellie.

"No! I said; it was Mary's question. It's got me thinking, that's all. Can't you see what she was getting at?"

"Of course. She thinks we're off our heads: that you can't run away from the world. Or your place in it, I suppose. Now that your mind has time, you've started wondering about your life plan?"

"You make it sound stupid. But yes, I suppose so. My education, for example."

"OK. Look, like I say, I really am very tired. How about we both think about that; I mean you especially, since you've raised it and then we can talk about it tomorrow. All day if need be. We have nothing else planned. You know, rather than starting now and risk having an argument. You know what I'm like when I'm tired."

Ellie sighs.

"Alright. I'm not angry about anything Mike, it's just that suddenly I'm thinking about the future and for nearly three months, down there on the beach, I haven't done at all. I don't know why."

Mike is too tired even to enjoy the novelty of going to bed in their new home. As soon as he lies down, he falls asleep. Ellie lies beside him, watching the pale shadows of leaves flickering on the ceiling, listening to the sound of the sea two hundred feet below and wondering why, so suddenly, a feeling of unease has come over her and a notion that the man beside her is avoiding a conversation.

In the early hours of the morning, they are both awoken by the unfamiliar sound of the wind tugging at the trees around them and the insistent thrumming of heavy rain on the roof of their new home.

CRAB AT THE WINDOW

As it turned out, it was more than three weeks before we got around to discussing what I'd raised on our first night. The next morning I think we just slipped back into the old ways and in any case we were both excited about starting to live in the new place and develop routines. It wasn't an ordinary house and we had to remember stuff like making sure there was enough wood chopped for the stove or that we weren't running out of drinking water.

Poor Mike! That first morning he kept looking at me oddly and he seemed on edge. I realised why after a while but it didn't seem as important as it had done the previous evening so I just left it. Maybe I shouldn't have. As it turned out, it would have been better to have talked it through that day. When we did get around to it, well, it was definitely the wrong moment. But there you are; we weren't really very good at talking through the things that mattered.

Afterwards, I was bothered that he didn't start the conversation. Because I didn't, he wasn't going to and that tended to confirm my feeling that he didn't want to talk about it anyway or didn't think it important enough.

I think I felt that he didn't trust me or our marriage enough to let me have the freedom that I was asking for. He was frightened and I reacted like a schoolgirl and got angry with him. Oddly, he wasn't able to explain his feelings to me and I wasn't mature enough at the time to be able to read the situation more accurately. Like, we were both to blame.

He chose to believe that I was worried about being in the shack all the time. I was, but that wasn't the whole story. Anyway, we did agree that we shouldn't spend all our time at home on the cliff and so we became regulars at 'The King's Head'. I suppose we liked the friendly atmosphere and we got quite matey with some of the locals. And it was warm and the heat was free! We used to go at lunchtime quite often. Mike had discovered from Patrick that Curly and Ginger didn't usually go there; it wasn't their local. But if they did, it would be in the evening. Neither of us wanted a repeat of the incident before. It wasn't always a good idea to go to the pub, though. Mike would often drink too much red wine and then he could get grumpy and we'd argue. Well, bicker.

We hadn't argued hardly at all on the beach but once we were on the cliff, it seemed to happen more. It really upset me. I don't know why things changed, but somehow they did. Anyway, we also got involved in the Butlers' social circle for a while which was great. I really hit it off with Mary; she was a sister and a

Mum rolled into one. We went off exploring the surrounding area; we walked for miles while the weather was OK and we went to Bere loads of times. We joined the public library. That was Mike's idea and I suppose it was his way of getting me back into the world of books and learning without any risk to him. That sounds a bit bitchy, but I think it's true.

So getting out cheered things up a bit and I didn't feel so isolated. But as the early winter days shortened and the temperatures dropped it was much more of an effort to do anything. Especially when any attempt to go out had to begin with a walk through soaking wet bushes and things on that muddy and slippery bloody track. By the third week of November, it became impossible. The freezing wind and rain coming in off the sea was unbelievable. So at that stage we kind of retreated into the house and huddled round the stove. That's when the stuff that had been festering for weeks came to the surface again.

I remember a grey afternoon towards the end November. Like, the weather had been so bloody awful that we hadn't been out for three days on the trot; I kept looking out of the windows every three minutes to see if the rain had eased off. I knew I was driving Mike mad but it was just too bad. I told him I was pissed off and bored. Real sulky teenager stuff.

He looked up from his book.

"I had noticed," he said in his best schoolteacher's sarky voice.

"Well, we've been shut in here for three days, haven't we? Not even been able to get out for a run along the beach or something," I replied irritably.

"Well, you could if you really want to. It's just that you'll get wet and you don't like that either, do you?"

"No, I bloody don't!" I snapped. "But getting wet is what living in this place is all about, isn't it? I mean, we even have to find a fucking umbrella to go out to the bog, don't we? Getting wet and being bored out of my bloody mind!"

"It's not my fault the weather is crap, Ellie," he said quietly.

"No, it's never your fault, is it? Sorry, sorry, no, I suppose not," I said, fidgeting at the edge of the rug with my foot.

"Have you finished your book, then?" he asked.

"No, but I'm sick to death of reading at the moment," I snarled. I wanted to kick something.

"OK, OK. Calm down. Do you want to brave the rain and go into Bere or somewhere for a coffee?"

I knew he was trying to help, but the suggestion just seemed so feeble. He knew well enough that going to Bere to some sad tea shop was not going to solve the problem.

"No!" I said. "They're all so dead those places now that the season's over. Depressing. Just ancient pensioners bloody doddering about with their noses dripping. Anyway, it's getting dark."

"You paint an appealing picture. Sex then? How about a quick one here on the sofa? Or, how about a knee trembler in The Facility? We haven't tried that yet. If we turn the shower on, that should liven things up."

That was typical Mike. When things got tense or something, he'd start on about sex. His view was that making love would solve any problem. Men! Well, it's true that it could smooth things out temporarily. Sometimes. We'd had a few petty squabbles and ended up in bed and in those situations he could be really tender and gentle and he'd look into my eyes the whole time we'd be doing it and I'd turn to jelly and then everything would be alright again for a while. Except that we wouldn't have talked through the problem, whatever it was. We took it to bed with us and got diverted but it was still there. Like under the sheets.

He completely misread the signals. I was obviously distressed and his answer to that was to bend me over the arm of the settee.

"For Christ's sake, Mike," I said. "Is that all you ever think about? Your answer to everything, isn't it? Anyway, I'm not in the mood. Which is obvious, surely?"

"Really? That's a first then. Ellen Amanda Chadwick is not in the mood, not even for a knee trembler. We should contact Reuters. What then?"

He was grinning rather stupidly and put his book on the floor. I could see what he was doing: trying to make me laugh so as to lighten the mood and divert me onto something else. Anything in fact, rather than having a serious conversation.

I gave another big sigh and slumped down onto the sofa beside him. We sat without speaking for a while, listening to the wind kicking the building and the rain lashing the roof. I wasn't going to be put off or diverted but on the other hand I didn't want a blazing row either.

"I suppose this is what I was on about, you know, a few weeks ago. The day we moved in."

Mike's brow furrowed and he looked at me nervously.

"I was wondering when you were going to come back to it," he said.

So he bloody knew all along what I wanted to talk about.

"You don't really want to talk about it, do you?" I said. I could feel my irritation rising again, despite my attempts to keep cool.

"What do you mean?"

"You know what I mean, Mike. I know you well enough by now. You're quite happy with things as they are, aren't you? I mean, please, please don't misunderstand me, Mike. I love you to absolute bits, you know that, and I really want to be with you and everything and nothing's changed over the way I feel, of course not, but, I don't know, since the day we came up here, I've been, like restless. For three weeks. Yeah?"

I looked him straight in the eye. He took my hand in his and squeezed it gently.

"Yes, I know. What happened that day, then?"

"I don't know. It's as if when we were down there on the beach I was in a trance or in limbo or something and now I've woken up. Can I ask you a question? You're a teacher and so you value education, right?"

I could hear the assertive tone back in my voice.

"Of course," said Mike. "Most people do. Not exclusive to teachers."

"No, alright, but you haven't asked me once since last July whether I want to continue at school. I mean, I haven't finished my 'A' Levels, have I?"

He raised his eyebrows. I suppose he wasn't at all used to me sounding so resentful but I couldn't help it.

"Well, no, I haven't mentioned it, I suppose. But neither have you, have you? You weren't waiting for my permission to introduce the subject, presumably? We're equal partners, remember?"

"I just think it's odd that as a teacher you haven't mentioned it, that's all," I replied. "Three weeks ago you said we'd discuss it the next day. We didn't."

I was right to say it, I know I was, but it certainly came out sounding like a really arsey kid getting the hump with her dad.

"Hey, hang on! What's this with apportioning blame? We haven't talked about all sorts of stuff, Ellie. Your mother. My kids. The possible effects on you of the trial. All sorts of crap. We've shut it all out. Maybe we still are shutting it out. But don't dump it all on me! So what are you saying? You want to go back to school or a college?"

He was beginning to sound angry too now. That's how it goes with arguments, sometimes, isn't it? I took a deep breath and thought to myself, keep calm!

259

"I'm not sure. But I think maybe I do. I mean, until all this, you know, us and everything happened I always wanted to go to University. Maybe now I'm thinking I still do. Does that surprise you?"

Mike hesitated. He didn't say anything for a while but I could tell from the way his eyes were shifting about that all kind of stuff was going through his mind.

"I don't have to explain it to you, Mike, do I? You're a teacher and you've been to University. So, you know, the opportunity to develop yourself intellectually; student life; young friends; the belief that you can conquer the world, I think you once said in class. You enjoyed it and benefited from it at my age, so why shouldn't I?"

"Well, I don't know. I suppose I'd kind of got used to you being, well, here," he said.

"I am here, Mike. And that's OK, of course it is. But does it have to be either, or? Can't it be both?" I said. I thought it was a perfectly reasonable comment. I was quite amazed at his resistance. He was against the idea; I could sense it in the way he was sitting and from the expression on his face.

"Well, I suppose so, but it wouldn't be easy, would it? Practically, I mean," he said.

"Mike! Sod the practicalities. I don't know about that yet. Yeah, maybe it would be difficult; but it doesn't matter about that now. Like, I'm talking about the principle of it. You're not saying you don't want me to finish my education and stuff, are you?"

"No, no, of course not, it's just that..."

He tailed off into silence.

"Bloody hell, Mike! That is what you're saying, isn't it? You've got used to me being what? A dutiful housewife and a sex machine?"

I expect I was shouting by then or at least I'd raised my voice quite a bit. I pulled my hand from his and stood up and started pacing about again.

"Come on, Ellie," he said, "you know that's not how I see it."

"Isn't it? How do you see it then?" I said. "How do you see the next ten, twenty, thirty years?"

Poor Mike. Like, he was just trying to read his book and I was ranting and raving like a complete loony. I was standing there with my hands on my hips. I think I was amazed at his refusal or inability to answer a simple question and he was amazed that I was on about the next thirty years. He was still on the beach; happy for that day and never mind too much about tomorrow.

"How do any of us know what he next few decades will bring?"

"Well, that's like, what? Pretty lame, isn't it?" I snapped. "You must have thought about it? I mean, maybe we should have talked about it before."

"Maybe," he replied.

He just sat there and like, I'm waiting for him to say something meaningful instead of just avoiding things or talking crap.

"Answer my questions, Mike! Are you against me finishing my education? Having a career, maybe? Where are we in ten years, let's say? Still stuck in this fucking shed on the cliff?"

He looked at me. I know that when I get really angry, that my eyes get really wide and they sort of flash. Mum says she can see green ice in there somewhere and it's not nice! Mike shuffled his backside on the sofa.

"I thought you liked it here? You were the one who waxed lyrical about the idea in August. In fact, it was your bloody idea! So now we're stuck in a shed? You've changed your mind about it, then, obviously?"

I tried to calm things down again in my mind and went to sit on the sofa again.

"Mike, I don't know. It feels like it might become a trap sometimes. Not always, right? Just sometimes. Perhaps it's just because the weather is so shit at the moment. Maybe we're coming at it from different angles. Look, I'm sorry. I'm not trying to be difficult, but this does matter to me and suddenly I just don't feel quite the same. Like, I feel maybe I'd be wasting an opportunity if I don't go back to school and everything. I know I couldn't go back this year. I've missed nearly a term already. It'd have to be next September anyway, I suppose."

I thought that by saying that it would take the pressure off him. And if it was next September, he would realise he would have time to get used to the idea.

He leaned his head on the back of the sofa and looked at the ceiling.

"We are coming at it from different angles," he muttered morosely. "Maybe it was only a matter of time. I mean, I've been there, done the student bit, got the degree, done the career, had the kids and you haven't even begun. I'm ready to stop and you're ready to start."

"Well, maybe. I'm not talking about kids, Mike! We're not doing that are we? But me going back to college and maybe University doesn't have to be a threat, does it? Mike, what exactly are you worried about? I don't think you want me to go off and do those things, do you? You want me to miss them out altogether. Why won't you answer my bloody questions?"

261

He didn't say anything but continued to stare at the ceiling. I think that if I was having that conversation now, I'd know how to deal with it better; you know, to get Mike to see that "different angles" wasn't the same as "opposite directions" and that there must have been a way of arranging things so that both our desires were met. But I don't know, I didn't seem to have the skills to draw him out then so I just kept blundering on with the same stuff.

"You said yourself I've got a brain. Not just big tits, you said. So I ought to use it, oughtn't I? Why shouldn't I, if that's what I want to do?"

"Yes, Ellie, you should use it. I'm not really arguing against that."

"So why are you obviously so anti? I mean, like, you're not saying, OK, let's go to the college and get the prospectus and get you signed up for next year or anything, are you? Or saying, OK, I'll help you with the reading and stuff until next September so that you're ready to pick it up again."

That was about as far as it got. We never did finish the conversation. Something happened at that moment that made things go from bad to worse. If you read it in Thomas Hardy you'd say it wouldn't happen in real life. But it does.

Mike was about to say something but whatever it was he didn't have time. He was interrupted by a hammering at the door and Paul Butler's voice shouting above the sound of the wind and the rain.

"Mike! Ellie! It's me; Paul! Open the bloody door, will you? I'm drowning out here!"

We looked at each other in surprise and then Mike jumped to his feet and opened the door.

"Paul! Come in, come in! Christ, you're absolutely soaked! Whatever's the matter?"

We could see from the expression on Paul's face, even though it was half-hidden under a sou'wester and streaming with water, that something was wrong.

"Not good news, Mike, I'm afraid. Your brother's been on the phone, about an hour ago. It's your mother. She's had a stroke, apparently and well, he says it looks serious and you need to go up to Essex straight away."

Mike didn't say anything for a moment, but the colour drained from his face. I can still see him standing there, his eyes closed and one hand on the back of the sofa to steady himself.

"Oh, God, no," he whispered.

"Yes, I'm really sorry, Mike. He wants you to phone him back before you leave. He, well, he asked me to impress on you that it's urgent," Paul blurted, wiping rainwater from his face.

Paul and I stood looking at Mike, waiting for him to say something. It felt like ages; I mean, it always does in those strange moments, doesn't it, while someone collects their thoughts.

"He didn't say any more than that?"

"No, that was about it," said Paul.

"I suppose that's enough. OK. We'd better go straight away then. It's really good of you to take the trouble to come up here to tell me. Us."

His voice sounded mechanical. He glanced across at me and reached for my hand.

"It's OK. I came as soon as I could. I'm sorry to be the bearer of bad tidings," Paul said.

Mike was just standing there. I suppose he was in a kind of shock. Not saying or doing anything. I thought that I ought to offer Paul a hot drink at least.

"Paul, do you want to take your gear off and warm up? Do you want a hot drink? Coffee?" I said.

He said he had to get back because the café was unattended.

"I hope things aren't as bad as they seem, Mike," Paul said, patting Mike on the shoulder and turning for the door. "Let me know if there's anything I can do, alright?"

Mike mumbled something. Paul patted his arm again, opened the door and was gone.

It was really weird. You know, one minute this was our life and then the next minute, everything had changed. The outside world came in that night, alright.

As soon as the door closed, Mike threw his arms round me and put his head into my neck. He was sobbing and saying that he wished he'd made more effort to contact his family. I know he did phone his kids about five times and his mother once, maybe twice, when we were in the chalet but it was no more than that. On the last occasion he came back from the phone box and said that she'd had a go at him about what he was doing: abandoning his kids, running off with a schoolgirl and how disgraceful it all was and she'd never forgive him. I don't think he even got so far as telling her that we were married. I think he'd slammed the phone down on her.

He didn't ever say much about his conversations with his daughters either, but they were obviously not easy for him. He'd look sad and tearful and tend to be very quiet for an hour or so. So Paul's message suddenly broke the dam and the tears of guilt came bursting through.

"I just hope that I'm in time," he said eventually, wiping tears from his eyes, "otherwise our last conversation will have been an angry one over the phone. I shall feel guilty for the rest of my life."

He sort of pulled himself upright, took a deep breath or two and spoke again, this time in a more controlled way.

"If we leave in about ten minutes, I reckon we can be there by about eight or nine, depending on the M25 traffic," he said.

He looked at me for confirmation and then paused because he could see the expression on my face.

"Ellie? I'd like you to come with me?"

I just shook my head.

"What? Why not? Ellie, I need your support. You're my wife!"

"Mike, don't make an issue of it, please," I said. "Now is not the time to be introduced to your family. You can see that, can't you? I can hardly sit at your mother's bedside, can I? What was it she called me? A little whore, I think you said. I don't know your brother or your kids, assuming they're around. Or your ex-wife, come to that, because if your kids are around, she'll have to bring them, won't she? No, Mike, please, it's really, really not a good idea."

He looked pained and hurt. I think he knew I was right but he kept on about needing my support. He wasn't very strong emotionally, I suppose. I think I had to learn from an early age to be quite steely. But Mike was really quite vulnerable.

"Anyway, I don't think I could face it, to be honest. Not yet and not like this. I'll be here when you get back, won't I?"

He went into the bedroom and started grabbing stuff out of the drawers and wardrobe and ramming them into a bag.

"We're bloody married, aren't we? The sooner they all get used to that, the better," he said.

"I agree, Mike, yes, but it's going to take time, isn't it? I just don't think we should force it on them now when there's other stuff going on. Anyway, see it from my point of view, can't you? Even if your mother wasn't ill and she'd invited us up there, which is highly unlikely, let's face it, I'd still feel like, totally bloody awkward and out of place, wouldn't I? Surely you can see that?"

He zipped up the bag and stood looking at me across the bed.

"OK, OK!" he said. He wasn't shouting, exactly, but very nearly. "I'm just really pissed off and disappointed, I suppose. But it sounds like my mother is lying on her death bed two hundred miles away and I'm going to find whatever's ahead of me very difficult and I'd like you with me for support but this is urgent and I haven't got the time to argue with you. If you won't come, then I can't make you, I suppose."

He almost pushed past me into the main room and snatched the pad and pencil out from the bookcase where we kept it. I stood there staring at the space he'd just left. I couldn't believe he was being so unpleasant. He was making me feel really bad; like I was a failure or something. All I was suggesting was that arriving in the sick room or the hospital with his new seventeen year old wife holding his hand was likely to be, well, like confrontational, wasn't it? I was sure I was right. And then I thought, well, he's upset, frightened, feeling guilty and everything so I tried to remain calm and not rise to the bait so that we argued as he left. My Mum always said that you should never leave the one you love with a cross word. They might be the last words you ever speak to one another.

"Look, this is my mother's address and phone number," he said. "In emergency, I'll call Paul at the café and leave a message for you so you'll need to check with him; otherwise, perhaps you could try to be at the phone box each morning at, say, eleven? And I'll try to call you then? At the moment, anyway. I mean, if you can persuade Paul or Patrick to let you use their phone inside that might be warmer than hanging about in a phone box if I'm delayed or something?"

"Yes, alright." replied.

He was putting his coat on and finding his boots when he paused and looked at me.

"Look, are you sure you won't come?" he asked again, but this time in a much warmer tone than he'd used a few minutes before. "I'm going to be worried about you here all on your own. I mean, I don't know how long I'm going to be up there, do I?"

"I'll be alright, Mike. I can cope. I know what to do and how it all works. I'm not a kid," I said.

He looked at me and was about to say something but obviously thought better of it. Of course, I was a kid, in a way and it was a stupid thing to say. I think he wanted to warn me about strange men and so on; you know the kind of stuff, but of course he bit his tongue in case he patronised me.

"I'm sure I'll be OK, Mike, but if not I can always stay at the pub, can't I? Let me at least try to be a grown up woman who can fend for herself," I said. I meant it to sound a bit, like, satirical, but it came out sounding like a snide dig at him. He looked hurt again.

"OK. I'm not convinced but, like I say, I haven't the time to argue."

There was no doubt he was really worried about it. I could see that from his face as he bent down to pull on his boots. When he'd done that, he put his arms around me again and kissed me. It was a beautiful, loving kiss and I wished we hadn't spent the afternoon bitching; well, I wished I hadn't been bitching at him now that he was going off into the cold darkness.

"Look, Ellie, I'm really sorry I've been such an arse; you know, earlier, when we were talking. I'll be back as soon as I can and we'll sort everything out. You know, your education and the rest of it. OK? I'd better go," he said, glancing at his wristwatch over my shoulder. "Can't say I'm looking forward to the drive in this pissing rain, but there we are."

"Be careful, Mike," I said and suddenly I felt that I was going to cry. All the resentments and hurt feelings fell away.

"I'm sorry too. I didn't mean to sound so much of a cow."

This time he kissed me for a long time.

"I'm off. I love you," he said, opening the door.

"I love you too, Mike," I replied, just about managing to get the words out through my constricting throat.

He waved, gave me a grin and was gone. He hated to say goodbye.

*

Of course, as soon as he'd gone, I burst into tears and I couldn't stop myself from crying for ages. I think I must have kind of dozed off in between bouts of crying. Then I decided I had to get a grip on myself and start coping if only to prove to myself and to him that I could. So I sat up, dried my eyes, listened to the wind slapping the house about and wondered what it was best to do.

I decided to build up the fire in the stove and cook myself something to eat. I realised that I was very hungry and looked at my watch. It was after seven o'clock, so it wasn't surprising that I was famished. I don't know what time Mike had left; just after five, I think, so I suppose I must have been grizzling to myself for well over an hour.

Once I'd chucked some wood in the stove and it started hissing and popping contentedly to itself, warming the place up, I felt a bit better. If you're miserable and cold, it's hell. Miserable and warm isn't so bad. I found some eggs to make an omelette and a can of beans. Not posh restaurant stuff, but it did the trick. After I'd washed up and tidied away it was about eight. I sat on the sofa and wondered what to do next. In the evenings, Mike and I would usually read or chat or play cards or something like that.

We could have had a television run off the solar and wind turbine thing but he didn't really want one. He said that most of what's on is utter crap and we'd be better off without it. It was one of those times when he kind of steam-rollered his opinion over me. I don't mean that I'm a wimp but sometimes he had a way of just saying how it was going to be that meant there wasn't going to be a discussion and in those very early weeks I just went along with it. It would have helped in the situation I was in to have something, crappy or not, to stare at to take my mind off everything.

I tried reading my book but I couldn't get into it and then I tried playing solitaire but that felt like, stupid. So in the end, I went to bed. Just before I turned off the light, I looked at Mike's wall calendar for some reason. It was November 29th and I realised that it was exactly a year to the day since we had first made love on that fantastic night in Emma's flat. So, of course, that started me crying all over again.

To be honest, I think I was crying not just because of the memory but also because of the realisation that things had changed in that year so far as our sex life was concerned. I mean, it was still fantastic and I wasn't complaining at all but that urgent excitement had waned a bit: that incredible high you get when it's new; when you don't know the guy all that well. Maybe that's how I like it best. Anyway, nothing stays the same, does it?

So I didn't sleep very soundly. I felt sad and wished Mike was there to cuddle up against. The wind got much noisier in the night and it was raining even harder. I wasn't frightened, exactly, but, well, uneasy. And, of course, I got cold. Usually, I used to sleep naked. Mike didn't like me wearing pyjamas or anything so as he could run his hands over me in the night. Anyway, that night I had on my thick pyjamas since he wasn't there, but I was still bloody freezing.

I woke up about two and I was shivering. It was really cold. The stove had gone out but there was no more wood in the basket. I'd forgotten to fill it before I went to bed. First mistake. So if I wanted to re-light the bloody thing I'd have to go outside onto the verandah where we had a stack of wood ready. I put on a pullover and also my dressing gown and then Mike's old coat which he kept on the back of the door.

And then I did something so bloody stupid, like, I'm embarrassed to mention it. I took the log basket, unlocked and opened the door and stepped out onto the verandah. It was blowing hard and it was very, very cold. The rain had eased a bit but it hadn't stopped and the wind was blowing it sideways onto the edge of the verandah. Some of the logs looked wet so I decided to take some from the back of the pile.

I was just leaning over to get some from the dry area when there was a strong gust of wind and the door slammed shut behind me. Mistake number two.

I shrieked and swore and then, like you do, I went and tried to push the door open. There was a mortice lock on the bloody thing and there was no doubt that the catch had engaged and that it wasn't going to open.

I was on my own, locked outside a posh shed on a cliff at two o'clock on a wild, freezing November night wearing an assortment of inadequate clothes and slippers. What a bloody idiot! How could I have been so stupid? I was really angry with myself.

I started shivering and shaking. My teeth were chattering and I couldn't feel my fingers properly. I knew I had to do something to get back inside and fast. Staying outside wasn't an option. At that moment I think I realised just how isolated we were. Running for help wasn't really on either. The pub was the nearest place but even that was a good twenty, twenty five minutes in daylight on a dry day. I'd freeze to death and they'd find me in the bushes, an icy corpse.

I realised I was going to have to break back in and cause damage in the process. All I could think about was that Mike would be pissy about it and then I thought, so what are you going to do? Stand here until he comes home with his key because you're worried he'll strop if you break in? Don't be bloody daft.

I grabbed one of the smaller logs and banged it against the glass of the window. Nothing happened. I hit it again and it cracked. I hit it really hard and there was this terrible splintering noise and some of the glass fell inside. I'd never smashed a window before so I didn't really know what to expect. I bashed out the bits that were still there. But once again, I'd been an idiot. I couldn't reach the stay thing at the bottom inside because I'd smashed the top pane. Instead of finding something to use to snag the stay and lift it up, I kind of panicked and smashed the bottom pane as well. There was glass everywhere.

I opened the window so that I could climb in. I had to use some logs to get high enough to get my leg over the window cill. As I was climbing in, the dressing gown cord got caught somewhere and I lost my balance and fell in, cutting my hand on some of the broken glass that was on the floor inside. It was quite a deep cut and now there was blood everywhere as well. Jesus, what a mess! Of course, the cut hurt and I was sobbing as I tried to find something to wrap round it. I used a tea towel in the end.

We had a First Aid tin and I found that, cleaned the cut as best I could and then put a clean dressing on it. The bleeding wasn't that bad. Then I went outside again but this time I put the catch up and wedged the door open as well, just in case. I grabbed some logs and filled the basket and brought it back in.

I was about to try to light the stove when I realised that although I had shut the door again, there was still a gale inside! I had to make a repair to the window. Fortunately, I remembered that there were a few pieces of plywood left over from the renovation work. They were round the back of the house under a kind of lean-to thing Mike had built. It meant going outside again! This time I put on some proper clothes and boots.

Eventually, I managed to find a piece the right size and to find the hammer and some nails. I nailed the thing to the outside of the window frame. Like, it wasn't very expert or very tidy but at least it kept the worst of the cold air out. It took ages to get the bloody stove to light as well but at last I managed to do it and I sat right up against it. I practically had the damned thing in my lap.

I can cope, I'm not a kid. Yeah, right.

I decided to go back to bed and before I went to sleep I made up my mind that when I spoke to Mike on the phone in the morning, I wasn't going to tell him about the window. I'd get it repaired and then maybe he'd never know.

*

I was waiting at the phone box at eleven like he said only he didn't call until nearly ten past. He was obviously having a bad time. He sounded strained, like choked. He said his mother was very ill and they didn't expect her to pull through. I said I was sorry but it didn't seem enough somehow. I heard myself say it and it sounded false. Then I started crying which I didn't want to do because I knew he had enough grief to be getting on with and he didn't need me blubbing down the phone as well. I was crying because I missed him and because everything felt wrong.

269

I said to phone me at the pub at twelve the next day if he could. I was sure it would be OK with Patrick. I said I couldn't stand in the cold outside the phone box anymore. And that was it. I kept sniffling and he was obviously distracted so we said goodbye. It was one of those phone calls that I'd rather not have had. Sometimes the phone can, like, make you love the person all the more, even though you can't see them. And sometimes, it just leaves you feeling empty and hopeless.

I went back up the cliff. If anything, it was even colder than the previous day. I stuffed the stove with logs and did a bit of tidying. Then I thought, shit to this, I'm going to go to the pub. I thought I could speak to Patrick about using the phone there. Also I thought he might know someone who could mend the window. Those were my excuses, anyway. I think really I just wanted to get out of that shack and have some ordinary human company. Like, I felt so miserable. It must have been about one when I got there.

Patrick had a fantastic fire blazing away in the inglenook in the public bar and that made me feel better as soon as I walked in. There were a few locals in there who smiled and said hello.

"Hello, gorgeous," said Patrick. "Where's your minder? Not let you out on your own has he? He wants to watch out, someone'll carry you off!"

I explained what had happened and he expressed surprise that Mike had left me on my own. He was quite critical, in fact. He thought I ought to stay at the pub.

"Be much more sensible for you, safer and more comfortable. It doesn't seem right, you all alone down there on the cliff in this weather," he said, frowning.

I said wanted to try to cope if I could, just to prove it to myself. He laughed.

"Women! All the same! Well, the offer's there. Just say the word."

I asked him if he knew a glazier or someone who could mend a window. I pretended that it had blown open in the gale and smashed. Like, I didn't want to tell him the truth.

Before he could answer, he was called to serve someone in the other bar. I took my drink and went to sit in the recess by the inglenook.

"Broken window? I can fix that for you," said a voice.

I looked up and over to the end of the bar and Curly was walking towards my table. Just like before, except that this time he didn't appear to be drunk and he looked considerably smarter. Very presentable, in fact.

"You remember me, don't you, Ellie?"

"I could hardly forget, could I?" I said.

He laughed, showing his lovely white teeth.

"No, I suppose not. I'm Dave. Dave Crabbe. Did I say before? I was a bit out of order that day. Sorry! Too much Happy Jack, I think!"

It was quite a gracious apology, really. And he just stood there. Didn't park himself uninvited like he did before. I didn't want to encourage him but he didn't seem so pushy and he had said something about mending the window. So I thought, what the hell?

"Apology accepted. Thank you," I said. "Are you a glazier, then?"

"No, I'm a car mechanic. But I can glaze a window, no trouble."

"Two windows," I said, smiling.

"Been having a smashing time, ey?" Dave grinned.

Like, it was a pathetic joke but I laughed anyway and told the lie about the gale again. We talked a bit about the weather, like you do. He seemed quite normal and friendly so I agreed that he could do the job. He asked about glass size and I gave him as best an idea as I could. He said he'd be able to fix it at ten the following day.

"You live in Old Jim Butler's place, don't you? I know it. See you at ten, then?"

And with that, he went back to his stool at the bar. He hadn't even sat down at my table or tried it on or anything. I was puzzled and, like, intrigued.

Later, when I'd got back home and sat down, I started to wonder whether I'd made another mistake. He knew that Mike wasn't around. But he hadn't asked me about Mike at all. Maybe he had set out to intrigue me, I thought. Well, if he did, it worked. Anyway, I needed the bloody window mending before Mike came back.

*

I slept better that night and woke up about eight. At ten on the dot, Dave appeared at the gate. He had some glass wrapped in thick paper and a bag of tools. He looked really smart, like the day before. I could see he'd had a shave and his curly hair was clean and shiny. I was amused: I mean, you don't need to make an impression if you're just there to mend a broken window, do you?

"OK?" he said.

"I'm fine," I replied. "Over there, look."

Within a few minutes, he had taken off the piece of plywood and was chipping out the old putty. I was raking up leaves. I decided that when he'd finished, I'd give him the money and make it clear that was that.

"This won't take long, Ellie," he called. "These are new windows, aren't they? The putty's very soft still, so I can get it out easily."

"Yes. OK, good," I said.

I watched him out of the corner of my eye. He was a very precise and quick worker. I mean, he obviously knew what he was doing. After a while, I decided I was getting cold so I put the rake away and went inside.

Now it was his turn to watch me through the window. It wasn't that kind of lecherous, lip-smacking stare that I was used to from some men, but it wasn't a series of idle glances either. I was certain he was looking at my figure: or what he could imagine of it under the baggy clothing I was wearing.

He was right about it being easy. The new glass was in place in no time.

"All done," he said. "You want to check it over?"

"OK," I said. I went outside and stood next to him, looking at the window. He'd made a really good job of it. The putty was expertly done and looked all nice and smooth.

"Leave it a couple of days and then you can clean the finger marks off and put some paint on, if you've got any around? As long as it's not frosty, that is."

He smiled and flicked his hair back with a jerk of his head. I shivered. It was cold but that wasn't the reason I had come up in goose bumps.

"Thanks, Dave," I said. "That's great. Yeah, we've got some of that paint. I can do it later in the week, then."

"Anywhere I can wash my hands? Linseed oil from the putty," he said, holding his fingers up in the air. He had very delicate hands. Not at all like a motor mechanic's.

"Oh, well, right, yes. In the kitchen," I replied, turning back to the door. "Come in."

He followed me through the door.

"Well! You've certainly improved this place," he said, as I directed him to the sink and found him an old towel.

"Thanks. It was a lot of hard work, though. Er, would you like a cup of tea or coffee? Before you go?" I asked. It seemed, like, rude not to offer but I thought I'd add, "before you go".

"Yeah, thanks, if it's not too much trouble. Coffee. Two sugars, please."

While I was making it, I felt that there was a part of me wanting him to go right away; a part of me that was very apprehensive about him being there. It felt, like, dangerous. And there was another part of me that wanted him to stay. That was the part of me that was watching his buttocks flex as he scrubbed his hands at the sink. I know! But I couldn't help it.

He leant with his back to the sink while he drank the coffee. I didn't invite him to sit down. I sort of fidgeted about the room while we were talking, moving things around. He watched me all the time, like he had done through the window. Like a cat and a mouse, but I'm not sure which of us was which.

I don't remember what we talked about: his job, what we'd done to the shack, where he lived; that kind of thing. Afterwards, I realised that he didn't give me any personal details; like whether he was married or anything. And he didn't ask about Mike. And I didn't mention Mike either. It was like this thing we both knew was there but we were going to ignore it. He knew that I knew why he wasn't referring to my husband. He was waiting to see if I would.

I should have done, to make my position clear. But I didn't. Like, it was a silent kind of conversation under the real one but it had more to say than the real one. But, I mean, dangerous. By not mentioning Mike I was giving him a signal, I suppose. I didn't think of it like that at the time, only afterwards.

"So, was I right in the pub before? You're not eighteen yet?"

He took a swig of the coffee, looking at me unblinkingly over the rim of the mug.

I wondered why he was asking that.

"My birthday's in August," I said. "I'm seventeen."

"Mmm," he said. It seemed he approved. "I thought so."

"How old are you then?" I said abruptly.

"Guess," he grinned.

He stood up straight and held his stomach in. Not that he needed to.

"Not bad, ey? What do you reckon?"

"Late twenties?" I said hesitantly.

"Spot on. Twenty seven. Well, twenty eight just after Christmas."

"Oh," I mumbled. I couldn't think of anything else to say. I started to feel hot even though it was quite cold by the stove.

I reckon it took him at least half an hour to drink that bloody coffee. It must have been stone cold by the time he finished.

"Thanks," he said, "that was great. Well, I'd better be off."

"Oh, right. How much do I owe you?" I asked.

"Favour for a friend, right? Just let me have the cost of the glass and the putty. Here, I've got a receipt," he smiled, pulling a piece of paper from the pocket of his jeans.

"Really? But I feel I should give you something for your time," I said.

He looked at me, raised an eyebrow and grinned.

"Well, just let's say it's a favour. For a damsel in distress."

I thought that was a patronising and puke remark but at the same time, I wished he wouldn't keep running his hand through his curls the way he did.

I took the receipt and then went into the bedroom to get the money. He was still leaning against the sink when I came back a few moments later.

"Here you are, then," I said, handing him some notes and coins. "Thank you very much. You've got me out of a hole."

He put his hand out but didn't actually take the money. He kind of wrapped his fingers around it and around my hand too. He looked at me, held my gaze and I could see his eyes twinkling. He didn't let go but I didn't pull my hand away either.

He took a step forward, put his other hand behind my neck and pulled me towards him. Before I knew what was happening, we were kissing. And I mean kissing, really passionately. The money fell to the floor and he put his other hand on my back. I think my arms had been at my sides but then I had them on his shoulders and his neck. I wasn't resisting. I could feel myself getting really aroused and he knew it too.

His right hand went under my pullover and he began to fondle my breasts. I groaned a bit and he squeezed me harder.

I suppose we were locked together like that for a few minutes. It was fantastic and it was awful at the same time. There were two voices shouting at me; one was like saying to go, go and the other one was saying you can't, you're married, this is wrong and you're cheating on Mike.

Dave started pulling my shirt out from the top of my jogging pants and then he ran his hand down inside my knickers and started feeling my backside.

"Jesus, Ellie," he whispered, "you've got a fantastic body! Come on, come on, let's fuck! You know you want to!"

Well, quite often that sort of crude stuff can really make me wild with desire, but not this time. It had the opposite effect and suddenly I was looking at myself being felt by this guy who was taking advantage of the fact that my husband wasn't around.

"No, Dave! No! Get off!" I shouted, pushing him away from me. "I don't want you to do that anymore!"

"What?" he said. "What are you on about? Come on, Ellie, you're hot for it! You want it more than I do. Give me a blow then, yeah?"

"No!" I said firmly and backed away from him.

He just stood near the sink, like before.

"Look, who's going to know? It's just between you and me right? A bit of fun. I'm not interested in a life commitment or a long-term relationship! It's just the sex, right? Come on, I know you want to!"

Well, a girl knows where she is with Dave!

"Dave, please go, will you? I want you to go now. Please!" I was almost crying.

"What happened? You were going like a steam engine just then?"

"It's not right. I'm married. You know that. I can't," I said.

"Right, wrong; who gives a toss? But you want to, yeah? I know you do; admit it. First time I set eyes on you, I knew it. I can always tell. A girl who likes it fresh, time and time again!"

"Look, Dave, I made a mistake. Maybe I gave you the wrong signals, or something. I don't know. I'm sorry if I did. I want you to go now, please."

"I know what bloody signals you were giving me, Ellie," he replied irritably, adjusting himself. I could still see his erection inside his jeans.

"I'm married," I said. I wasn't going to say that I really did want him to do it to me.

There was a pause for a while. Then he made a fist and slammed it on the drainer.

"Alright, alright," he said moodily, bending down to pick up his bag of tools. "But you'll regret it. I'm bloody good you know!"

"Go away!" I shouted.

"OK, OK, I'm going. But you know what? I've been with a lot of women, so I know a thing or two. I know I'm right. You wanted it just then, alright. You want it most of the time, don't you? Even when you say you don't, yeah? You're desperate for it. I know all the signs. Yeah? Fucking is what you do best, isn't it? Yeah? Not relationships, right? Move on to a new fuck; I know. And I know why. Well, when he can't get it up anymore or you get tired of him or you just want an orgasm like you've never had in your life, you know where to reach me. My number's on the back of that receipt."

"You're disgusting!" I said. "Now get out of my house!"

He laughed and opened the door.

"Ellie, I don't know anything about you; but I know all there is to know. And you're kidding yourself with the faithful little housewife act. You'll change your mind," he said. "Girls like you always do. Remember? Fucking's what you do best, yeah? And if it's this afternoon, I'll be in the pub! See you!"

With that he slammed the door and was gone.

I grabbed a cushion from the sofa where I'd ended up and threw it across the room, giving a scream of anger, self-disgust and, yeah, he was right, frustration. It was so true, what he said. I was hot for it; hot for him. What a slut. And I'd forgotten to go up to the pub to take Mike's call.

IV THRENODY

I felt so dirty and yet so full of desire.

I nibbled at some cheese and crisps. Then I went back outside to do some more clearing up to try to take my mind off the stuff that was starting to bother me. The sky was like a sheet of lead. It was so cold that I only managed about an hour before I had to come in again.

There was a knock at the door at about half past four. It was dark by then and I jumped out of my skin with fright. My immediate thought was that it was Dave come back with a belly full of beer and not prepared to take no for an answer this time. If it had been Dave, he wouldn't have got no for an answer. In the previous couple of hours I'd come to the conclusion that if I was a slut, I might as well have fun behaving that way.

"Ellie, it's only me, Patrick. Are you alright?"

With a mixture of relief and stinging disappointment, I opened the door.

"Patrick? Come in, it's freezing out there."

As he came in and took his jacket off, I was wondering whether he was going to try it on with me as well, but he's not like that. That's what I'd always thought about Patrick; then a voice said that they're all like that. Especially with young women.

"I thought I'd better make sure that you're alright," he said, looking concerned.

"Oh," I replied, "shouldn't I be, then? I'm fine."

He looked at me and I saw doubt flicker across his face. And curiosity.

"It's just that Dave Crabbe came stomping in at about half twelve, looking like thunder. There are usually only two things that make him mad: drink or women. I assumed it was the latter," he said.

He looked at me again and left the remark hanging in the air to see whether I'd offer any explanation.

"He told you he'd been here, then?" I said, trying to sound off-hand.

"Well, yes, he said he'd been repairing your broken window."

"That's right. He did it very well," I said, inclining my head towards the curtained window behind me.

"Mmm. It's just that, well, I'm not trying to pry, Ellie. But we all know what Dave Crabbe is like, especially with young girls. Sorry, that sounds a bit patronising, but you know what I mean?"

I thought he was prying. The creep.

"I'm OK, Patrick, as you can see. I'm fine," I said.

"He's pretty insistent, I believe and they say he usually gets his way. Been a rumour going around that he's been, well, you know, with a girl of fourteen over at Chine. She looks a lot older, apparently. That's how he likes it," he said.

I wasn't sure how I was supposed to respond to that piece of information so I thought it best to tell him what he obviously wanted to know.

"Oh, right," I said. "Well, he did try it on but it was no big deal, Patrick. I just told him to piss off and that was that."

"I thought as much," he said. "It explains his bad temper when he got to the pub. Anyway, good for you, Ellie. You can look after yourself, then?"

I gave a rather feeble smile and nodded.

"Patrick, did Mike phone earlier? I was expecting to be at the pub at twelve but, of course, Dave was still here so I couldn't," I asked, trying to move the conversation on.

"Yes, that's the other reason I came down," he said. "Mike did phone but not at twelve. It was about three, just as we were bottling up. He sounded pretty grim. He asked whether you'd been in and I explained to him why you weren't there. I'm sorry, but it seemed like the right thing to do at the time, but, well, maybe not?"

I didn't want to ask him exactly what he'd told Mike otherwise he'd see that it did matter.

"It's alright, Patrick," I said as confidently as I could, "you haven't dropped me in it. There is no need for you to worry."

I stood up and went over to the kitchen area and started banging things about to make it clear I thought the conversation was over.

"Oh, good, well that's OK, then," he mumbled. "Mike said he'd phone again tomorrow at twelve."

*

That night was stormy and the wind started making this really weird cooing, hissing sound and then a screeching noise after I'd gone to bed. I think it was whistling in the water tank gantry or something. At one point it sounded like a small child crying.

In my dreams, I was back in the courtroom and the whining noise that the wind was making became, like, laughter and hissing from the jury and the public gallery as Sowerby questioned me.

Sowerby is like a giant pig: all red and fleshy. His nasal hair is about six inches long. Bristly. He has tusks.

"A vigorous and enthusiastic participant in sexual intercourse," says Sowerby, feeling himself under his gown whilst jerking his hips backwards and forwards. A belly-dancing pig.

A whistling sound comes from the jury.

"He says she screamed with pleasure too…ooooh… and so he did it even harder!" Sowerby is spluttering; spittle hits the polished rail of the jury box.

Check-suit in the jury wolf-whistles and shouts out, "Cunnilingus, cunnilingussssssss in all manner of positionssssssss and placessssssssss…ooooooh…whoooo…ooooh!"

He begins to waggle his tongue suggestively, like Jimi Hendrix.

Sowerby has exposed himself and is beckoning to me to come and touch him. I can see Dave in the public gallery. He is leaning against the safety rail and his impossibly large erection is visible in his jeans.

He is hissing through his teeth and says, "She told me to push harder, push harder, pusssssssssssssshhhhh harder…your Honour…what can a man dooooooo?"

I can hear a screaming noise and I think it's coming out of my mouth but it isn't. I look around the courtroom and I see my mother in the middle of a cheering crowd. Dad is there and he's pushed her onto all fours. He is crouched behind her, pawing and ripping at her underwear. She is the one who is screaming. There is blood on her skirt. Dad is laughing a high-pitched sound like a hyena. I recognise the sound.

"Ladies and Gentlemen of the Jury," says Sowerby, fondling the rigid enormity of himself, "the complainant wants vigorous sex …ssssssssseeexxxxxx…as the norm in a relationsssssship with a much older maaaaan, mmmm, oooohhh, aaaah, as I shall now demonstrate. If the complainant would care to dissssssssrobe?"

There is a roaring, thundering sound as the men in the jury cheer and bang their fists on the seat backs. I look down and see I have only a small towel, barely covering myself. My breasts are bulging over the top and I feel that my rear is completely exposed. The Judge indicates that I should take off the towel.

Dave is suddenly beside me and is running his engine-oiled fingers around my nipples. I'm wriggling with pleasure but my mother is still screaming horribly somewhere.

"Perhaps the complainant is frightened of what she has unleasssssshed in herself?" shouts Sowerby.

"Unleasssssssssshed...unleasssssshhed...After you, Mr.Crabbe! Take the slut for all she's worth! Which isn't much! Ha...aaaaah!"

"Aaaah! Waaahhhh!" the jury whine and shout.

Dave begins to unbutton his jeans.

"Come on Ellie, letsssssss fuck...sssssssuuucck. Cck...Cck..."

I am completely naked and the eyes of all the men are on me, boring into my visible openings with hot pokers. I bend down to do Dave's bidding and flashbulbs go off.

I smile at all the men and they grin and gesticulate.

"Me next...aaaaaahh!"

They begin to jostle for places in a queue which snakes around the courtroom. I am on my knees like a dog.

Suddenly I see Mike elbowing his way through the screeching crowd. He is punching at the ogling men and he is waving our marriage certificate over his head. Someone makes a grab at it and it tears, falling in wet shreds like seaweed.

"Ellie! Ellie! It's me! I have the boat and the sssssssppooooooooon! Ruuuuuncibbbble spooohhhhhnnnn."

He stops and sees me naked, kneeling in front of Dave. It is clear to him what I am about to do. I try to stand up and cover myself.

"What the? What the hell are you doing?" he wails. "Ellie! Ellie! No, no, please, no! You bitch! You whore!You slut! Slut! SSSSSSSssssslut!"

"Ooooooooh!" howl the people.

*

All the next morning, the Monday, I kept looking at my watch. I had to make sure that I didn't miss Mike's call a second time. Of course, I was like a cat on a hot tin roof, jumping about, unable to sit still or settle to doing anything. I just didn't know how I was going to explain away to Mike what had happened the day before: I didn't know how Patrick had said what whatever he'd said and I didn't know how much to tell Mike. Sometimes I thought it would be best to tell him the whole lot and, like, throw myself on his mercy and at other times I was working out how I could lie to him effectively.

And then I felt really shit that I was thinking that way at all.

I was putting my coat on about quarter past eleven when I was aware of a shadow flicking across the window at the front. Then a key went into the lock, the door opened and Mike was standing there.

I was so pleased to see him! I'm sure I looked totally surprised and then I kind of just threw myself in his direction.

"Mike, oh, Mike!" I cried, "You're back! What happened?"

I tried to kiss him but, although he gave me a peck, he looked really grey and tired and he was, like, tense. He didn't push me away exactly, but it was like embracing a lamp post. I sort of stepped back a bit and we were just standing there facing each other with our coats on. He didn't say anything for a minute but just looked at me. There was a terrible sadness in his eyes.

"Mum died yesterday in the hospital about quarter to twelve. That's why I didn't phone," he said quietly. He sat on the sofa, took his glasses off and put his head in his hands.

I didn't know what to do or say. All I could think about was that his mother had died just as Dave was slipping his searching hands inside my damp knickers.

THE CRYING GAME

After the stroke, Mum didn't regain consciousness at all. She lay motionless, white and crumpled, like discarded old newspapers, until she died. There was no sudden dramatic moment; no scream of pain or moans or a calling out to the Lord. In fact, the only way that Andy and I knew she'd gone was because something on one of the machines stopped ticking or beeping. There was nothing else to tell us that the woman who had given us life had left us behind.

Although I was supposed to call Ellie at twelve, by the time I was able to think about doing so, it was gone three. I knew it was unlikely that she'd still be waiting in 'The King's Head', but I thought she might have left a message with Patrick.

"To be honest she didn't show in the first place," he said when I finally got through and explained I had expected to call her at twelve.

I was immediately gripped with fear and panic, thinking she'd hurt herself or had slipped down the cliff or something bloody awful.

"Mike, it's alright. I think so, anyway," Patrick said. "She had a problem with a broken window; something to do with Friday's gale and she was getting it repaired at lunch time today."

I knew there was something else he wanted to tell me and I knew I wasn't going to like it. Eventually he told me that Ellie had asked him whether he knew a glazier but before he'd had a chance to find the number of a local man, Dave Crabbe had approached her and, apparently, she'd accepted his offer with alacrity. I didn't know who the hell he was talking about at first but when the penny dropped, I was alarmed and angry. How could she be so stupid and gullible as to ask that lecherous bastard? Or was there no broken window at all? Jealousy and fear of what might be were shaping themselves in my mind.

"Is he a glazier, then?" I snapped.

"He's a car mechanic, actually. Maybe he does windows on the side. I don't know; not heard that he does. He's a bit of a lad, they say. There's a rumour going round that he's got an underage girl from over Chine way pregnant and of course there was that business with Madge Potter's daughter last year," he said. "He likes them young, they say."

"Thanks for that, Patrick, that's just about made my day that has. All I needed to hear, isn't it, that my young wife has invited the local ram to come and service her needs while I'm on the other side of the fucking country? Really has cheered me up no end, that has, Patrick," I said, snarling with sarcasm.

By about seven that evening I was ready to get in the car and come back to 'The Crows' Nest' as fast as I could but Andy dissuaded me on the grounds that I was too tired and distraught and that if I must do the drive, let it be after some sleep. He said he was happy to sort out the funeral arrangements and so by six the following morning, I was on the M25.

*

As soon as I got back to the cliff and walked through the door, I could tell that something was wrong. When you have been completely absorbed and mesmerised by another person's very being, you can tell straight away when the balance of things has been disturbed. I had hoped all the way down in the car that when I walked through the door, everything would be like it was before; like the elation and harmony we had found on the beach, in fact and that the doubts which had been in my mind periodically before I left and then which Patrick had made worse, would be shown to be without foundation. Blown away.

As I came through the door, I could see that she wasn't holding my gaze properly; her eyes would rest on me briefly but then would start flicking about all over the place. Her movements were somehow nervous and unsteady. She was jittery; apprehensive.

She wanted to embrace me and I wanted to embrace her too and kiss her but something in her apparent enthusiasm seemed false and, for my part, I felt wooden and unable to initiate any warmth. I remember collapsing into the sofa. Emotionally exhausted by the events of the weekend, tired by the journey and impaled by spears of doubt as I came through the door, I broke down and wept.

Ellie just stood by me for a while, unable to do anything. That in itself spoke more words than all the following conversation. Eventually, she sat beside me and held my hands and wiped my eyes with her handkerchief. It was probably a good five minutes before I managed to calm myself, after which I took my coat off and splashed some cold water on my face. I went out to The Facility and when I came back, Ellie had taken her coat off too and was standing looking out of the window at the sea.

"We need to talk," I said.

"Yes, OK," she replied.

There was a long pause.

"Are you going to tell me or do I have to drag it out of you?" I said.

I knew it was a confrontational remark. Dr. Chadwick commencing his interrogation of naughty Ellen Amanda Fortune. Yes, but what I didn't know was just how naughty Ellen had been.

"Tell you what?" she said feebly.

"Oh, for Christ's sake, Ellie," I said angrily, "don't let's piss about! Let's save ourselves the mental energy, shall we? You know what I'm talking about. I've spoken to Patrick who's given me the theme but not the entire melody. Sing it to me, why don't you?"

She backed away a little. I suppose my body language must have been very threatening but even so, I was surprised.

"What's the matter? Why are you backing away like that?"

"I don't know, Mike. You're frightening me. It feels like you're going to smack me one," she whined.

"What? You ought to know me better than that. OK, OK!"

I took a step backwards.

"So what happened? I'd like you to tell me, please."

"Well, I was stupid, I locked myself out and I had to smash the window."

"Look," I said, "I'm not really interested at this stage in the fucking window!"

I was being really aggressive, I suppose. I ought to have let her chunter on about the window so she could come to the main event in her own good time, but I was so distressed and bloody angry, I didn't have the patience. She was indicating the window with one hand and we both looked at it. The rain was weeping great tears down the glass.

"Oh, I don't know, though," I laughed hollowly.

"Look!" I pointed at the glass. "Oily fingerprints made by the grease-ball Crabbe! And where else did his grubby fingers end up?" I yelled. "Let's deal with the real issue here, shall we?"

"Mike, please stop shouting," she said.

"Why? Are you worried the neighbours will hear? I'll stop shouting if you'll stop being evasive! Tell me what happened!"

She looked as if she was going to cry. I was getting really angry.

"Well?"

"Mike, please calm down. You're really frightening me," she sobbed, moving away from me and pressing herself into one end of the sofa.

"Right, look. Let's short-circuit this, Ellie, shall we, otherwise we'll be here all night going round in circles. You broke a window. It doesn't matter how at the moment. For reasons best known to yourself, you asked or agreed to Crabbe coming here yesterday morning to mend it. Correct so far?"

"Yes," she whispered. "He offered . I didn't ask but I wanted it done quickly, so..."

"OK, progress. I'm sure he did offer. Now, I'm speculating on the basis of what I have already seen of Mr. Crabbe's behaviour towards you last August and further, on the basis of information or gossip, maybe, which has been forwarded to me in this context by our friendly publican, Patrick. To whit, the bastard likes them young!"

"So do you," she said.

That stopped me in my tracks for a fraction of second.

"Indeed," I said, recovering myself, "but at least I have the grace and integrity to profess undying love and to propose and undertake marriage. Apparently, he just fucks them and leaves them. Am I right?"

"How should I know?" Ellie said petulantly.

"Good question," I replied, "but you are the only one here who can answer it. Yes? So, I speculate that Crabbe, having mended the window and gained some favour, wheedled his way in here and then tried it on?"

She didn't say anything, but stared at her feet. I shouldn't have been surprised. As on more than one occasion in the past, she was reacting to my sarcastic, savage schoolteacher with her sulky, uncommunicative pupil.

"Ellie?"

"I suppose so," she said.

"Jesus, Joseph and Mary," I said. "You suppose so? Look, Ellie, I just need to know what happened. He tried it on. OK, then what? I'd like you to tell me. Please. At least be honest with me, even if what I have to hear is going to hurt."

She looked up at me and there were enormous teardrops welling up in those green eyes.

"Promise me you won't be angry and hit me or something," she said very softly.

"Where's this coming from, Ellie? Hit you? When did I ever lay a finger on you? I can't promise not to be angry, but of course I won't hit you. Jesus Christ! Has it come to that already?"

I couldn't believe what she was saying and what I was forced to say in return.

There was a long pause. She fiddled with her socks, her sleeves and her hair. She looked up at me several times but wasn't able to say anything. I realised that standing over and above her was not helping, so I smiled a kind of wan smile and sat on the other end of the sofa, keeping a distance between us.

"So?" I said encouragingly.

She started crying and threw herself at me, putting her arms around my neck.

"Mike, Mike, I'm so sorry, I don't know what happened or why..."

I pulled her close to me and put my face into her hair.

"Ellie, this is torturing me. You haven't told me anything at all yet. Put me out of my misery, for God's sake. A simple question, OK? Did you have sex with him? Commit adultery? Ellie?"

She shook her head furiously.

"No, Mike, I didn't! No. You must believe me!"

"OK. I believe you. Thank you."

Suddenly she sat up, wiped her eyes and looked me straight in the eye. Here it comes, I thought.

"I offered him a coffee and he stood over there and I went to get the money to pay him and then he grabbed my hand and pulled me to him and snogged me and put his hand inside my pullover and my pants and he felt me, you know. And then I pushed him away and told him to sod off. Eventually he did."

She had looked away when she'd talked about him feeling her and now she looked back at me, no doubt gauging my reaction.

"Mike, I'm so sorry, forgive me, please forgive me!" she started crying and sobbing all over again.

I knew that there was more that had to come. It wasn't over yet.

"He snogged you and felt you up? He had time and encouragement to do that, then? You didn't fight him off straight away, for crying out loud?"

Ellie drew in a large breath and seemed to pull herself upright. I could tell that what she was about to say was the most difficult of all for her.

"I didn't stop him, Mike, to begin with. I don't know why, I don't know; I think maybe I was a bit hacked off about the argument we had about my education and so maybe I was getting at you in a kind of way. I don't know, it doesn't seem to make sense now. I mean, I suppose I wanted him to, you know, do what he was doing, but then, but then he wanted to go to bed and suddenly I realised what I was doing and where it was leading and I pushed him away."

I just looked at her.

"He's not important to me, Mike. It was just animal stuff, I suppose, you know?"

I could feel my fists clenching and unclenching. Despite what I'd said, I did want to hit her; to slap her all around that room, treating her like the whore that I felt she was.

She began screaming almost hysterically.

"I am a slag, aren't I? You married a slag!"

She jumped up, ran into the bedroom and threw herself on the bed.

I smashed my hand into the door as I opened it violently.

"I need some air," I said coldly.

I crashed all the way down the track to the gulley and out onto the rough pebbles of the beach. It was freezing but I didn't mind. I felt physically sick so the cold air and the rain lashing my face were a positive benefit. I stayed down there, stumbling backwards and forwards in the lee of the brooding cliff face, the breakers' roar drowning all other sounds, until the middle of the afternoon.

*

When I got back to the shack, she had fallen asleep on the bed. Her face was red and blotchy and I could see she had cried herself to sleep. I closed the bedroom door and went and sat on the sofa.

After a while, I started to think that my largely unarticulated fears about what might happen if she went off to college and then University had been shown to be well-founded. She was susceptible to temptation, simple as that. Of course, I was hardly in a position to adopt any moral high ground, although I had been doing just that. Odd how blind you can be when there is emotional hurt involved.

What I had done myself with her twelve months previously when I was still married to Barbara and she was my pupil was worse. Or what about the moment of surging, priapic lust with Simone under the olive trees at Gassin? We didn't know each other; there was no relationship between us of any kind; she didn't even know my name, I don't think. But as Barbara had put it so adroitly at the time, we would have fucked like dogs out in the open. That's what I wanted and what stopped us was not my conscience as Ellie's had stopped her. Could her actions be considered worse than Old Nibber's, decades ago, turning his back on his wife to run after a nubile kitchen maid he found among the runner beans?

289

Let he who is without sin cast the first stone. One of the few things you can find in the Bible which makes sound sense. I wanted, despite the burning hurt, the anger and the sickness of jealousy, to forgive her. To push the matter away, just as other matters had been buried for the previous five months. Put another way, I saw that I could rationalise a path through it; what I couldn't tell was whether my heart would let me. Only time would tell, I said to myself, recalling with a wry grin Barbara's mother's phrase. But I had to try. We had to try.

I went back into the bedroom and sat on the edge of the bed next to Ellie. She was still asleep. I stroked her hair for a while until she woke up. She looked at me, her eyes red with weeping.

"I feel so worthless, like a piece of shit," she whispered at last. "I've failed you. How can you ever trust me again?"

"That's the issue, Ellie, you're dead right. You want me too?"

"Of course I do, Mike. I love you, whatever's happened," she replied.

"I love you too, Ellie, that's why this is hurting me so much."

"I know. I'm sorry. Give me time to show you I can be trusted again, please?"

We held on to each other for a long time, crying more tears of anguish and regret.

ELEGY IN AN ESSEX CHURCHYARD

It is bleak mid-winter on the misty edge of the oozing Essex marshes. In the distance, through a flapping curtain of fine rain, is a reedy landscape stretching in an unbroken flatness from the graveyard wall to the sea. In the foreground is a raw gash in the sticky ground.

A group of silent mourners is gathered loosely around the grave. They lower their heads, lift the collars of their heavy, black coats or press together under the glistening domes of umbrellas.

A blustery, cold wind has possession of the marshlands. Carried in its invisible skeins, the mourners smell fishy saltings, silted oyster pits, the distinctive tangs of wet sea grass and the distant, icy, green waters of the North Sea. It whines and sighs in the hawthorn hedges, tugs at the umbrellas, pries open coats with its insistent, chilled fingers and it makes raw even the sweetest of young lips.

Two little girls stand close to their father by the grave. One of them has cold tears running down her cheeks, for it is her grandmother's funeral. Her sister is crying, not just for her dead Gran but also because she confronts the primeval horror and mystery of the burial. Her mewling, keening cries are tossed over the wall by the wind and lost in the creeks and swatchways encircling the little church.

Someone has draped tarpaulins over the edges of the wound in the soil, perhaps so that it looks like roadworks and not a grave at all. Not a dark place in which to deposit a dead grandma. They cannot see the bottom of the hole but they suppose it must be very deep. They will put Gran in that deep hole in the earth; lower her in with straps under the coffin, their Daddy says and then throw wet earth on top. One of the little girls knows a song about John Brown's body, a-mouldering in the grave. They wonder about mouldering.

Waiting silently under a clump of yew trees on the far side of the churchyard there is a neat, yellow, mechanical digger. Inside a man is smoking and studying page three of 'The Sun'. Across the dun fields, somewhere on the other side of the church, comes the thick, muffled sound of a shotgun as a farmer shoots a rabbit.

Standing to one side of the group at the graveside there is a young woman, not much more than a girl, who holds the collars of her coat under the exquisite curve of her throat. She is very beautiful, especially in black. The voluptuous swelling of her bust and the trim undulations of her hips and thighs are enveloped by the thick material of the coat, but they are not lost. She is very cold, for this serrated north east wind is unfamiliar to her.

She attends the funeral out of duty. She did not know the deceased. Her husband has insisted that she accompanies him, since it is the proper thing and anyway he is no longer sure whether he can trust her to stay at home alone. Whatever sadness or despair is in her heart, it is not for the departed who is now making her last, short journey from the church. She is in mourning for another loss, for something she found once but discarded on a Devonian cliff.

On the other side of the grave, behind the little girls, is a stouter woman of middle age. Her face is creased with the pain of standing in this bitter spot and is lined with the sadness that comes from a betrayed and broken heart. She can see the tall, slim figure of the girl who has drawn her husband into the silken folds of her nubile bed. But she senses that something is strained between them.

The coffin is borne shoulder high between the mossy stumps of the gravestones of yore. The rain silvers the hats of the undertaker's men as they move slowly into the gloom of the shadow cast by the Norman tower. The bearers are paid to look serious but one of them is watching for the beautiful young woman whose figure he has already assessed during the church service. To take his mind off the discomfort of the coffin's insistent weight on his shoulder, he imagines himself stripping and raping her.

The bearers' heavy shoes scrape the flint in the path; one of the men wheezes and coughs cloying phlegm.

The other middle-aged man at the graveside turns to watch the halting progress of the coffin. As he turns, his eyes meet those of his brother's fabulous new wife. She holds his gaze for a moment, smiles imperceptibly and then her eyes flick away. His own wife, graying, thickening in the middle and devoid of a bust, stands loyally at his side. He watches the coffin but he is thinking of what it might be like in bed with a seventeen year old girl with a body like his new sister-in-law's. He sighs loudly, wistfully; a sound somehow out of harmony with other noises in the graveyard.

The officiating cleric adjusts his robes and finds his place in the dampness of his book. A drop of rainwater runs off his stubby nose and further wets the page. His voice intones flatly.

The bearers move forward. The one who has been wheezing and coughing is fighting to subdue a bronchial spasm. They grasp the straps and lower the soaking coffin into the dankness of the grave. There are more words from the

292

book and a handful of earth is thrown; the mourners hear it hit the coffin six feet below with a wet, echoing thud. Ashes to wet ashes, dust to viscous mud.

The church bell begins to sound a single, mournful note which carries across the marshes and out into the vastness of the empty sea.

As the mourners turn from the grave, the man in the digger looks up, takes a last look at page three, folds his newspaper, flicks a dog-end at a nearby headstone and starts the engine. Moments later, he is shovelling grey clay into the hole. If he's quick, there'll still be time for a wet at 'The Dog'.

*

The mourners return to the warmth of the house. The new young wife is introduced by her husband to his relatives. She makes a great effort, smiling and moving as gracefully as a cat in her slinky black dress. She is a resounding success, especially with the men.

When all the mourners have gone, the little girls have said goodbye to their Daddy and their Uncle has kindly agreed to re-unite them with their Mummy who made a tactful retreat after the interment, the man and his beautiful young wife are left alone in the house. His house, he tells her, for his parents have agreed to leave it to him. His brother inherits the freehold premises of the family business. A tidy split of the spoils.

Later, in the warm darkness of the bedroom, the middle aged man lies next to his beautiful, naked, teenage wife. He whispers to her and runs his hand down the firmness of her belly. She tenses a little. She is surprised that he wants to make love when only a few hours before, he has buried his mother. But there is more than one urgent need in him tonight.

Usually, she is quickly and easily aroused, but tonight she is not. Her husband's movements inside her become more insistent and he urges her response. She has tried to prevent it, to push the thought away but now she gives in.

She allows herself to imagine the face and the probing hands of a much younger man with curly hair.

She arches her back and jack-knifes her hips. Now she is able to cry out in ecstasy.

SILENT CONCEALMENTS

The early months of 1992 weren't always easy. Mike was obviously still very upset about his mother's death. It took weeks to clear the place and even longer for Mike to begin to smile again.

I think he would have stayed there, in that house at that time, if I had agreed. But there was no way I was going to live in that bloody gloomy place, sitting in the muddy marshes in Essex! It's a really awful part of the country. No, living there would have been worse than being in the shed on the cliff! So, after he'd cleared it, we went back to Devon and he let it out. He didn't want to sell it. I think he still lives in it now.

In the January Mike said that he thought I should start at the local sixth form college. Amazing! He was trying really hard to make things work. I think now that what he was doing was showing that he recognised that he couldn't, like, lock me up. And that he had to trust me and I had to behave accordingly. We couldn't have a marriage based on anything else, he said. He was right.

It was excellent. I really enjoyed the classes and although, of course, some of the syllabus was different to Cumbria and Somerset before that - I didn't stand much bloody chance, when you think about it - I didn't really care about that too much. I mean, I wasn't fretting about getting the 'A' Levels or University and all that crap. I was happy to be studying again and enjoying the company of people my own age.

I think I just felt that I re-established contact with the real world. It was a real release. I mean, it sounds terrible, but I couldn't wait to get out each morning and away from that shed on the cliff. The weekends and holidays were a real drag! I don't mean I wanted to get away from Mike; it wasn't that, although he could be a bit moody at times; no, the place made me feel caged. Strange, because I'd been fine down on the beach: the chalet wasn't that much bigger and the idea of the shack had been so exciting and romantic. I couldn't believe that just a short time before, I'd been so keen to do it up and move into it!

When I got back in the evening I felt, like, invigorated and if Mike was in the right mood, it would give us something to talk about. I wanted him to help me with the set texts and he did sometimes and those were the really good days. But some evenings I felt he was reluctant about it. He said that it put us back into the pupil-teacher relationship. He reckoned we had enough trouble establishing a proper relationship as it was without emphasising the age gap and going back to behaving like it used to be. He said something about the problem being that we would live forwards but think backwards.

I suppose he was right. The whole thing about the age gap, which we hadn't really bothered about for months, suddenly seemed to be an issue. Maybe it always was but we just dumped it when we were on the beach, along with everything else.

Mike wanted me to be a wife; an adult companion. His equal socially and intellectually. But he also wanted me to look young and he was more than happy that I was a schoolgirl in his bed. Being sexually involved with a young girl was what turned him on. Simple as that. So he didn't want to emphasise the age gap and then again, he did.

I wanted to be worthy of his trust. My big problem was that I wasn't sure that I could be. Well, that day when Dave Crabbe snogged me rather proved it, there was no doubt. I didn't like what I was beginning to see in myself and I couldn't altogether understand why it was like that, but I had to acknowledge that it was there.

The most gorgeous guy in the whole place was my History teacher. He was always asking if I wanted any extra help after school, to catch up on what I'd missed! Oh, really? Yeah, right. I won't say I wasn't tempted because I was, but I wasn't going to make that mistake again. Older men!

I don't mean that I had stopped loving Mike. No, definitely not. Maybe I never have. Things had cooled down a bit, like they do, but at that time and at that age I didn't really know that's what to expect. It was just that, well, I did sometimes wonder what it would be like with someone else. I mean, that's normal, isn't it?

One afternoon in late March I could see that he was hacked off when he came to pick me up at the college as usual. Public transport was total shit so we didn't have much choice but I think it made us both feel irritable. I wanted to be independent and he didn't want to be thrown into the role of a parent picking up his daughter, because, of course, that's how it felt to us and how it looked to the outside world, especially all my mates.

"You know, Ellie, this sodding college thing is tying us down. Stopping us from doing things or going places. I'm sure that sounds selfish because I know you're enjoying it and getting a kick out of it but at the moment it's pissing me off. Sorry," he said, looking up at me from under a frown.

"What things?" I replied.

"Well, I don't know. I mean, it's pretty restricting being here in this bastard weather and under different circumstances, we might have buggered off somewhere warmer for a couple of months. Seen something of the world. You know. I can afford it," he said.

"We can do that in the holidays, can't we?"

"Yes, but what I'm suggesting is long-term, not just a couple of weeks. And I'm also on about spontaneity. We can't say today, let's go tomorrow, can we?"

"You mean that you're bored and I'm not?" I suggested.

"Yes, I suppose that's about it," he mumbled.

There was more to it than just boredom on his part, of course.

We had loads of those bickering and bitching sessions. But they weren't really about what was getting at him. He'd never come out with it and say, like, I don't trust you and you're going to be tempted and shag someone else, but that's what was at the root of it. Of course, he wasn't stupid.

There was a May Ball; well, a disco at the college towards the end of May and I wanted to go. I'd made friends with a couple of girls by then and one of them, Katy, said I could stay at hers that night to save the problem of getting back to the cliff afterwards when it would be late. Mike was not amused.

He had met Katy and Claire and that didn't help my arguments for going to the disco at all! A couple of times when he'd picked me up, he was in a good mood and took us all for a coffee. Afterwards, he was quite blunt about Katy.

"I don't know about her personality but I spotted the way she wiggled her tits about, fluttered her eyelids and pouted those juicy red lips while she was licking her spoon," he said. "She's up for it."

I laughed out loud.

"You're imagining things, Mike! I didn't notice any of that."

"Well, you wouldn't. It wasn't for your benefit, was it?"

I raised the question of the disco about a week before the date and told Mike about Katy's invitation. It was difficult. I mean, I felt I couldn't just say, "I'm going" but on the other hand, I wasn't going to ask his permission, either. Maybe it was me that was being unreasonable? After all, I was married. I shouldn't have expected to go to things like that in the first place. But I was so young.

He knew as well as I did that sixth form discos can be, like, a bit of a meat market. I didn't seek to argue against that, I just said that even if it was a market, I wouldn't be buying or selling. It was that old trust thing again.

And I had no intention of breaking that trust, really I didn't. I wasn't angling to go to the disco so I could cheat on him. I didn't want to mess things up or cause loads of pain. Eventually, he agreed. I think he could see that sooner or later, he was going to have to accept that sort of thing, so it might as well be now. He made it sound like he was giving his permission and that hacked me off a bit.

The disco was great. I hadn't been to one for ages and we spent forever getting ready at Katy's, like you do. I was just a teenage girl again, out with her friends for the night. Usual stuff: shrieking; giggling; rolling your eyes; flirting with guys. It was about ten o'clock when I saw Dave come into the college hall. It was really crowded and people were jumping about all over the place, but even so, I saw him straight away. Before he saw me. The effect was, like, electric.

"What's the matter?" yelled Katy over the music.

I'd stopped dancing and was just standing there. At that moment, it occurred to me what I should do: dash out through the other door, get a taxi and go home quickly. But of course, I didn't.

"Someone's just walked in who I wish hadn't!" I yelled back.

"What?" shouted Katy.

"Never mind," I mimed.

Of course, he spotted me within a few minutes. After all, that's what he was doing there, wasn't he? I don't mean he was looking for me, because he had no idea I was a student there. No, he'd managed to wangle a ticket somehow and he was there because he knew it would be heaving with young girls. He looked good. I mean, really hunky. Dressed for the kill.

He came over to me and the others. We danced for a while and when the slow stuff came on he got really close and horny. Claire was scandalised and Katy looked jealous. Towards the end of the evening, he said, "Let's go" and I didn't utter a word of objection. By then I knew what was going to happen. And I wanted it to. I just signalled with my hand to Katy that I was off; she smiled, whispered, "Be careful!" and we were gone.

In his oily smelling and rattling car that he told me that Mike had sought him out, warned him off and threatened him. He was quite open about the girl over Chine way that he'd got pregnant. There was no pretence with Dave. You knew exactly what he was interested in and exactly what you were walking into.

He rented a flat above a dry cleaner's in Bere High Street. Opposite the chip shop. Romantic? I don't think so. It was seedy but I didn't expect it to be any different. I wasn't there for the interior décor or for romance. I was there for sex and he knew it. He had told me the previous November that fucking is what I do best and that night I proved his view of me correct.

He'd got me back to his flat and into his grubby bed by turning on the charm but once he'd got my pants and bra off me, he didn't need to charm me anymore. He was like a machine, designed solely for screwing. It was like he was plugged into a socket. He just kept going, with hardly a pause. He didn't say anything, he just groaned and grunted. Seamless sex and orgasm.

Of course, I wasn't falling behind and he knew I wouldn't; that's why I was there. I was a pneumatic nympho, not a girl with a name or a personality. And that was OK by me. I lost count of how many times we actually did it. I shouldn't think his neighbours got much sleep that night.

At six, he got out of the bed, said he worked Saturdays, pulled on some grimy overalls and went over to the door. I thought he was going to go without saying anything, but in fact he paused, turned to look at me and spoke.

"Thanks, Ellie. I was right, wasn't I? You just love fucking, don't you?"

And with that, he was gone. I never saw him again.

LOVE HURTS

I lay there for a few minutes and thought about what he meant and what I had done. I was really ashamed of myself and I felt dirty and used. I had been used. But I wanted to be used; I wanted the animal sex-without-strings. I was some bloody mixed-up cow.

The dawn was slow in arriving. There's nothing to lift your spirits like lying on sex-soiled sheets after a night of noisy fornication with a near stranger in a dank and filthy flat, even if some of the soiling probably wasn't mine. I felt like absolute shit.

I had committed adultery. I started crying because I had and because I didn't think of it the night before. A bitch on heat. Mike doesn't deserve this, I thought. He put me on trust and this is how I repay him.

I understand now why animal sex has been such a powerful drug for me. Somehow, it's the absence of commitment; the newness of it that is the driving force. I can't seem to resist it and it makes me feel like filth every time. And after I've had it, I can push it away or persuade myself that I didn't really do anything too awful. I can even persuade myself that the person I'm in a relationship with has only got himself to blame for my actions. It's his fault for abusing me or my right to freedom.

Mike had said he'd pick me up at ten and so I had about an hour and a half to decide what to do. I went back to Katy's to get my stuff - and, boy, was she snotty - and went out into the road and down to the junction. He picked me up from there. I didn't want him coming into the house and having a cosy chat with her.

I decided that I wasn't going to tell him anything. I told myself that it was a one-off thing, like, an experiment and it wasn't going to happen again. When he asked me how the disco was, I told him that the whole thing had been bloody boring and that I wasn't going to another one. He looked visibly relieved and stroked my thigh.

I started to make a real effort at the shack and with the marriage. Why not? I loved Mike and where was the sense in hurting the guy? I knew I was being dishonest but I wasn't deliberately trying to delude Mike so that I could go off and do it with someone else at some other time. No, I wanted it to be alright between us. I didn't want to blow it all out of the water and telling him what I'd done would sink it without trace.

So, what had happened with Dave Crabbe hadn't happened. Gone. Erased. Wiped out along with the rape, the trial, Mum; other stuff I don't want to talk about; everything, just as ever. I stopped being so wrapped up in the college life; I did keep on with it but I put it in perspective. I made sure there was time to do the things that Mike liked; the things we both liked; could enjoy together like the summer before, on the beach. And the sex was good too.

It worked; it was really great. We were happy, the weather was glorious, the garden at 'The Crows' Nest' started to look so pretty and Mike was back to his usual loving, laughing self. Just for a few brief weeks we managed to re-discover the magic of those earliest times.

By the middle of June, I began to worry that I'd missed my period. They were never that regular, but even so. Like, I know I should have made Dave use contraception. I mean, I wasn't on the pill, was I? There was no need. But I didn't. Stupid, irresponsible whore!

As the days went by and my period still didn't arrive or show, I began to panic. I spoke to Katy about it one time but she wasn't very sympathetic. After college one afternoon I bought one of those kits you can get in the chemist's. Of course, it tested positive.

I suppose that it was at that moment that I knew what I was going to have to do. I didn't have the courage to talk to Mike, so I left him a note. What a bloody coward.

THE SPACES IN BETWEEN

July 18th, 1992

My dear Mike,

I'm so, so sorry. Please don't be angry with me. You have to promise me that you won't be angry, ever.

I can't do this anymore. None of it, Mike. Not at the moment, anyway. I need time out. I need my own space for a while. Maybe it'll be alright one day. I hope so, but if I'm honest with you, it doesn't feel like it at the moment.

It's not really your fault and I do still love you. You have to believe that. It's my fault. Maybe you chose the wrong girl. Sometimes I feel I'm no good for you and I cause you so much pain, don't I?

I'm sorry to do it like this in a note. I wanted to talk to you but I just couldn't. Can you forgive me that too? I've taken most of my stuff, except the really heavy things. I'm going to Em's or Mum's, I'm not sure which yet. I'll make up my mind later. You can phone me tomorrow if you want, but please, please don't come to find me. I have to have some space.

Guess what? I just realised something. We arrived here last year on July 17th. Do you remember? So it's true what it said in that poem. We sailed away for a year and a day. Now I'm crying. I think you know that under my laughter there are often some tears. It's always been like that. I know that I have to do this for your sake and for mine. Otherwise I shall hurt you too much. And I've already hurt you more than enough.

Sorry again,

Ellie xx

FADING VOICES

"Mrs Shepherd? This is Mike Chadwick. Is Ellie is with you? I've just spoken to Emma who says she's not there. I'd like to speak to her, please."

There is a pause.

"I'll see if she wants to speak to you. She's still in bed."

Michael waits. He can hear voices at the other end of the line, disembodied and distant. Eventually the hand-set crackles as Ellie picks it up.

"Hello?"

"Ellie! Are you alright? What's going on? I don't understand," he says, choking back the tears.

"I'm alright. I'm sorry."

"I got your letter. It was...well, a terrible shock. I've hardly slept all night, for worrying myself sick. I don't understand what's wrong, Ellie. Why have you run away from me?"

"I said in the note."

"No, you didn't Ellie, not really."

"I just need some space; to get my head around some stuff," she says, quietly.

"Stuff? But what stuff? I mean, I know you've been a bit withdrawn just lately, the last two weeks, but things are better than they were last Christmas, aren't they?"

"Well, not really, Mike. I thought they were, but they're not. Not for me."

"I thought we were doing better. You know, with the college business on a more even keel."

"Look, Mike, it's got nothing to do with college. It's to do with us. Well, me, really. I just need to have time to think."

"Think? About what? You're not being very clear," he says, an exasperated tone in his voice. "If there's something troubling you, then surely we can talk it through together, at home, face to face and sort it out, can't we? Running away isn't going to help, is it?"

"It might. I don't know. There are so many things I need to get straight in my head," she says.

"Like what for instance? Come on, Ellie, please! You owe me some sort of explanation; I'm going crazy here."

He starts to choke again.

"Well, you know, the age gap and everything, for a start. It's always going to be there. Like, social stuff, when you want to be with older people and I want to be with teenagers. Like, you take charge of things all the time; you know, I'm the kid and you're the grown up. And you and your kids. Me and my Mum. All of it. Stuff from my childhood, maybe. I dunno, Mike. It's never going to work."

"Ellie, since when did any of that matter to us? You haven't even mentioned anything like that for weeks and weeks."

"Mike, it matters. It's bugging me, more and more. That's what I mean, I need to think it all through."

"I don't see that any of that, even if it is bugging you, justifies you running off like this, does it?" Michael asks, plaintively. "How do you mean, I take charge?"

"Look, Mike, I don't want an argument with you. I really don't. Please just let me have some space, like I said in the note," Ellie says firmly. "Please?"

"If you feel that I'm rail-roading decisions, Ellie, I'm sorry. I didn't realise. You've never said anything about it before. I mean, you should have said and then we could have sorted it. We still can, if that's what this is all about. But I don't think that this is what it's about. Is it? It feels like there's something you're not telling me, again."

Ellie sighs.

"Mike, it's part of it. I need to think about me; what I want in life and what sort of person I am."

"What? What's that supposed to mean, Ellie? You agreed to get married about a year ago. We got you sorted at college in January. Isn't that enough of a start on what you want in life?"

"I don't know," Ellie's voice is strained.

"You mean you want something else?"

"I don't know."

"You've changed your mind about being married, is that what you mean?" Michael can hardly believe that he's asking the question.

"I don't know. Maybe. I don't know."

"You need to think about yourself? Which means what? You don't know what sort of person you are? This isn't making any bloody sense at all," he snaps.

"Mike, I know this is shitty for you. I mean what I said in the note. All of it. I'm sorry, I really am sorry. No, I don't know what sort of person I am, since you ask," she says. Silently, she sees a picture of herself, spread-eagled on the squalid sheets of a bed in a seedy flat, fornicating enthusiastically with Dave Crabbe. That is what I am, she thinks, a slut, and that's why I'm here but I can't hurt him with that. Not that.

"That's what I mean about maybe I'll hurt you. What you want from me; I mean, how you want me to be; I'm not sure I can be that person. I'm not sure if I am that person, so I have to try to sort that out in my mind. Do you see?" Ellie hopes that this comes close enough to the whole truth to satisfy him for now.

"Not really. What are you saying? You're not who I think you are? There's some part of you I haven't discovered yet, in all the months of intimacy and closeness we've had? Is that it?"

"Something like that. Mike, just let me be, please?"

"Ellie, this is madness. You're really not making any sense. Look; I have to ask. Has this got something to do with that bastard Crabbe? My instincts say it has?"

Ellie closes her eyes and squeezes them hard. This is what she's dreaded.

"No, Mike, I just said, it has to do with me," she says.

"Are you sure?"

Ellie grunts affirmatively. It's a lie but at the same time, it's the truth.

"Look, won't you please come home? I mean, let me come and pick you up and bring you back and we can talk it through. Or we can arrange for you to talk it through with someone. You know, a counsellor?"

"No! Mike, I'm asking you, please don't come up here and cause a scene. I'm not coming back. I've got to go now; I need to go to the toilet. Sorry, Mike."

"Ellie! Ellie! I love you!"

Ellie puts the receiver down and runs to the bathroom where she is violently sick.

MELANCHOLY LARGO
Ellie's Journal

Sunday, July 26th, 1992

Mike phoned again today. He's phoned every day this week. He cries a lot and so do I but I try not to let him hear me. There is nothing new to say. I can't tell him any more without causing even more pain than I'm causing him anyway. He hasn't asked about Dave again. Maybe he's afraid to. Was sick again this morning, three times. Felt really depressed this afternoon and went to bed about six.

Saturday August 1st, 1992

I miss Mike terribly. I thought today of asking him to come and get me and telling him everything when we got back to the cliff. Then I changed my mind. I don't seem to be able to think straight or do anything without bursting into tears. I feel really down all the time. Mum says it is because of my condition. She's right, but not in the way she thinks. She presumes the baby is Mike's. I haven't told her. No point. I just said it wasn't working out with Mike. She said, I told you so. I wish it was Mike's baby.

Friday August 7th, 1992

There haven't been quite so many phone calls this week. But about eleven o'clock this morning, Mum said he was outside the house in his car! I couldn't believe it! I went and looked through the net curtains and he was. He was just sitting there, the car window open, staring at the house. He sat there for about an hour. I didn't know what to do. Eventually, he came to the door. Mum told him to go away or she would call the Police. He said he wanted to see me. I leaned out of the upstairs window. That way he couldn't see all of me. I'm starting to show a bit now.

He looked terrible. Grey, thin and old. He just looked at me and said he loved me and he wanted me to come home with him. I could see the tears in his eyes. It was just awful. He said it didn't matter whatever had happened and that we could work it out. I wondered if he'd guessed or something. I'm sure he has. He's not stupid. But he's waiting for me to tell him. He would reckon that an unforced confession from me would be better than a reluctant admission which he dragged out of me. Maybe I should have said? The neighbours were watching from behind their curtains. Nosey bastards.

No, I couldn't say I shagged Crabbe all night and now I'm pregnant. I really wanted to say I'd go with him because I know I still love him. But it wouldn't work. He couldn't trust me or respect me ever again. I can't respect myself. I said no and asked him to go and leave me alone, otherwise Mum would cause trouble. He said "please" a couple of times and then turned away, got into the car and drove off.

I cried all day. Can't believe what I've done. So, so stupid.

Thursday August 20th, 1992

My birthday. Eighteen today, so now I'm a grown-up. Yeah, right. Just as well, really. I've already been raped by my step-father, been in the newspapers, run off with my teacher, got married to him, committed adultery, got pregnant and walked out on my husband without telling him why, poor bastard. And I still love him, so much.

Mum wanted to organise a celebration! I told her she must be joking. What is there to celebrate? Everything feels like shit. And today is our Wedding Anniversary as well. If I wasn't pregnant, I'd have bought a bottle of whisky and drunk myself into oblivion. But then, if I wasn't pregnant, I wouldn't need to, would I?

What a difference a year makes. I expected Mike to call, but he didn't. I was relieved and very sad too. He's only called about three times since he turned up here. Same conversation, round and round. He pushes and probes. I resist and evade. It just upsets both of us. Maybe that's why he didn't call today of all days. I'm sure he'll be thinking about last year. The afternoon in the meadow. I wish I could go back to that day now and have another try at getting it right. Too late, though. Always too bloody late.

And something really weird happened. I decided yesterday that today I would take off my wedding and engagement rings and put them away. A year to the day. I don't want to be divorced from him. Do I? But having the rings on my finger seems wrong. As if I'm being a hypocrite. And seeing them every few minutes is a constant reminder of what I've done. So this morning I took them off. I opened the jewellery box that Mike bought me last year to put them inside. I haven't opened it for ages. My necklace is in there and I took it out to have a look at it. So beautiful. As I went to put it back later, I noticed that there was something wedged behind the lining of the box. I could see that it was a piece of paper. Mike must have put it there. I can't understand how I'd never noticed it before, but it was pushed right down.

It was a letter he wrote me a year ago. I read it over and over and just bawled my eyes out. I couldn't stop for hours.

BEFORE THE DARKNESS

20th August 1991

My dearest Ellie, my wife!

This morning we were married, this afternoon we made endless, intoxicating love on a bed of sweet grass scented with crushed cranesbill and this evening we danced on our beach under the moonlight. What more could a man so deliriously in love hope for in one day? And now I cannot sleep! I tried but the day's experiences have been so intense that I was not able to say goodnight to them just yet. Perhaps I feel that by staying awake I can somehow prolong my time with you in Paradise.

What is there to say at the end of a day like this? Everything. But how do I put onto the two dimensions of a page the tenderness of our wedding day and the rich texture of my love for you? Such a thing has defeated many great men of letters.

I think you know that I wanted this day to be very special and memorable for both of us. Until I happened upon that meadow a few days ago, I had no idea quite what to do after the Registry Office, or where to go, that would appropriately seal our formal vows; seal them in a way which would be fitting, romantic and which would burn into our memories. I'd left it a bit late. Not like me, really. Then I found that meadow and it all fell into place.

I shall never forget it and nor will you. An American writer called Mark Twain said that grief can take care of itself, but that to get the full value of joy, you must have somebody to share it with. He was so right. I am so lucky to be sharing such joy with you.

In a life time we must all live countless hours which are gone as soon as they are spent. They are unremarkable or repetitions of what has gone many times before, perhaps. It is wrong of us all to be so dismissive of our allotted span, to be so profligate in spending our Life's hours, but we are. We ditch much of lives and put it out for the dustcart. We do not care about it, we cannot recall it and it appears to be of no use to us. But not so the few hours we spent in the meadow this afternoon. I shall put them in the safe cabinet which I keep for memories which are special and irreplaceable. I bring them out once in a while and polish their precious stones.

I have never felt like this before. Ever. The sensations which have me in their thrall excite, engulf, mesmerise and sometimes, yes, they frighten me with their consuming fire. But I am helpless to do more than be enthralled. I have no say in this at all. I dare to hope that it is like that for you too although, I suppose, you cannot be as sure as I am, can you? I am your first (and only!) lover.

I want this to go on forever and ever. But fears and apprehensions stalk me and sometimes overtake me when my guard is down. At night sometimes, when I awake in that terrible dead time just before dawn when, unaccountably, doubts can prosper. I tell you this not to frighten you or worry you but because I want you to understand.

We live in a land of perpetual light where the sun always shines and the clocks never chime. Can we defy our time forever? Things will impinge; they must. I will get old. You will too, but much later. Maybe it is this which sometimes sits black on my horizon. You have yet to come to full bloom but I can feel an autumn chill.

Ellie, I am frightened of losing you. Frightened that something, or someone, will come between us. Frightened that one morning you will awake, see autumn beside you and hear the call of a more vibrant spring. I know you say that you will not. And I believe you. I believe that you mean it. But now is now and cannot be forever. I grew and changed and arrived here. You have yet to begin. And that is why sometimes I cannot sleep. To sleep is to throw away Now in the hope that it will still be there tomorrow.

So I am frightened that to try to keep you I will tether you and constrain you. That I will somehow not let you grow. Ellie, if I do, forgive me. Ellie, I think that to grow you may have to leave me and this place behind. That is my darkest fear. And I do not know how to dispel that terror.

Should I ask for your help or will that inevitably bring the thunder rolling in from the moor?

It is very late. I must return to bed where I belong, close to you. Even though you are asleep, I shall whisper three simple words with far more force than they can show on the page:

I love you.

Mike

ODES TO A LOST SUMMER

January 18th, 1993

My lost Ellie

It is six months now since you walked out of my life. In that time I have telephoned you about twenty times, written you five letters and once, ignoring your entreaties, I came to find you to ask you to come home. That is still my wish.

You have been variously polite, distant, uncommunicative, confused and confusing, implacable and evasive. Once, you did come close to being affectionate, for a few minutes giving me false hope that you would return to me where you belong. We belong together. You know and I know it. Why will you not acknowledge this simple truth?

I lie awake at night; I pace the cliffs and the beach by day, trying to make some sense of what you have done, what you might have done, what you have said and what you have not said. Some days I think I see the answer; some days I do not. I speculate that something happened that you have chosen not to tell me or have not the courage to tell me. I have asked you about this but you won't give me a straight answer.

The worst days are when I imagine all kinds of horrors. But it is not for me to say what they might be or to accuse you of a role in the sordid dramas of my mind. It is for you to tell me, if you can and if I am right that there is some piece of the jigsaw puzzle in your possession which you will not let me have. I think you would feel better if you unburdened yourself, wouldn't you? And it would help me too, to know the truth, however unpalatable.

I have spent six months living in miserable, fading hope. Now, I feel I have to draw a line somewhere to preserve my own sanity. The winter is already well advanced and you know how it is in 'The Crows' Nest' at this time of year. The environment there cannot help my mood or assist me to overcome this grievous hurt. Some days, truly, I think I am going insane with this grief.

I shall remove what is valuable (some of your things are there; I will take them with me) shut the place up and go to live in Essex. The tenants there have vacated. If you want or need to contact me, you have the address and the phone number.

I have asked both Paul and Patrick if I may place a For Sale card for the shack in their respective premises. Even if you said you wanted to come back tomorrow, it could not be to this place. It is clear it was a mistake. A mistake for which I take full responsibility, incidentally. It must be sold. I do not wish to live here anymore.

You say that you still love me and that you do not want a divorce "at this time". Those are your exact words. So, since I take it that there may still be some slim chance of reconciliation, which is what I want, I shall write to you occasionally if only to give you what news I have, to ask after your welfare and to ascertain whether, perhaps, you have changed your mind. In other words, I regard our marriage as still "live" but in some kind of abeyance. In the meantime, I have to find a path somewhere; anywhere that leads away from this cliff and the beach. What else can I do? The memories of yesterday's summers torment me.

Accordingly, I ask just one thing. Please let me know when you have finally made up your mind about the state of our relationship and marriage. Please don't now just ignore it. I'm sure that you agree with me that some kind of final resolution, whatever it is, will be better than this limbo of separation, this "space" as you call it. For me, it is a dead, dark space.

Finally, Ellie, I must write this. It is no surprise, or it should not be. Maybe by now you will have found the love letter I wrote for you on our wedding day? (Look in your jewellery box if not.) You probably wonder why I didn't give it to you at the time. Perhaps it's obvious now. It doesn't matter, anyway. What matters, Ellie, is that what I wrote in August, 1991 of my feelings for you remains as true today as it was then.

Whatever you have done, however awful.

I love you,

Mike

*

February 3rd, 1994

Dear Mike,

Thank you for your letters during the last year. I suppose that I should apologise for not replying but, you see, I have had nothing new to say. I'm sorry if that sounds harsh, but it's true.

You asked me a year ago to let you know when I had made up my mind about things so that's why I am writing. I am sorry that I am probably not going to say what you would like to hear. Maybe after all this time it won't be too much of a surprise, though.

Of course, I have thought about us a lot. I know you think I must have made an impetuous decision in July '92 to leave you. Maybe it was, but it was the right decision. It was hard, very, very hard and it still is but what I felt then, I feel now only more so. I am sorry, because you are a really lovely, loving guy, but it's no good. Especially not now because so much has changed for me. I cannot go back.

In the last year, I have had to grow up fast. It won't be long before I'm no longer a teenager! I know myself better now than I did before, although back then the truth was beginning to emerge. I know I have hurt you, Mike, and I regret that with all my heart but it would be to hurt you more and for longer if I were to come back now. I am sure of that.

I do not want a reconciliation. Please, please do not try to make me change my mind. It is made up. I ask you to let me go. If you love me enough and I believe you when you say you do, you will. You have to love me enough to let me go.

I don't know what you want to do about a divorce, if anything. I suppose that would be best? I really don't know; I leave it up to you. That sounds ridiculous, I know. I think maybe it is that although I am saying that we must live apart, to destroy the marriage through the finality of a divorce court seems terrible? I'm not making much sense, am I?

We both have the same memories. They are beautiful and they are there for all time. Thank you for what we did have, once. I treasure it. Thank you for taking me to the land where the bong tree grows. I suppose if we'd listened to the words properly, we'd have realised it wasn't for ever.

Please look after yourself. And forgive me,

Ellie

SWEEPING AUTUMN LEAVES
September 2004

I was exhausted this morning after only ten minutes of sweeping leaves out the front. I must be getting old. But I'm not even sixty yet, so surely not "old" as in dribbling, doubly incontinent and preparing to shuffle off this mortal coil? But I do seem to have gone off the boil.

I can't be arsed with lots of stuff now; what's the point? When you're young there's a purpose, but as things go on and the shit happens, well, you lose interest. Too much sitting about moping about the past and too much vin rouge as well, no doubt. Yes, Doctor, I'll try to cut it down to just six bottles a day if you insist. You miserable, self-righteous bastard.

I suppose it doesn't help living on my own. People are funny when they hear that: always wanting to put a label on it. Bachelor? No. Oh, widower? No. Ah, divorced? No. Separated?

No, abandoned; she pissed off; years ago now. That shuts them up; there's nothing worse than self-pity.

There have been one or two opportunities with women, of course, but in the early days I still held hopes that Ellie would suddenly appear on the doorstep. I wanted to be able to say I'd held to the vows and when it became clear that she was not going to appear, well, by then I'd lost interest. The fires had died down. Sometimes I wonder whether a very young woman around would kick-start the engine again. She could surprise me occasionally by appearing ripely nubile and topless in the shower. Maybe that would stiffen the sinews and summon up the blood.

Ha! Looks like you've had that, Michael my boy. Young and ripe! Eat your heart out. Delicious like a peach? Simone's peach!!

"You're 'aving a laugh, son," as they say in Essex these days.

I haven't had a woman for more than ten years. Not since Ellie. When John Major was Prime Minister! I'm not suggesting any connection or significance in that, merely noting it as an historical fact.

I know that I should have let it all go by now. I do try; some weeks or months are better than others. I visit the grandchildren; take a walking holiday in the Peak District – not Cumbria! – and then my mind is occupied. But otherwise, I think of her every day. I wish I didn't in a way, but there it is.

Of course, she's not eighteen anymore; extraordinary to think she's in her early thirties. Maybe she's got kids; another man. I have no way of knowing, but I bet she's kept her looks.

Why does it hurt, even now? Time is supposed to be a great healer, isn't it? "This day too shall pass" and all that crap.

If I shut my eyes, I can see it all. The beach. The cliff. The birds riding the currents; the sun silvering the sea. The salt taste of the air; the surf thundering through the nights as we held each other and made love until dawn. And the dark clouds over the moor. Oh, yes, there were always dark clouds over the moor.

Old Nibber! Don't pretend it isn't about the sex, he said. Who's pretending, Nibber? Of course it was about the sex. Jesus, I've never had sex like it! Not before, not even as a student and certainly not since.

But it was love too. If it was just sex, I wouldn't have been thinking about her every day for fourteen years. I'd probably have forgotten her sodding name by now.

It engulfed me. There was no possibility of controlling it. We were small leaves, a tangle of stems sucked into a vortex, clinging to one another, breathing one another's tinctured breath. We lived in a small, enclosed space, protected from the screaming maelstrom and the floodwaters by the obsessive intensity of ourselves and the force that was carrying us along in its thrall.

It put us down, in time, on a deserted beach and we lay in the sand, calm. God knows, I'd have happily stayed on the beach with her at the time, for all time. Bloody memories! And here I am again, now, this piss-wet, lachrymose September morning, distressing myself by allowing those memories and sensations the space and air to return.

How I can I not weep for the folly and the heartache of it all?

MEMOIR
October 2004

Dear Mike

I hardly know how to begin, now that I've written your name. I have thought about you so often that to write it now, here, is somehow to acknowledge the pain I have caused you. As I wrote the letters that are your name, I had to stop to cry. Again!

I'm sorry. Maybe you don't want all this. Well, then just screw this up and throw it away. Is it inappropriate for me to write? I don't know.

We are still married. Weird, or what? But I know it is in name only. Academic, as you used to say. Perhaps you have a partner? Somehow I don't think you have because if you did, unless you had lied to her about your status, which I don't think you would, she would have wanted you to get a divorce. No, I think you are still on your own. Am I right? Call it Ellie's intuition.

I found out from Directory Enquiries that you are certainly still at your place in Essex. I nearly phoned this morning and then I thought that really would be an intrusion.

I am troubled by what feels like unfinished business. It has troubled me for ten years. You told me then that I should tell you the truth and you were right but it has taken me a decade to be able to do so. Just goes to show how unbalanced I was.

OK, confession time. This is hard for me but it may be even harder for you; I'm sorry, but I want to set the record straight. You told me once that it didn't matter what I'd done, you still wanted me. Hang on to your hat.

Well, you were right, Mike. And you knew you were. On the night of that disco I went to at the college (it was May 22nd 1992 - seems like a lifetime ago) I didn't go back to that girl Katy's. You remember her?

After the disco, I went back to Dave Crabbe's sordid flat and spent the night with him. A one-night stand and I never saw him again. At the time I was disgusted with myself and not quite sure why I did it; why I let him. I know now.

In the morning I felt terrible, like shit, but I persuaded myself it was a one-off and that it wouldn't happen again and that I wouldn't tell you. What you didn't know, you wouldn't be hurt by. That was my feeling at the time. I am so sorry. It was stupid; it was naïve but I was only seventeen, for Christ's sake! Of course I felt dreadful guilt but it was the thought of the hurt and pain I'd cause you that stopped me from speaking and made me run away.

It seems absurd to apologise now. To say that I am so, so sorry that I behaved so badly. But I have wanted to say it for all those years; I wanted to say it then, but I just couldn't. I wanted to tell you how much I loved you, but I couldn't. I choked on the words because of what I'd done.

All I could do was to ask you to forgive me. I don't know whether you could or did.

Anyway, you knew, didn't you? I lied to you and you didn't really want to press me for the truth. You wanted me to confess; that was your test of our strength and I failed it miserably.

If I hadn't discovered I was pregnant, it's possible that you would never have known, although I think that something else like it would have happened anyway, sooner or later. Dave Crabbe, Fred Bloggs; whoever. You will find that difficult to understand, but I know now that it's true. I understand myself better.

I called my little girl Hannah. I hope you don't mind. She's eleven now and a lovely little girl. They say she looks like me. Same green eyes.

I have been in a number of relationships, none of which have lasted. When Hannah was a baby I got involved with a guy. Gary was a lot older than me. Yes, that's right, there is a pattern in all this. He ended up abusing me physically and emotionally. Awful. Violent. Frightening. I managed to get out of it for my sake and Hannah's. The next two relationships weren't much better. Older men again, one of them a teacher! You can't accuse me of being unpredictable.

By early 1997 I was a real mess. I had no self-esteem, behaved like a whore and was physically ill. I lost about two stone. Fortunately, our GP intervened and I ended up having extensive counselling which really helped, although it was hard. Some pretty vile crap from my past, to do with my father, came out. I don't really want to go into detail, but I'm sure you can put two and two together. A girl abused in childhood will always have problems with maintaining relationships in later life, apparently.

Both my Mum and Emma were really supportive. Surprised? What is it they say? Blood is thicker than water. Thank God, because Hannah needed some stability while I was going through it. It was hard going with Mum for a while, when the crap about my father was coming to the surface – she had probably suspected at the time but pushed it from her mind. That's Mum!

In 1998 I got a place of my own and things began to look up a bit. I met Alec who was only eight years older than me, so I was doing well and after a while, he moved in. Things were OK for a couple of years. The relationship was sound-ish because I was OK. I understood my problem. What was it you used to say? Knowledge is power, right? He was kind and gentle but it lacked real passion. You know what I mean about that!

Two years ago, Alec was killed in an awful accident on the farm where he worked. How come some people get all the crap in life and others get off unscathed?

Well, since Alec's death, I have concentrated on Hannah's welfare and her schooling. She's a lovely young lady. She had an uncertain beginning. I want to make up for that now.

You may not believe this, but in all those years, barely a day has gone by that I haven't thought about you. I have worn the beautiful necklace you gave me many, many times. Even when I was with Alec and we were getting along, I thought about you and it never seemed that I was being disloyal to him. Strange.

I am older, wiser and saner now. I am not contacting you now for the wrong reason. Alec left me well-provided for. Hannah and I are pretty self-reliant. I'm not a basket case or a sponger. Don't misunderstand.

I don't think I ever stopped caring about you. More than that, I suppose. We had something very special and I blew it. I have never found it again, nor anything that came anywhere close.

Those days are clearer than yesterday. And you know what? Without seeing you or speaking to you in any form for more than ten years, I know you feel the same. How's that for confidence? Or delusion?!

I still have the wedding ring and that beautiful letter you wrote me on our wedding day. Probably about once a year I read it and cry myself silly for those lovely, lost days.

Mike, I have told you some dreadful things and it's taken me over a decade to do it, so, maybe you'll not want to respond to this. I know forgiveness can be hard.

Therefore you might think I have a bloody nerve, but I'd like to see my husband again, if he's willing. I hope with all my heart that you are. I am wearing the necklace as I write this.

Mike, you told me many times that there is a beginning and there is an end in all things. I was confused and doubtful all those years ago but I never felt there was an end for us. Please, please call me.

Love hurts,

Ellie xx

PS I'm sure you remember our wedding picture at Hooken? There was only ever one copy and I also have the negative. I am sending you a copy I had done. I hope you don't mind.

PICTURE POSTCARD

In a café by the sea in a cove in Devon, the owner has allowed a local photographer to display his postcard shots of the nearby coast and beach. They are beautifully composed, sepia images that speak of yesteryear. They are popular with the few tourists and walkers who find their way to the remote, pebbled shore.

The café owner is intrigued by one particular photograph, for it seems to him that the figures within it are familiar, although he cannot be sure for time plays tricks and the photographer has taken the picture through the early morning sea mist with the figures half in silhouette in the distance. It is unclear.

The café owner knows the place. There is a rock half a mile down the beach to the west with an odd, white cap. It is in the centre of the picture and standing beside it, motionless and staring out to sea, is an old man who wears spectacles. Next to him, holding his hand, is a much younger woman whose luxuriant tangle of hair is suffused with light from the rising sun.

Lightning Source UK Ltd.
Milton Keynes UK
UKOW04f1456041213

222373UK00006B/321/P